## Also by Jessica Sorensen

*The Secret of Ella and Micha*

*The Forever of Ella and Micha*

*The Temptation of Lila and Ethan*

*The Ever After of Ella and Micha*

*The Coincidence of Callie & Kayden*

*The Destiny of Violet & Luke*

*Breaking Nova*

*Nova #2*

# The Redemption of Callie & Kayden

JESSICA SORENSEN

sphere

SPHERE

First published in Great Britain in 2014 by Sphere

A CIP catalogue record for this book
is available from the British Library.

ISBN 978-0-7515-5261-4

Printed and bound in Great Britain by Clays Ltd, St Ives plc

Papers used by Sphere are from well-managed forests
and other responsible sources.

MIX
Paper from
responsible sources
FSC® C104740

Sphere
An imprint of
Little, Brown Book Group
100 Victoria Embankment
London EC4Y 0DY

An Hachette UK Company
www.hachette.co.uk

www.littlebrown.co.uk

*For everyone who survived*

# Acknowledgments

A huge thanks to my agent, Erica Silverman, and my editor, Selina McLemore. I'm forever grateful for all your help and input. And to everyone who reads this book, an endless amount of thank-yous.

# Prologue

## Callie

*I want to breathe.*

*I want to feel alive again.*

*I don't want to feel the pain.*

*I want it all back, but it's gone.*

I hear every sound, every laugh, every cry. People move around the room frantically, but I can't take my eyes off the sliding glass doors. There's a violent storm outside and rain is hammering against the concrete, dirt, and dry leaves. Lights flash as ambulances drive up under the port and the glow reflects off the rain on the ground, red, like blood. Like Kayden's blood. Like Kayden's blood all over the floor. So much blood.

My stomach is empty. My heart is hurting. I can't move.

"Callie," Seth says. "Callie, look at me."

I take my gaze off the door and stare into his brown eyes filled with worry. "Huh?"

He takes my hand in his and his skin is warm and comforting. "He's going to be okay."

I stare at him, forcing back tears, because I have to be strong. "Okay."

He lets out a sigh and pats my hand. "You know what? I'm going to go see if he can have visitors yet. It's been almost a damn week. You'd think they'd let him have visitors by now." He gets up from the chair and walks across the packed waiting room to the receptionist's desk.

*He'll be all right.*

*He has to be.*

But in my heart, I know he won't be all right. Sure, his wounds and broken bones may heal on the outside. On the inside, though, the healing will take longer, and I wonder what Kayden will be like when I see him again. Who will he be?

Seth starts talking to the receptionist behind the counter, but she barely gives him the time of day as she multitasks between phone calls and the computer. It doesn't matter, though. I know what she'll say—the same thing she's been saying. That he can't have visitors, except for family. His *family*, the people who hurt him. He doesn't need his family.

"Callie." Maci Owens's voice rips me out of my daze. I blink up at Kayden's mother with a frown on my face. She's dressed in a pinstripe pencil skirt, her nails are done, and her hair is curled up into a huge bun on the top of her head. "Why are you here?" she asks.

I almost ask her the same thing. "I came here to see Kayden." I sit up in the seat.

"Callie, honey." She speaks like I'm a little kid, frowning

as she stares down at me. "Kayden can't have visitors. I told you this a few days ago."

"But I have to go back to school soon," I say, gripping onto the arms of the chair. "I need to see him before I go."

She shakes her head and sits down in the chair next to me, crossing her legs. "That's not going to be possible."

"Why not?" My voice comes out sharper than it ever has.

She glances around, worried I'm causing a scene. "Please keep your voice down, honey."

"I'm sorry, but I need to know that he's okay," I say. There's so much anger inside me. I've never been this angry before and I don't like it. "And I need to know what happened."

"What happened is that Kayden's sick," she responds quietly and then starts to get up.

"Wait." I get up with her. "What do you mean he's sick?"

She slants her head to the side and gives me her best sad face, but all I can think about is how this is the woman who let Kayden get beaten by his father for all those years. "Honey, I don't know how to tell you this, but Kayden injured himself."

I shake my head as I back away from her. "No, he didn't."

Her face grows sadder and she looks like a plastic doll with glassy eyes and a painted-on smile. "Honey, Kayden's had a problem with cutting for a very long time and this...well, we thought he was getting better, but I guess we were wrong."

"No, he doesn't!" I scream. Actually scream. I'm shocked. She's shocked. Everyone in the crowded waiting room is shocked. "And my name is Callie, not honey."

Seth hurries up to me, his eyes wide and full of concern. "Callie, are you okay?"

I glance at him, then at the people around the room. It's gone quiet and they're staring at me. "I . . . I don't know what's wrong with me." I reel on my heels and run for the sliding glass doors, bumping my elbows onto the trim when they don't open quickly enough. I keep running until I find a cluster of bushes around the back of the hospital, and then I fall on my knees and throw up all over the mud. My shoulders shake, my stomach heaves, and tears sting at my eyes. When my stomach is empty, I fall back on my heels and sit down in the wet dirt.

There's no way Kayden could have done that to himself. But deep down in the center of my heart, I keep thinking about all the scars on his body and I can't help but wonder: What if he did?

## Kayden

I open my eyes and the first thing I see is light. It burns my eyes and makes my surroundings distorted. I don't know where I am. *What happened?* Then I hear the deep voices, clanking, chaos. There's a machine beeping and it seems to match the beat of my heart as it hits my chest, but it sounds too slow and uneven. My body is cold—numb, like the inside of me.

"Kayden, can you hear me?" I hear my mom's voice but I can't see her through the bright light.

"Kayden Owens, open your eyes," she repeats until her voice becomes a gnawing hum inside my head.

I open and close my eyelids repeatedly and then roll my eyes back into my head. I blink again and the light turns into spots and eventually into faces of people I don't know, each of their expressions filled with fear. I search through them, looking for only one person, but I don't see her anywhere.

I unhitch my jaw and force my lips to move. "Callie."

My mom appears above me. Her eyes are colder than I expected and her lips are pursed. "Do you have any idea what you put this family through? What is wrong with you? Don't you value your life?"

I glance at the doctors and nurses around my bed and realize it's not fear I'm seeing, but pity and annoyance. "What..." My throat is dry like sand and I force my neck muscles to move as I swallow several times. "What happened?" I start to remember: blood, violence, pain... wanting it to all end.

My mom puts her hands next to my head and leans over me. "I thought we were over this problem. I thought you stopped."

I tip my head to the side and glance down at my arm. My wrist is bandaged up and my skin is white and mapped with blue veins. There's an IV attached to the back of my hand and a clip on the end of my finger. I remember. *Everything.* I meet her eyes. "Where's Dad?"

Her eyes narrow and her voice lowers as she leans in even closer. "Gone on a business trip."

I gape at her unfathomably. She'd never done anything about the violence when I was growing up, but I guess I was kind of hoping that maybe this would have pushed her to the end of her secrecy and her need to always defend him. "He's on a business trip?" I say slowly.

A man in a white coat with a pen in his pocket, glasses, and salt-and-pepper hair says something to my mom and then he exits the room carrying a clipboard. A nurse walks over to a beeping machine beside my bed and starts writing down stuff in my chart.

My mother leans in closer, casting a shadow over me, and whispers in a low tone that conveys a lot of warning, "Your father's not going to have any part of this. The doctors know you cut your own wrists and the town knows you beat up Caleb. You're not in a good place right now and you're going to be in a worse place if you try to bring your father into this." She leans back a little and for the first time I realize how large her pupils are. There's barely any color left except for a small ring around the edge. She looks possessed, by the devil maybe, or my father—but they're kind of one and the same.

"You're going to be all right," she says. "All the injuries missed anything major. You lost a lot of blood, but they gave you a blood transfusion."

I press my hands to the bed, trying to sit up, but my body is heavy and my limbs weak. "How long have I been out?"

"You've been in and out for a couple of days now. But the doctors say that's normal." She starts tucking the blanket in around me, like I'm suddenly her child. "What they're more worried about is why you cut yourself."

6

I could have yelled it—screamed to the world that it wasn't all me. That it was my dad, that he and I had both done the damage. But as I glance around the room, I realize there's no one here who really cares. I'm alone. I did cut myself. And for a second I kind of hoped it would be my end. That all the pain and hate and feelings of being worthless would *finally*, after nineteen years, be gone.

She pats my leg. "All right, I'll be back tomorrow."

I don't say anything. I just roll over and seal my eyes and mouth and let myself go back into the comfort of the darkness I'd just woken up from. Because right now, it's better than being in the light.

# Chapter One

*#62 Don't break apart*

## Callie

I spend a lot of time writing in my notebook. It's like therapy for me, almost. It's extremely late in the night and I'm wide awake, dreading going back to campus tomorrow morning and leaving Kayden behind. How am I supposed to just leave him, bail out, move on? Everyone keeps telling me that I have to, like it's as simple as picking out an outfit. I was never good at picking out outfits, though.

I'm in the room above the garage, alone, tucked away in the solitude with only my pen and notebook for company. I sigh as I stare at the moon and then let my hand move across the paper almost on its own accord.

I can't get the image out of my mind, no matter how hard I try. Every time I close my eyes, I see Kayden, lying on the floor. Blood covers his body, the floor,

9

the cracks in the tile, and the knives that surround him. He's broken, bleeding, cracked to pieces. To some people he probably seems like he can't be repaired. But I can't think that.

I was once shattered to pieces, destroyed by the hand of another, but now I feel like I'm beginning to reconnect. Or at least I did feel that way. But when I found Kayden on the floor it felt like part of me splintered again. And more of me broke when his mother told me he did it to himself. He cut himself and has probably been doing it for years.

I don't believe it.

I can't believe it. Not when I know about his dad.

I just can't.

My hand stops and I wait for more to come. But that's all I seem to need to write. I lie down in the bed and stare at the moon, wondering how I'm supposed to move forward in life when everything important to me is motionless.

❧

"Wipe that sad frown off your face, Missy." Seth is holding my arm as we walk across the campus yard. It's cold. Rain is drizzling from the gloomy clouds and the sidewalks are covered in murky puddles. There's practically a river running off the rooftops of the historic buildings that enclose the campus. The grass is sloshy beneath my sneakers and the icky weather matches my mood. People are running to and from class and I just want to yell, *Slow down and wait for the world to catch up!*

"I'm trying," I tell him, but my frown still remains. It's the same frown that's been on my face since I found Kayden a little over a couple of weeks ago. The images hurt my mind and my heart like shards of glass. I know part of this is my fault. I'm the one who let Kayden find out about Caleb. I barely even tried to deny it when he'd asked me. Part of me had wanted him to find out and part of me was glad when Luke had told me Kayden had beat up Caleb.

He nudges me with his elbow and constricts his grip when I trip over my feet and stumble to the side. "Callie, you need to stop worrying all the time." He helps me get my balance. "I know it's hard, but always being sad isn't a good thing. I don't want you going back to the sad girl I first met."

I stop in my tracks and step right into a puddle. The cold water fills my shoes and soaks through my socks. "Seth, I'm not going back to that." I slip my arm out of his and wrap my jacket tightly around myself. "I just can't stop thinking about him… how he looked. It's stuck in my head." It's always in my mind. I didn't want to leave Afton, but my mom threatened me, saying if I failed the semester she wasn't going to let me stay at the house for Christmas break. I'd have nowhere to go. "I just miss him and I feel bad for leaving him there with his family."

"It wouldn't have mattered if you had stayed. They still won't let you see him." Seth brushes his golden blond hair out of his honey brown eyes and looks at me sympathetically as rain drips down on his head and face. "Callie, I know it's hard, especially when they said he did it to...he did it to himself. But you can't break apart."

"I'm not breaking apart." The drizzle of rain suddenly shifts to a downpour and we sprint for the shelter of the trees, shielding our faces with our arms. I tuck damp strands of my brown hair out of my face and behind my ears. "I just can't stop thinking about him." I sigh, wiping away the rain from my face. "Besides, I don't believe that he did it to himself."

His shoulders slump as he pulls down the sleeves of his black button-down jacket. "Callie, I hate to say it but...but what if he did? I know it could have been his dad, but what if it wasn't? What if the doctors are right? I mean, they did send him to that facility for a reason."

Raindrops bead down our faces and my eyelashes flutter against them. "Then he did," I say. "It doesn't change anything." Everyone has secrets, just like me. I'd be a hypocrite if I judge Kayden for self-infliction. "Besides, they didn't send him. The hospital transferred him there so he could be watched while he heals. That's all. He doesn't *have* to stay there."

Seth offers me a sympathetic smile, but there's pity in his eyes. He leans forward and gives me a quick kiss on the cheek. "I know, and that's why you're you." He moves back from me, turns to his side, and aims his elbow at me. "Now come on, we're going to be late for class."

Sighing, I link elbows with him and we step out into the rain, taking our time as we head to class.

"Maybe we could do something fun," Seth suggests as he opens the door to the main building on campus. He guides me into the warmth and lets the door slam shut behind us. He releases my arm and shakes the front of his jacket, sending raindrops everywhere. "Like we could go to a movie or something. You've been dying to see that one…" He snaps his fingers a few times. "I can't remember what it's called, but you kept talking about it before break."

I shrug, grabbing my ponytail and giving it a good wringing so the water drips out of the end. "I can't remember either. And I don't really feel like seeing a movie."

He frowns. "You need to quit sulking."

"I'm not sulking," I say and massage my hand over my heart. "My heart just hurts all the time."

His shoulders lift and descend as he sighs. "Callie, I—"

I raise my hand and shake my head. "Seth, I know you always want to help me out and I love you for that, but sometimes hurting is just part of life, especially when someone I lo—care about is hurting too."

He arches his eyebrows because of my almost-slip. "Okay then, let's go to class."

I nod and follow him up the hall. My clothes are wet from the rain and there's water in my shoes. Even though it's cold and the water sticks my clothes to my body, it reminds me of a beautiful time full of magical kisses and I need to hold onto that.

Because for now, it's all I've got.

❧

Time drags on. Classes are ending, wrapping up for winter break. I've been staring at my English book for so long it feels like my eyes are bleeding and the words look identical. I rub my eyes with my fingertips, pretending like the room doesn't smell like pot and that Violet, my roommate, isn't passed out in the bed across from mine. She's been like that for the last ten hours. I'd be worried she was dead, but she keeps muttering incoherently in her sleep.

On top of studying for the English exam, I'm supposed to be writing an essay. I joined a creative writing club at the beginning of the year, and at the end of it, I'm supposed to turn in three projects: a poem, a short story, and a nonfiction piece. As much as I love to write, I'm struggling with the idea of putting truth down on paper for other people to read. I'm afraid of what might come out if I really open up. Or maybe it's because it seems silly to write a paper about the truth of life when Kayden's in an institution living the truth. All I've typed so far is: *Where the Leaves Go by Callie Lawrence.* I'm uncertain of where I'll go with this.

The rain from earlier has frozen into fluffy snowflakes that sail from the sky and a silvery sheet of ice glistens across the campus yard. I tap my fingers on the top of my book, thinking about home and how there's probably three or four feet of snow and how my mom's car is probably stuck in the driveway. I can picture the snowplow roaming the town's streets, and my dad doing warm-ups inside the gym because it's too cold to be outside. And Kayden is still in the hospital under supervision because they think he tried to kill himself. It's been a few weeks since it happened. He was out of it for quite a while from the blood transfusion and lacerations to his body. Then he woke up and no one could see him because he's considered "high risk" and "under surveillance" (Kayden's mother's words, not mine).

My phone is sitting on my bed next to a pile of study sheets and an array of highlighters. I pick it up, dial Kayden's number, and wait for his voicemail message to come on.

"Hey, this is Kayden, I'm way too busy to take your call right now, so please leave a message and maybe you'll be lucky enough that I'll call you back." There's sarcasm in his voice like he thinks he's being funny and I smile, missing him so badly it pierces my heart.

I listen to it over and over again until I can hear the underlying pain in his sarcasm, the one that carries his secrets. Eventually, I hang up and flop back on my bed, wishing I could travel back in time and not let Kayden find out that it was Caleb who raped me.

"God, what time is it?" Violet sits up in her bed and blinks her bloodshot eyes at the leather-band watch on her wrist. She shakes her head and gathers her black-and-red-streaked hair out of her face. She gazes out the window at the snow and then looks at me. "How long have I been out?"

I shrug, staring up at the ceiling. "I think, like, ten hours?"

She throws the blanket off herself and climbs out of bed. "Fuck, I missed my chemistry class."

"You take chemistry?" I don't mean for it to sound so rude, but the shock of her taking chemistry comes through in my voice. Violet and I have shared a room for three months, and from what I can tell, she likes to party and she likes guys.

She gives me a dirty look as she slips her arm through the sleeve of her leather jacket. "What? You don't think I can party *and* be smart?"

I shake my head. "No, that's not what I meant. I just—"

"I know what you meant—what you think of me, and everyone else thinks of me." She snatches her bag from the desk, sniffs her shirt, and shrugs. "But some advice: Maybe you shouldn't judge people by their looks."

"I don't," I tell her, feeling bad. "I'm sorry if you think I judged you."

She collects her phone from the desk and tosses it into her bag, then heads for the door. "Listen, if some guy named Jesse comes by, can you pretend that you haven't seen me all day?"

"Why?" I ask, sitting up.

"Because I don't want him to know I've been here." She opens the door and glances back over her shoulder. "God, you've been a little snippy lately. When I first met you, I thought you were like a doormat. But lately, you've been kind of cranky."

"I know," I say quietly, with my chin tucked down. "And I'm sorry. I've just been having a rough few weeks."

She pauses in the doorway, eyeing me over. "Are you…"

16

She shifts her weight, looking uncomfortable. Whatever she's trying to say seems to be hard for her. "Are you okay?"

I nod and something crosses over her face, maybe pain, and for a second I wonder if Violet's okay. But then she shrugs and walks out, slamming the door behind her. I release a loud breath and lie back down on the bed. The need to shove my finger down my throat and free the heavy, foul feelings in my stomach strangles me. Damn it. I need therapy. I reach for my phone without sitting up and dial my therapist's number, aka Seth, and my best friend in the whole world.

"I love you to death, Callie," Seth says as he answers after three rings. "But I think I'm about to get lucky so this better be important."

I scrunch my nose as my cheeks heat. "It's not...I just wanted to see what was up. But if you're busy, I'll let you go."

He sighs. "I'm sorry, that came out a lot ruder than I planned. If you *really* need me, I can totally talk. You know you're my first priority."

"Are you with Greyson?" I ask.

"Of course," he replies with humor in his tone. "I'm not a man-whore skank."

A giggle slips through my lips and I'm amazed how much better I feel just from talking to him. "I promise I'm fine. I'm just bored and was looking for an escape from my English book." I shove the book off the bed and roll onto my stomach, propping myself up onto my elbows. "I'll let you go."

"Are you really, really sure?"

"I'm one hundred percent sure. Now go have fun."

"Oh, trust me. I'm planning on it," he replies and I laugh, but it hurts my stomach. I start to hang up when he adds, "Callie, if you need to hang out with someone, you could call Luke...You two are kind of going through the same thing. I mean, with missing Kayden and not really understanding."

I bite at my fingernails. I've spent time with Luke, but I'm still uncomfortable being alone with guys, except for Seth. Besides, things are weird between Luke and me because we haven't officially talked about what happened at Kayden's. It's the white elephant in the room, the massive, sad, heartbroken elephant. "I'll think about it."

"Good. And if you do, make sure to ask him about yesterday in Professor McGellon's class."

"Why? What happened?"

He giggles mischievously. "Just ask him."

"Okay..." I say, unsure if I really want to. If Seth thinks it's funny then there's a good chance that whatever happened might embarrass me. "Have fun with Greyson."

"You too, baby girl," he says and hangs up.

I hit END and scroll through my contacts until I reach Luke's number. My finger hovers over the DIAL button for an eternity and then I chicken out and drop the phone down onto the bed. I get up and slip on my Converses—the ones stained with the green paint—because they remind me of a happy time in life. I zip up my jacket, put my phone into the pocket, and collect my keycard and journal before heading outside.

It's colder than a freezer, but I walk aimlessly through the vacant campus before finally taking a seat on one of the frosted benches. It's snowing but the tree branches create a canopy above my head. I open my journal, pull the top of my jacket over my nose, and begin to scribble down my thoughts, pouring out my heart and soul to blank sheets of paper because it's therapeutic.

I remember my sixteenth birthday like I remember how to add. It's there locked away in my head whenever I need it, although I don't use it often. It was the day I learned to drive. My mom had always been really weird about letting my brother and me anywhere near the wheel of a vehicle until we were old enough to drive. She said it was to protect us from ourselves and other drivers. I remember thinking how strange it was, her wanting to protect us, because there were so many things—huge, life-changing things—she'd never protected us from. Like the fact that my brother had been smoking pot since he was fourteen. Or the fact that Caleb raped me in my own room when I was twelve. Deep down, I knew it wasn't her fault, but the thought always crossed my mind: Why hadn't she protected me?

So at sixteen, I finally got behind the driver's seat for the very first time. I was terrified and my palms were sweating so badly I could barely hold onto the wheel. My dad had also had a lifted truck and I could barely see over the dash.

"Can't we please just drive Mom's car?" I asked my dad as I turned the key in the ignition.

He buckled his seat belt and shook his head. "It's better to learn on the big dog first, that way driving the car will be a piece of cake."

I buckled my own seat belt and wiped my sweaty palms on the front of my jeans. "Yeah, but I can barely see over the wheel."

He smiled and gave me a pat on the shoulder. "Callie, I know driving is scary, like life. But you're perfectly capable of handling this; otherwise I wouldn't let you."

I almost broke down and told him what happened to me on my twelfth birthday. I almost told him that I couldn't handle it. That I couldn't handle anything. But fear owned me and I pressed on the gas and drove the truck forward.

I ended up running over the neighbor's mailbox and proving my dad wrong. I wasn't allowed to drive for the next few months and I was glad. Because to me driving meant growing up and I didn't want to grow up. I wanted to be a child. I wanted to be twelve years old and still have the excitement of life and boys and kisses and crushes ahead of me.

"Fuck, it's freezing out here."

My head snaps up at the sound of Luke's voice and I quickly shut my journal. He's standing a few feet away from me with his hands tucked into the pockets of his jeans and the hood of his dark blue jacket tugged over his head.

"What are you doing out here?" I ask, sliding my pen into the spiral of the notebook.

His shoulders rise and fall as he shrugs and then he sits down beside me. He stretches his legs out in front of himself and crosses his ankles. "I got a random call from Seth telling me that I should come out here and check up on you. That you might need to be cheered up."

My gaze sweeps the campus yard. "Sometimes I wonder if he has spy cameras all over the place. He seems to know everything, you know."

Luke nods in agreement. "He does, doesn't he."

I return his nod and then it grows quiet. Snowflakes drift down and our breath laces in front of our faces. I wonder why he's really here. Did Seth tell him I needed to be watched?

"You want to go somewhere?" Luke uncrosses his ankles and sits up straight. "I don't know about you, but I could really use a break from this place."

"Yeah." I don't even hesitate, which surprises me. Does that mean I'm getting over my trust issues?

He smiles genuinely, but there's intensity in his eyes; something that's always there. I used to be intimidated by it, but now I know it's just him. Besides, I think he hides behind it—maybe fear, loneliness, or the pain of life.

I tuck my notebook underneath my arm and we get to our feet. We hike across the campus yard, heading toward the unknown, but I guess that's okay for now. I'll know where I'm going when I get there.

# Chapter Two

*#22 Make a decision that frightens you*

## Kayden

Whenever I close my eyes, all I see is Callie. *Callie. Callie. Callie.* I can almost feel the softness of her hair and skin, taste her, smell the scent of her shampoo. I miss her so fucking badly I can't breathe sometimes. If I could sleep forever, I would, just so I could hold onto the one thing that makes me happy. But eventually I have to open my eyes and face the reality I put on myself.

The torture.

The brokenness.

What's left of my life?

I probably don't deserve to think about Callie, not after what I did, after she found me...like that. She knows my secret now, the darkest one I've hidden inside me since I was a kid, the one that's the biggest part of me. The worst part of it is that she didn't hear it from me. She heard it from my mother.

It's for the best, though. Callie can go on living her life and she can be happy not having to deal with my problems. I'll stay here and keep my eyes shut and hold onto the memory of her for as long as I can because that's what keeps me breathing.

❧

I'd never been afraid of death. My dad started beating the shit out of me when I was young and an early death always kind of seemed inevitable. Then Callie entered my life and my acceptance of an early death was wrecked. I'm afraid of death now, something I realized after I cut my arms. I can remember watching the blood drip onto the floor and then staring at the bloody knife in my hand. All this doubt and fear had washed through me and I'd regretted it. But it had already been done. As I lay down on the floor, all I could see was Callie's sad face when she'd hear the news that I was dead. There would be no one to protect her from the world if I was gone. And she needed protecting—deserved it more than anyone. And I was such a fuckup that I couldn't even give her that.

About two weeks after the incident, I was transferred to the Brayman's Facility, which isn't much better than the hospital. It's located over on the side of town near the garbage dump and an old trailer park. The room is bare, with plain white walls, no decorations and a stained linoleum floor. The air smells a little less sterilized, but the garbage dump odor drifts into my room sometimes. There's not so much death lingering over everyone's heads, but people really like to talk about it.

I've been here for only a few days and I'm not sure when I'll be ready to leave yet. I'm not sure about a lot of things.

I'm lying in bed, which I do a lot, staring out the window, wondering what Callie is doing right now. I hope something fun that makes her happy and smile.

It's almost time for my checkup so I slowly sit up in the bed, placing my hand over my side where I was stitched up. The knife miraculously missed my organs and it was actually the less severe of my injuries. I was lucky. That's what everyone kept telling me. I was also lucky I didn't cut any major arteries on my wrist. Lucky. Lucky. Lucky. The word keeps getting thrown around, like everyone's trying to remind me how precious life is. I don't believe in luck though, and I'm not even sure I believe that surviving means I'm lucky.

Several times while I was in the hospital, I thought about telling someone what really happened, but I was so doped up on painkillers that I couldn't seem to clear my head enough to get around to it. When the fog in my brain finally cleared, I saw the situation for what it was. I'd just kicked Caleb's ass, I was considered unstable, and the scars on my body raised concern for self-mutilation. I'd be going up against my father and I'd lose, like I always have. There was no point in telling anyone what really happened. People would see only what they want to.

The nurse enters my room with my chart in her hand and a cheery smile on her face. She's older, with blonde hair and dark roots, and she always has red lipstick on her teeth.

"How you doin' today, hun?" she ask in a high voice, like

I'm a child. It's the same tone the doctors use on me because I'm the kid who tried to slit his wrists and then stabbed himself with a kitchen knife.

"I'm fine," I reply and take the little white pills she offers me. I don't know what they're for, but I think they're some kind of sedative because every time I swallow them I fall in and out of consciousness. Which is fine. It numbs the pain, and that's all I've ever wanted.

Ten minutes after the pills go down my throat, drowsiness takes over and I lie down in the bed. I'm about to fall asleep when the familiar scent of expensive perfume burns at my nostrils. I keep my eyes shut. I don't want to talk to her and pretend everything's okay and that my father didn't stab me. I hate pretending that she doesn't know and that she's worried about me.

"Kayden, are you awake?" she asks in a sedated tone, which means she's on something. She pokes my arm with her fingernail and the gesture is rough and scratches my skin. I shut my eyes tighter and cross my arms, wishing she would scrape it harder, cut the skin open and erase everything I'm feeling.

"Kayden Owens." Her sharp voice is like nails on a chalkboard. "Listen, I know you don't want to hear this, but it's time to get your shit together. Get up, start eating better, and prove to the doctors that you're okay to come home."

I say nothing and don't open my eyes. I just listen to my heart beat. *Thump, thump. Thump, thump.*

Her breathing accelerates. "Kayden Owens, I will not let you ruin this family's reputation. Now fix this mess." She grabs the blanket and flings it off me. "Get up, go to therapy, and prove you're not a threat to yourself."

My eyelids gradually open and I turn my head toward her. "What about Dad? Is he still a threat to me?"

She looks like shit, dark circles under her eyes and she's wearing a heavy amount of makeup to try and cover it up. She's still all done up in a fancy red dress, with jewelry and a fur coat, her elaborate façade to hide the ugly in her life. "Your father did nothing wrong. He was just upset at what you did."

"You mean beating the shit out of Caleb," I clarify as I put my hands on the bed, push myself up, and lean against the headboard.

Her eyes turn cold. "Yes, I mean that. Getting into fights is not acceptable. You're lucky Caleb's okay. Although he's still deciding if he's going to press charges. Your dad's working on trying to make a bargain with him."

"What?" It feels like a thousand razor-sharp needles have slid underneath my skin. "Why?"

"Because we're not going to let you drag this family's reputation down the drain with your pathetic life. We're going to keep this as quiet as we can."

"So you're bribing him with money," I utter through clenched teeth. *Fuck.* I want to hit something hard, ram my fist into a metal wall, split open my knuckles, and watch them bleed. I don't want my father taking care of this. I don't want to owe him anything. He'll hold it over my head for the rest of my life. Fuck. This whole situation is so messed up.

"Yes, with money," she snaps and takes her makeup compact out of her purse. "Your father's hard-earned money, which you should be very grateful for."

"Let Caleb press charges." I honestly don't care anymore. Almost every part of me has died and what's still alive is just waiting until the next incision. "I don't give a shit. It'd be better than letting Dad pay him off."

She checks her reflection, pursing her lips, and then clicks the compact shut. "You're so ungrateful." She storms toward the door, her high heels clicking against the dingy linoleum. "You're the most frustrating child in the world. Your brothers never gave me problems like this."

That's because they escaped during the storm and were gone for the tornado. "I'm not a child." I rotate onto my side and close my eyes. "I've never really been a child."

The click of her heels stops. She waits, like she expects me to say something or wants to say something herself, but then the clicking picks up again and soon she's out in the hall. I let the numbness of the pill slink into my body and drag me into the dark. The last thing I see before I pass out is the most beautiful blue-eyed, brown-haired girl I've ever laid eyes on. The only girl who's ever owned my heart and I hold onto the image with every ounce of strength I have. Otherwise I'd probably lose the will to breathe.

# Callie

"I have a quick question," I say to Luke. We're standing in front of the entrance to a small ice rink, getting ready to go ice-skating, something we've both never done (which we admit to each other on the car ride over here). It's not too crowded, but there are a few couples skating and holding hands and a girl getting lessons in the center. "What happened in Professor McGellon's class?"

Luke shakes his head as he runs his hand over his shortly shaven brown hair. "Did Seth put you up to that?"

I bend over to tighten the lace on my skate. "He mentioned on the phone that I should ask you."

He rolls his eyes as I stand up. "You really want to know?"

I hesitate at the note of warning in his tone, but decide to be a bit of a daredevil and nod my head. "Yeah, I do. I guess."

"I got caught doing…something in his class." He ventures out onto the rink and dips the toe of the skate down so the blade cuts the ice. "With a girl."

Seth and his need to push me out of my comfort zone. I'm blushing, but I act like it's just a flush from the frigid temperature, adding a shiver from my body. "By the professor?"

He progresses forward and his knees wobble as he inches toward the middle of the rink where a girl is spinning in circles with her hands above her head. "No, by Seth."

I grip onto the wall and edge out onto the ice, deciding it's probably best to change the subject before my cheeks ignite. "So this is what people do to cheer themselves up?" With my hands out to my side and my palms flat, I try to keep my balance as I slide my feet across the rink.

Luke has his hands spanned to the side of himself, and his knees are bent as he skates in a zigzag pattern. "That's the rumor I was told," he says and reaches for the wall when he stumbles.

"By who?" I clutch onto the wall for support as my knees begin to buckle and remain there briefly to let the poor people behind me skate by.

He grins as his feet make a circular motion against the ice. "By this hot chick I hooked up with the other night. She insisted that we needed to go ice skating."

I inhale a deep breath and fight back another blush creeping across my cheeks. "Why didn't you just bring her here then?"

He snorts a laugh. "What fun would that be? I like hanging out with you, Callie. It's relaxing." He pushes his feet along the ice and attempts to skate backward but trips over his feet and slams into the wall. His hand shoots out and he clutches onto the edge of the plastic section.

"Are you okay?" I stifle a laugh as his eyes pop wide open.

"You think that's funny?" He gets his feet underneath himself and then, with very little coordination, skates toward me with his knees knocking together and his arms flinging to the side of him.

I stifle a laugh, moving my feet inward and outward, going backward to get away from him. "I thought football players were supposed to be coordinated."

His lips curve into a grin and he winks at me. "On grass, Callie. Football players don't spend much time on ice."

"How about a ballet studio," I tease. "I've heard you guys sometimes like to twirl around and point your toes for"—I make air quotes and smile—"athletic purposes."

He shakes his head, rolling his tongue into his mouth to force back a grin. "You know, Kayden's right about you. You can get kind of cocky when you want to."

My heart sinks to my stomach and Luke's face falls. We both stand there, immobile, and my thoughts drift to Kayden.

I stumble to the gate to sit down on a bench. "I think I need a break. I'm not very good at this," I say, changing the subject.

"Me neither." Luke skates to the exit and his toe clips against the rubber threshold as he follows me off the rink. He takes a seat beside me on the bench and stretches his legs out in front of himself.

For a while we just stare out at the other skaters, watching them laugh, smile, fall, and have fun. They look like they're having a great time, and I envy them. I want to have fun too, but with Kayden. I want him here with me.

"So have you heard from him?" Luke asks casually, gazing across the ice rink.

I look at him, creasing my forehead. "Who? Kayden?"

He nods his head once without making eye contact. "Yeah."

I blow out a breath and it puffs out in front of my face in a cloud of grayish smoke. Even though it's an indoor rink, it's still as chilly as it is outside. I have my jacket and gloves on, along with my hood over my head, and I'm still frozen to the bone. Or maybe the cold's from the direction the conversation's heading.

"No," I mutter, fastening my gaze on a young couple skating hand in hand. They look happy and if I stare for long enough I can change their faces into Kayden's and mine. "I haven't heard anything except for the latest gossip from my mother."

Luke hunches over as he reaches for the laces on one of his skates. "And what's the latest gossip?"

I swallow the massive lump in my throat. "That Kayden's in a facility under surveillance."

He cocks his head to the side and glances up at me. "Because they think he did it to himself?" There's insinuation in his tone. He knows what I know: that Kayden's dad is an evil monster who could have stabbed his son.

I tried to talk to my mother about it, but she told me it was none of our business. She's angry with the Owenses because Kayden beat up Caleb. I should have told her why... I wanted to, but sometimes wanting to isn't enough.

When I'd finally worked the courage to go tell her, it was right after Kayden's mom had told me he'd cut himself. My mom had been sitting at the kitchen table eating a bowl of cereal as she read the newspaper.

"Mom, I have to tell you something," I said, shaking from head to toe. I'd just walked in from outside, so I pretended it was from that, but really it had been my nerves.

She glanced up from her cereal, holding the spoon inside the bowl. "If it's about Kayden, I already know."

I sat down at the table across from her. "I know what you've probably heard, but I don't think he did it to himself."

She stirred her cereal with the spoon and lines crinkled around her eyes. "What are you talking about, Callie?"

"I'm talking about...I'm talking about what happened to Kayden." I crossed my arms on the table and balled my hands into fists. "And why he's in the hospital."

The lines disappeared from around her eyes as she frowned. "Oh, I don't care about that. I'm talking about what he did to Caleb."

My heart compressed at the sound of Caleb's name and I wanted to scream at her for saying that. "That wasn't his fault."

She shook her head and grabbed her bowl as she stood up. "Look, I know you care about him, Callie, but he's obviously got a temper on him." She walked over to the sink and put the bowl in it. "You need to stay away from him."

I pushed back from the table and my knees shook. "No."

She turned around and the iciness in her eyes reminded me of why I couldn't tell her stuff—because she only ever looked at stuff from her own point of view. "Callie Lawrence, you will not talk to me that way."

I shook my head, backing toward the door. "I'll talk to you like this when you're wrong."

Her eyes widened, shocked. I'd never talked to her like that before. "What is wrong with you? Is it because you've been hanging around Kayden? I bet it is."

"A few weeks ago you were so happy we were together," I said, gripping the doorknob.

"That's before I knew what he was capable of," she said. "I don't want you hanging out with him. And besides, you should be on Caleb's side in all of this. He's been part of this family for longer."

A cold, yet hot wave of anger ripped from my toes and rushed to my mouth. "You don't even know the whole story! And you don't care enough to ask!" I wasn't sure what I was referring to anymore but I didn't stay long enough to find out. I jerked the back door open and ran outside into the snow.

She didn't follow me and I wasn't surprised. I'd never expect anything more from her.

"Earth to Callie." Luke waves a hand in front of my face and I flinch. "Did you hear what I asked? About Kayden?"

"Yeah." I press my lips together, thread my finger through the laces, and begin to unfasten them. "That's what everyone's saying—that he cut himself."

Grabbing the gap between the blade and the bottom of the

skate, he slips off his skate, tosses it to the side, and stretches out his toes. "You don't believe that, do you?"

Part of me does, whenever I think about that night when Kayden and I had sex and there were all those fresh wounds on his arms. I didn't think about it at the time, but they could have been track marks from self-inflicted injuries. But I don't believe that he stabbed himself.

"I think it might have been his dad." Saying it aloud changes everything, makes it real, true. I'm breathless, not just because of the idea of Kayden's father stabbing him, but because Kayden hasn't said anything and it aches to think about what his silence could mean. I know the pain that causes that kind of silence way too well.

Luke kicks off his other skate, then relaxes back in the bench and crosses his arms. "You know, I remember when we were kids and Kayden used to sleep over at my house all the time. I always thought it was weird because he wanted to stay at my house and not his. Mine was a fucking shithole and my mother's fucking crazy. I didn't get it, until the first time I stayed over at his house."

I want to know why he thinks his mother is crazy, but the tension in his jawline is an indicator not to ask. "What happened?"

He pulls off his gloves, balls them up, and puts them into the pocket of his jacket. The intensity in his liquid brown eyes carries the severity of what he's about to tell me. "I broke a cup. Not on purpose, but still the fucking cup was broken and that's all that mattered. I remember when it happened, Kayden flipped out. We were like ten and I didn't get it. It was a fucking cup, right?" He exhales loudly and I notice that his hands have a slight tremble to them. "Anyway, Kayden's panicking and yelling at me to get the broom from the storage closet. So I go to get it, but it's not in the storage closet. So I start looking everywhere and finally find it in the hallway closet. At this point, I can hear all this yelling coming from the kitchen." He pauses and his throat muscles move as he swallows hard.

I realize my own hands are shaking and my heart's hammering inside my chest. "What happened? When you went back into the kitchen?"

He stares at the other side of the rink. "Kayden was on the floor and his father was standing above him, with his knee bent, like he was getting ready to kick him. Kayden had blood all over his hands because he was crawling through the shards trying to pick them all up. He had this huge cut on his face and there was a piece of the cup in his dad's hand." He pauses. "Kayden denied his father did anything to him, but I can put two and two together."

I breathe through my nose over and over again, fighting back the tears. "Did he ever tell you the truth?"

"About that day?" He shakes his head. "But there was one time I was over there and he got into this huge argument with his father and his father hit him right in front of me, so after that the cat was kind of out of the bag."

I wiggle my foot out of the skate, shut my eyes, and let my

lungs expand as cold air fills them. "Do you ever feel guilty for not saying anything?"

He's quiet for a very long time, and when I open my eyes, he's watching me. "All the God damn time," he says with fire in his eyes.

There's a moment when Luke and I are connected by a piece of thread that's frayed and thin and very breakable. Then it's over and he gets to his feet, collects his skates by the laces, and heads for the locker that's holding our shoes. I follow him, grabbing my skates before rounding the bench. We put on our shoes and walk to his truck, not speaking and allowing the guilt to seep into our already chilled bodies. He starts up his old battered truck but dithers when he's about to shove the shifter into gear.

"Maybe we should go see him," he says and pushes the stick shift forward into drive. He cranks the wheel to the right and turns up the heater before pressing the gas and pulling out of the parking spot. "I've got only one more class before Christmas break, but I can blow it off. I already took the final."

"But they're not letting anyone see him except for family," I remind him as I bend my arm and reach behind me for the seat belt. "At least that's what my mom told me yesterday when I called her. She said that Maci told her he wasn't allowed visitors except for her and that he can't even talk on the phone."

His gaze cuts to me as he stops the truck at the exit and looks both ways at the empty street. "You believe her?"

I pull the seat belt down and buckle it, and then my

shoulders lift and slump. "I don't know. Maci Owens is a lot of things, but why would she lie about that?"

"To cover up what really happened." The truck fishtails as he pulls out onto the main road, which is slippery with snow. It's late, the sky is gray, and the lampposts lining the street highlight the flakes falling from the sky.

I'm about to tell him yes, let's drive down the highway and fly toward Afton. I was planning on heading back in a few days anyway, but then my phone starts playing "Hate Me," by Blue October.

I frown. "It's my mom." I take my phone out of my pocket and stare at the glowing screen. I briefly consider letting it go to voicemail where she could yammer to it about how messed up she thinks it is that Kayden beat up Caleb. But giving her an open door to a one-sided conversation is like Christmas morning for her and I don't want to have to listen to her go on and on in hopes of hearing something important.

I press TALK and put the phone up to my ear. "Hello."

"Hi, sweetie," she singsongs and my face instantly sinks. "How are you?"

"Fine." I ignore Luke's questioning stare and watch the road.

"You don't sound fine," she replies and then sighs. "Callie, you're not going back to being depressed again, are you? Because I thought college was healing that."

"I was never depressed," I respond flatly. "Just quiet."

She sighs exaggeratedly and I grit my teeth. "Look, honey,

I just wanted to let you know that Caleb's probably going to be pressing charges against Kayden for what he did."

"What!" I exclaim, startling Luke enough that he jumps and swerves the truck a little and the side of the tire clips the curb, causing the truck to lurch. He quickly regains control and I lower my voice and press my finger to my ear to hear better as I huddle toward the door. "What the fuck do you mean he's pressing charges?"

"Callie Lawrence, you will not use that kind of language on the phone with me, young lady," she warns. "You know how much I don't like the *F* word."

"Sorry," I apologize. "But why is Caleb pressing charges? They both beat each other up."

"No, Kayden hit Caleb for no reason," she says. "Caleb was just defending himself."

"He didn't hit him for no reason. He hit him because of me." It slips out like poison vapor and I choke on each syllable.

There's an extensive pause. "Callie, what do you mean he hit Caleb because of you? Why would he do that?"

My shoulders curl in as the shame and the dirtiness floods my body and I remember her limited ability to understand things. "It's nothing. I'm just upset and saying stuff. It doesn't mean anything."

She pauses again and I wonder if for a split second, she's contemplating my words on a deeper level. "Callie, is there something you want to tell me?"

When I breathe again, it's deafening and I swear the whole world can hear it and they know my secret. "No, Mom."

"Okay then." She sounds disappointed, like I was just about to give her the secret locked in a box inside me. But only Kayden has the key to it. "Well, I just wanted to let you know in case it comes up. I know his best friend goes to school there with you and I don't want you to have to hear it by gossip."

I shake my head. "All right."

"I'll talk to you later, Callie."

"Okay, bye."

We hang up and I clutch the phone in my hand, strangling the life out of it. My palms start to sweat and I can't stop thinking about Kayden. *He did it for me. He did it for me. I need to save him.* "I think we should go to Afton."

When Luke looks at me, there are lines on his forehead and his hands are gripping the steering wheel. "Really?"

"Yeah." I raise my hips and slide the phone into the pocket of my jeans. "My mom said Caleb's going to press charges against Kayden."

He keeps some of his attention on the road as he turns the truck into the parking lot in front of my dorm. "Are you shitting me?"

I zip up my coat and put my gloves on. "No, and I need to fix it . . . somehow. It's my fault it happened to begin with."

He parks the truck near the front, puts his hand on the shifter, and pushes it into park. The radio plays and the engine keeps cutting out. I wonder if he knows why Kayden beat up Caleb that night, if he ever told him.

"All right, it's a deal." Luke stares at the McIntyre residence hall in front of us. It's the tallest of the residence halls at the University of Wyoming and it looks lonely, towering above the others. "You want to leave tonight or in the morning?"

I grab the door handle and pull on it. "In the morning. I'd like Seth to come, too, if that's okay."

He nods and reaches for his pack of cigarettes on the dashboard. "That's fine as long as you guys don't mind squishing into this thing. It's a piece of shit, but Seth's car's never going to make it to Afton with all the snow."

I shove open the door. "He'll be fine with it I'm sure." I swing my feet over the edge of the seat, getting ready to jump down.

"Callie," Luke calls out. "Is there any way we can fix this? Stop Caleb from pressing charges? You know, if he does, Kayden's going to get suspended from the team. He'll probably never play again. And he'll probably get suspended from school. Plus, he might have to go to jail or pay a huge fucking fine that he can't afford without his father's help." He pauses, deliberating with his forehead bunched. "I just really want to make sure that everything's okay with him . . . Sometimes when people hit bottom, they give up . . ." His voice grows softer, like the weight of a fall leaf. "Kind of like my sister."

The gravity of the situation pushes on my chest as I hop out, grabbing the door for support. I remember that Luke had a sister. He never said how she died, but after what he just said, I wonder if it was suicide.

Pressing my palm to the nagging ache in the center of my heart, I turn around toward the cab. "I'm going to try. I just have to figure out how." I already know how. The big question is, can I do it? Can I finally say it aloud, confront him, threaten him, make it so that he's so terrified he'll walk away from it. Can I tell my mother, father, and brother? Can I trust them to believe me and be on my side?

Do I have that much power? Do I have that much courage?

In the end, I know I'm going to have to answer those questions and make a decision that's frightened me for the last six years of my life, but maybe it's time to face it.

Maybe it's time to quit being so scared.

# Chapter Three

*#46 Transform yourself*

## Kayden

I've been here six days, almost a week, but it seems so much longer. It's just after lunch and I'm in the middle of my daily individual therapy session, which is better than group (I don't bother talking in that one). I'm sitting in my room in an uncomfortable metal fold-up chair. My side hurts like hell and I can't stop picking at the wounds underneath the bandage on my wrist. It's cloudy outside and thunder and lightning keep snapping and booming, lighting up the room with a silver glow.

"Tell me how you feel," the therapist says.

He says it every God damn time.

And every God damn time I give him the same response.

"I feel fine," I reply and flick the rubber band on my wrist over and over again until the skin on the inside of my wrist stings. This is what they gave me to help my self-mutilation, like a tiny sting can replace a lifetime of cuts, stabs, broken bones, the raw pain of life.

My therapist's name is Dr. Montergrey, but he told me to call him Doug because using his professional name makes him feel old. But he is old, well into his sixties, with gray thinning hair and lots of wrinkles around his eyes.

Doug puts his finger to the bridge of his nose and adjusts his square-framed glasses as he reads over the notes he has on me. I can only imagine what they say: a threat to himself, angry, irrational, uncooperative, self-damaging. He jots down some notes and then looks up at me. "Look, Kayden, I know sometimes it's hard to talk about how we feel, especially when we have so much hate and rage going on inside, but you might find it helpful to talk about it."

I flick the rubber band again and the snap is covered up by the deafening clap of thunder. The room lights up and the rubber band breaks, the pieces falling to the floor. I stare at them as I rub my swollen wrist. I still have a bandage on one of them, the one that I made the deepest cuts on. The other one is starting to heal and soon there will only be scars. More scars. One day I wonder if I'll be one big scar that will own every ounce of my skin.

Doug reaches into the pocket of his brown tweed jacket and retrieves another rubber band, a thicker one that's dark red. I take it, slip it onto my wrist, and begin flicking it again. Doug scribbles some notes down, closes the notebook, and then overlaps his hands and places them on top of the note-book. "You know, the longer you stay in denial, the longer they're going to keep you here." He gestures around at the room. "Is that what you want?"

I stop flicking the rubber band, fold my arms, and lean back in the seat with my legs kicked out in front of me. "Maybe." I know I'm being a pain in the ass and I don't know why. I feel bitter on the inside, unworthy to be here. I feel everything and maybe that's the problem. I clench my hands into fists and jab my fingernails into my palms, which are tucked to my side so the therapist doesn't see them.

"I just don't want to be here," I mutter. "But it's fucking hard, you know?"

He leans forward with interest. "What's hard?"

I have no idea where I'm going with this. "Life." I shrug.

His gray eyebrows dip underneath the frame of his glasses. "What's hard about your life, Kayden?"

This guy doesn't get it, which might make it easier. "Feeling everything."

He looks perplexed as he reclines in his chair and slips off his glasses. "Feeling emotions? Or the pain in life?"

Fuck. Maybe he does get it. "Both I guess."

Rain slashes against the window. It's weird that it's raining instead of snowing and by morning the ground is going to be a sloshy mess.

He cleans the lenses of his glasses with the bottom of his shirt and then slips them back on his nose. "Do you ever let yourself feel what's inside you?"

I consider what he said for a very long time. Sirens shriek

outside and somewhere in the halls a person is crying. "I'm not sure . . . maybe . . . not always."

"And why is that?" he asks.

I think back to all the kicks, the punches, the screaming, and how eventually I just drowned it all out, shut down, and died inside. "Because it's too much." It's a simple answer, but each word conveys more meaning than anything I've ever said. It's fucking strange to talk about it aloud. The only person I've ever said anything to was Callie and I sugarcoated it for her, to keep her from seeing how ugly and fucked up I am on the inside.

He removes a pen from the pocket of his jacket and his hand swiftly moves across the paper as he scribbles down some notes. "And what do you do when it becomes too much?"

I slide my finger under the rubber band and give it a flick, then do it again harder. It breaks again and I shake my head as I catch the pieces in my hand. "I think you know what I do, which is why I keep breaking these damn rubber bands."

He chews on the end of his pen as he evaluates me. "Let's talk about the night you got in a fight."

"I already told you about that night a thousand times."

"No, you told me what happened that night in your own words, but you've never explained to me how you felt when you were making your decision. And emotions always play a large part in the things we do."

"I'm not a fan of them," I admit, slouching back in the chair.

"I know that," he responds confidently. "And I'd like to get to the bottom of why."

"No, you wouldn't," I tell him, dragging my nail up the inside of my palm to soothe the accelerating beat of my heart. "No one wants to hear about that. Trust me."

He drops the pen on top of the notebook that's on his lap. "Why would you think that?"

"Because it's true." I stab my nails deeper into my skin until I feel the warmth and comfort of blood. "I'm nineteen years old and everything that's done is done. There's no point in trying to save me. Who I am and what I do is always going to be."

"I'm not trying to save you," he promises. "I'm trying to heal you."

I run my finger along a thin scar on the palm of my hand that was put there when my dad cut me with a shard of glass. "What? Heal these? I'm pretty fucking sure they're not going anywhere."

He positions his hand over his heart. "I want to heal what's in here."

Usually I bail on these situations. Otherwise I'll end up feeling things I don't want to, and then I have to take it out on my body just to cope. But I can't here. They won't let me anywhere near anything sharp, especially razors. My jawline and chin are extremely scruffy because I haven't shaved in a week.

"This is getting way too heart-to-heart for me," I say and grab onto the sides of the chair to push myself up.

He holds up his hand, signaling for me to sit back down. "Okay, we don't have to talk about your feelings, but I want you to answer one thing for me."

I stare blankly at him as I lower myself back into the chair. "That depends on what that one thing is."

He taps the pen against the notebooks as he deliberates. "Why did you go to the party that night?"

"It's always the same question with you."

"Because it's an important question."

I shake my head as my pulse speeds up with either anger or fear—I can't tell. "I went there to beat Caleb Miller up. You know that."

"Yes, but why?"

"Why what?" I'm getting annoyed, frustrated, and pissed off, and the anger snakes through my veins underneath my skin.

"Why did you beat him up?" It's like he's stuck on repeat and I want him to shut the hell up.

My heart knocks inside my chest like a damn jackhammer and all I want is something sharp or rough—anything that can calm my pulse down. I'm glancing around in a panic, searching for something, but the room is bare. *I can't do this. I can't do this. Fuck!* "Because he hurt someone." My voice comes out piercing and uneven and makes me sound weak and pathetic.

He sits forward in the chair. "Someone you care about?"

"Obviously." I shake my head, annoyed. My heart is still beating too loud and I can barely think straight.

He raises his eyebrows. "Someone you love?"

My pulse speeds even more, erratic and without a distinct beat. I feel it pulsating underneath every wound and scar on my body. *Love? Do I love Callie? Can I?* "I don't think I even know what love is."

He looks like he's struck gold and found an insight into what's locked away in my soul. "Can you answer just one more question for me?"

I throw my hands in the air exasperatedly. "Do whatever the hell you want. You're already on a roll."

He asks, "Do you think you deserve love?"

"I already told you I don't even know what it is," I mutter and he waits for me to divulge more information. What does he want from me? To tell him that my dad beats the shit out of me? That my mom's a drug-addicted zombie? That the only exchange of love I've ever gotten is from Daisy and that felt about as plastic and as fake as things can get.

He writes down a few notes, then clicks his pen and tucks it away in his pocket before shutting his notebook again. "I think we might have made some progress today." He checks his watch and then gets to his feet, retrieving his trench coat from off the back of the chair. "Keep it up, and maybe you can have visitors who are not family."

I slump back into the chair. "I'm not sure if I want visitors," I mumble.

He doesn't seem to hear me. When he reaches the door, he slips his arm through the sleeve of his jacket, secures the belt around his waist, and sticks his hand into his pocket. "And Kayden, keep using this, no matter how many times it breaks. We can always get you a new one." He throws a rubber band at me and I catch it effortlessly. For a second I'm back on the field, running and catching the ball, free from life.

I wish I were back there, fixed and mended. But unlike the rubber band, I'm not sure I can be fixed so easily.

## Callie

"I can't believe your truck doesn't have a CD player," Seth says with his arm extended across the front of me as he fiddles with the volume on the stereo. He has on a jacket, with the sleeves pushed up, and skinny jeans. "Or an iPod hookup. I swear I'm having flashbacks of mullets, spandex pants, and crimped hair."

"I think you're going back a little too far." Luke has his hood pulled over his head and a leather band on his wrist that has the word *redemption* on it. I wonder if it means something to him or if he believes in redemption. I wonder if I believe in it. He stretches his arm in front of me and flips open the glove box. "Back to the eight-track era."

I cringe at how close he is, but then release the tension, refusing to go back to that place. I zip up my jacket, because it's cold inside due to the fact that they keep rolling down the windows to smoke.

It's early in the morning, the sun is kissing the frosted

land, and the highway is a hazard from last night's storm so we have to drive slowly. There are a few cars stuck in the mounds of snow in the strip of land in the center of the opposing traffic and people have turned off onto the ramps because they're too afraid to drive. Luke and I are used to it though. It's the conditions we grew up in.

Seth slaps his hand away from the glove box and Luke looks at me in disbelief, but I just laugh. "No, eight-tracks were still in play in the eighties."

"Early eighties," Luke corrects. "They faded out by mid-decade."

I laugh because they are fighting over something so ridiculous and I'm tired and nervous and my head's in a very strange place. "You guys are fighting like an old married couple." As soon as I say it, I want to take it back, because I'm not sure how Luke will take it.

When I look at Luke, he seems perfectly fine. He shrugs and then sticks his hand into the glove box and pulls out a tape labeled *Let's Get High*. "Whatever," he says and feeds it into the tape player. "As long as I'm the guy in the relationship, it's all good."

Seth rolls his eyes. "Whatever, you'd totally be my bitch and you know it."

That's it. I can't hold it in any longer. My body falls forward as I cover my mouth and my shoulders shake as I laugh into my hand. "Oh my God, I can't believe you just said that."

"Yes, you can." Seth pats my back. "I wouldn't be me if I didn't say the first thing that pops into my head."

51

He's right. Seth is blunt and funny and he totally says whatever the hell he wants. And I love him for it. I sit up, wiping the tears from my eyes, and then give him a quick kiss on the cheek. "Thank you for making me smile," I say.

He grins. "Anytime, sweetheart."

Luke shakes his head, but there's a grin on his face so I know he's not offended. I like Luke. He's not judgmental and he seems accepting. I almost lean over to hug him and then realize how weird it is because it doesn't freak me out. What does that mean? *Crap*. What *does* that mean?

"Come on Eileen," by Dexy's Midnight Runners, blasts out from the speakers.

"This is so eighties," Seth says and begins snapping his fingers and bobbing his head. He really starts to get into it, shaking his hips and shimmying frontward and backward. "Come on, Callie, you know you want to dance. It'll make you smile even more."

I grin from ear to ear. "No way."

Cold air fills the cab as Luke cracks the window. The lighter flicks and then the smell of cigarette smoke flows through the air. Seth keeps dancing as he reaches into the pocket of his hoodie and takes out his pack of cigarettes. Out of the corner of my eye, I see Luke bobbing his head as he sucks on the end of his cigarette. He takes a long drag, and then puckers his lips and a thin trail of white smoke laces out of his mouth. Seth starts thrusting his hips wildly as he flicks the end of his lighter and puts it up to the tip of the cigarette.

The paper curls in and turns black as he takes a long drag. The car starts rocking as the chorus comes on and both the guys really start getting into it. The smoke burns my lungs and the cold causes goose bumps to sprout all over my arms. I experience almost every single detail of the moment and I decide to experience it all.

"Oh fine, what the hell." I start lifting my shoulders up and down to the rhythm and Seth grins at me.

"That's my girl," he says and blows out a cloud of smoke with his lips puckered out.

We both start doing this funny jiving thing with our hands and Luke laughs as he cranks up the music. For a second I transform myself into a dancer. When the chorus hits again we all take a deep breath and belt out the lyrics at the top of our lungs. I raise my hands above my head and shut my eyes. *It'll be all right. It'll be all right. Kayden will be all right.*

Because I'm here, dancing, smiling, and sitting between two guys, and if that can happen, then anything's possible.

## Kayden

I've been in the clinic for a week now and today should be a really good morning. Doug has informed me that I can have visitors outside of family and that I can make a few phone calls throughout the day. When he gives me time to make the phone call, however, I get stuck on who to call. My first instinct is to call Callie, but I haven't talked to her since it happened and

I'm not sure she wants to talk to me after finding me like that. The idea of finding out scares the shit out of me. Besides, I'm trying to keep my distance and protect her from me because the last thing she needs is my instability and fucked-up head.

I dial Luke's number and lean back in the bed, watching the storm outside my window as the phone rings and rings.

"Kayden?" he says, sounding confounded. There's an eighties song playing in the background and I can hear a lot of giggling.

"What's up?" It sounds so stupid after I say it. There's a long pause and then someone starts singing really loudly and really off key. "Is that Seth in the background?"

"Yeah." He hesitates again. "Are you okay?"

I flick the rubber band with my finger. It snaps back, hits my wrist, and sends a sting through my arm. "Kind of... Why are you with Seth?"

"Because... we're in the truck." He seems conflicted. "We're headed to Afton to see you actually."

I snap the rubber band against my wrist a few more times, but it's not stilling the anxiety twisting inside me. "When you say *we* you mean..."

"I mean, Seth, me and..." He trails off. "And Callie."

The singing stops and so does the music.

"Who are you talking to?" Callie asks.

When I hear her voice I swear to God my heart stops. I clutch at the chord and wrap it around my wrist until it's tight and cuts off the circulation. I stare outside at the slush on the ground and the banks of snow around the mostly vacant parking lot.

"Umm…" Luke struggles for words.

"You can tell her," I say, because if they're headed here then I'm going to have to face her soon.

"It's Kayden," he tells her and then it gets quiet.

"Oh…" She's perplexed and I don't blame her. "Can I… Can I talk to him?"

"Hold on," Luke says and then asks me, "You want to talk to Callie?"

"I…" I never get to discover my answer, and it sucks because I'm dying to know how I feel. My response would have revealed the truth about my fear and how bad it's going to be when she gets here. But like always, my mother walks in just at the right moment and steals everything away from me.

"We need to talk." Her chin is tipped high like she's better than everyone in the building and she's carrying around a duffel bag on her shoulder. *"Now."*

"I gotta go." I hang up, knowing I'm being a pussy and dodging my feelings. I unravel the cord from my hand and lean back in my bed, putting my feet up on it. I'm wearing a pair of plaid pajama bottoms and an old blue T-shirt that has holes in it. I've worn the outfit five times since I've been here and it's getting old.

She heaves the duffel bag onto the foot of the bed and then positions her hands on her hips. "You need to work on getting better and getting out of here. It's making our family look bad."

I carefully hunch forward, because moving too fast still hurts my side. "And what do you suggest I do, Mother, because the doctors seem to think differently. They think I need to stay here and heal."

"I don't give a shit what the doctors think." She unzips the bag with a tug. "What I care about is that you get dressed in some normal clothes, get everyone thinking you feel better, and then come home so we can start planning what we're going to do if Caleb Miller presses charges."

"I could always plead mental insanity." Sarcasm drips from my voice. "Maybe they'd just keep me here instead of sending me to jail."

Her face flushes red and she shifts the handle of her purse higher onto her shoulder. "You think this is funny? Maybe I should have your father come down here and talk some sense into you."

No matter how hard I try, I'm sent straight back to that place where I'm lying on the floor bleeding to death and completely ready to accept it. I rub my hand across my face and then say through clenched teeth, "I'll see what I can do."

She smiles and it looks out of place, like she's the evil villain about to execute her evil plan. She kisses my cheek and I can smell the wine on her breath. Then she moves back and rubs her thumb across my cheek. "I got lipstick on you." She pulls her hand away and smiles again. "Let's work on getting you out of here." She pats my leg and then walks out of the room, leaving the door open. I hear her say something to one of the doctors and then a nurse shuts the door.

I take a long-sleeve thermal shirt out of the bag, which is filled with jeans, shirts, and socks, and slip it on over my head. Then I reach for a pair of jeans, ready to put on my full costume and go lie to the world, just like I've been doing my entire life.

# Chapter Four

*#67 Reunite with something you thought you lost*

## Callie

We arrive in Afton late at night when the moon is a ginormous orb in the charcoaled sky and the blizzard is creating a veil in front of the truck, making it hard to see. We would have made it here by dinnertime, but Seth made us stop for lunch and play in the playhouse at McDonald's. But it was kind of all our faults for getting so carried away and staying until we got in trouble by the manager.

I think we were all avoiding something. But what that is, I'm still trying to figure out. After a very long, exhausting drive, Seth and I sneak up into the garage and crash on the bed without having to talk to my mother. The place holds one of the strongest memories in my head, and when I'd first walked in, I'd nearly fallen over as I remembered how it felt when Kayden touched me, kissed me, became a part of me.

"I'm bummed," Seth states as we lie face to face on the bed

in our pajamas. The space heater hums in the background and the glow of it and the lamp highlights the spackled spots on the walls. He fakes a pout. "I was totally looking forward to meeting your mother."

I gently pinch his arm. "You liar. You're so glad she's asleep."

He giggles and then rolls to his side, propping himself up on his elbow. "I know. I wish I was, but from what you tell me about her, she's not going to be that fond of my colorful personality."

I sit up in the bed, take the elastic out of my hair, and then refasten my ponytail. I let my arms fall into my lap and I chew on my lip, thinking about tomorrow and seeing Kayden.

Seth touches my bottom lip and my initial reaction is to flinch, but I work at it and keep it under control. "A penny for your thoughts?"

"It's nothing." I sigh and flop down on the bed on my side. "I'm just wondering what it's going to be like...seeing him again."

He considers this as he sweeps his bangs off his face. "It'll be like the first time I decided I was going to talk to you. You have to think of Kayden like a skittish cat. If you say the wrong thing, he might flip out."

"You thought of me as a skittish cat?"

"A skittish kitten." He grins and winks at me. "You looked like you were going to claw my eyes out the moment I approached you."

I fluff the pillow and tuck my hands under my head. "What if I say something wrong, though, and he gets upset?"

He unlatches his watch and rolls to the side to set it on the Tupperware bin next to the bed. Then he pivots to his hip and faces me. "You won't."

I lift my legs up and slide them underneath the blankets. "How can you be so sure?"

He smiles and touches the tip of his finger to the tip of my nose. "Because he opened up to you the first time, which means you've already said the right things. So all you have to do is go there tomorrow and be yourself."

"I hope you're right." I click the lamp off and the room goes dark. The pale glow of the moonlight filters in through the window. "I really hope you are."

"I'm always right, darling," he says, and then squeezes my hand. "Just don't overthink it."

I shut my eyes and hold onto the thought that tomorrow I'll see him, alive, and not bleeding on the floor. Maybe then I can finally get the god-awful image out of my head.

## Kayden

It's mid-December, the start of winter break. If I weren't here, I'd be heading home from school, probably with Callie and Luke. It's weird knowing she's probably driving into town right now, just getting home, so close to me in distance, and yet she still seems far away, almost unreachable, since I'm stuck in here and she's out there.

I've secretly been collecting rubber bands and I have five of them on my wrist. Not that Doug knows it. I kept pretending that I broke them until I had a collection. The thickness gives more of a sting and it settles me on the inside each time I flick them. I need a lot of settling because my mother showed up tonight and has been here for over an hour trying to work things out with the doctor and Doug to get me released.

They're over by the doorway having a conversation about me like I'm not even here. It's actually more of an argument than a conversation.

"But we'll be there watching him at all times." My mother talks with her hands a lot and she's got long fingernails. Every time she says something she swings her arms animatedly and almost nails the doctor in the eye.

Doug fans through his yellow-sheeted notebook and reads through his notes. "Look, Mrs. Owens, I know this must be hard for you, but I don't think it's healthy for Kayden to leave the facility just yet. In fact, I'd advise against it."

My mother taps her foot on the floor and crosses her arms as she stares Doug down like he is a small, insignificant piece of shit. "Look, I understand what you advise, but I'd rather not take advice from a doctor who got his PhD from some low-budget college."

"I got my PhD from Berkeley," he says, pulling out a pen from his pocket.

Her gaze sweeps over him and she elevates her eyebrows. "Really? Then why are you here?"

Doug stays calm as he balances the notebook on his arm and writes something down. "I might be asking you the same thing."

I think I like Doug at that moment and I smile to myself as I wiggle my finger under the bands and flip them against the inside of my wrist and let the burn soothe me. I'm sitting in the corner of the room, not the one I sleep in but a larger one with a lot of tables and chairs scattered around. The walls are brick and cracked with old age, but it's more comforting than the dull white ones in the room. Some people eat lunch in here, but I choose to eat in my room because there's always too much going on, like fights and yelling and crying.

My mother stabs her fingernail against Doug's chest. "Don't you dare insinuate anything."

"I wasn't," Doug says simply, wincing as he grips the spot on his chest where my mother stabbed her finger. "It just seems like you're awfully eager to take Kayden out of here when it's clear he's not stable."

I scan the scars on my arms and the bandage on my wrists. I've been picking at the scab that's underneath it a lot, which is why it's not healing. But it's a fucking habit and I can't seem to break it.

"He's perfectly stable," my mother insists. There's a slight slur to her speech and I wonder if the doctor can hear it. "And it's my call, since I'm the one who signed him in to be here."

I stand up, stunned. "You did that? I thought that was the hospital?"

She glares at me with annoyance. "I put you here for your own good. You needed to be watched for a while, but now... you've been here for a little over a week and it's time to move on and get your act together."

Or kept away from my father. "Then I want to leave," I say, walking across the room. "And I want to go back to school, not back home."

"You can't," she replies curtly. "It's Christmas break."

"Okay, then maybe I want to stay here." I back up to the chair and sit down. I tip my head forward and rub the sides of my temples with my fingers. "Fuck." I have no idea what to do. I don't want to be in this God damn room anymore, but leaving means facing the world, myself, my father, Callie.

"If Kayden wants to stay here," Doug interrupts. "Then he can."

"I'm sure as hell not paying for it," my mother snaps venomously. She reaches into her purse and takes out the car keys. "I'm signing you out first thing tomorrow morning and then you're coming home—that is, unless you want to fork out your own money."

She clutches the keys in her hands and storms out the

door, taking my hope with her. I wonder why she's doing it. Why she'd put me in here for barely over a week and then suddenly want me out. There's got to be something going on.

Whatever it is, I don't want to go home. If I do, there's a good chance my father's going to finish what he started.

Doug sighs as he returns his pen to his pocket, and then he turns to me. "Well, that didn't go so well."

"It never does with her." I shove the sleeves of my long-sleeved shirt up and rest my arms on my knees. "There's no use trying to fight her on anything. She always wins."

He grabs a chair from the corner and positions it in front of my chair. He doesn't bother taking his jacket off, which means he's probably not staying long. "Does she win fights with your father?" he asks as he lowers himself into the chair.

Warning flags pop up all over in my head. I know the drill. *Lie. Lie. Lie.* "What do you mean? What fights?"

He crosses his leg over his knee and the bottom of his pants ride up. He's wearing these socks with smiley faces on them. "Your mother and father never fight?"

I shake my head because it's the truth. They really don't because my mother is a yes-dear kind of person. "No, not really."

His brows pucker and I get the feeling I might have said something wrong. "Kayden, what's your dad like?"

My fingertips automatically jerk inward and my nails slice at my skin. "He's...he's a dad. A normal dad."

"Do you have a good relationship with him?" he questions.

"Because I find it kind of strange that he hasn't visited you once."

"Our relationship's fine." My throat feels thick with tar. "He just works a lot of hours."

His hand whisks across the paper as he writes something in his notebook and then proceeds into the conversation with caution. "Has he ever hit anyone in your family?"

It is the perfect opportunity to tell him everything: about my life, about the pain, about the unworthiness. But it feels like betrayal and I realize that I'm basically my father's puppet. It's a terrifying and confusing conclusion, like the strings that attach me to him have wound into knots. "I-I don't know."

"You don't know?" He's skeptical. "Are you sure?"

I nod my head as I stare at the floor in front of me. There's a pink stain on it and a lot of the linoleum is cracked and chipped. "I really don't know."

He evaluates me, then takes a card out of his front pocket and extends his hand toward me with it between his fingers. "I want to see you first thing Monday. My office address is on the back." He flips over the card and shows me where the address is written in his handwriting. "My number's also on the front. If you ever need to talk about anything, you can call me anytime."

I take the card, realizing that committing to his request means committing to more than just a visit. It means opening up doors I nailed shut a long time ago and facing all the demons I locked inside. It means telling him everything, even about my dad. And then what? What if I actually do? Then what happens to my family? My mother? My father? Do I care? I don't know. I don't know anything. I think I'm the most fucked-up, confused person who's ever lived.

Doug drags the chair back to the corner and then tucks his notebook underneath his arm as he heads for the door. "I want to see you a few times over Christmas break, and then we'll find you a therapist to talk to in Laramie when you go back to college."

A measured breath eases from my lips as I clench my hand around his card and bend it in half. I get a paper cut and it momentarily stills the stirring inside me. "What if I don't want to?"

He offers me a positive smile. "You do, otherwise you would have just said no."

I don't say anything and it's a silent agreement. I'll see a shrink in Laramie. That is if I make it back to school.

*Shit.* I'm suddenly reminded of the bigger picture. I have more problems than just dealing with my father. How the hell am I going to get out of that mess? Let my father buy Caleb off? Then what? I owe my father for life? And carry his secrets—our family's secrets forever.

Doug exits the room and I let my head fall into my hands. I drag my fingers through my hair roughly and pull hard on the roots. For once, I wish that things were easy. That I could relax. Breathe.

Really, what I wish for is Callie.

# Callie

I wake up early the next morning, before the sun has completely risen over the curves of the mountains. I slept terribly last night, tossing and turning, unable to get comfortable. I kept having this dream where I'd run into Kayden's house and find blood on the floor and knives, but he wasn't there. I searched the whole house but all I kept finding were piles and piles of leaves. I woke up dripping in sweat and ended up throwing up in the bathroom.

I lie awake in bed, and Seth is snoring next to me, content in his sleep. I listen to him breathe until I can't sit still any longer and then get up and grab my notebook from my bag. I take a seat in the makeshift windowsill that looks out at the snowy driveway. My mom's car is buried in a foot of snow and my dad's truck has chains on the tires.

I pull my knees up and station the notebook on them before pressing the tip of the pen to the paper.

I dream that I get to have cake before Caleb takes me into my room. When I blow out the candles and make a wish, I wish to have the happiest and best birthday in the world and the wish comes true. Caleb never shows up that day to hang out with my brother, and I get to play hide-and-go-seek outside with the other kids. I rip open paper and smile at my presents.

Lately in the dream, instead of making a wish for myself, I make a wish for Kayden. I wish that he never met me and that he never learned my secret. I wish that he never had any reason to beat up Caleb and that he never ended up on the floor, bleeding to death.

I wish for happiness in a world full of sorrow.

There's always so much pain and I wish for all of it to be gone.

Of course, wishes are just wishes, just hope for a speck of light in a dark field.

When I analyze my wish for Kayden, I get terrified at what it means. If I'm willing to take brokenness and shattering of my childhood in exchange for the removal of his, then how deep are my feelings for him? And am I ready to handle them?

I pause to think about what I wrote and I spot my mother walking out the side door of the house as she tromps through the snow toward the garage. I let go of the pen and it falls to the floor. I glance over at Seth sleeping in the bed and then I panic, hop up, grab my jacket and phone, and run out the door. She's reaching the top of the stairs when I shut the door.

"Oh good, you're awake." She hugs her arms around herself and bounces up and down as she shivers.

I slip my arms through the sleeves of my jacket and flip

my hair over the collar. "Yeah, I was just getting ready to head inside."

My mom glances out at the mountains and the sky is tinted pink from the sunrise and reflects in her eyes. "You're up early." Her brown hair blows in the breeze as she looks at me. Even though it's been only about a month since I've seen her, she's aged a lot, but that might be because she's in her pajamas and her hair and makeup aren't done. "I don't remember you being a fan of getting up early."

I shrug as I zip up the jacket and then pull the hood over my head and hug my arms around myself and shiver. "I slept in the truck during the drive over here," I lie. "So I wasn't very tired."

She eyes me over with skepticism. "Who gave you a ride here?"

I'm wary to answer. "Um, Luke."

"Luke who?"

"Luke...Price."

Her shoulders stiffen and she wraps her robe tighter around herself. "Kayden's friend?"

I nod. "Yeah."

She thrums her fingers restlessly against her hips as she clenches her jaw and stares at the door to the garage, trying to see through the frosted window. "Callie, I don't want you hanging around Kayden."

The wind decides to kick up and snowflakes sting my skin as they swirl around us in a flurry. The wind howls against my eardrums and the reflection of the daylight discomforts my eyes.

"Why?" I chatter, rocking my body to attempt to keep warm.

"Because I don't want you having any association with Kayden." She looks at me and I see loathing in her eyes. Or maybe it's fear. "He's obviously got a temper and even your father said he was trouble when he was on the team."

"I doubt Dad said that," I argue. "He always liked Kayden. And besides, you talk to Kayden's mother."

"Not by choice." There's judgment in my mother's eyes like she's blaming Maci Owens for Kayden's mistake. If that's the case, would she blame herself if I told her what happened to me?

I hide my hands in my sleeves and tip my chin down into the collar of my jacket. I'm wearing a pair of pajama bottoms and the fabric is thin and the cold air easily trickles through. "Can we go inside and talk about this? It's cold."

She glances at the door of the room above the garage again and then redirects her attention to me. "Is your friend in there? The one who..." She lowers her voice and her eyelashes flutter against the snowflakes gusting around us. "The one who likes guys?"

I sigh, turn sideways, and squeeze between her and the railing without uttering an answer. Thankfully, she follows me and Seth is off the hook. At least for now.

When I walk into the kitchen, that night smashes into my chest, the night Jackson sat at the table eating pie and Caleb tormented me with my secret. The night Kayden found out who broke me. The night where he let me cry and then slipped out of my life as effortlessly as if he were made of sand.

I walk over to the cupboard and take out a bowl and a box of cereal. I set the bowl down on the counter and open the box as my mom walks in, letting the cold air and snow in. She slams the door and then slips off her boots beside the door and winds around the table, heading across the kitchen toward me.

"I was going to make you breakfast." She reaches for the drawer above the oven that holds the pans.

I shake my head as I pour cereal into the bowl. "That's okay. I'm not hungry enough to eat a big breakfast."

She drops her arm to her side and scans my tiny frame. "You look like you're losing weight again."

I look down at my short legs and my petite waist hidden under my pajamas. "I'm just stressed out."

"Stressed out over what?" she asks. "About school? Or about what happened with your friend?"

I can't hold it in. It's too much and it's pissing me off. "Oh, now he's my friend, but back when you first found out, you were so excited we were a couple. In fact, I think you told everyone in the whole damn town."

"Watch your language." She reties her pink robe and gathers her hair out of her face. "Callie Lawrence, you will not talk to me that way." She turns around and extends her arm toward the cupboard that holds all her prescription medication. "This is my house and while you're here you will follow my rules."

I close the cereal box, stirring in my fury. "I'm eighteen years old and I can be friends with whomever I want."

She grabs one of the bigger bottles and slowly turns around to face me with her hand over the lid. "Even ones who beat up your brother's best friend."

I dig my nails into the granite countertops as the pain of the last six years chokes my oxygen away. "That's all you care about? Caleb?" His name tastes toxic in my mouth.

She battles to unscrew the lid from the bottle, pressing the bottom against her hand as she squeezes the lid with her fingers. "Callie, Caleb has been part of this family since he was six years old. You know his parents barely talk to him. We're the only family he has."

"I don't give a shit about Caleb!" I shout and my lungs nearly combust. But it feels good. Really, really good. I press my hand to my chest, calmly let go of the countertop, and straighten my shoulders. "I'm going to go out to breakfast with Seth."

Her eyes are amplified and her lips start to part in protest, but the look on my face quiets her. She cinches her mouth shut as the lid slips off the bottle. "Fine, have fun." The pills rattle as she pours a couple into the palm of her hand.

I put the cereal back in the cupboard, set the bowl in the sink, and hurry out the back door. I run across the driveway and jog up the steps of the two-story garage. When I open the door, I'm surprised to find Seth sitting on the edge of the bed, awake and dressed in a red T-shirt and a pair of dark denim jeans.

"You're up," I say as I shut the door.

He tousles his hair into place with his fingers. "I woke when you ran out of here like there was a fire. What was up with that?"

I shuck my jacket off, ball it up, and toss it onto the bed. "I saw my mother heading out here and I didn't want you to have to deal with her."

He hooks his watch onto his wrist as he wanders over to his shoes that are at the foot of the bed. "Callie, no matter how many jokes we make, I can handle your mom." He slips his foot into his boot. "Trust me, if I can handle my own mom, then I can definitely handle yours."

I frown as I sink down onto the edge of the bed. "But you haven't talked to your mom since you told her about Greyson."

He shrugs as he laces up his shoe and fastens a knot. "She'll get over it. It'll just take some time, just like it did when I told her I was gay."

I flop back onto the bed and drape my arm over my forehead. "How do you decide what's worth telling your parents and what's not?"

He's silent for a while and then I hear his footsteps as he walks around to my side of the bed. He lifts my arm off my head and looks down at me. "If you're asking me if I think you should tell your parents about what happened with Caleb, then the answer is yes. I think you should."

He releases my arm and I lean up on my elbows. "How can you be so sure?" My mouth sinks to a frown. "She could get mad at me. Or she could hate herself as much as I hate… hated myself."

Seth brushes my bangs out of my eyes with his fingers. "Callie, if she hates herself for a while, then she hates herself for a while. You've been carrying around the burden for the last six years and it's about time someone else took a little bit of the weight off of you."

"I'm not sure I can," I whisper, clutching at the dull ache inside my chest. "There's just so much…so much acceptance in telling her the truth."

"Like you might have to accept that it's finally real?"

I nod as I gaze at the clear sky outside. The sunlight is beaming down on the houses across the street. Sunlight is a rare occurrence in Afton, but maybe it's a sign that not everything is caped in darkness. That light does exist even in the darkest of corners.

He moves back as I sit up and head for my bag on a fold-up chair near the door. "I was thinking we could go out to breakfast this morning. There's this café in town that has the best pancakes in the world." I take a purple shirt out of the bag and a pair of jeans.

"I was thinking we could go see Kayden first," Seth says as he texts something on his phone.

"But he's not allowed visitors." I hold my clothes to my chest and head for the bathroom to change.

"Yeah, he is." Seth sets his phone down on his knee and takes a deep breath. "I just got a text from Luke saying that not only is Kayden allowed to have visitors but he's leaving the facility today."

I stop in the middle of the room as reality finally catches up with me. Although I'd never admitted it aloud, I'd wondered if I'd ever see Kayden again. That maybe he didn't even exist and that everything that had happened between us was just my imagination attempting to force my mind to thrive again. "Should we wait for him to get out and then go see him?" I stare at the open bathroom door.

The mattress squeaks as Seth gets up from the bed and steps into my line of vision. "I think we should go pick him up. Luke said that his mother's supposed to and then she's going to take him home, but he thinks we should go pick him up and take him somewhere."

I raise my chin up and meet his eyes. "Like kidnap him?"

Seth laughs at me and his face turns red and his eyes water over. "He's nineteen years old, Callie. We can't kidnap him if he wants to go."

"But isn't he supposed to be watched?"

"What? At his parents' house? With his *dad*?"

I free an unsteady breath from my lungs. "But I worry that we might be doing more harm than good . . . running away."

Seth steps closer to me, places his hands on my shoulders, and fixes his eyes on me. "You want to know what I think? I think that you're afraid."

I hug my clothes tighter against my chest because I need to hold onto something. "Of what?"

"About hearing the whole story about that night. I think you're afraid of the truth."

"But what is the truth exactly?" I ask.

Seth gives a lopsided smile and gently shakes my shoulders. "That's for you to find out because he needs you."

He's right. I'm afraid of everything that night holds and that I'll have to admit that it's my fault. I'm afraid I'll learn that Kayden was really trying to kill himself, trying to leave me alone in the world. That he'll leave me again, and I need him like I need air.

"Where will we take him, though?" I wonder. "My mom's made it really clear that she doesn't want him here."

A devilish grin spreads across his face. "You leave that to me. All you need to do is bring your bag and tell your mom you're going to be gone for a couple of days."

My eyebrows dip together. "You're not going to tell me where we're going?"

His grin widens and his hands leave my shoulders and reunite with his sides. "It's called a surprise road trip, Callie."

I drag my hand across my face. "You think that's a wise idea, considering everything?"

"No, but I've never been one for wise ideas," he says. "I believe in irrational, fleeting decisions that keep life interesting. And life needs to be interesting because we've got only one of them to live."

I smile and it almost feels real. "You are the most wise...I mean, irrational, fleeting person I've ever met."

He wraps his arms around me and embraces me in a tight hug. I drop my clothes to the floor and hug him back. I don't cringe. I don't panic. I just enjoy it. Because Seth is home. And I hope one day Kayden will be too.

We hug for a while and then let each other go. I gather up my clothes and head to the bathroom. "All right, let's go get him," I say, knowing it's not going to be that easy.

Because reuniting with something you've lost rarely is, especially when you're not sure who exactly you're reuniting with.

# Chapter Five

*#41 Eat a lot of pancakes*

## Kayden

My mom came to pick me up the next morning, just like she promised. They stopped giving me my meds so I feel drained and piercing on the inside, like shards of glass are roaming through my bloodstream.

"Are you ready to go home?" she asks as she enters my room. There's something in her tone I don't like, a warning maybe of what waits for me at home.

There's an instant where I think about telling Doug what really happened. At least I'd finally be getting it off my chest. But then I think of what that means—of what I'll have to admit and face. Every punch, every kick, a childhood packed with torturous memories. I'll have to feel it and I don't have a knife or razor to turn it off.

"Yeah," I finally answer as I fold up a pair of jeans and put them in the bag.

She looks relieved and horrified. "Good."

She spends a few minutes chatting with the doctor near the doorway, collecting the papers they give her with a mildly tolerant look on her face. I gather the last of my stuff from the dresser drawer beside my bed. My stitches are out, but there's still some pain when I twist my midsection, although the doctors assure me that I'll make a full recovery eventually and will probably be able to play football again next season.

I can't even look that far ahead, because I have no idea what lies before me. Felony charges? My dad? College? Callie? Maybe nothing.

I zip my bag up and swing it over my shoulder, deciding not to think about my future for now. All I need to focus on is getting out the door and then my attention can go to making it to the car. My mom and the doctors have disappeared so I head out, unsure where I'm supposed to go.

Fate takes matters into its own hands, though. I'm halfway across the room when fate steps into the room in the form of a short, tiny little thing with big blue eyes and brown hair. She looks smaller than the last time I saw her. Her waist is a little thinner, and she has dark circles under her eyes like she hasn't been sleeping very well.

"Callie," I say, dropping my bag to the floor.

She fidgets with her fingers, wringing them in front of her, looking upset as she takes in the bandage on my wrist. "Hi," she says in her tiny voice as she meets my eyes. Her hair is pulled up and pieces of it frame her face.

I can't help it. I smile like a stupid idiot, but then I quickly frown. "You shouldn't be here."

She sucks in a sharp breath. "Seth and Luke and I decided to come pick you up...I thought Luke told you on the phone that we were coming."

"Yeah...but it still doesn't mean you should be here." I know I sound harsh, but I can't help it. I honestly didn't really think she'd show up and now that she has...I hate letting her see me in this kind of place.

Her eyes widen like I've slapped her and I feel like the biggest douche. She takes a step toward me and I ball my hands into fists to stop myself from touching her, running my fingers through her hair, kissing her lips. "Luke and Seth think we should go on a road trip."

"A road trip?" I say in disbelief. "Right now?"

She shrugs, like she has no clue what to do or say. I opt to let her off the hook, because she doesn't need to be standing in a facility staring at a guy who nearly cut himself to death and who let his father almost beat him to death.

"Look, Callie." I pick up my bag and swing the handle over my shoulder. "I can't go on a road trip with you." I feel the throbbing beneath the bandage and I focus on that, instead of the glossiness in her eyes and her quivering bottom lip. "I can't really do anything with you right now." I step toward her and then inch around to the side. "I'll talk to you later, okay?"

It's the stupidest thing that's ever left my lips, but it needs to be done. She deserves better than the broken piece of shit that I am.

## Callie

I'm standing outside the door to his room, fidgeting nervously as I wait to go inside and see Kayden. His mom's in the room with him and I don't want to go in until she leaves. I'm not sure what to say or if there's anything I *can* say when I get inside. There's no magical word that will make it easier, and it's terrifying.

The hallway is packed with people and chatter, and the chaos is disconcerting and adds fire to my jittery nerves. I've been writing for days in my journal about what I would say to him when I first see him. *I'm glad you're okay. I'm sorry. Thank you.* The last thought I always feel guilty about, but I can't get it out of my head.

"You look like you're going to throw up, Callie." Seth's voice interrupts my thoughts. He's standing across the hallway, beside Luke, with his arms folded behind him as he eyes me worriedly. "Do we need to get you a bucket or something?"

I shake my head. "No, I'm fine. Besides, where would you find a bucket?"

The corners of his lips tug upward and in three long strides he crosses the hall and stops in front of me. "You know he's okay, right? He's still Kayden, just a banged-up one who probably needs *you* now more than anything."

"Yeah, I guess." I fold my arms over my chest and then uncross them, unable to hold still.

He swings his arm around me and pulls me in for a hug. "Just take deep breaths and breathe."

I nod and suck air through my nose and let it out between my lips just like he instructed. But as the door swings open, my chest constricts along with my heart as Maci Owens comes walking out. She's dressed like she's going to a fancy dinner and it seems ridiculous to me. Her hair is done up in a neat bun and she has on heavy eyeliner and lipstick. She's wearing a navy blue dress and black high heels. My dark feelings toward her outfit and looks may be stemming from the fact that she's here and doesn't look the least bit upset.

Her high heels click as she exits beside one of the nurses. She has her phone in her hand and a pair of leather gloves in the other. She passes by me and the woman who once greeted me with a cheery smile barely acknowledges me. She's probably still upset about how I reacted when she tried to tell me Kayden injured himself.

I keep my gaze fixed on her as she walks down the hall, and then Seth nudges me with his elbow and I tear my gaze away from her and fix it on him. "Huh?"

He nods his head at the doorway. "Quit worrying about her and go in."

I glance at Luke. "Maybe you should go in first."

He quickly shakes his head. "I think he'd rather see you first."

I'm not sure if he's right, but I decide to go in. I inhale another breath in preparation and then enter the room. I've always thought that hospital rooms were the most depressing rooms that existed, but this facility is much worse. The walls are unembellished, the floor is blemished, and the bed is made up neatly for the next patient.

Kayden is standing in the middle of the room with a bag over his shoulder. In my head I'd been picturing that he'd be lying in a bed, looking helpless and scared. He's taller than I remember and I instantly tip my head up to meet his emerald eyes. His brown hair is a little longer and shaggier, hanging over his ears and in his eyes and he looks like he hasn't shaved in a while, his face scruffy. There's another scar on his cheek and a bandage on his wrist along with an array of rubber bands. His body looks solid, but his expression looks breakable and fragile.

"Callie," he says, looking stunned and a little upset to see me. His bag falls down his arm and hits the floor.

"Hi." It seems like the silliest thing I could ever say, but it's the first word to pop into my head.

The corners of his lips start to turn up, but then it vanishes and I question if I ever really saw it. "You shouldn't be here," he says.

My heart tightens, twines into knots, binding so tightly it begins to wilt into pieces. I don't know what to do or say so I tell him about my road trip. He's not happy and suddenly he's leaving, walking past me with barely a glance. Then I'm alone, unable to move or breathe. All I can think is that this is the end of it. The end to my happiness.

After standing in the middle of the room for an eternity, Seth finally walks in. He approaches me like I'm a skittish cat and I glance down at my nails, wondering if he thinks I'm going to scratch him.

"Hey." He stuffs his hands into his pockets and takes cautious steps until he's right in front of me. "You want to go get that breakfast? The first set of pancakes is on me."

I love that he doesn't ask what happened. If I had to speak I'd probably crumble into teeny tiny pieces that would get stuck in the dirty cracks of the floor. I nod and he swings his arm around me and leads me outside, holding me together.

❧

The restaurant is crowded and filled with the voices of people enjoying their breakfast with their families. Dishes clank in the kitchen and the air smells like coffee and waffles. Luke came with us, but he's been distracted by one of the waitresses behind the counter pretty much since we walked through the door. I wonder if he did it on purpose, to distract himself from what happened at the clinic. Luke actually tried to chase Kayden down after he ran out of the room, but he came back minutes later, looking upset, but he never said what happened.

"You know what I just realized?" Seth points a syrupy fork at me as he chews a mouthful of pancakes. "This needs to be added to our list."

I glance down at the barely touched stack of pancakes on the plate in front of me. "What? Eat pancakes?"

His neck muscles move up and down as he forces the overly large mouthful of pancakes down. "No, eat *a lot* of pancakes."

I pick up the bottle of strawberry syrup that's in the tray at the end of the table. I press my thumb down on the handle, tip the bottle, and douse the pancakes with red syrup. "That doesn't seem significant enough for the list."

Seth stabs his fork into his pancakes as he shakes his head. "No way. Everyone in the world should sit down and stuff themselves with pancakes at least one time in their life." He shoves a bite into his mouth and then closes his eyes and inhales deeply. "Especially ones this damn good. I swear I'm having a foodgasm."

A laugh flees from my mouth and he opens his eyes looking happy. It's the first time I've shown a sign of life since I left the facility. "Foodgasm?" I ask.

He nods his head and swallows his food with a forceful gulp. "The gasms of champions."

"Champions of what?"

"Life."

I can't stop smiling as I shovel up a forkful of pancakes and stuff them into my mouth. "All right, we can add it to the list and then cross it off because we're doing it right now."

He grins from ear to ear, then grabs a napkin from the tin case and dabs the syrup off his lips. His fingers circle the glass of milk in front of him and he wraps his lips around the straw and takes a sip. He sets the glass down, wipes his mouth off with the sleeve of his shirt, and then leans back in the booth and drapes his arms over the back of the seat. He watches me eat with an anxious expression on his face.

I cram my mouth with pancakes and then look up at him. "What?"

His shoulders move up and down as he shrugs. "I was just wondering if you wanted to talk about what happened."

I extend my hand toward the butter in the middle of the table beside a plate full of toast and a bowl full of jam packets. "With Kayden?" I ask and he nods. I grab the knife and slide it through the butter, getting a thin slice on the blade. "Nothing. I just messed up. That's all."

"You looked like you were going to cry," he says. "And Kayden, well, he looked upset when he walked out. I mean, he practically ran away from me when I said hi."

I smear the butter all over the pancakes and it makes a mess with the syrup. "I just didn't approach him like a skittish cat. I threw the road trip idea out there way too quickly and he freaked out. At least I think that's what happened."

"So he just decided to go home to his mother and father." Seth lowers his hands down from the back of the booth and rests his elbows on top of the table. "Why would he do that?"

I divide the half-eaten stack of pancakes as I prop my elbow onto the table and rest my chin in my hand. "Maybe he's not ready to admit the truth aloud yet."

"Are we speaking about you or him now?"

"I'm not sure."

I continue to demolish my pancakes with my fork, trying to figure out what could be going through Kayden's head. If his dad did it to him then maybe fear, but why would that make him afraid of me? I think about the bandage on his wrist and the rubber bands.

I drop the knife onto the table. "Seth, why would someone have rubber bands on their wrist?"

He shrugs as the waitress walks up to the table with the bill. He takes it from her and she smiles at him.

"Thanks for coming in." She coils a strand of her blonde hair around her finger as she chomps on her gum and tries to dazzle him. "I hope you'll come back."

Seth shakes his head as he reaches his hand into his pocket to get his wallet. "As much as I loved the pancakes, I probably won't be coming back." It's his attempt to politely turn the waitress down.

She pouts out her lip and takes the bill and Seth's credit card when he offers it to her. "Well, okay then." She pierces me with a death glare, and then stomps off in her bubblegum-pink pumps and matching waitress uniform.

"You know, I'm starting to wonder about the female sex," Seth remarks as he sets his wallet down on the table. "Always looking for love in the wrong places."

"Am I included on that list?" I sip my orange juice and then place the empty glass back on the table.

He rolls his eyes like it's the most ridiculous thing he's ever heard. "Absolutely not, darling. You just need a better way to approach it." He fiddles with his watch, twisting it around and around as he watches the time. "Why did you ask that question about the rubber bands?"

I circle my fingers around my wrist and rotate my arm. "Because Kayden had a whole bunch on his wrist."

Seth thrums his fingers on the table and then his brow knits. He retrieves his phone from his pocket and runs his finger along the screen before typing something in.

"What are you doing?" I ask, reaching for my purse.

He holds up a finger as he taps the screen. "Just a sec."

I take out a few dollar bills and lay them on the table for a tip, then drop my wallet back to my purse. I eye the waitress over at the counter who's whispering something to another waitress. They both glance over and glare at me like I'm the devil.

"I think they think I'm your girlfriend," I say, slumping down in the chair.

Seth glances at them, then shrugs and starts reading the screen again. "Then it was really wrong of her to hit on me."

"I guess so." I direct my attention to the flurry of snow outside. It's everywhere, white and crisp and completely innocent looking as it shines under the sun. It's a false innocence though, because the icy roads here have caused many accidents and taken many lives.

Seth slaps his hand down on the table and the ice in the glass shakes as I jump, startled. "I knew it sounded familiar," he mutters. Shaking his head, he puts his phone down on the table. "I know what the rubber bands are for."

"What?" I sit up in my seat.

He reaches across the table and takes my hand in his. "It's a form of treatment used on cutters and people who self-mutilate."

I already knew that Kayden might have hurt himself, but now it seems real. I slip my hand out of Seth's and fold my arms over my stomach as I curl inward. "I don't feel good."

"Callie, it'll be okay," he reassures me and seeks my hand again.

I recoil, shaking my head as I get to my feet. I feel the vile burn in my stomach and it aches like a forming bruise. "I need to use the restroom." Before he can respond, I get up and run across the café, bumping into one of the waitresses on my way there. I knock her tray out of her hand and feel bad, but I don't have time to apologize.

As I run past the counter, where Luke is sitting, I hear him call out, "Callie . . . what's wrong?"

I don't respond. I need to get it out. *Now.* I need to get rid of the vile feeling in the pit of my stomach.

I slam my hand against the door and fling it open. I run to the nearest stall and collapse to my knees. I start to shove my finger down my throat, when suddenly I see Kayden lying on the floor. Helpless. He needs help. He needs someone who can help him. It hits me hard, like a kick to the stomach, what I need to do. Maybe I can change that wish I'm always dreaming about, the one where I erase everything that happened to me on my twelfth birthday. I might not be able to take away Kayden's past pain, but maybe I can help with his future pain. I just need to be strong. I move my finger out from my mouth and it's one of the hardest things I've ever had to do. I'm shaking and sweating as I sit back and lean against the wall, letting my head fall back. Then I just sit there. Not feeling better, but knowing it's for the best.

# Chapter Six

*#35 Walk, don't run*

## Callie

Seth and I have been spending a lot of time at the café, partly because Seth thinks we need to eat pancakes all the time and partly because we're avoiding eating breakfast at my house as a result of my mother and Seth's first meeting. It was nothing but awkward right from the very beginning.

"It's nice to meet you, Seth." My mom stuck her hand out and Seth politely shook it. She was wearing a white apron over a floral dress, looking very 1960-ish. The kitchen smelled like cinnamon and the pans hissed on top of the oven.

"It's nice to meet you too." Seth let go of her hand and took in the excessive amount of Christmas lights strung around the top of the walls and the Santa and reindeer figurines all over the shelves and counters. "You like to decorate, huh?"

My mother flipped the eggs in the pan, then picked up a mixing bowl from the counter and began to whisk the batter.

"Oh yes, I love the holidays. They're so much fun. What about you?"

Seth raised his eyebrows at her as he pulled out a chair at the table. "Do I like the holidays? No, not really" He sat down and I joined him, reading the text I got from Luke.

**Luke:** Did you hear from him?

**Me:** No . . . have you?

**Luke:** No, I stopped by his house, though.

**Me:** Is he okay?

**Luke:** I don't know. His brother answered and said he hadn't seen him. I think he was drunk, though.

**Me:** I texted him a couple of times. He never texts back.

**Luke:** I'm sure he's fine. He's probably just working through some stuff.

Working through some stuff? Alone. In that god-awful house.

"Callie, did you hear me?"

I glanced up from my phone and my mother and Seth were staring at me. "Huh?" I said.

Seth's eyebrows dipped beneath the square-framed glasses he was wearing, not to correct his vision but because they are fashionable. "Are you okay?" he asked.

I nodded. "I'm fine."

"Who are you texting?" my mom asked, mixing the bowl with a whisk.

I quickly locked the screen on my phone and set it down on the table. "No one."

My mother dropped the whisk on the counter and batter splattered all over. "You were texting Kayden, weren't you? I can't believe this, Callie. I told you I didn't want you spending any time with him after what happened—after what he did to Caleb."

Seth looked at me with astonishment in his eyes and I shrugged, shaking my head, trying not to cry. "It's not Kayden," I told my mom again.

"Even if it was, I think Callie's old enough to decide who she wants to talk to," Seth chimed in calmly. "In my opinion she is an excellent judge of character." He said it with an attitude and any chance of my mother and him getting along fell apart right there. "More than most people, who seem to miss the mark all the time."

She didn't fully understand the depth of his words, but his snippy tone was enough for her to decide she didn't like him, something she told me later when she pulled me aside.

"He's rude," she said. "Does he talk to his own mother that way?"

"He doesn't talk to his mother," I'd said and that was another strike against him.

After that, I decided it'd be better to keep them separated, because Seth wouldn't keep quiet if my mother said something ridiculous and my mother would never stop saying ridiculous things.

❧

I've been home for almost a week. Time seems to move in slow motion. Each hour feels like days, and days like months. Christmas is only four days away and my mom keeps trying to make me spend time shopping and wrapping presents with her. I do as much as I can, but every time she brings up Caleb, I bail. I even took off during our trip to the mall and had to call Luke to come pick me up.

"I'm not sure if I'm even hungry," I tell Seth as I pour syrup on the stack of pancakes in front of me. We're in the café again, enjoying the same light chitchat after a very uncomfortable morning with my mom. "Six days in a row is putting me on pancake overload."

He butters his toast and then adds some strawberry jelly. He's wearing a blue shirt with a logo on the pocket and his hair is still a little damp from the shower he took right before we left the house. "Well, you don't have to order pancakes every time," he says and sets the butter knife down on the table.

"Or maybe you should order me something different," I reply, grabbing some sugar packets from the bowl. Seth had taken it upon himself to order for me while I was in the restroom, and I wasn't planning on ordering pancakes.

"I think we should eat pancakes every morning that we're on break." He takes a bite of his toast. Crumbs fall to the front of his shirt and he dusts them off with a sweep of his hand. "It'll be fun."

I stare down at my pancakes buried in a puddle of syrup. "Are you sure?"

"I'm always sure when I say something aloud." He sets the toast down on the smaller of the two plates.

I seal my lips and try not to laugh at him because Seth is never sure of things, just like I'm not, just like most of the world isn't. "All right, we can try to eat pancakes every day over break. But if I end up puking you have to promise to hold my hair back."

"I promise." He smiles and raises his hand in front of himself. I slam my palm against his, giving him a high-five. For a moment it's just he and I in the café, maybe even in the world. But the bell on the door dings and my eyes instinctually wander over to it. Suddenly, I remember that there are a lot more people in the world who need to eat a lot of pancakes over Christmas break.

Kayden walks into the café and the few people at the tables promptly look up at him. There have been rumors going around about him throughout the small town, ones that are horrible. I struggle not to hit every single person looking at him.

He has a coat on and there are snowflakes stuck in his wet hair. He's wearing an old pair of jeans with holes in them and black boots on his feet. The Christmas lights that trim the windows reflect in his eyes and make them look red instead of green. His gaze sweeps the room but misses me, and then he walks up to the counter where one of the older waitresses with gray hair and a hairnet greets him at the register.

"Callie, what are you staring at?" Seth tracks my gaze and then his eyes bulge. *"Oh."*

It's like my feet don't belong to me as I bend my knees and stand up from the booth. As soon as I'm on my feet, Kayden's eyes lock on me. We stare at each other from across the café and the tables and chairs and people blur away. He crosses his arms over his chest and presses his lips together before shaking his head. He looks away as the waitress hands him a plastic to-go bag. I'm not sure what it means, but I need to talk to him.

"I'll be right back," I say and start to step away as Kayden pays the waitress.

Seth catches my sleeve and draws me back a little bit. "Be careful, Callie."

I nod, even though I'm not sure if he means to be careful for Kayden or myself. He releases my sleeve and I weave around the tables, tucking my elbows in. Kayden is putting his wallet into his back pocket when I reach him and the plastic bag is hooked over his hand. His jaw tenses as he grabs some napkins from the metallic dispenser near the register without looking up at me.

"Hi," I say, and again I'm frustrated with myself for such a silly start.

"Hey," he mutters, shoving the napkins into the sack.

"I just...I just wanted to come over and see how you're doing." I take a breath because I'm nervous and forgetting to breathe.

His eyes rise up to me and I'm taken aback at the coldness in them. "I'm fine."

"That's good." My throat is shrinking, reducing airflow, and I don't know how to react. He starts to head for the door and I follow him. "Kayden, wait."

He doesn't, pressing his hand to the door and shoving it open. I know I should back off, but I can't convince my feet to stop moving. I hurry out the door after him, wrapping my arms around myself as the wind hits my bare arms.

"Maybe we could talk?" I suggest as he opens the door to his mother's black Mercedes.

He pauses, shaking his head, and then he looks over the roof at me. "Callie, I have to go. I've got stuff to do today."

I walk through the slush and the puddles and around the back of his car, not ready to give up. "You're staying at your house?"

He tosses the bag of food across the center console and onto the passenger seat. "Yeah, where else would I go?"

The water is seeping through my shoes and it's cold. "You could come stay with me."

His eyes focus on me. "And what? Your mother's just going to welcome me there?"

I hesitate and it's the wrong thing to do, but I can't think of anything to say. "I don't care about my mother."

He shakes his head and ducks over to climb into the car. "Callie, I can't stay at your house, not after everything that's happened."

Why does it feel like he's not referring to my mother anymore but to our relationship? "Please don't run away," I sputter. I'm no longer thinking rationally. I run around the front of the car and open the door to the passenger side, prepared to make him feel better. *Somehow.* I just need to find out how. The inside of the car smells like him and I breathe in the scent as I move the food bag out of the way, climb in, and close the door. "I don't want you going back there."

Shaking his head, he slams the door and adjusts the seat back, giving himself more room. He meets my eyes and there's a hollowness in them. "Callie, I never really left there. Just escaped for a little while." He turns the key in the ignition and the engine roars to life. "My father isn't there anymore."

I shake my head. "Where is he?"

He shrugs, biting his lip, staring out the window at the surplus warehouse next door. "On a business trip I guess."

I want to ask him—want to know if he had any part of it. "Kayden, did he—"

"Look, Callie," he cuts me off and his gaze slices into me. "I have to go. I got shit to do."

I swallow hard and my insides tremble. "Please talk to me," I whisper, sucking back the tears.

He inhales through his nose and his solid chest puffs out and then descends as he releases the breath. His hand is turning pallid as he clutches onto the steering wheel and I swear I can hear his heart beating. "I…" His breathing quickens as he struggles to speak.

I prop my elbow on the console and place my hand on his cheek. He flinches but stays motionless, looking at me. My heart is racing passionately and pumping adrenaline through my body. I don't know what I'm doing or if it's wrong or right. All I can do is hope I'll get to him. "You know you can tell me anything, right? I'll understand." He swallows hard as I brush a shaky finger under his cheek. He still looks like he hasn't shaved. His skin is rough under my touch. *"Please."*

He shakes his head. "I-I can't."

"Yes, yes, you can." I lean over the console, needing to get close to him. "I'll help you." *Like you helped me.*

His warm breath feathers against my cheeks and his breathing quickens as his gaze flicks to my lips. "Callie, I…" He drifts toward me and then his mouth crushes urgently against mine. I instantly part my lips and allow his tongue to slip inside as I release a pent-up breath. I've missed this—him—more than I let myself admit. I need him. So much.

I grip the front of his shirt as he cups the back of my neck, pulling me closer, kissing me and exploring my mouth with his tongue in rough, almost desperate movements. His other hand moves around and frantically grabs at my hip. The console is jabbing into my stomach but I don't care. I just want to keep kissing him forever. I never want to let him go or have him let me go. I need him.

But then he's pulling away, breathing profusely, with his jaw clenched shut. When he looks at me, his eyes are cold. "You need to go...I'm sorry, Callie." He looks like he might cry. "I can't be with you."

I try to tell myself that it's because he's hurting but suddenly I'm back in high school, back to being no one, back to being the invisible girl filled with shame.

*"Freak," Daisy said as I walk down the hall with my head hung low. "Nobody wants you around."*

*I hurried down the hall, clutching my books as I ran outside. I kept running and running until I was safely underneath the bleachers near the football field where no one could see me. I shoved my finger down my throat and forced my lunch out of my stomach. Then I sat down in the dirt and through the cracks in the seats watched the football team practice, wishing I could stay there forever.*

My breath falters as I climb out of the car, into the snow and the wintry air. As soon as I slam the door, the tires spin in the slush as he peels away without looking back. Even though I feel like chasing after him, I turn around and walk back inside with my head hung low.


## Kayden

I'm officially the world's biggest asshole as I pull out of that parking lot. I've snubbed the world's saddest girl not once but twice, and on top of that, I kissed her. I'm a fucking prick. I can see her watching the car as I peel out onto the road, her head hung low, and she probably feels like shit.

But it's for her own good; that's what I have to keep telling myself. One day she'll look back at all of this and be glad she didn't have to deal with it her entire life. My burdens and problems should be mine and mine alone.

Still...kissing her again has made it a huge problem. I'm driving away from the café, the slush on the roads whipping up against the windshield as I fly down the main road in my mom's car. My heart is acting stupid, flying about as fast as the car is and my lips are burning from the feel of hers. The inside of the car smells like her too and I can't stop thinking about how good she smells when I'm close to her and how it feels to touch her.

I should have never left the house. My mom was wasted, though, and wanted something to eat. I didn't want her driving drunk so I offered to go. But being out in public wasn't a good idea. Too many people I know, and too much judgment. And then Callie...being there...seeing her...

Tears threatened to come out of my eyes as I leave her behind at the café and the pain and sadness is making me want to pull over. I can't let the feelings surface, not when I have no way to turn them off. I'll have to deal with them and I can't. But my eyes keep pooling with water and it's become harder than hell to see. Everything looks white and sloshy and I can't focus on the road. I need to stop the tight knot in my chest from tightening any more.

Holding onto the steering wheel, I reach across the console for the glove compartment, hoping my mom will have a screwdriver or something sharp inside there. I just need a quick fix to temporarily turn it off. I keep glancing up at the road as I dig through the glove box. There's a stack of papers, a tube of lipstick, and a packet of air fresheners. "Fuck!" There's nothing sharp. I slam the console and sit up just in time to see a small blue car stopped in the middle of the road with the exhaust huffing a cloud of dark smoke into the air.

I slam my foot down on the pedal and my car screeches to a halt. Snow and slush flip up into the air as the back end of the car loses control and glides to the side. It stops sideways about a foot before ramming the other car.

I slam my hands against the wheel as the car inches forward and angles to the side. I'm losing control over everything— over how I feel, and it's going to end up killing me.

The thing is I'm not sure if I'm terrified about that or relieved.

# Chapter Seven

*#2 Don't overthink so many things*

## Kayden

It's been a little over a week and a half since I got released and I'm fucking pissed. And shocked. And a whole lot of other stuff I can't sort through. The last time I saw Callie was when I left her at the café. She's tried to call and text me a few times since I ran away from her, but I never respond.

Being stuck in the house is tough, though, and kind of depressing, especially since Christmas Day was yesterday and it went unnoticed. But it's always kind of been like that I guess. My mother has cleaned out the knives and razors and every sharp object in the house. Whether it's for my dad's benefit or my own, I'm not sure. My oldest brother, Tyler, is still hanging out. I guess he lost his job and house, so now he's crashing in the downstairs room we used to hide out in when we were kids. He's also drinking about as much as my mother. My father hasn't been home since I came back. My mother says he's on a business trip but I secretly wonder if he's hiding until they can be sure I'm not going to talk about what happened that night.

"Good news," my mom says when I enter the kitchen. It's early in the morning, but she's dressed up, her hair's done, and she's already got her makeup on. She's sitting at the table sipping coffee with a magazine in front of her and a half-empty wine bottle.

I head for the cupboard. "Oh yeah."

She picks up the coffee mug. "Yes, if you consider not going to jail good news." She takes a sip of the coffee and then puts the cup back down on the table. "I think Caleb and your father have come to an agreement. We'll give him ten thousand dollars and in exchange he won't press charges."

"Is that even legal?"

"Does it matter if it is?"

I open the cupboard and take out a box of Pop-Tarts. "Kind of...And besides, how do you know he won't just take the money and still press charges. He's not a good, honest guy."

"No, he's the guy *you* beat up." She picks up the creamer and pours some into her coffee. "Now quit arguing. This is how your father's handling it. And be grateful that he's handling it."

I unintentionally snort a laugh. "Be grateful." I gesture at my side, which is starting to scar over. "For what? For this?"

She raises the cup to her mouth and scowls at me over the brim. "What? The injuries you put there yourself?"

I slam the cupboard and it makes her jump. "You know

that's not true...and I wish...I wish..." I wish for once she'd just admit that she knows but doesn't care. It'd be better than her pretending that none of this exists.

She lowers the cup to the table and flips a page of her magazine, shrugging nonchalantly. "All I know is that you cut yourself and that your father wasn't even here that night."

"Mom, you are so full of—"

She smacks her hand down on the table and her body is shaking. "Kayden Owens, we're not going to talk about this anymore. It's being taken care of and we're moving on because that's what we do."

I lean back against the corner, bend my arms behind my back, and grip the countertop. "Why are you always protecting him? You should be protecting your kids...but you won't even admit the stuff that's going on."

She shoves back from the table, grabs her magazine and coffee, and hurries toward the doorway. "Do you know what it's like growing up so poor that your mother has to sell herself on the corner all so you can have a used pair of shoes from the local surplus store?"

My mother has never really talked about her childhood or her mother, so I'm stunned. "No...but I'd rather grow up without good shoes than grow up getting my ass kicked every day."

She swings her arm back and throws the cup at me. It zips past my head and shatters against the wall. Sharp fragments sprinkle all over the floor and get stuck in the cracks of the tile.

"You ungrateful little shit. You have no idea how lucky you are." She's shaking from her anger and her eyes are bulging.

I glance from her to the shards on the floor and then back at her with my mouth hanging open. She's never been this upset before. She's usually subdued. But as quickly as the wildfire came, it's gone and the flames and rage in her eyes dissipate. She runs her hands down her hair, combing it back into place before she walks out of the room and leaves me to clean up the mess.

I get a broom from the closet and sweep it up, watching the broken pieces fall into the garbage can as I empty out the dust pan. I notice some travel itinerary to Paris and also Puerto Rico in the garbage and wonder if that's where my dad went. These places seem more like a vacation, though, than a business trip.

As I put the broom away, I get lost in that night, the uncontrollable anger in my father's eyes, and the feeling of not knowing surfaces in my chest. What is going to happen to me? How do I make myself fit back into life when I thought I'd fallen into death? And will I even ever have a life to fit back into again? My mom can pretend all she wants that this is going to go perfectly—that they'll pay off Caleb and he'll keep his mouth shut—but I have my doubts and I won't be the least bit surprised if he takes the money and still presses charges.

I continue to analyze my plans as I go down to the room in the basement and sit in the quiet. I take my phone out of my pocket and stare at the screen with my finger hovering over the TALK button. I want to call Callie so fucking bad. Because it feels like she could help me, let me know some of the answers, give me a reason to revive again.

"Hey, man." Tyler stumbles into the room and slams the door shut with his elbow. He's got a brown paper bag in his hand and he tips his head back and takes a swig from whatever is inside and then wipes his face with the sleeve of his shirt and directs the bag at me.

I shake my head and put my phone away, taking Tyler's interruption as a sign not to call Callie. "No thanks, man."

He shrugs and takes another gulp before flopping down in the leather sofa across from mine. He looks more like he's in his late thirties than his twenties and his clothes are ragged and worn. He's missing one of his teeth, which he says is from a fight, but I wonder if he's a crack addict or something by all the sores on his face. His brown hair is cropped and it's thinning out and he reeks of smoke and booze.

"How long are you staying here?" He kicks his feet up on the table and there's a hole in the bottom of his shoe.

"I have no idea." I pick up the remote from the coffee table and aim it at the television screen. "I guess it depends on what happens with this Caleb thing."

He removes the paper bag from the bottle of vodka and puts the tip of the bottle up to his mouth. "Yeah, what was that about?" He knocks a shot back and then slams the bottle down on the table. There's a red ring around his mouth from pressing the bottle against it and I wonder if it hurt or if he even felt it.

I turn on the TV and begin flipping through the channels. I don't want to talk to him when he's so trashed that he won't remember a word. Even though it's probably wrong, I still have bitter feelings toward him for bailing on me when I was a kid so he could turn into this. "It's called life."

He laughs incredulously. "Life's called beating the shit out of someone?"

"It was our life for a while," I say and he fidgets uncomfortably. I crack my knuckles and my neck, resisting the urge to ram my fist into the table in front of me. "I didn't beat the shit out of him. I broke his nose, knocked out a few teeth, and bruised the shit out of his face. That's it."

"Yeah, but what did Caleb Miller do to you?" he presses. "The last time I was here, he seemed like an okay guy."

I pop my knuckles again, pushing on them as hard as I can, until the skin feels like it's going to split open. "He's a fucking prick who got away with something he should be in jail for. What I did to him was minor compared to what should be done to him." I get up because I don't want to talk about it anymore.

He turns around in the chair, following me with his bloodshot eyes. "Didn't you beat him unconscious?"

I shake my head as I jerk open the door. "Nope." I thought I did, but it turned out he was just playing it up. Yeah, his face looked like a fucking lumpy blueberry, but by the time the police put me in the back of the car, he was up and milking it for all it was worth.

I walk outside, done with the conversation. I don't have a coat on, just a hoodie, but I welcome the cold as I hike across the icy front yard, tromping through the snow, with my arms at my sides. Both cars are gone from the driveway, but the motorcycle is in the garage with the key in it. I run my hand along the leather seat, thinking about the last time I rode it and how I wrecked it trying to jump it over a hill. It's black, sleek, and not made for jumping, but I was showing off for a bunch of girls and ended up skidding into the dirt and giving myself killer road rash. It was minor compared to some of the things my father's done to me and even some of the things I've done to myself.

Rolling my wrist and feeling a slight pain inside the muscle from my cuts, I swing my leg over the seat, turn the key, and floor the throttle while I hold down the brake. The engine and exhaust huff to life and for a split second I feel alive. I pick up my feet, release the brake, and fly out of the garage onto the road. It's colder than hell, but it could be worse. It's actually a warm day for Afton and the roads are clear. I can deal with it as long as I drive slowly. I just need to go somewhere.

Anywhere, but here.

## Callie

It's been a little less than a week since I saw Kayden at the café. I've texted and called him a couple of times and always end up crying because he won't answer. I can't stop thinking about the emptiness in his eyes and the anger in them when he pulled away. Seth's texted him a few times, but it always goes unanswered. It kills me that there's been no contact with him and that he's up in that house, alone with his terrible family, keeping silent about his life. Silence. Silence. Why is it always about silence? I wish both of us could tell the world and be free from the chains we drag around.

Seth and I have been spending a lot of time away from my house, hanging out at the café, eating too many pancakes, and driving the roads aimlessly, anything that will keep me away from my mother. It's not like she's been terrible, but she keeps reminding me about my obligation to my brother and Caleb, since they're a "package deal." But yesterday was Christmas, and she forced us to hang out at the house all day. It didn't go very well and we ended up getting into an argument when she pulled me away and told me she thinks I shouldn't hang out with Seth anymore.

"He has quite a mouth on him," she'd said. "And I don't like his attitude."

"You don't have to like it, Mom," I'd replied. "But he's my friend and he's going to stay my friend."

That didn't go over very well and she started lecturing me about the little girl she lost, the one who didn't sass off.

"What are you thinking about?" Seth asks. We're up in the room above the garage. It's a fairly nice day, the sunlight spilling all over the snow and ice and melting it. I've been analyzing it for a while, watching it reflect against the ice, looking so perfect, yet I know if I step outside, the cold and slipperiness won't hold up the perfection. "You have this strange look on your face...like you're thinking about killing someone."

I'm standing next to the windowsill kicking a punching bag with my bare foot. My dad hauled it up into the room a few days ago, after my mom gave it to him for Christmas as a way to "get into shape."

"I'm just thinking about stuff."

He flips a page of the magazine he's looking through as he lays on his stomach on the bed. "Like what?"

I shake my head and ram my fist into the bag, barely budging it. Sweat beads down the back of my neck and my ponytail is slipping loose from the elastic. "Nothing. It's nothing...just the weather."

He cocks an eyebrow as he peers up from the magazine. He's got on a pair of jeans and a striped shirt and this leather string necklace around his neck. "The weather?"

I shrug, pivot my hip to the side, and then spring my knee up, flattening my foot against the bag one more time. Breathless, I pad over to the bed, the concrete floor cold against my bare feet, and I hurry and hop onto the mattress. "Yeah, sometimes I like to analyze it and what it all might mean in relation to life."

He turns a page as he gapes at me. "You're a very strange girl. You know that?"

I nod as I tuck my feet underneath the blanket. "I've been told that a few times."

He sighs and then eyes my outfit. I still have my pajamas on, no makeup, and I smell like sweat. "Are you planning on staying dressed like that all day? I was hoping we'd go out."

I lean back against the wall, fanning my hand in front of my face to try and cool off. "To where?"

"Anywhere but here."

"This place is already wearing on you, huh."

He shakes his head and starts reading the page in front of him. "No, but this room is and the fact that you keep dazing off into Callie la-la land. You're bumming me out... You've been bumming me out since that day you ran into Kayden at the café." He peeks up at me through his long black eyelashes. A strand of his hair falls into his eyes, but he doesn't bother brushing it back. He looks like he's waiting for me to tell him something.

"What's wrong?" I ask, draping my arm across my stomach.

He scowls at me as he roughly flips another page and he accidentally rips the corner. "You're keeping something from me that happened at the café... when you ran outside."

"No, I'm not," I lie because I'm afraid to talk about it, afraid of what Seth will tell me it means.

He points a finger at me with his eyes narrowed. "Don't you lie to me, Callie. Just tell me you don't want to tell me. Don't lie."

My face sinks as I frown. "I'm sorry. I just really don't want to talk about it. It'll be too hard... to find out what it means... to find out how I feel."

He pauses as he assesses me and then his gaze glides to the window where my notebook lays. "Have you written about it?"

I shake my head and wipe some of the sweat off my face with the back of my hand. "And I don't want to."

"Have you ever written about how you felt that night... about Kayden?"

"I haven't," I tell him. "And like I said, I really don't want to."

He straightens his arms and pushes up from the bed. He kneels and scoots closer to me until he's by my side. "Maybe you should. Maybe you should write Kayden a letter, telling him how you feel, not just about what happened, but how you feel about him."

"Seth, I don't think I can." I roll onto my back and stare up at the patches on the ceiling. "I'm afraid of what I'll end up writing... I'm afraid of what I really feel and how he'll react to it." I'm afraid that what I'm forcing to stay locked away inside my heart will break free and I'll have to deal with it.

He takes my hand in his and one side of his mouth quirks upward. "Callie, honey, I think if both of us have learned anything in our lives it's that being afraid is not the way to live."

"I know," I say softly, realizing just how much I've been holding in. Ever since it happened, my chest and feelings and heart have vined into this warped knot. "But what if I find out something that I don't want to?"

"It's better than hiding it and repressing it, isn't it?"

I smash my lips together and listen to the space heater

hum as I consider his words carefully. Then I compel myself to sit up. "You're a very wise man, Seth."

"Well, duh." He rolls his eyes and smiles. "That's clear to everyone who meets me."

My smile grows because despite whatever ends up coming out on that paper when I jot down my thoughts, I'll have Seth and I know that unlike in the past, I won't be alone.

I retrieve the notebook from the windowsill and curl up in a ball on the bed holding the tip of the pen to the paper, ready to admit what really lies inside the darkest spots of my heart, the things I'm afraid of but want more badly than anything in my life.

⌒

An hour later, I walk out of the garage, feeling lighter, almost like I'm flying. Seth was right. Writing down everything I'm feeling was a good idea. I feel much better. It's strange because I write about Kayden all the time, but it was different actually writing *to* him because I know that one day, if I ever get the courage, he might read it.

I'm headed out to the driveway where Luke is waiting for me in his truck, ready to take Seth and me away for a little bit. Seth beat me out already and as I head down the steps he's laughing about something and it makes me smile. It's a breezy day, the clouds heavy. It isn't snowing yet, but it probably will be by the end of the day.

I'm halfway down the driveway, eager to get away from

the house for a while, when the door to the house swings open and Jackson walks out.

His brown hair is damp and he has on a heavy green coat, jeans, and a pair of boots with the laces undone and dragging in the snow. "Hey, I need to talk to you." He trots down the steps, trailing his hand down the railing.

I slow down and wait for him near the stairway, drawing the hood of my coat over my head and tucking my hands into my pockets. "About what?"

He halts on the bottom step and I crane my neck to look up at him. "About your loyalty to this family," he says.

The icy breeze pinches my cheeks. "I am already loyal to this family."

He shakes his head and targets his finger at Luke's rusty 1980s Chevy truck parked at the end of the driveway. "Not if you're hanging out with him."

"With Luke?"

"With Kayden's best friend."

I start to walk away, but his fingers snag my arm and he stabs his nails aggressively into the fabric of my coat as he wrenches me back toward him. "You know he was there that night?" he growls. "Luke was, when Kayden beat up Caleb and he didn't even try to stop him."

I jerk my arm, but he constricts his grip. "Jackson, let go of me." I bend my elbow and twist my arm again and jerk on it, but he won't let me go. "Please, you're hurting me."

His eyes are as icy as the snow beneath my feet and his

fingers unwrap from my arm. I stumble to the side and press my hand to the side of the house to get my footing. "I've been best friends with Caleb since I was six, Callie, and you used to be friends with him too."

I back down the driveway away from him, shaking from the confrontation. "I don't want to talk about this anymore."

"You never want to talk about anything, Callie." He bends his knee and steps up to the next stair without turning around. "You just shut down and go to your own weird little place."

"Because I have to!" I whirl around and sprint down the driveway. That weird little place he's referring to is more of a home than this place will ever be. This place holds memories that stab at me every time I step foot inside it.

I hop into the truck and the warm air flowing out the vents comforts me. I climb over Seth's lap, because he refuses to "sit bitch" and I settle in the middle. Once I'm situated and my seat belt's buckled, Luke shoves the truck into reverse and backs down the driveway. My brother is standing at the top of the stairs, watching us with his hands in his pockets.

"What's his deal?" Seth asks, nodding his head at Jackson.

"He's upset about stuff." I position my hands in front of the heater vent to warm them up. I can feel Luke and Seth's eyes on me, but I don't want to look at them. With my head hung low, I breathe through my nose to force back the hot tears wanting to spill out.

The truck bumps up and down as Luke floors it over the small snowbank at the end of the driveway, and then he rams it into drive and we're speeding down the snowy road. The radio plays peacefully in the background and the engine makes these clinking noises. Halfway across town, Seth and Luke take out their cigarettes and crack the windows so they can smoke. It's chilly and smoky and my head is falling into a very dark place.

I wish I could do it. I wish I could walk into the house, when my mother and father and Jackson are all sitting down at the table. I'd have a loud voice, not a shaky one, and I'd finally tell them. They would hug me, comfort me, and tell me that it was all going to be okay.

But I know that's not how it would go. It's been six years since it happened and each year I spend in the shadows of silence is another weight added to my shoulder. It makes it harder to tell the truth and time makes it harder for people to understand.

Seth and Luke flick their cigarettes out the window as we turn into Luke's driveway. Flakes of gray ash blow back into the cab and land on my clothes. I've seen his house before, when my mother was driving me to school, but I've never actually been there, nor do I know much about his mother and father, other than that they got divorced when he was young. It's a smaller home, with green siding in desperate need of a paint job. There is a few feet of snow in the yard and a tree in the center near a salted pathway that leads up to the front porch.

Luke shoves the truck into park and turns the key, silencing the engine. He stares at his house as he removes the key from the ignition and stuffs it into the pocket of his black hoodie. "My mom's not here," he explains. "And I suggest we leave here before she comes back."

"What exactly are we doing here?" Seth wonders as he pushes his thumb on the buckle to unlock his seat belt. Then pushes the button on mine, releasing my waist from the strap.

"We're making a plan," he states with a pensive look on his face as he rubs his hand across his cropped brown hair.

Seth and I trade a look. "A plan?" we say simultaneously.

"To get out of this place." He flips the handle and pushes the door open. "I don't know about you, but I'm sick of being here. It's depressing."

"Where would we go?" I wonder as Seth opens the truck door and hops out into the light layer of frost covering the slender driveway.

Luke jumps out and looks back into the cab at me with his hand resting on top of the door. "Anywhere but here."

I glance at his house, wondering what's so bad about it. I scoot across the seat toward the open door where Seth is waiting for me with his hand extended for me to take. "Any exact ideas of where we'd go?" Slipping my fingers into his, I jump out and slip on the ice, but Seth catches me by the arm and saves me from a very painful fall.

"Somewhere cheap," Seth says as he helps me get my balance. "I don't know about you, but I'm pretty much broke after buying all those Christmas presents."

"I still can't believe you bought all your Christmas presents from the Quickie Mart," I tell him as he slams the door. I fiddle with the fifty-cent machine bracelet he gave me that has a gold teddy bear charm on it to remind me of "better times" he told me when he gave it to me. He was referring to the carnival where Kayden and I first kissed and where he also won me a teddy bear, which we dressed up and left with a *Take me home* sign on it.

"Oh, you know you loved yours." He smiles at me and then loops his arm through mine and we skip after Luke up the pathway to the front door of his house.

Luke shoves the door open and steps to the side to hold it for Seth and me. We turn sideways so we can fit through the doorway without letting go of each other and Luke follows us in and shuts the door.

I get the feeling that something's wrong the moment I step inside. There are heavy striped curtains blocking the windows so it's very dark and musty. The orange-and-brown-plaid couches are covered in plastic and there's a plastic rug sprawled over most of the shaggy brown carpet. There are shelves built into the walls and each one is lined with rows of animal figurines that are coordinated by breed. Plants decorate the windowsills and are lined up from smallest to largest, but they're all brown and dying. It's cold too and I can see my breath puffing out in front of my face and it mixes with the dust.

"What's with all the plastic?" Seth asks as Luke makes his way to a hallway at the back corner of the room.

Luke shrugs as he flicks the thermostat with his fingers. "My mom's insane."

We don't utter another word. We leave the living room and head down the hall. I notice how bare the walls are, no photos, no pictures, no decorations, and it gets colder the farther back into the house we go. I'm getting kind of nervous, especially because the air is really dusty and it's making it hard to breathe. When we reach the end of the hall, however, Luke opens a door and I step into the room and the air clears.

"So this is my room," Luke tells me awkwardly and then cracks a joke. "You two are the only two people besides Kayden who have dared step foot into the shithole."

I turn in a circle as I take in the made bed, the band posters tacked to the walls, and the desk with a computer on it that looks like it's from the nineties. Everything is very clean and very orderly, but not in an uneasy way like out in the living room. "It's not a shithole," I assure him. "It's your room."

He seems happy with my response and his rigid shoulders relax a little. "Well, I'm glad you think so because I sure as hell don't." He pats the front pocket of his jacket and takes his pack of cigarettes out. "Oh, and by the way, it's fucking hilarious when you swear." He doesn't light up a cigarette; he just holds the pack in his hand like it's his security blanket.

Seth sits on the bed and bounces up and down a little and the mattress squeaks. "So what's your brilliant plan?" he asks, crossing his leg over his knee.

Still holding his cigarettes, Luke rolls up his sleeves and scoots out a chair that's in front of the computer. He presses the power button on the tower and then sits down in the chair, waiting for the computer to boot up. He holds up his finger and reaches for an iPod beside the computer. He hums under his breath as he scrolls through songs and I give Seth a questioning look.

Seth raises his eyebrows and twists his head toward Luke. "So, are you going to tell us, or are we going to have to guess?"

"You're going to have to guess." Luke sets the iPod down and a song clicks on, "Running Away," by Hoobastank.

"Are we guessing by this song?" Seth's face lights up with enthusiasm as he straightens up his posture.

Luke nods as he opens a search engine and types a few keys on the keyboard. "Yep."

Seth taps his finger on his chin, enjoying the game. "Are we running away?"

Luke pops a cigarette into his mouth and then claps his hand. "Bravo. Nicely done."

I shoot Seth a confused look and he just shrugs. "What? I love games."

I sigh. "Am I the only one who seems to mind that we're talking about running away?"

They both shrug and I roam around the room looking at all Luke's posters and little knickknacks scattered about. Seth takes out his phone and starts texting while Luke types on the keyboard and clicks the mouse. There are photos all over his room, some of him with a woman who looks a lot like him, and I think it's his mother. There's also another woman he's in a few pictures with who's a lot older than Luke, and she has the same brown eyes as him. Maybe it's his aunt or his sister, but I thought she was much younger. There are a few pictures of him with random girls and a handful where he's with Kayden. They're standing next to a black motorcycle and smiling and they look happy. The bike has a huge dent in it and Kayden's arm is scraped and bleeding.

"He wrecked it," Luke clarifies. When I turn around, I find that he's watching me from the computer desk as he leans back in the chair. "He was trying to jump it over a hill and he wrecked it."

"I think I remember." I glance at the photo again. "That was the year he couldn't play for a few weeks because he'd hurt his arm, right?"

"Yeah, that was the one. And we lost three games in a row because of it."

"My dad was so mad." I turn around to face him. "He used to chew him out during dinner."

"Oh, I bet." Luke's mouth turns upward and I realize he doesn't smile very much. "He used to chew us out all the time at practice."

Thinking of Kayden hurts my heart. "Maybe we should go see him," I suggest.

"I was planning on it." Luke clicks the mouse on the PRINT PAGE button on the screen and the printer beside the tower illuminates. "Right after I plan our running away."

"Aren't we a little too old to be running away?" Seth asks,

looking up from his phone. "Isn't it more like a road trip, which is something I suggested a few days ago?"

"It sounds more adventurous when you say running away," I admit. "Like we're doing something scandalous."

Seth's shoulders jerk forward as he sputters a high-pitched laugh. "Oh my God, I've been such a bad influence on you."

My mouth droops into a frown. "What did I say?"

He stands up to shove his phone into his pocket. "*Scandalous*. That's something I would say." He bounces back down on the bed.

I shrug and shuffle my toe across the carpet in a half-circle in front of me, feeling silly. "So? It's a compliment being like you."

All the humor evaporates from his face and his honey-brown eyes. Within seconds he has me in his arms and he hugs me like I'm the most important thing in the world to him. "Don't ever change, Callie Lawrence," he whispers in my hair. "Promise me you won't."

I enfold my arms around him and set my chin on his shoulder. "I won't. I promise."

The printer starts making shrill noises as buttons glow and flash and Luke clears his throat. "I hate to break up your little moment, but I'm ready to share my plan."

We break apart, but still hold hands as we turn to him. He swivels in the chair, back and forth and back and forth as the printer spits out pieces of paper stained with ink. When it stops, he collects the papers and holds one up. It's a picture of a light-blue beach house that sits near the ocean. The sky is unblemished and the sunlight reflects off the water and makes it look like crystal.

"You want us to go to the beach?" Seth squints at the photo as he bends forward, leaning in.

Luke nods as he gathers the papers and lines them up by tapping them against the desk. "Yep, my father has a beach house in California that he hardly ever uses and I have a key and everything."

"You want us to *drive* to California?" Seth gapes at him like he's insane.

Luke shuts off the computer, grabs the papers, and strolls toward his organized closet with the papers secured underneath his arm. "It's only, like, ten hours."

Seth glances at me with skepticism. "Really? Only ten hours?"

"I've never been to the beach," I admit. When Seth and Luke gape at me, I shrug. "What? My family doesn't like to travel. My grandparents even live in Florida, but in the central area and every time we've been there my mom refuses to drive anywhere besides the closest grocery store. And my dad always just wants to watch the sports network."

Luke blinks as he shakes his head, and then he begins yanking shirts off hangers, some falling onto the brownish carpet, but he doesn't bother picking them up. "Well, that gives us even more reason to go."

Seth bobs his head up and down in agreement. "Agreed

124

completely. And might I say that it's a brilliant plan. Much more brilliant than my lame old road trip I was planning to a cabin up at the ski resort."

Luke throws a few shirts and pants into a large navy blue duffel bag that he gets from the top shelf and then he adds a pair of striped shorts and a pair of sandals and sets the bag onto his bed. "I'm just desperate to get away from here, man. That's all."

I wonder what he's running away from. "How long are we going to be gone?"

Luke's shoulder moves up and down as he zips up the bag. "Until break's over, I guess."

I look at Seth to see if he agrees and he merely nods his head. "We have nothing better to do than hang out with your mom." He makes a disgusted face. "And I for one don't want to do that."

"Yeah, but telling my mother that I'm not going to be here for New Year's . . . she's going to flip," I tell them.

"Then don't tell her," Seth says simply. "Text while we're on the road."

I contemplate the idea for a briefer amount of time than I expected. "I can do that."

Seth beams and points a finger at his chest. "I'm a very bad influence and I'm glad."

Luke slings his bag over his shoulder, folds the papers neatly in fourths, and then stuffs them into his back pocket of his pants. "Ready to hit the road?" He walks toward the door, scooping up his car keys off the desk. "We'll stop and pick up your things and then we'll go get Kayden."

"But how are we going to get Kayden?" I ask as Seth and I follow him across the room. "He wouldn't even talk to me when I went to see him. And what if he doesn't want to go?"

His fingers wrap around the doorknob and he jerks the bedroom door open. "I don't give a shit what he wants. He needs to go and get away from that fucking torture chamber known as his house. It's fucked up that he's there." He steps out into the hall and glances over his shoulder at me. "Besides, we're going to teach you how to be a little bit more persuading."

"We?" I ask, confused. I try to breathe through my mouth as I enter the hallway and the air becomes asphyxiating again. "As in…"

He tips his chin at Seth, who flashes us a brilliant smile. "As in Seth and me."

My shoulders slouch as we head down the gloomy hallway, the air pressurizing the farther down we go. "I just worry we're going to do more harm to him by taking him away."

Luke stops abruptly. Hitching his thumb underneath the strap of the duffel bag, he reels to face me and his bag bangs against the wood-paneled wall. "Callie, I've known Kayden for forever, and trust me, that house is going to do more harm to him than going away with us will."

"All right," I agree, but my stomach twines into thorny, firm knots. Not because I want him to stay at his home, but because I'm worried. Worried I'll do something wrong—mess it up for him again. I worry he'll end up lying on the floor in a puddle of his own blood.

Unexpectedly, the front door slams shut and a bustle of banging sounds fill up the house. "Luke," someone singsongs in a high octave.

Luke's body stiffens and his breath hitches. *"Shit."*

"What's wrong?" I whisper, but Luke doesn't respond. He just stands there with his hands limp at his sides and grinding his teeth.

The bag starts to fall from his shoulder and I reach for him and then withdraw as he turns on his heels and motions at us to move backward. Seth drags me by the shirt as I hurry backward and Luke takes energetic strides as he ushers us into the room and toward his bedroom window.

"We'll have to go out this way," he insists as he unlatches the lock and boosts the window up. Arctic air rushes in and breezes through my hair and kisses my cheeks.

"What?" Seth peers down at the high mound of snow below the window. "Are you crazy? We'll get stuck in the snow."

Luke shakes his head as he backtracks to the desk. "No, we won't. I promise."

"Luke!" the woman shouts. "I know you're here so come out, come out wherever you are."

"Please," Luke begs with dread in his large brown eyes as he scoops up the iPod from the desk.

I've seen that kind of fear in my own eyes and in Kayden's.

Without any more hesitation, I swing my leg over the windowsill.

Seth's fingers fold around my skin as he snatches me by the elbow. "Callie, are you crazy?"

I wiggle my elbow out of his hand, and before he can grab me again, I step up onto the windowsill. Bending over, I spring onto my toes and launch myself out the window. When I hit the ground, my legs sink knee-deep into the snow and the wetness instantly seeps through my jeans and into my shoes. Seconds later, Luke lands beside me. He doesn't allow enough time to sink too deep as he bends his knees, falls forward, and summersaults down the hill. He lets go of his bag and climbs back up the hill, offering his hands to me. I take them, even though my initial reaction is to recoil. With a soft tug, my legs are freed and I slide down the hill on my stomach, my shirt riding up a little and the ice stinging my skin.

When I roll onto my back and look up at the window, Seth's feet are dangling out. He peeks over his shoulder into the room and then shakes his head. "What about the window?"

Luke picks up his bag and brushes the snow off it before fastening the handle over his shoulder. "What about it?" He hikes toward the side of the house and stomps his boots in a bare area of the yard. "Leave it open for all I care. I just want to get the fuck out of here."

Seth sighs and then, giving a push with his hands, he dismounts from the windowsill and falls into the snow. Like me he sinks, but he shimmies his hips and gets his knees bent. He easily slips his foot out and drops down on his hands. He claws at the snow with his fingers and gets his other leg free, then rolls down the rest of the way.

"Fuck." He flips onto his stomach and pushes up to his hands and knees, panting from the fall. "That wasn't fun."

"What do you think that was about?" I ask, giving a peek over my shoulder at Luke flicking his lighter and firing up a cigarette. He's standing near the corner and raking his hand through his hair as he mutters to himself.

Seth shakes his head. "I have no idea, but I have a feeling that this beach escape plan is to run away from whoever that was."

I offer Seth my hand and he interlocks his fingers with mine. "I think it's his mom." I pull him to his feet and then he holds onto my arm as we trample through the snow toward Luke, stomping the snow off our shoes when we reach a flat area near the corner.

We don't ask him questions because Seth and I both understand the need for secrets. If he wants to talk to us, he will. We understand that. We step out onto the driveway, onto a thin sheet of ice and Luke leads the way down the fence line toward the road. When we curve around the last of the house where Luke's truck is parked, my hand falls from Seth's hand. Kayden is there and so is the motorcycle from the picture, dent and all.

"Kayden." I gasp at the sight of him. His lips are tinted blue and he doesn't have a coat on, just a hoodie. His brown hair is sticking up all over the place and his cheeks are bright red. He looks like a frozen ice statue and my instinct is to run to him, so I do, moving my feet quickly, completely forgetting that I'm standing on ice.

Two steps forward, I slip and my feet shoot out from underneath me. I go flying in the air like an injured bird. Seth's hands snap out to catch me, but he misses and I fall flat on my back and my head slams against the ice. It severely hurts and I don't get up right away. But I'm not sure if it's because of the pain or the fact that once I get up, I'm going to have to find out if he's going to run away from me again.

## Kayden

I drive through town for what seems like forever, until I can no longer feel my fingers and my lips are as numb as the inside of me. Then I head for Luke's because it's better than going back home. For a split second I consider going to Callie's house on the other side of town, but I can only imagine how that would go since her parents are so fond of the douche bag I beat the shit out of.

Besides, I need to stay away from her. It's important that I do. For her.

I park my motorcycle next to the curb, relieved to see that Luke's truck is out front. But my face falls when I see his mom's Cadillac parked next to it. I don't want to talk to anyone and

Luke's mom is weird and likes to talk about nonsense. She'll want to talk too, especially if she's heard the rumors about me.

I pry my frozen fingers from the handlebars and climb off. Then I stand there, staring at the house, deciding if I really want to go in. It's not like Luke would press me for what happened, but it'd be hanging in the air.

I'm about to climb back on the bike and drive away when Luke comes strolling around from the back of the house with a bag on his shoulder. I start to walk toward him when Callie and Seth step out behind him. They're holding hands and Callie looks like she's struggling to walk across the ice. Her attention is focused on her feet, but her blue eyes slide up from the ground and land on me. They widen and her hand falls from Seth's. Her brown hair waves in the wind as she starts to run toward me. I begin to back away, but she hits a patch of ice and her feet go flying out from underneath her. In a few lengthy strides, I've made it across the snow-packed front yard and to her. Her hair is spread around her head and her eyes are enormous and glossy. The pale, smooth skin that I know covers her entire body almost matches the shade of the snow. She blinks up at me as she clutches her head and lets out an agonizing groan that tears at my heart.

"That hurt." Her chest ascends and falls as she sighs with her lip pouting out.

It's the most fucking adorable thing I've ever seen and it briefly flings me back to that place in her bed where she's looking up at me and trusting me as I thrust inside her. But as I reach my arm out to her, I catch a glimpse of the scar on my arm and I'm back on the floor at my house and my father is stabbing me. I'm cold and helpless and I don't know where I'm going to end up.

Callie puts her hand in mine and warmth envelops my body. I pull her to her feet, and unable to help myself, slip an arm around her waist and balance her in my arms. It feels so good to hold her and I start to choke up. *What the fuck is wrong with me?*

She tips her head up and peers at me with her big eyes. "Hi." She bites on her lip, like she's embarrassed by her word choice.

This time I decide to do better than the last time she said this to me. "Hi." I run my hand through her hair, brushing some snow out of it.

Her lips tug up into a smile. "Are you okay?" She skims across my frozen skin and her lips go slack. "You look frozen."

I can't help but smile. "You just fell and slammed your head on the ice and you're wondering if I'm okay?"

She nods like it's not a strange question. "Did you drive your bike here?" She glances over at the motorcycle and then back at me. "Without a coat on?"

My fingers dig deeper into her hips, mainly because I'm looking for an excuse to cling onto her. "Maybe."

She frowns. "You have to be cold."

"Not really," I lie.

"Ummm...guys?" Luke interrupts and Callie and I blink out of our own little world.

I look at him, pulling Callie closer to my chest. "What?"

Luke signals at his house where his mother is staring at us through the front window that's surrounded by icicles. "Do you mind if we head somewhere and talk. I'd like to get the hell away from here."

"Yeah, of course, man." I start to let go of Callie, but she slides her hand from my shoulder and down my arm.

"I'm going with you," she says as she laces her fingers through mine.

I shake my head and try to remove my fingers from hers. "No way. You'll freeze to death."

She straightens her shoulders and fixes me with a look of determination. "Yes, I am."

I look at Seth, who's fiddling with the strings on the hood of his jacket. "You mind helping me out with this one?"

"Sure." Seth unzips his jacket and slips his arms out of the sleeves. "Put this on." He chucks the jacket to Callie and she catches it with a smile on her face.

"She'll freeze to death," I say as Callie puts her arms through the sleeves. The jacket nearly swallows her tiny body.

Seth raises his eyebrows as he yanks down the sleeves of his black shirt, and then he backs toward Luke's truck. "She'll be fine. She's a lot tougher than you give her credit for."

Callie zips the jacket up all the way to her chin and then

gathers her hair at the nape of her neck and pulls the hood over her head. She looks up at me and her eyes are filled with so much willpower I'm not sure what to do with it. She's usually so fragile and vulnerable.

"Are you sure?" I ask, hoping she'll change her mind. "Because it's colder than hell."

She steps past me toward the bike with her chin elevated even when her small legs sink deep into the snow concealing the front yard. "Absolutely." A smile touches her deep-red lips and humor creeps into her voice. "Besides, hell is warm."

I restrain a laugh and walk behind her, the snow up to my ankles. "Okay, if that's what you want."

"Kayden." Luke calls out my name and I reluctantly turn around.

"Don't do anything stupid," he says, and for a second everything's normal between us. He's just my friend, not the guy who saw me lying on the floor in a pool of my own blood and cuts on my arms that I put there myself. He tosses me one of his spare coats, a thick tan one with a thermal insulated layer that he keeps in the truck in case it breaks down. He likes to always be prepared.

I catch it and put it on, even though I was enjoying freezing the pain out of me. I pull the hood over my head and when I turn around Callie is sitting on the bike. She looks good on it, like she belongs there, and it makes me uneasy because I don't want her to belong with me. I want her to belong with someone who will make her happy, even if it means I have to hurt for the rest of my life.

I proceed to the bike cautiously, deciding if I should put her in front of me or behind.

She slides back without looking at me and runs her fingers along the dent in the side of it. "You wreck this once?" Her eyes are massive when she glances up at me.

I swallow the rock-size lump in my throat and resist the overwhelming impulse to lean forward and kiss her. "Yeah, it was a while ago though. I promise I'll drive safely, especially with you on the back...I would never let anything hurt you." I feel stupid for saying it because I've hurt her many times.

She gives me a dead-serious look as she says, "I know you won't." She swivels her hips and inches back a little farther with her hands on the seat. "I trust you, Kayden. Even if you don't want me to."

She doesn't know enough about me to trust me so much, but I can see in her eyes there's no use arguing with her. I hop on and rev the engine. She scoots forward until her chest is pressed up against my back and the fronts of her legs are touching the backs of mine. Her arms circle my waist and she buries her face into my back. It's the most contact I've had with someone since it happened and I swear my heart practically ruptures and bleeds out into my chest. I wish I could die right there with her holding onto me, because it would be a very peaceful death. I wouldn't be alone and empty inside. She would be there with me and she'd be the last thing I'd ever feel and breathe.

I start to panic at how calming the thought is, but I shove it way down where I can't feel it. I stop overthinking everything and give the motorcycle some gas, before releasing the brake. We take off, just Callie and me and the wind.

# Chapter Eight

*#16 Make someone understand that you understand them no matter what it takes*

## Callie

I thought I'd be more scared than I am. The roads are icy and there's nothing but two wheels and a small amount of metal between the ground and my body. But I'm holding onto Kayden and my head's resting against his back and I'm happier than I have been in the last month. I let the cold air flow over me as he winds back and forth, following the curves of the road. We pass people in cars and on the sidewalks in front of the stores bordering the main road in town. They look at us like we're insane. But that's okay. We can be insane together.

I shut my eyes and block everything out, breathing in the smell of the crisp winter air as I tighten my arms around Kayden's waist. I feel his chest contract, like he gasped, but the lull of the engine is all I hear.

When the motorcycle starts to decelerate, I open my eyes.

We're pulling up in front of the café where Seth and I get our pancakes almost every morning. I don't move right away. I don't really want to.

Kayden parks the bike at the front, near the entrance doors. Red and green twinkly lights are flashing and reflect across the snow. The air smells like sausage and coffee and it makes my stomach growl.

"You alive back there?" Kayden asks, turning his head and looking over his shoulder at me.

I nod, but don't move my face away from his back. I'm afraid if I do he'll disappear.

"Callie?" Kayden says. "Are you okay?"

My shoulders lower as I let out a breath and then force myself to let him go. I lean back and look him in the eyes. "Yeah, I'm fine."

He frowns and draws a line across my cheek with his finger. "You look frozen."

I touch my cheeks and either they're numb or my fingers are. "Maybe we should go inside."

Kayden swings his leg over the bike and gets to his feet. I start to climb off when my phone vibrates inside my pocket. I take it out and scroll through to check my messages.

**Seth:** We'll b there in a bit. We had to stop at the store.
**Me:** For what?
**Seth:** For stuff.

**Me:** Is something wrong?

**Seth:** No . . . we just think you two might need a few
    minutes to yourselves.

**Me:** When will you be here?

**Seth:** Soon. And remember: skittish cat.

"Skittish cat?" Kayden says.

I look up at him and realize he's leaning over me, reading the screen. "It's nothing." I shove the phone into my pocket, bend my knee up, and draw my leg to the side to get off the bike.

Kayden lifts an eyebrow as he circles his fingers around my wrist and helps me off the bike. "So they're giving us time?"

Damn it. Why did he have to read the message? He lets go of my arm and I lower my chin down into the jacket and tuck my hands into the pockets. "Seth's just being weird."

He eyes me with suspicion and I'm worried I've already messed my chance up. But then he says, "Isn't Seth always weird?" And I feel like he's giving me an easy exit because maybe he wants a few minutes with me.

I nod. "Yes, he is, but he wouldn't be Seth if he wasn't weird."

He returns my smile and then moves his hand toward mine, hesitating momentarily before he interlocks our fingers, slipping his large ones through my tiny ones. I glance up at him and his chest puffs out as he liberates a stressed breath from his lungs. We don't say anything else. We just cling onto each other as we head toward the front door of the café that's decorated with a picture of Santa holding a bag of toys.

When I step inside, I realize how frozen I am. The coziness of the warm air encloses me and prickles the life out of my cooled skin. It's not very crowded today in the café, but we still pick one of the corner booths hidden away at the back to get as much privacy as we can. Christmas tunes play from the speakers in the ceiling and on each table are unlit silver and white candles. It's that time of year where people are happy and they try to sprinkle things with magic. I wish they would sprinkle some on us.

Once I'm in the booth, I wiggle my arms out of Seth's jacket, ball it up to the side of me, and then remove my own jacket that was beneath it. I'm a little disappointed that Kayden chose to sit across from me, but I just remind myself *skittish cat, skittish cat.*

He instantly reaches for the saltshaker and rotates it between his hands, channeling his nervous energy. It's quiet, except for the flow of chatter and the clinking of glasses and pans coming from inside the kitchen. I struggle to think of something to say as Kayden stares at the saltshaker in his hands. I retrieve a menu from the stack on the table near the napkin dispenser and begin reading it over.

The waitress comes to take our orders. She's the same one who flirted with Seth and she gives me this knowing look, like I'm a slut. Her hair is braided to the side and her name tag says

"Jenna." I think I remember her from school. She was a grade lower than me and was friends with Daisy McMillian.

"Hey, Kayden," she says, adding a giggle at the end.

He glances up and then shoves the saltshaker to the side. "Hey, Jenna."

"How are you?" She touches his arm with her manicured fingers, petting his muscles like he's a dog. I have this insane impulse to slap her hand away. I don't like it because it's not me. "I heard you were in a car accident or something."

Kayden rolls his eyes and mutters, "Yeah, or something."

She laughs, but her eyebrows knit. "You're so funny."

Kayden looks at me as he stretches his arm toward the stack of menus and my gaze darts to the table. I tuck my hands between my legs and focus on the list of appetizers.

Kayden and she start conversing about their old high school days and how everyone's missed seeing Kayden play and hanging out with him at parties. Kayden smiles at her every once in a while and it hurts a little because he's barely said anything to me since I've seen him.

"You know she misses you," Jenna says, smacking on her gum with the pen poised against the order book.

Kayden peers up from the menu at her, his eyes glazed over, looking lost. "Who?"

She pops a pink bubble in out of her lips and glances at me from the corner of her eye. "Daisy."

I inch lower into the booth, wishing I were smaller or

invisible, and position my hand to the side of my face, pretending to be fixated on the beverage list.

"Yeah . . ." Kayden focuses on the menu. "I think I'll have the pancakes."

I smile, thinking of Seth and our pancakes endeavor and a little bit of courage surfaces in me. I sit up a little straighter and scoot my menu to the side. "I'll have pancakes too, and coffee."

Her nose scrunches as she writes down my order and then smiles charismatically at Kayden. "Do you want anything to drink?"

Kayden closes his menu. "I'll have a cup of coffee too."

She scribbles that down, flashes a grin at him, and when she turns around to head to the counter, she scowls at me. I look away from her and focus my concentration on Kayden. I have more important things to worry about than Jenna and Daisy.

"I want to talk to you," he starts, looking at the cracks in the table. "I just don't know how."

"You don't know how to talk to me?" I don't know how to take what he said. I always thought we were great at talking, which is why I shared my secrets with him. "Why?"

He traces his fingers along the oval-ringed patterns in the wood as he reaches up with his other hand and draws his hood off his head. He rakes his fingers through his hair and rearranges his brown locks into place so they're out of his eyes and flipping up at his ears. "Because you saw me like that. And I've never wanted anyone to see me like that, especially you."

I pick at the cracks in the table, knowing I have to choose my words wisely. "Kayden, I've told you a thousand times that I'll never judge you and I mean it."

"It's not about judgment, Callie." He glances up at me and the misery in his eyes matches what lies inside my heart. "It's about what you deserve." He sighs, rolls up his sleeves, and traces his finger along a fresh scar running vertically down his forearm. "You deserve better than this."

"No, I don't." I think about the last time I threw up in the bathroom because I couldn't deal with the pain, something I've done for years and years. "You and I aren't that different."

He looks even gloomier as he jerks his sleeve back down and covers up the scars. "We're nothing alike. You...you're beautiful and amazing and the sadness and pain in you was put there by someone else." He lowers his voice and sucks in a breath. "I put the pain there myself."

I keep my voice soft as I lean over the table. "No, your father does."

He shakes his head, staring at the counter. "I cut myself that night."

My chest compresses and squeezes my heart into a miniature ball. "*All* of the cuts?"

He doesn't answer and his scruffy jaw goes taut. Carefully, so I don't scare him, I slide my hand across the table and place it over his. "What happened isn't your fault. It's mine. It all started because of me."

His head snaps in my direction and the fire in his eyes

makes me recoil. "In no way is this your fault and in no way do I regret doing what I did to him." His gaze is piercing, but his voice is calm. "Are you mad that I did it?"

I promptly know the real answer because I feel it every time I think of Caleb getting beat over and over again. "I wish I could say that I was, because I never ever wanted you to be the one to do that, but I can't be." Tears start to pool in the corners of my eyes, but I force them back because it's not the right time or place to cry. "I'm sorry, Kayden. I'm so sorry for bringing you into this mess."

He edges his hand out from under mine and positions it on top of my fingers. "You have nothing to be sorry about... I'm the one who should be sorry, for bringing you into this mess. I can't...I can't even imagine how hard it must have been to walk in on me when I was like that."

I shake my head and focus on the unequal beat of his pulse in his hand. Everything is real and it's hard to keep up. "It was only hard because I...because I thought you were dead."

He looks like he's about to splinter apart and I'm verging into the same place. I want to clutch onto him. I want him to clutch onto me, because I know if we can just hold onto each other then we can make it through this. But suddenly he's pulling away and getting to his feet and I don't know what to do or say.

"I need to walk away," he says, not looking at me but at the door at the front of the café. "It's better for you...You don't deserve this...I don't deserve you."

Just as quickly as I found him again he's walking out of my life. I watch him weave around the tables and then he's out the door, leaving me. I need to make him understand that I understand him. I need to make him see that he deserves to be happy and that he doesn't ruin me. I get up and hurry around the tables, not caring that everyone is looking at me like I'm crazy. I slam my hand against the glass door and throw myself out into the cold, completely defenseless without my jacket on.

"I sometimes make myself throw up," I stammer as I run up to the bike with my feet slipping on the snow.

He freezes with one foot on the ground and one foot off and turns his head. His eyes scroll across my body and I feel naked and exposed. "You *what*?"

I press my fingertips to my nose and shake my head because I can't look at him when I say it again. "I sometimes make myself throw up." I give him a moment and then I drop my hands to my side. "And not because I think I'm fat. It's because..." I take a step toward him and angle my head back, looking up into his emerald eyes. I can see the reflection of myself in them and I look as scared as I feel. "It's because I'm trying to get rid of all the vile, foul feelings inside me. The ones I can't deal with."

He's looking at me, and I mean really looking at me, and there's this connection, this understanding that we are two people who have been fractured, not by ourselves but by someone else and we're doing everything we can to not shatter to pieces.

I wait for him to react and when he doesn't budge I decide to do it for him. I walk up to him, getting close enough that I can feel the heat emitting from his body. Then I stand on my tiptoes, throw my arms around his neck, and hug him, praying to God he'll hug me back, because, even though it's a simple gesture in theory, sometimes hugging is complex.

His arms stay slack at his side as his chest rises and falls. I'm about to give up, back away, and allow myself to cry when his arms wrap around my waist. He grips me tightly and it gives me hope that maybe there might be some hope left.

He holds me for what feels like forever, nuzzling his face into my hair. At some point it starts to snow, but we don't move. We are frozen in a moment neither of us wants to leave.

"For how long?" he finally asks, his breath warm against my cheek.

I shut my eyes and bask in the feel of him. "Since it happened."

His arms tighten around me and he presses my body against his. "I'm sorry."

"It's not your fault." I tenderly run my fingertips up and down his back, working up the courage to ask. "Kayden?"

"Since I was twelve." He reads my mind and trusts me enough to answer.

I constrict my arms around him, sealing us together in every way possible. Maybe if I try hard enough, we'll fall into each other and become one single person and we can share our pain instead of carrying it by ourselves.

146

## Kayden

I'm shocked by what Callie tells me and at first I don't understand. She makes herself throw up. Tiny, barely there Callie makes herself throw up. But then she explains why and it makes more sense to me than anything else in my life. I realize how perfect we are for each other and also how disastrous we could end up being. Because even though we can help each other pick up the pieces of our lives, we could also break at the same time and then nothing would be left to catch us as we crumble.

"Maybe we should go inside," I finally say even though I don't want to. I want to stand in this very spot and hold onto her forever, but we'd freeze to death.

She puts a sliver of space between us as she leans away and slants her chin up to look at me, her hair falling back from her eyes and forehead. "I'm not sure I want to go back in after I ran out like that."

I tuck a strand of her hair behind her ear as her palms travel up my arms. "How about I go in and get your jacket while you call Seth because I don't want you riding on that bike."

"But what will you do?"

I cup her cheek with my hand, desperately needing to touch as much of her as I can. "I can put the bike in the back of the truck and then we can go for a drive or something."

There's a trace of a smile on her lips. "Where will we go?"

I return her smile as I sketch my finger across her yielding bottom lip. "Wherever you want."

A sly look comes over her and then she stands on her tip-toes and kisses my cheek. "How about the beach?"

I cock my eyebrow and give her a funny look as she moves back, and then I glance around at the mounds of snow in the parking lot, near the fence line, and below the roof where the snow is sliding off. "The beach?"

She glides her hand down my arm and places it in mine. "Yeah, I'll explain when Seth and Luke get here."

I don't know what she's up to and I'm scared to find out. I had a plan. I was going to stay away from her, but she's standing here and she understands me so much more than anyone ever has and I'm not ready to let that feeling go just yet. "All right, you call them and I'll go get your jacket from inside."

She nods and starts to take her phone out of her pocket as I head inside. A few of the people at the tables give me notable glances as the door swings shut behind me. They're probably the ones who have heard the story. Gossip spreads quickly around here and I wish I could get the hell away from their stares. From the snow, from the town, from my home, from life.

I hurry up and grab Callie's jacket and ignore Jenna's penetrating stare as I wind around the tables and hurry out the door, relieved when it swings shut behind me. Jenna was a friend of Daisy's and I don't want word to get back to Daisy that Callie and I are together. I'm worried Jenna's already called Daisy and she'll show up here any minute. That's the last thing I ever want Callie to have to deal with.

I immediately bust up laughing as soon as I see Callie. I haven't laughed in forever and it cramps up my chest. "What are you doing?"

The sky has blackened and snow showers down from the vapory gray clouds. Callie has her hands on the handle of my bike, trying to push it forward so it's underneath the shelter of the carport and out of the snow. Her feet are slipping against the ice and she's barely getting it to budge.

I step up behind her and feel her tense as I place my hands on top of hers. "You're going to hurt yourself," I say, dipping my head forward and sneaking a smell of her hair, remembering the first time I did it. I lift her hands off the bike and step back, guiding her with me. "The snow's not going to hurt it."

She leans back, tips her chin up, and looks up at me. "Are you sure? I thought I read somewhere that motorcycles were not made for snow."

I press my lips to her forehead and leave them there for a moment, savoring the feel of her skin before pulling back. "Where on earth did you hear that?"

She shrugs. "I don't know. Somewhere, like in a magazine or something."

Shaking my head, I smile and hold up the jacket for her to put her arms in. It's been so long since I've smiled that the muscles around my lips kind of hurt. She turns to the side and slips her arm through the sleeve, then rotates to the other side and puts her other arm in.

I let go of the jacket and glide my palms down to her waist. Pressing my fingertips into her, I spin her around to face me and her eyes snap wide. I inch my fingers around to her stomach, never taking my eyes off her as I pull the zipper up to her chin and her breath eases out in a thin fog. My fingers shiver as I draw them away, and then I bend forward and kiss her forehead, shutting my eyes as I inhale her, fighting to keep my eyes open. I've missed the feel of her skin over the last month and touching it instead of dreaming about it is surreal. But it's also wrong. I'm not the best thing for her and she should have the best. More than that. She should have everything and I am far from everything. Numbness drains through my body as I realize that eventually I'm going to have to let her go.

"Seth and Luke will be here in a minute," she whispers, clinging onto the bottom of my shirt, with her face pressed into my neck.

I can't feel my fingers, my arms, my heart. "Okay." I feel fucking helpless, but all I can do is stand and shiver and pretend like it's just from the cold.

# Chapter Nine

*#6 Run away—run to the beach*

## Callie

I'm confused. I can tell that Kayden wants to hold me, but he keeps pulling away, fighting the urge to touch me. What we need is a long talk so I can understand what he's thinking and what he wants, and so he can understand what I want because I don't think he knows. We need a week at a beach house with plenty of alone time, which is what Seth and Luke are trying to give us.

Later that day, we're in Luke's truck, which is parked out back of the grocery store. It's getting dark, but the lampposts light up the snow dancing from the sky. It's the day after Christmas but it still looks and feels like Christmas. The buildings around us are decorated with various colored twinkle lights and the sidewalk has flashing candy canes and wreaths bordering it.

"I thought Callie was joking about that," Kayden says. I'm

sitting on his lap with my back leaning against the door. The window is wet and my hair keeps sticking to the glass. "But by the serious looks on you guys' faces I'm guessing I was wrong."

Seth squirms his shoulders forward and squeezes out from between Kayden and Luke. He reaches in front of Luke, sticks the end of his cigarette out the window, and ashes it into the snow. "Why would we ever joke about going to the beach?" He turns around and leans against the dash, angles his head back, and stares up at the cloudy sky. "Does it constantly snow here? I swear I haven't seen it stop since I've gotten here."

"From December to April," I clarify as Kayden's fingers sneak up to my face and he smoothes his hand over my head. I can't stop my eyes from closing and an almost noiseless but embarrassing sigh slips out. My cheeks start to heat, so I keep talking to distract everyone. "So are we going to do it?"

"Go to the beach? To San Diego?" Kayden asks with doubt in his voice. I nod my head and soak up the comfortable feeling of his hand on my cheek. "I'm not sure I can."

My eyes open and he's watching me. "Why not?"

He shakes his hand. "There's just stuff…things I need to deal with."

"Can't you deal with them at the beach?" Seth sits forward in the seat and lowers his feet back onto the floor, and then he nods his head at me. "With this beautiful girl over here?"

Kayden looks torn as he glances from me to Seth and then out the front window and into the night. "I have something on Monday that I have to be here for."

"We can be back on Monday," Luke chimes in, rotating the defroster up as the windows fog. "That'll give us four days of freedom and that's four days we don't have to spend here."

I stare into Kayden's eyes and see something I don't like—overpowering fear. "We don't have to go," I say to him because he's the only one who matters at the moment and I can tell something's wrong.

He rubs the pad of his thumb across my bottom lip, flipping it down a little. "Do you want to go?"

"Only if you want to go," I reply, and to add emphasis, I lean in and whisper, "And you *can* go."

He stares at me with the strangest expression, like I'm this amazing, unique creature that no one knows about, and then his mouth tilts up into a small but breathtaking smile. "I can go until Monday."

Seth squeals, claps his hands, and kicks his feet against the floor as he screams, "Road trip, here we come!"

"Thank fucking God." Luke sighs with relief. He cranks the heat up and then flips the lever next to the steering wheel, turning the wipers on. They move back and forth and back and forth, wiping away the snow from the glass and making it dewy. "Now we just have to go get everyone's shit."

"I'm good," Kayden says as I sit up and put my feet on the floor. He combs his fingers through my hair, gazing out the window with his eyebrows knit. "I'll just get some clothes and stuff when we get there."

None of us press him because it's obvious he doesn't want

to go home. "What about your bike?" Luke turns around and puts his arm on the back of the seat, looking in the bed of the truck at Kayden's motorcycle obscured by a sheet of fluffy snowflakes. "You want to take it?"

Kayden shrugs. "All I want is to not have to go home yet." His fingers fall from my hair and settle on my hip where he delves into my skin just beneath the hem of my shirt. "So we can take it or ditch it somewhere."

Luke rotates back around in the seat and shoves the shifter forward, the gears grinding a little before slipping in. "We'll just take it." He presses on the gas, inching the truck forward. "What about you?" He looks at me and then at Seth. "Do you guys need to go get your stuff?"

I start to open my mouth to say no, but Seth interrupts. "I don't go anywhere without my kit."

Luke doesn't even bother asking. He just rolls his eyes and aims the truck in the direction of my house. I watch the homes zip by as I sit on Kayden's lap, hoping I'm not doing anything wrong, hoping I'm not doing more damage than good. Really, I don't know what I'm doing and all I can hope for is the best. It's the worst feeling in the world because hope has never been that kind to me.

❧

I rapidly get thrown into a state of anxiety when Seth and I climb out of the car. There are four figures that I can see through the kitchen window of my house and I recognize that the dark-haired fourth member isn't part of my family. My mom, my dad, Jackson, and Caleb are sitting at the kitchen table as I walk up the driveway to the garage and Kayden is in the truck with Luke at the end of the driveway.

I smell a storm coming in, like the aroma of rain that laces the air before a thunderstorm. But the scent I smell is foul, like dirty water that stains the grass after the rainstorm.

"What are you looking at?" Seth says, tracking my gaze to the window of the kitchen. The lights are on and the inside can be seen clearly. My mother is serving everyone, my dad is talking heatedly, and Caleb and Jackson are laughing at him.

I shake my head, wrap my hand around his upper arm, and haul him up the driveway. Seth is looking at me like I've lost my mind, but I keep walking, step by step until we're inside the room above the garage. I flip on the light and shut the door, panting as I lean against it.

"This is so bad," I whisper and then hurry for my bag. "We have to get out of here now."

Seth follows me at a slow pace and veers to the side for his kit that's in the bathroom. "What's wrong with you, baby girl?" There's clanking as he gathers his cologne and razor from near the sink. "You're acting like a weirdo."

I toss my shirts and a few pairs of jeans into my bag and then zip it up. "There's…there's…" I can't get it out and he steps out of the doorway zipping up the mini bag he carries his toiletries in.

"Callie, whatever it is, just tell me." He drops the smaller bag into the larger one on the bed. "It's okay."

"There's someone in the house," I sputter, dragging my bag to the door.

"Obviously." He raises his eyebrows at me and then scrutinizes my bag. "Did you put any shorts or sandals in there? It's going to be a hell of a lot warmer there than it is here. Plus, you don't want to walk around in the sand wearing sneakers."

"I don't own anything else," I say and then swiftly shake my head as I jerk open the door. "Seth, we have to go. *Now*." Everything's about to fall apart, just like it did last time.

Seth rolls his eyes and slings his bag over his shoulder. "Fine, but you're going to eventually tell me what the panic is all about." He turns sideways and squeezes through the doorway.

I flip off the lights, close the door, and trot down the stairs after him, wrestling my overly large bag down the steps behind me. I should have left some of my stuff here, but I'm too afraid that Caleb or my brother or my mom will walk out.

I dash past the side door, my legs nearly trotting in the rush, but Seth snags my elbow as he slams to a halt. "Don't you want to tell your mother where you're going?"

I glance at the side door, the light spilling through the window in the center, and I shake my head. "I don't think I should."

His brow creases as he examines my face with concern. "Are you sure? I know she's been bugging the crap out of both of us, but she seems like she's going to panic if we just bail and not tell her."

My body ripples with a tremble when I see Caleb rise

from the table and head across the kitchen. "It'll be okay." My voice is insignificant like the snowflakes drifting down from the starless sky, touching the ground, and instantly melting.

"Callie, I…why are you shaking?" He glances back at the house as the side door flings open. Pale yellow light floods the darkness but then suffocates out like a flame as a tall figure emerges in the doorway.

It's Caleb carrying a trash bag in his hand. He's probably trying to win my mother over and she's probably letting him, because she always wants to see what she wants to see. *Why is she so blind?*

Caleb's demeanor doesn't change as he steps out onto the porch and into the snow, making sure to close the door behind him to smother out whatever he's going to say from my family's ears. "What are you doing out here? Standing out in the snow?" His gaze cuts to Seth as he steps down a stair. "You got another one, huh? Decided to dump that crazy football player after he kicked my ass."

"Fuck," Seth breathes, suddenly understanding who it is. His fingers plunge into my arm as he begins to tow me back, one foot after another, the snow crunching beneath our shoes.

Caleb moves down a stair, reducing the distance between us with a smirk on his face. His eyes are black like coals and his face is masked by the shadow created by the hood over his head. Sometimes I wonder why he doesn't seem to care or show any remorse for what he did. What is wrong with him? Is he so warped and split that he likes torturing me?

"Come on over here and introduce him," he calls out as he arrives at the bottom step.

"Fuck you!" Seth shouts, taking longer strides, practically dragging me backward down the driveway as my tiny legs work to keep up with him.

My legs feel like rubber and won't work right and I keep tripping over my feet. I wish I could find some kind of strength that has to be suppressed inside me and shout at him, take him down, scream, throw things. Do anything to wipe the pleased smirk off his face.

But in his presence I'm still the child he pinned down on the bed. He has his hand forced over my mouth while he shatters me into fragments. I allow Seth to haul me down the driveway toward Luke's truck, watching Caleb through the curtain of snowfall. His eyes are fixed on mine and I feel tears beginning to leak out of my own. I'm crying and weak and I want to crumble into the ground and melt with the snow-flakes.

"Callie." The sound of Kayden's voice snaps me back to real life and the bigger picture.

I have more problems at the moment than how I feel, like getting Kayden away from Caleb before a reenactment of that night happens. I spin around and Seth's hand falls from me. Kayden is standing in front of the bumper of the truck with his arms folded. His eyes are not on me but locked on Caleb. His face looks like a shadow as he stands with the rays of the headlights aimed at his back.

I shift my bag higher onto my shoulder and my shoes lose traction against the snow as I run to him. His eyes don't leave Caleb even as I approach him and then he steps forward, dodging to the side, out of my path. I drop my bag and before he can get any closer to the house jump up, fling my arms around his neck, and latch onto him.

Every muscle in his body hardens as I hook my legs around his waist, clutching onto him like I'm a leech because that's what I need to be at the moment—something he can't get rid of without a lot of work.

"Callie," he says in a low tone, not holding onto me. "Let me go."

I rapidly shake my head. "No, please just get back into the truck."

His hair brushes against my cheeks as he shakes his head. "Callie...I can't." He sounds strangled and I really believe that he thinks he can't walk away.

"But you can." I breathe against his ear as I bury my face into his neck. "For me."

It's like I've discovered the magic words and unexpectedly he's backing up toward the truck, slowly, but he's going.

Then I hear Caleb say, "Oh, so she didn't ditch you. I guess she's turning into a little slut then."

"Please, please, please," I chant as he starts to walk forward. "Please don't do this. I need you. I need you. I need you." I close my eyes as I hear a door creak open and then another one opening. Suddenly everyone is shouting.

I hear Luke's voice first. "Why don't you shut your fucking mouth and go back inside before you get yourself hurt again."

"Oh, I'm so going to press charges now," Caleb replies. "The epic, favorite—and apparently suicidal—football player is going down."

And then I hear my mother's. "Callie Lawrence, you get in here this instant. I told you to stay away from him."

I feel Kayden's chest stirring with mine as he seeks oxygen with me, treading forward and then backward, like he can't decide where to go or what he wants to do.

"Callie Lawrence!" my mom shouts and her voice echoes through the streets and dogs start to bark. "It's Christmas break. You should be in here with your family."

*But I am with my family.* I summon every last ounce of courage I still have thriving inside me, push back from Kayden's shoulders, and forcefully meet his gaze. "Please take me out of here," I plead in an uneven voice. The anger fleetingly diminishes in his pupils as he blinks at me. "I can't do this without you."

Just like that we connect again and our hearts beat together, erratic and untamed but still together. And that's all that matters. It's just him and me, shielded from the shouting and yelling going on around us. He backs up to the truck, holding onto me, and opens the door. Without taking his eyes off me, he climbs in and slams the door shut. The warm air engulfs us as we hold onto each other. Seconds later the driver's-side door opens and Seth hops in and Luke follows.

The shouting enters the cab, but the cranking of the heater and stereo stifle it. As we're backing away, I realize that I'm not alone in the world. I have a truck full of people who care about me enough to not ask what the fuss was about. One day I'll give them all hugs for it.

Kayden starts smoothing his hand down the back of my head and his pulse is beating through his fingertips. He keeps kissing my head and mutters that it'll be okay. I'm not sure if he's talking to me or himself.

When I feel the truck driving down the road, I finally look back at the house. My mom is standing in the middle of the driveway in the snowfall without a jacket or shoes on. She has to be cold, but her face looks red in the dim porch light. My dad's on the steps, dressed in jeans and his favorite jersey, scratching his head. And Caleb is nowhere to be seen.

I wish that's how it always was. I wish he would just disappear and my mom and dad would wave at me from the driveway, letting me live the life I should have had a long time ago.

## Kayden

I can tell she's worried about me and I'm pretty sure that if we were alone, she'd tell me that we shouldn't go on the trip. She thinks I'm going to break apart, but the only time I'm not completely broken is when I'm around her. At least that's what I'm thinking while Luke and I wait for Seth and her to come out of the garage.

Luke lights up a cigarette as we wait. Neither of us speaks as he inhales and exhales puff after puff and the heater drowns out the chill in the air as he cracks his window.

"Okay," he says as he sticks his arm through the open window and ashes the cigarette. "I just want to know one thing."

I stare at the garage in front of us and at the headlights lighting up the tire tracks in the snow. "And what's that?" I ask, unsure if I want to hear his response.

He puts the end of the cigarette back into his mouth as he tosses the pack onto the dash. He sucks in a deep breath and exhales the smoke as he relaxes back in the seat. "Was it worth it?"

"Hitting Caleb?" I check without looking at him.

The smell of smoke gets stronger as he sucks in another lungful. "Yeah."

My gaze elevates past the stairway to the upper section of the garage. The light is on inside of the small room and I can see Callie and Seth's figures moving back and forth in front of the window. I remember what Callie and I did the last time we were up there, how she felt while I was inside her—how I felt.

"Yes." It's a small word that doesn't really mean anything, yet it does. In fact, I think it means something more than I'm ready to admit to myself.

He puts the cigarette into his mouth again and the paper withers and glows orange as he sucks in a deep drag. "So…are you doing okay with everything?"

I drum my fingers on top of the door handle. "Yeah, I'm okay."

He clips his fingers around the cigarette and removes it from his mouth, breathing out the smoke and it fills up the cab. "Are you sure...because if you ever need to talk or anything, I'm here."

It's the deepest conversation we've had and I think I know why we're having it. Luke's older sister, Amy, took her own life. Right after it happened, he got really wasted one night and started crying in front of me, blaming himself because he didn't notice any signs.

I nod. "I promise I'm good."

Luke and I stay quiet until Callie and Seth come out and I start to relax again. Then all hell breaks loose as the side door to the house swings open.

"No fucking way," Luke says as Caleb steps outside. "Shit, Kayden..."

I'm already climbing out. My fists are balled, adrenaline is thrashing in my body, and I don't know what I'm going to do. Every emotion I felt that night consumes me again, the good and the bad ones. Caleb sees me and smarts off, adding fuel to the flames raging inside me. I'm about to do something that'll probably ruin my life forever when Callie throws herself onto me. She keeps begging me to stop, for her, please. But Caleb keeps going, calling her a slut, and I want to kill him. I actually feel it, the need to beat him to death, and for a divided second it's all a feel, possessed to make it happen.

Then Callie's gazing at me with her beautiful blue eyes and she looks like she's about to cry. She utters six little words that change my life and scar my soul forever.

"I can't do this without you," she whispers, hugging me like I'm her lifeline.

All of a sudden I know I can't do anything to him, because it'll hurt her more than it'll probably hurt Caleb. So I back away and climb into the truck, holding onto her to keep myself from falling into the darkness.

❧

No one speaks for most of the drive. It's like we're all too afraid to be the first voice heard and too afraid of what might come out of our mouths. Callie has her head resting on my shoulder and she keeps running her finger along the inside of my wrist. I know she can feel the healing scars on my skin and it makes me uneasy, but I don't pull back. If she needs to touch me, then she can touch me.

Her phone keeps going off, playing Blue October's "Hate Me," but she keeps silencing it.

"It'll be okay," she whispers, and then minutes later she drifts asleep, practically balling herself onto my lap because there's barely any room to move with four people squished in the single cab. But it is what it is and we don't need any more.

Luke drives for half the night, determined to get there as quickly as possible. I offer to drive a few times, but he declines each time. The radio is blasting a little Chevelle and the clouds fade the closer we get to the ocean and the stars dot the sky. I wonder if it's possible to fix myself and turn into someone else. Someone I've never known. Someone who doesn't cut himself, who doesn't want to feel pain over emotion, someone who can be worthy to hold her like I am right now.

I glance down at Callie in my arms. Her hair is hanging in her face and she's hitched her leg over mine. One of her hands is on my lap and she holds the other one against her chest. I know I need to tell her everything but I'm not sure how she'll handle it. She's barely said her own secrets aloud, which is why I took matters into my own hands, why I beat up Caleb, and why I was willing to beat him up again in the snap of a finger.

And I don't regret what I did.

I never will.

❧

"Rise and shine, Sleeping Beauty." Something heavy slams into the side of my head. I jolt awake, flinging my arms in the air. The sunlight strikes my eyes and I blink several times against the brightness. Luke is standing to the side of me with the door open and a shit-eating grin on his face. "Shit, I thought you were never going to wake up."

I glance to my side at the bag he must have thrown at me and then at the sand stretching out in front of me that connects with the ocean. The backdrop of the bright blue sky mirrors the water and blinds the hell out of my eyes. I've been to the beach before, during the few times my mother and father decided we needed to try and be a family. It always ended shitty, with someone getting pissed off, and the trip would get cut short.

"How long have we been here?" I yawn and I set my feet to the ground and climb out and stretch my arms above my head.

Luke leans into the cab, grabs the duffel bag, and slams the door shut, swinging the keys around on his finger. "Like ten minutes. Callie told me to let you sleep, but I didn't see the fun in that."

I'm glad that he's being an ass and not treating me like a suicidal freak. "Well, thanks, I guess."

He lifts his eyebrows as he heads for the front of the truck. "No problem."

The beach house belongs to Luke's father—I know that much. What I've never got was how his father could afford it, and yet he couldn't afford to pay for Luke's tuition for school, among other things. I asked him about it once and all Luke did was shrug. He doesn't like to talk about his dad, even before his parents got divorced. I've met him only once, when I was six, right when Luke and I became friends. He seemed a little off, like he didn't know what to do with himself or Luke. A week after I met him, he packed his stuff and left. Luke's probably visited him, like, ten times since then and each time he comes back, he never talks about his trip. And I never ask.

The wooden porch bounces slightly as I walk on it, heading toward the side door of the house. The screen is shut, but the door behind it is agape, so the warm air can flow in. I hear the waves of the ocean rolling against the sand and music playing from inside that mixes with the sound of Callie's laughter.

"Warning," Luke says as he pulls open the screen door.

"Seth has already claimed one of the two rooms that has a bed. Callie says she'll bunk up with him, but there's no way in fucking hell I'm sharing with you."

I walk inside and the door swings shut behind me. "I'm fine with sleeping on the couch." As much as I would love to share a bed with Callie, hold her, spend the night with her, it's probably better if I don't, because I'm unsure how close I want to get to her yet.

"Good, because I hate sleeping on the couch." He heads across the kitchen to the hallway with his bag slung over his shoulder and I'm left standing alone. There are a few barstools around a small island and a sitting window that shows the view of the beach. I take a seat on a stool and pull one of my legs up, resting my arm on top of my knee. I remember when I was little the ocean was one of the most amazing things I'd ever seen. I was fascinated by the way the waves rolled up and washed away the sand, leaving their imprint on the world. Sometimes I would stand right at the edge and let it crash against my feet as I considered taking one more step and my feet would eventually move forward. One more step and it'd take me away—

"Kayden." Callie's voice rises over my shoulder. I hear her walk closer to me and feel the warmth of her body when she's right behind me. "Are you okay?" She places a hand on my shoulder and there's a tremor in her fingers.

I remember the first time I kissed her, up in that playground carnival ride, on the bridge, pressed up against the net.

She trembled under my touch and I loved every second of it, yet hated it because it made me feel things I wasn't ready for.

"I'm fine." I plaster a fake smile on my face and turn around. "I was just thinking." I reach up and move her hand off my shoulder, slipping my fingers through hers as I get to my feet.

"About what?" she wonders with a tilt of her head and strands of her brown hair fall into her eyes. "About what happened last night...with..." She struggles to say his name and I quickly let her off the hook to remove the pain in her eyes.

"No, not that." I sweep her hair back with my free hand and then let it drift down to her cheek and I enjoy the feel of skin. "The last time I was by the ocean."

She lays her hand over mine as it lingers on her cheek. "How old were you?"

"Twelve." My mind flashes back to the feeling of the ocean and the power of the violent waves. I shake the feeling from my head. "You know what? I don't really want to talk about it." My hand drops from her face and I bring her hand down with mine. "What do you want to do today?" It seems like such a stupid question when we have so much shit hanging in the air.

But she just smiles as she swings our arms and plays along with me, giving me what I need. "We should probably go shopping so you won't have to wear the same clothes the entire time."

"Shopping, huh?" I arch an eyebrow and sigh. "All right, let's go shopping."

## Callie

What an insanely ordinary thing to do, I think as we walk up the busy street fenced by buildings and neon-colored shops and a mob of people who are dressed in beachwear. I feel over-dressed in my fitted blue shirt and skinny jeans. My Converses are not made for a sidewalk that has sand in it and I keep wishing I'd brought my sandals the way Seth had suggested when we were packing.

I thought it was an absurd thing to say, but now looking at the sand everywhere, I do want to sink my toes into it. I'm staring at my feet as I walk and dodge from left to right through the crowd. I'm never comfortable in crowds because I always wind up getting touched, no matter how hard I try not to be. But as I keep getting prodded in the shoulder by men and women I realize my internal cringing instinct has diminished over time.

"I told you," Seth whispers in my ear.

I blink up at him and he has a huge smile on his face. His eyes are hidden behind silver sunglasses and he has on a thin red T-shirt, jeans, and sandals. "Told me what?"

"That you'd regret not wearing sandals." He sticks his arm out for me to take and I loop it through mine, like we are two ordinary people taking a nice stroll down the sidewalk. Only we're not and I'm reminded of that when he opens his mouth again.

"Do you…do you want to talk about it?" he asks as we

pass by a store displaying a collection of sunglasses in the window.

I shake my head, taking in the stores beside me, trying not to think about how I felt seeing Caleb again, the things he said to me, or the fact that my mom has called and texted me at least a hundred times and left me countless messages I refuse to check. "I'm okay," I say. "And despite the fact that I don't have shorts or sandals, I'm enjoying the sun and sand."

He grins at me and it beams in the sunshine. "Well, I'm glad." The smile fades. "But if you need to talk…"

"Then I'll come to you." I point to the candy canes hanging on the streetlamps just above our heads. "It's kind of strange seeing Christmas decorations without snow on the ground."

"Indeed it is." His phone rings inside his pocket and he reaches his hand in to silence it without even looking at it.

I eye him over, but he only smiles, and I don't press, returning the favor of limited questions because that's what he's doing for me.

Kayden and Luke are walking just a little ways in front of us, talking and laughing. Luke keeps checking out girls as they walk by, particularly the ones dressed in tight dresses.

"I don't understand how they can be so comfortable dressed like that," I say as Seth jerks me to the side to swerve me around a man who's dressed as a taco and handing out fluorescent-pink flyers.

"How can who be dressed like what?" He steers us back over to the center of the sidewalk.

"People." I glance around the busy street with my shoulders slouched. "I mean, most of the girls are wearing nothing."

Seth laughs at me and then draws me closer to him. "I think you should try dressing like that."

My eyes widen and I start to panic as I take in the limited fabric on almost everyone. It's not like they're naked or even in swimsuits but a lot of women are wearing short dresses and it makes me uneasy. "Seth, there's no way I'll ever be able to wear a dress." I think back to Caleb and how he called me a slut on the porch. I know it shouldn't bother me, but it does.

"I doubt that," he assures me with certainty. "I think that one day you'll be just as comfortable in your own skin as all of these people are in theirs."

I frown with doubt. "I don't think so."

He scans the street and his eyes land on a tall woman with flowing blonde hair the color of sunflowers who's wearing a white-and-pink sundress. Her hair is dancing in the light breeze that smells like salt and fish and everything that is linked to the ocean. "How about something like that?"

I shake my head, breathing in the fresh air to still my accelerating heart. "No way."

He fires a death glare at me, his brown eyes darkening as his eyelids lower. "Why not?"

"I was twelve the last time I wore a dress," I say quietly,

with my head held low as shame washes over me. It was pink and had flowers on it and I loved spinning in it.

Suddenly he understands. "Oh Callie, I'm sorry." He hooks a finger below my chin and forces my eyes away from my feet.

"It's fine." I shuffle my feet along the boards of the slightly arched bridge as we walk over it. "You didn't know."

He's quiet for a while and I return to staring at my feet. "How about you just try it?"

I blink up at him, stunned. "I thought we moved past the subject."

He shakes his head with his gaze fastened on me. His blond highlights glimmer in the sun and he's paler than most of the people around here. "I don't want you to stop moving forward."

I wave my hand in front of me. "But we *are* moving forward."

He smiles. "That's not what I meant."

"I know." I sigh heavily, with the heat of the sun kissing my cheeks. "It doesn't really matter either way. I don't own a dress."

A grin expands across his face and he starts bouncing with excitement and swinging my arms. "Oh my God, I should totally buy you one."

I glance around at the store windows. A few of them are clothing stores with half-dressed manikins on display. Others have knickknacks and beachwear, and there's an Umbrella

172

Hut near the corner of the street, and a man is walking around in front of it with floral board shorts, a tank top, and a Santa hat. "Seth, I really don't think I can."

He nudges me with his shoulder. "We can at least try." He jerks me to the side by the arm and then we cross the street to a fluorescent-pink store with daisies painted on the window and dresses hanging up on a rack underneath the outside deck. "We'll buy you one and then if you feel like wearing it you can."

"And if not?"

"Then we'll have had the pleasure of buying a dress."

I sigh but don't argue and he takes that as a yes. He speeds up and weaves us through the people, and I keep my shoulders in to stop anyone from touching me.

"Hey, where are you two going?" Luke calls out from the sidewalk with his hands cupped around his mouth.

Kayden's looking at us like he thinks we're running away from him. He's got on a pair of dark denim jeans and a fitted black shirt. His bangs are hanging in his eyes and the ends flip up around his ears and neck. He's still scruffy on his chin and strong jawline and I wonder how long it will be before he can shave again—be around a razor again.

He mouths, *Are you okay?*

"Yeah, go get your clothes," I call out as I wave and then Seth tows me backward and we step up onto the curb of the opposite sidewalk. "We'll catch up with you."

Luke looks puzzled, but then shrugs and heads up the

sidewalk with Kayden behind him. I tear my gaze off them and turn around, tripping on my shoelace that's come untied. I kick up sand as we head to the daisy store. In the distance, there are the whispering sounds of the waves washing up on the sand.

"And some sandals too," Seth adds, and he braces me by the arm as I trip over a hole in the sidewalk.

I nod as I regain my footing. "Sandals do sound nice."

We rummage through the racks outside for a while, but don't find anything that is "Callie first-time-dress-worthy," Seth tells me. We wander inside, out of the sun and into the cool temperature of the air conditioning. The cashier is reading a magazine behind the counter and she glances up before returning her attention to her reading.

Seth fans his hand in front of his face. "It's hot here and it smells like cherries."

"I think the temperature is actually normal here," I point out. "It's just that we've come from one of the coldest places in the world."

He shoots me a doubtful look as he starts flipping through a T-shirt rack. "In the world?"

I walk up to one of the circular racks in the center of the small shop and run my finger along the tops of the hangers. "Okay, maybe in the country."

He laughs and I join in as we flip through the hangers. Each time he holds up a dress, I shake my head and decline. It's not like they're all ugly; it's just that I really don't want to wear one. I want to stay in my clothes and keep covered up, except maybe my feet. It feels like if I put a dress on then I'm going to go back to that day.

I wander over to the flip-flop section and pick up a pair with pretty purple jewels on the top. I check the size and they're the perfect fit. I'm about to head up to the register to pay when Seth strolls up with his hands behind his back.

"Okay, I think I found one," he says, stopping in front of me. He has a sucker in his mouth and I wonder where he got it from but I don't ask because with Seth sometimes being confused is better than understanding. "But before I show it to you, I want you to clear your head."

"Clear my head." I riffle through one of the racks holding more sandals.

He nods, taking the sucker out of his mouth. His lips are stained red and so are his teeth. "Shut your eyes and clear your head of that place you keep going to every time I hold one up, because if you do it, I think you're going to love this one."

The store is vacant except for the clerk, who's very distracted by the magazine. I'm glad there's no one, otherwise I'd feel silly. I close my eyes, inhale through my nose, and then exhale through my mouth. "All right, trying to clear head in T minus five seconds."

He laughs at me and then pinches my arm. "Don't just try to clear your head. *Clear* your head." I feel him shift as he moves closer. "Here, do this. Picture Kayden."

I peek one eye open. "I don't think that will clear my head. In fact, I think it will cloud it even more."

He shakes his head and pops his sucker back into his mouth. "No, it won't. I promise." His voice sounds funny as he rolls the sucker into the pouch of his cheek.

I sigh and shut my eyes, picturing Kayden and his gorgeous green eyes. His amazingly perfect smile and his soft, deliciously tasty lips. Yeah, his lips, those might be my favorite part. My head is clearing. "All right, I'm thinking of him."

"Now think about how much you trust him."

"Okay…" My mind promptly floats back to that night when I lay under him, helpless but unhindered as he held me, kissed me passionately, felt me from head to toe, our sweaty bodies united. He took me to a place I didn't think existed and made me feel things I never knew I could.

"He's not going to let anything happen to you, Callie," Seth says in a soothing voice that steadies my nerves. "And neither will Luke and I. You have three strong guys. You're not alone and you don't need to hide anymore."

I get what he's saying and it overwhelms me. For six years I felt so alone in the world, hiding in my room. But now I'm here and I have Kayden, Seth, and even Luke. I'm not alone. I have friends. Tears start to sting at my eyes and one drop slips down my cheek.

"You're the best friend in the whole world," I say, holding back the tears as I open my eyes. "And I mean that."

"I know you do." A smile lifts at his lips and he brings his arms out in front of himself, showing me the dress he picked out. "Ta-da."

It has thin straps and is a few different shades of purple, kind of like tie-dye, and there's a lacey trim along the top and bottom of it. It looks like it's made of silk, but it's not low-cut and it looks like it will go to my knees.

I run my fingers along the soft fabric and check that the size on the tag is correct. "You think this is the one? The one to cure me of my fear?"

"No, I think you're the one to cure you of your fear," he says, waving the dress at me. "This will just look really good on you *and* it matches the shoes."

I glance down at the purple flip-flops in my hand and then back up at the dress. "Yeah, they do kind of match," I say and he waits for me to take the dress. Finally, I snatch it up and head to the counter.

"Aren't you going to try it on?" Seth meanders around the racks after me.

I pile the dress and the shoes onto the counter next to the register and tub of pens with furry ends. "No way. Not until I get back to the house."

He rolls his eyes and then backs away toward a section of shorts. The cashier takes her time getting up from the chair and she heads to the register, yawning. Then the phone rings and she's backing up toward it.

"Just a second." She holds up her finger and wanders over to the phone on the corner desk.

I wait patiently with my arm on the counter and my hand on the dress. I remember when I was younger and I used to wear dresses all the time. I would run around and play catch in them and would always skin my knees.

"Maybe you shouldn't play catch," my mom would say to me all the time. But I refused to listen because I loved feeling like a princess who could play sports. I would run up and down the football field, letting my tiny legs carry me as my dress and hair blew in the wind. I was so happy and I realize it's probably one of the last times I've ever felt so carefree.

The cashier laughs as she says something into the phone. "No way. Are you freaking kidding me? He did not."

"Yes way, he so did," Seth mutters mockingly and he drops a pile of clothes down on the countertop. The cashier glares at him as she coils the cord of the phone around her finger. Seth makes a face at her and she turns her back on us.

"Now we're going to be here forever." I flip through a selection of necklaces on a small rack near the register. Most have seashells on them and one even has a miniature bottle of sand.

"Well, I'm going to file a complaint to her manager," Seth says loud enough for the cashier to hear.

I pick up the top item that Seth set down: a pair of denim shorts. "Are you planning on wearing these?" I say sarcastically.

"Ha-ha. You must be feeling better if the sarcasm is coming out." He sets a tank top down on the counter. "And no, these are for you."

I pick up the tank top. "I'm okay with this." I pick up a pair of black lacy panties and then drop them like they're toxic. "But this is too much."

I move my hands toward the pile to scoop it up and take it away, but he slams his hand down on top of it. "Just in case," he says and then a sly smile curves at his mouth. "Like maybe if you feel like being scandalous."

My cheeks are as flaming hot as the black asphalt shimmering in the sunlight just outside the store. But I'm smiling and I momentarily surrender. I figure I'll get the clothes and then argue with him when we get back to the house and out of sight of anyone.

"Fine," I say and then smile as I point to a man walking down the street in a pair of mini pink shorts and a T-shirt. I'm trying to act cool and control my blush but it's hard when there's so much skin showing everywhere. "But if I have to dress in this stuff, you have to dress in one of those."

He follows where I'm pointing and then grins. "Deal, but I'm totally getting one in blue. Pink doesn't look good on me."

"God, he has to be cold. It's not *that* warm." I start to laugh at the idea of Seth in them and then my laughter picks up when he joins in. We're laughing hysterically by the time the cashier hangs up the phone. Tears are streaming down our cheeks and there are temporary laugh lines around our mouths. We keep laughing even when she gives us dirty looks, because we're on the beach, trying to have fun. And laughing is the first step to fun.

By the time we walk out of the store, it's gotten even hotter, but maybe that's because of Seth's last few items he threw on top of the stack. I have a bag in my hand and Seth is carrying several more at his side. The sun is at its peak and shining down on everyone. But I feel terrible. Guilty. Sad. I'm walking around in the sunlight and laughing when Kayden is bearing so much darkness inside himself.

# Chapter Ten

*#14 Let the niceness be*

## Kayden

The sun's bright. Like really fucking bright. Maybe it's because I've been trapped indoors for the last few weeks. Or maybe it's because I feel so dark inside. Who the fuck knows. I'm trying not to think about it too deeply because then I'll have to think of the pain—feel it—and I don't want to yet. Maybe not ever.

Luke and I are strolling up the sidewalk beneath the sun. We stopped and grabbed some clothes at a local shop and I also ended picking up something for Callie. I'm not sure when—or if—I'll ever give it to her, but it was just too perfect not to get. One day, maybe, I hope.

Since Callie and Seth still haven't showed up, we decide to walk down to the beach. Luke keeps checking out every girl who walks by. He's acting weird, even for him. But he's always been this way whenever something bad is going on at home.

"Are you okay?" I ask as we cross the street at the corner where the two roads converge.

He glances at me with his eyebrows creased. "Yeah, why wouldn't I be?" When we reach the other side of the street he asks, "Are you doing okay?"

"I'm fine," I lie, weaving around a woman shoving through the crowd while talking really loudly on her cell phone. Luke checks out her too, angling his head to the side so he can watch her until she disappears around the corner. "I'm just a little tired." It's the stupidest excuse I've ever given, but he doesn't press.

We walk the rest of the way down the street without talking and pause at a crosswalk at the end. There aren't any cars coming but we both just stand there staring at the land as it opens up to the ocean. The waves are fairly quiet and the sun hits the water and creates a blinding reflection.

I shield my eyes and start to cross the street. There aren't too many people, but I don't want to be around even the small amount who are headed toward the water. I just don't want to be around people right now. I want to be inside somewhere in the dark, because I feel like they all know what's inside me by the bandage on my wrist and the rubber bands. It's like everything I worked so hard to hide is out in the open. Luke knows it. The people half-dressed on the beach know it. Callie knows it.

"So what do people do around here?" Luke asks as we hike through the sand to where the frothy waves collide with the shore and wipe away the footprints in the sand.

I shrug, lowering my hand from my eyes. "I'm not sure. Your father's the one who lives here."

His jaw tightens. "Yeah, doesn't mean I know anything about this place...or him."

"How did you even get a key to his place?"

"I don't have a key."

I give him a questioning look. "You don't have a key?"

"Nope," he says simply.

Great. Just what I need. I'm already facing charges if Caleb doesn't accept my dad's bribe. And after what happened last night, I'm wondering if he'll decide to turn it down. I got a text from my mom this morning saying that he blew her off on the phone when she called to check up on their deal. Part of me doesn't want him to accept. Part of me wants to be cut off from my dad. As I think this, a hint of rage and agony surfaces inside me and I quickly choke it down because I'm not capable of dealing with it without a sharp object to transfer the tearing inside of me to the outside of me.

"Are we going to get into trouble?" I ask, fidgeting with the bandage on my wrist, peeling the tape away and then pressing it back down.

"Nah," he says and inches up to the brink of the water. "He hardly ever comes here. And if he does, he won't be pissed. He'd probably be happy."

I end the conversation there because I know it's bothering him. Setting the few bags of clothes on the ground, I lower myself down to sit in the sand and I bend my knees up and rest my arms on top of them. Luke plops down too and we just sit there, letting the silence wash away the pain like the water does to the sand.

I'd probably have stayed that way if my phone didn't start beeping. I move my arms off my knees and take my phone out of my pocket.

**Callie:** Where r u?

**Me:** We r at the beach. Where r u guys?

**Callie:** At the shopping center looking for you guys.

**Me:** Go to the end of the street and head toward the beach. We r right there on the first opening.

**Callie:** OK

I put my phone away and rest back on my hands. "They're headed over here."

Luke bobs his head up and down as he stares off at the horizon. "What are we going to do tonight? I don't want to just sit around and do nothing. I came here to do . . . something."

"I think I'll just stay in." I stretch out my legs. "I don't feel like going out."

He mulls over what I said with his brown eyes squinty against the light. "Look," he says. "I know you've been through a lot, but . . . but I think the last thing you need is to sit around and think about it."

"We don't have to go out." Callie's voice floats over my

shoulder and my body immediately goes as rigid as a board as emotions rush through me.

I turn my head and look at her. The sun is shining in her big blue eyes that are shielded by her long lashes. Her hair is pulled up and her skin glistens from the heat. She has a bag in her hand and a skeptical look on her face. Seth's next to her, carrying an extensive amount of brown paper bags with a purple flower logo on them. He's staring at the ocean with a puzzled look on his face.

I stand to my feet. "What did you get?" I nod toward the bag and force a smile to my lips. "Anything good?"

Her brow puckers as she glances down at the bag in her hand and then back at me. "I don't know."

The way she says it, with such perplexity, makes me wonder what's in the bag. I start to reach for it to tease her. "Can I see?"

She shakes her head quickly and moves her hand around to her back, her cheeks turning a little pink. "No way."

Okay, now I'm even more curious. I look at Seth for an explanation but he just shrugs nonchalantly. "Callie's just being Callie."

I'm not sure what that means because Callie being Callie means her being sweet and adorable, but she's acting offish and twitchy. "Okay...do you guys want to go get something to eat?"

Callie nods and I can't help but think about how she told me she makes herself throw up. I'm not sure what to do with this or if there's anything I *can* do. I understand bad habits and how they own you.

Luke grumbles something as he pushes up to his feet and brushes the sand off his jeans. "No sushi or crab or anything seafood related."

A smile forms at my lips. "I think we established the first time the four of us went out that none of us like seafood."

Seth raises his hand above his head and then points a finger down at himself. "Um, hello. I'm pretty sure I said that I love sushi."

"You did," Callie tells him and then peeks through her eyelashes at me. "It was Kayden and me who said we didn't."

"It seems like forever ago," I mumble as my mind travels back through time, back to when I first met her, back when everything was nothing. God, she's incredibly gorgeous in more ways than most people will ever know. As stupid and as cheesy as it may sound, she'll perpetually own my fucking soul—or the pieces of it that are left, anyway.

I don't know how she does it. How I can be feeling so shitty one minute, and then she smiles and for a second the pain is gone.

I can't take this anymore. I need her like I had her before. I need her right fucking now before I lose it.

I grab her hand, surprising her, and lead her with me as I stride across the beach toward the street, because at the moment I don't give a shit about anything but touching her. Her shoes shuffle against the sand as she hurries along with me. I search for a place out of the way, because what I want to do can't be done in public. I spot a gap in between two small shops, one an alarming yellow and the other a clear blue, like the sun and the sky. They are shaded by slanted roofs that nearly connect over a narrow alley.

"Kayden, what are you doing?" Callie stammers as she trips over her feet, struggling to keep up with me.

I shake my head as I push through a group of people and head down the trail toward the shoreline. "Just hang on."

I cross the street and then when I reach the front of the yellow store, I round to the side and tuck us between it and the building next to it. There's a large Dumpster near the back end and a pile of crates at the other. It's not the perfect place, but perfection is overrated.

"Are you okay?" she asks, breathless as I slow us down.

I take a breath and face her. I don't give her, or myself, time to react as I wind my hand around her waist and press her small body into mine. She gasps as I attach my lips to hers, knowing I'll probably regret it later when I'm by myself. But I need her now.

When our mouths unite, I can finally breathe again. It's like I've been drowning for the last month, only coming up for air when my lungs are about to burst. But her kiss has brought me to the surface.

"Kayden," she murmurs as she grips handfuls of my shirt. "Oh my God."

I slip my tongue inside her mouth and she opens her lips

to let me in deeply. I devour her, realizing how starved I've felt over the past month. I press her closer as I back us into the wall, our legs tangling as we fight to keep our balance. Her bag falls from her hand and my hand comes down on the side of the building. The wood scratches at my palms and I savor the small abrasions. But the most pain comes from my heart rupturing open from kissing her.

She lets out a quiet moan as my hand slides up her back and to her neck. The sound nearly drives me mad. The small kiss heats like a flame and my heart comes to life again. She opens her mouth wider and I slide my tongue in as far as it will go, running it along the inside of her mouth, tasting her, breathing her in. Her hands move around my midsection to my back and she holds onto me.

I want to stop it, but I've lost all control. I move my hand away from the wall and the other away from her back and quickly glide my palms down her side to her thighs. Spreading my fingers around her legs, I pick her up and she latches onto me, crossing her ankles behind my back.

Her bottom lip trembles as I gently nip at it and I'm reminded of how innocent she is and how I'm the only one she's ever trusted to touch her like this. And that's got to count for something. Because Callie is the most stunning, incredible, kind, loving person I've ever met.

It has to mean something that she cares for me.

# Callie

I forgot what it was like, how scary it is, but equally as wonderful, to be touched, felt, held by him when he's letting go of his pain. At first I have no idea what's going on. One minute we're talking about sushi and the next he's dragging me away from the beach. I start to ask him why, but he silences my thoughts with a brush of his lips and all thoughts about life—about everything—vanish. He's kissing me and not pulling away and that has to mean something, like we might have just stumbled forward from our standstill.

He tastes like mint and need, as he overpowers me with his tongue. His scruffy face is like sandpaper against my skin as I clutch onto him, wanting him to touch me all over and terrified by the thought of him ever letting go. I'd latch onto him endlessly if I could, so I know he'll be okay—we'll be okay.

He has to be thinking the same thing too because he picks me up and presses me close to him. My legs are like magnets and attach to his back. He lets out a deep, throaty groan and I'm shocked by the images that flash through my mind, back in the garage, nervous, but eager to be with him in every way possible. I want to breathe, be alive again.

I open my mouth wider and his tongue seeks every square inch of my mouth. I'm shaking from head to toe and it only gets worse when he nips at my lip, dragging his teeth along the inside of it.

"Kayden," I moan and fasten my arms around his neck. I

pull him against me and he crushes us against the side of the building. His hands start to stray down my body and my hips curve into him. Smothering heat sizzles off our bodies as our tongues melt and twine together. A shot of ecstasy shoots up between my legs as I feel his hardness pressed against me and the sensation amplifies when his hand cups my breast. I forget where we are and how hard it is to exist sometimes. I just want him. So badly. I want him to hold me forever.

But then his lips are leaving me and he sets me back down just as quickly as he picked me up. We slam to a standstill again and I try not to fall apart. My lips feel swollen, my lungs are heaving ravenously, and everywhere his hands touched, brushed, and grazed tingles, and all I can think about is doing more with him.

His emerald eyes are glossy and he pants erratically, looking away from me to the beach and out to the side of the building. "I shouldn't have done that."

I shake my head and place a hand on his cheek. "Kayden, look at me."

He blinks his eyes against the sunlight and then forces his eyes to meet mine. "Callie, I can't be doing this. We need to be...we need to be just friends."

"Just friends?" I frown because I don't want to be friends. But at this moment it's not about what I want. It's what he needs. "That's what you really need?"

He nods his head, with his jaw clamped tightly. "For now..." He swallows hard as he stuffs his hands into his pockets, the muscles in his lean arms wound tight. "And this isn't about you. I promise." He's not looking at me, but just over my shoulder. "It's me."

I bite at my lip, considering my next words carefully. "Whatever you need, Kayden. I'm here. You can talk to me."

He conclusively meets my gaze and there's a spark within his pupils that I haven't seen since we reunited. "I know that."

A smile touches my lips, and daringly, I reach forward and lace my fingers through his. "Let's go get something to eat, before Seth ends up throwing a tantrum. He's been complaining the last hour about how hungry he is."

Kayden nods, his fingers twitching as I stroke my thumb across the palm of his hand for reasons that are unclear to me. "Okay." He fakes a smile and I hate that he's faking it in front of me. It means he's closed off, and I don't want that. I want him to trust me like I trust him. I owe him that much.

I owe him a lot more.

I owe him everything.

❧

An hour later we're seated out on the deck of a restaurant that's right by the ocean. The air smells like salt and there's a light breeze that kisses my cheeks and blows strands of my hair into my eyes. The sun is lowering and the heat is a little bit more bearable. There are a few people sitting at the round wooden tables scattered around the deck, but for the most part it's quiet.

The four of us are sitting silently as we read our menus. Kayden's seated next to me and he has his knee resting against mine. I'm not sure if he notices or not, but I don't dare move, afraid that he'll move it—pull away again.

"So how about some sushi?" Seth jokes, shattering the silence. "Or some crab."

Luke rolls his brown eyes as he pops his knuckles. "I think I'm going to go with a burger."

Kayden is biting his lip and I watch him as he reads over his menu, fantasizing about his mouth back on mine. He has his hand tucked under the table and he keeps flicking the rubber bands on his wrists over and over. By the sound of the snap, it has to hurt, but I don't dare try to stop him. If that's what he needs, then it's what he needs.

"I think I'm going to have the same." Kayden closes his menu and places it into the middle of the table beside the ketchup and mustard rack.

It goes silent again and Seth starts texting on his phone while Luke stares out at the beach to the side of us. The waiter finally comes and takes our orders and brings us our drinks. We sip on our straws quietly, with the rush of the waves filling up the empty miles of space between our thoughts.

"That's it," Seth abruptly says and pounds his hand down onto the table. All three of us jump, startled, and Kayden almost knocks his drink to the ground.

Luke's head whips in his direction and he shoots Seth a death glare. "Next time a fucking warning would be nice."

Seth brings his straw to his lips and slurps on his drink. "I'm sorry, but the dead silence is maddening." He sets the drink back down and wipes his lips with the back of his hand. "We need to have some fun."

Kayden immediately stiffens and the rubber band on his wrist snaps and snaps. "Yeah, I think I'm just going to head back to the house."

Seth shakes his head as he rips the wrapper of the straw into tiny pieces. "No way. We did not drive out here to hang out at the house. We came here to have some fun."

"Seth, I don't think—" I start.

He talks over me, flicking the pieces of wrapper into the center of the table. "No. This isn't going to happen. We all have our problems we've been dealing with and we all need a break from life. So we're going to get dressed up and go have some fun."

"Where?" Luke questions and moves the straw to his lips, taking a drink. "At, like, a club or something?"

"No clubs," I beg with my hands overlapped in front of me. "Please."

Seth aims a weighted look at me. "Miss Callie, we've gone over this. Clubs are fun. And you have big, strong Kayden here to protect you."

My shoulders tighten and hunch as I think about just how far he went to protect me and his hand grabs mine from beneath the table. It's like he can read my mind and he leans over and puts his lips to my ear.

"It'll be okay," he says softly, meeting my eyes and giving me a crooked smile. "If you want to go, we can go."

I lean in until there's a sliver of space between our lips. "I want to do whatever you want."

His pupils are huge and his breath caresses my cheeks. "If you want to go out then so do I."

We'll never be able to reach a conclusion this way and I guess Seth sees that too.

"Then it's settled," Seth says and it makes me kind of irritated because I can tell Kayden doesn't want to go out. "We're all going out and have a fucking fun night."

Luke sets his drink down on the table and I catch him glancing at Kayden. Maybe I'm not the only one concerned.

"Is everyone okay with this?" Luke asks, but he's looking at Kayden.

Kayden leans away from me and shrugs as he reaches for his soda on the table in front of him. "I'm good, man."

"I don't think—" I start to protest.

Setting his drink down on the table, Kayden squeezes my hand with his free hand, then slants over and places a soft, moist kiss on my cheek. "Callie, I'll be okay." He breathes against my neck as his finger grazes my wrist. "I promise... you need to... you need to stop worrying about me."

"That'll never happen," I whisper, letting out a slow breath and I nod, my cheeks burning from his kiss. I don't want to go out, and not for the reasons Seth thinks. I'm worried about Kayden. We haven't talked about what happened and it needs to be talked about. Because I don't understand any of it. All I want is to go somewhere and talk so I can ask him all the questions I have bottled up in my head for the last months.

Seth raises his glass in the air to make a toast. "I say, from now on, or at least for the next couple of days, we let the niceness be."

Luke heaves a heavy sigh and tolerantly stretches his arm, bringing his glass up to Seth's. "As long as we're not sitting around in the house, I'm all for the niceness."

Kayden still keeps hold of my hand, and using his free one, lifts his glass up. "I'm in."

They all look at me and I feel tinier than I already did. Wrapping my fingers around my damp glass, I sigh and tap it against theirs. "Fine, but no trouble."

Seth giggles. "Darling, trouble is my middle name, so just roll with it."

Luke snorts and even Kayden cracks a smile. But I keep frowning because it feels like we're running away from our problems. If I've learned anything in my life, it's that running away from them only allows them to chase you.

"To the niceness," Seth says and clinks his glass against ours, spilling a little soda onto the table.

"To the niceness," the three of us mutter and our glasses collide, making a promise I'm not sure we'll all be able to keep. Even though I'd like to believe that the next few days will be filled with laughs and giggles and sunshine, I'm worried a storm may roll in.

# Chapter Eleven

*#45 Don't let the man bring you down*

## Callie

"Seth, I don't think I can do this." I'm super squirmy as I take in my reflection in the mirror. My skin is pallid and even though the dress goes to my knees, I feel naked. The straps barely cover my shoulders and I'm showing more skin than I've shown in the last six years. The freckles on my skin are exposed, along with my boney collarbone and somewhat flat chest. Even the sandals on my feet make me feel bare. And my hair is down, which I've never been a fan of.

"I look weird," I say, tugging the bottom of the dress down. "And...naked."

Seth shakes his head as he steps back to examine me. His hair is swept to the side, with a slight fluff in the front. He has on a pair of tan shorts and a gray button-down shirt with the sleeves rolled up. "You look beautiful."

I cross my arms over my chest. "I don't think I can do it."

"Of course you can," he says simply, turning back to the mirror.

I shake my head. "Seth, why are you so dead set on this?"

He's fiddling with his hair and pauses. With a determined look on his face, he turns away from the mirror and looks at me. "Callie, I'm dead set on it for the reason you aren't. You have to let it go. I know it's hard, but you need to move forward—we all need to move forward and let go of the past."

"Is that what you're doing?" I ask. "Because it feels like you're running away from something."

"I'm not running away from anything." He fastens the bottom button on his shirt. "I let go of the running away the day I started dating Greyson. It was like I'd been freed from the fear of what happened and I finally could be myself again."

"But how do you forget what happened?" I wonder, smoothing the wrinkles out of the dress with my hand. "How do you not think about it?"

He gives me a small smile and sets his hands on my shoulders, looking directly into my eyes with a fire of determination. "You don't forget. You just move past it. Let go. Be who you were supposed to be instead of who they make you feel like you should be."

"But how do I divide the two of them," I say, letting my hands fall to my side. "Because sometimes I feel like they mix. Like right now. It feels wrong how I'm dressed, but I don't know if it's because I'm associating the dress with what happened or because I just don't like dresses."

The corner of his mouth tips up and then he kisses my forehead. "Wear it and find out."

He backs away from me and walks over to his bag that's on the twin bed. He pulls out a bottle of cologne, takes the cap off, and douses his shirt in it. I head over to my bag and quickly skim the letter I wrote to Kayden. I'm still unsure of what it revealed and I'm debating if I should run away from it or embrace it. Maybe it's time to face the inevitable.

"Oh, I forgot to ask." He clicks the cap back on the cologne. "What did you wear underneath that dress?"

I bite down on my lip, battling my embarrassment because I did wear the black lacy panties he made me buy. "Nothing."

"Oh, you decided to go commando?" he says with a devious grin. "That's even better."

I let my lip pop free and a smile sneaks through. "You know that's not what I meant."

"I know." He winks at me. "But it was funny." He chucks the cologne back into his bag. "Are you ready to do this?"

I glance at the mirror, noting the vastness in my eyes— they take up my entire face. Sure, I trusted Kayden to see all of me, but I'm uncertain about the world, because it's big and scary and always shifting. One minute it feels like home and the next, distant and unfamiliar.

I submit though and Seth opens the door for me. My knees wobble as I amble out into the kitchen where Luke and Kayden are laughing about something at the table. There's a tall bottle filled with a brownish liquid sitting on the table.

When I step closer I realize it's a bottle of Jack Daniels. There's also a lit cigarette in Luke's hand and smoke is filling the air.

I halt in the doorway, watching how Kayden's eyes light up every time he says something. I wonder if he's drunk because he's gone from sad to happy in a matter of a couple hours. There's a huge smile on his face and his eyes are a little glazed over.

"Drinking already?" Seth rubs his hands together, looking eager as he swings around me, bumping into my shoulder. I grab hold of the countertop to catch myself and then step to the side so I'm slightly hidden behind the counters.

Kayden's eyes brighten when he sees me and I know right then and there that he's buzzed. "Yep, we thought we'd get started early," Kayden says to Seth as he picks up the bottle and hands it to him. His eyes lock on me and I'm thrown back to all the fun moments we had together, the ones that leave me hope even though things look grim right now.

He smiles as he pushes up from the table, the legs on the chair scraping against the tile. He takes long uneven strides as he curves around the table and Seth steals his seat.

Kayden's hair is styled and flips up around his ears. He has on a dark gray shirt and a pair of loose-fitting jeans that hang at his hips. He's also put a few leather bands on his wrists to try and cover up the bandage on it and his face is clean-shaven, which makes me worry because that means he had to use a razor.

"Hey," he says as he crosses the kitchen in long strides and winds around to the cupboard area.

"Hey," I reply, rotating around, so I'm facing him and my back is pressed into the edge of the counter. I give a fleeting glance at his arms, checking for fresh wounds. Everything looks great, except I can't see underneath the bandage.

He abruptly stops and his forehead creases as his eyes lazily scroll up my body, lingering for a moment on my chest before resting on my eyes. "I don't think I've ever seen you wear a dress."

I shake my head with my elbows bent and my fingers gripping the counter. "That's because I haven't. Not for a long time anyway."

His gaze is relentless and makes me grow fidgety. Finally, his eyes lock on mine and even through the subdued sea of alcohol, I see the real Kayden still lives on the inside. "You look beautiful."

"Thank you," I say quietly and tuck a few strands of my hair behind my ear. "I think—"

His lips come crashing down on mine and I suck in a deep breath through my nose as my legs start to give out. His warm tongue enters my mouth and he tastes like Jack and smells like cigarette smoke. His hand grabs my waist and he holds my weight up as our bodies crush together. He angles us back, our legs entwining, and my heart knocks in my chest. The edge of the counter jabs at my back, but I don't care. All I care about is him.

My hands slip up his strong arms and knot through his hair. In the back of my mind, a rational voice is screaming at me to stop, because he's drunk and confused and I need to stop it.

"What are you doing?" I slant my head back a little. "I thought you needed us to be friends."

"I do," he assures me, sounding choked up and then his lips touch mine. I'm trying to pull away, yet at the same time I'm pulling him to me. I'm conflicted. Muddled. I'm a terrible person.

His long fingers spread around my hips and his fingers dig into my skin as he picks me up and sets me down on the countertop. My head bangs against the cupboard as his hands move around to the front of my thighs and he splays my legs open. Moving between them, his fingers sliding farther up my legs until his thumbs are grazing the sensitive inner section. For a moment, I forget where I am and who I am and open up my legs wider, allowing him to get closer.

"Um, I hate to break this up." Seth's voice slaps me back to reality and I instantly jerk away, panting and slamming my head against the cupboard again. "As much as I love you guys, I'd rather not see how far this is going to go. You guys should probably save the groping for later, when you're alone."

Kayden rests his head against my shoulder, breathing abundantly, and his body is tense under my hands. "Sorry," he whispers to my collarbone and then he's pulling away, leaving me more exposed than I already was.

I blink my eyes and adjust my dress as far down over my legs as it will go, and then I hop off the counter. I run my hands through my hair, trying to fix it in place, and I struggle not to cry from the stabbing sensation in my heart.

Seth arches his eyebrows at me. "See, dresses aren't so bad."

I press my lips together, because it's not funny, and yet it is. "I guess not." My mouth sinks to a frown. It aches in every part of my body. All I want is to be with him in a stress-free situation where we can enjoy one another, be real, be us.

His shoulders move up as he lets out a low laugh and then extends his hand out to me. "Come on, baby girl." He touches my bottom lip that's pouting out. "Don't let the man get you down. Let's go have some fun."

I nod and follow him into the kitchen area and we stop beside the small wicker table. Seth's carrying the bottle of Jack in his hand and he swings his arm around toward me, offering it to me. "Here, this will relax you."

I glance around at Luke and Kayden waiting by the screen door, and then back at Seth. "That's okay. Someone needs to drive."

Luke shakes his head, smiling as he rubs his hand across his cropped brown hair. He has a loose-fitted red shirt on and a pair of worn jeans. "I'm having a weird sense of déjà vu, because I'm pretty sure you said the same thing that night we went to the club."

"I did," I admit, flipping my hair off my shoulders. I don't know if it's the night's heat or the kiss, but I'm suddenly very hot. "But what are we going to do? Take a cab everywhere?"

Luke nods as he picks up his phone and rises from the chair. "Already taken care of. One should be here in, like, five."

Seth wiggles the bottle in front of my face and the liquid inside splashes against the glass. "Come on, relax." He leans in, lowering his voice. "You need to relax, Callie. You've been so stressed out lately."

He's right. I have been stressed and I want to relax—to forget for just a second about the unbearable weight on my shoulders. I grab the bottle from him and without any preparation put the glass to my lips and tip back my head, gulping way too big of a swallow. My gag reflexes instantly kick in and I drop the bottle as I clutch at my chest.

Kayden's arm dashes forward and he catches the bottle before it hits the floor. "Holy shit," he says and then steps up beside me to pat my back. "Take it easy."

I cough and fight the urge to vomit. I'm not a big drinker and I usually take it in small doses. "I went a little overboard," I say between coughs, with my hand pressed against my chest.

He smoothes my hair back with his hand and his palm lingers on my cheek. He keeps touching me, yet he acts like he shouldn't. I'm confused and choking and I just want to be free again. "Callie, you don't need to drink if you don't want to." He says it so quietly only I can hear him.

I stand back up and straighten my shoulders. "I know. And that goes for you too."

He eyes me over and then his throat muscles work as he

swallows hard. "Here." He hands the bottle to Seth and hurries toward the door, pushing it open. He steps outside and the door slams shut, leaving the three of us lost and confused. I don't know what to do or if I should follow him. I have no idea what he needs.

Suddenly, I realize I don't know much about him at all.

## Kayden

She thinks I'm mad at her, but I'm not. I'm mad at myself. For coming here. For kissing her. For touching her the way that I have. She deserves better. I'm not even strong enough or good enough to stay away from her.

I strategically make Luke and me sit in the front of the cab so Seth and Callie have to sit in the back. That way I can cool down and stop thinking about her in that damn dress. All I want to do is take her back to the house, rip it off, and make love to her again. But I need to stop thinking about that. And I need to stop drinking because it brings out the feelings I'm trying to keep locked away inside my steel heart.

Luke and Seth keep passing the bottle of Jack back and forth and taking shots with their heads tucked low so the cab driver, a younger man with long hair and a goatee, won't see. Seth offers it to Callie a few times, but she shakes her head and declines each offer. She hasn't looked at me since we left the house and she keeps fiddling with the straps on her dress as she stares out the window. The sky is dark and the Christmas lights light up the street and glow into the cab and in her eyes. Her eyes look sadder than they did when I first met her, if that's even possible.

There's some sappy song playing on the stereo. Some guy's singing about love and I find myself wanting to stab my eardrums or at least make a few cuts to my skin. I don't want to think about love or what it means to me. I don't want to think about anything.

I'm about to ask Luke to pass me the bottle when the cab pulls up in front of a tall brick building wedged between similar buildings. There's a crowd lined up in front of it and the music playing from inside can be heard all the way to the curb.

Luke takes some money out of his wallet, hands it to the cab driver, and then glides the door open. "You guys are paying for the drinks." He hops out and I shake my head as Seth slides over and climbs out.

I wait for Callie, but she doesn't move. When I finally dare to glance over my shoulder at her, I find that she's watching me. I rest my arm on the back of the seat and twist my stomach so I can turn to face her.

"Is everything okay?" I ask her.

She brings her bottom lip into her mouth and shakes her head. "No."

I fight the urge to touch her. "What's wrong?"

She releases her lip and slides to the edge of the seat. "I don't know who you are."

My jaw nearly drops to the ground. "What?"

She lets out a shaky breath as she swings her feet out of the cab. "I don't know who you are. Not really, and it hurts." She doesn't say anything more as she climbs out, pulling at the bottom of her dress, and joins Seth and Luke on the curb.

I don't know how to feel about what she said. I've told her more than anyone else. But really, when I think about it, I've told everyone else nothing and her the bare minimum. My boots scuff against the gravel on the road as I slam the door. The cab drives off, tires skidding, and I'm left standing on the curb.

Callie has taken ahold of Seth's arm, but I can't tell who's holding onto whom. Luke is already reaching for his cigarettes and pops one into his mouth. We walk up to the end of the line and Luke flicks the lighter and the paper burns. People are talking, laughing, having fun, but the inside of my head is twisting.

She doesn't know me.

She really doesn't.

And that's because I won't let her.

Suddenly I feel like an asshole. I owe her an explanation for why she found me bleeding out on the floor.

I'm stuck in my own head as the line moves forward and we walk inside the building. Luke found an eighteen-and-over club so we don't need fake IDs to get in. As soon as we step over the door's threshold, the atmosphere becomes suffocating. There are too many damn people crammed tightly into the small room. The air is stifling, but luckily there's no smoking allowed. The music is deafening and the floor is vibrating from it. I've never minded these kinds of places before, but suddenly I'm feeling a little claustrophobic. I think Callie is too, because she's clinging onto the back of Seth's jacket like her life depends on it as he walks in front of her, shoving through the crowd. Luke disappears into the mob completely.

Someone stumbles back from the bar and spills beer all over the floor next to Callie's feet. As she jumps out of the way, her fingers lose hold of Seth and she reaches for him. But the people are closing in and I can tell she's trying not to panic.

I take a few long strides and grab hold of her waist. Her body goes rigid, but I quickly kiss her head and whisper, "Relax, it's me."

She nods at the sound of my voice and her shoulders unravel. I inch closer to her until my chest is pressed against the back of her head, and then I circle my arms around her waist and pull her securely against me as I maneuver us through the crowd. I make sure to keep my elbows out so no one can get close enough to touch her and when we finally break out of the crowd and into the table section we both take a deep breath.

My arms relax around her, but I don't let her go as we walk to the corner table where Luke and Seth are sitting. I let go of her only to pull a chair out for her and she gives me a tentative smile as she sits down. I round to the other side of the table and take a seat myself, wishing I wasn't here.

"God, it's fucking crazy in here," Luke says, ruffling his hair as he glances around at the bar, the crowd near the door, and the dance floor over in the corner. "And hot."

Seth nods in agreement as he reaches for his cigarettes that are in his front pocket. But then his face sinks and he gazes at the tables around us. "Wait a minute. There's no smoking in here, is there?"

Luke shakes his head as he leans back into the chair and his muscles flex as he crosses his arms. "No...It's going to fucking kill me."

"I think it's the cigarettes that are going to kill you," Callie jokes nervously as her eyes flick to the dance floor.

Luke shoots her a death glare, but then shakes his head and grins. "Well, if I can't smoke then I'm at least going to drink." He pushes the chair away from the table and rises to his feet. "What's everyone's poison?"

"The least potent thing that exists," Callie says, wringing her hands on her lap and picking at her nails. She's anxious and I want to know why. Is it because of me, or is it something else?

Seth takes out his phone and starts pushing at buttons. "I haven't talked to Greyson since yesterday." He sighs. "I think he might be upset with me."

Callie rests her arms on top of the table. "Why?"

Seth shrugs as he slides his fingers across the screen of his phone. "Because I might have said something mean about our relationship."

"Like what?" Callie asks.

"Like I wanted a break." He sets the phone down and sighs as Callie frowns at him. "Don't look at me like that. I didn't mean it. I was tired and overthinking things and I didn't mean it."

Callie runs her hand across the top of the table, sweeping some salt that's on it onto the floor. "Did you tell him that?"

"Not yet," he says. "But I'm working up to an apology."

"Seth." She extends her hand across the table and touches his arm. "Since when do you hold things in? You should never do that. It's not healthy."

He shrugs, glances at me, and then grabs onto Callie's arm. "Come with me for a minute," he says, getting up from the table and pulling her to her feet.

Nodding, she follows him without looking back at me. All I hear are their words echoing in my head. Never hold anything in. It's unhealthy.

If that's true then I'm the unhealthiest person alive. I feel it rushing up inside me. What I am. What I feel. My life and the emptiness that will always own me. If it doesn't then I have to feel the past years of my life. I can't even think straight as feelings overtake me and I push to my feet. Rushing across the room, I head back to the bathroom and shove the door open. There are a few guys in there, so I go into one of the stalls and lock myself in. Pressing my hands against my face, I take deep breaths and then slide my fingers down to my wrists, snapping the rubber band. I do it over and over again until my wrist has a large red welt on it, but it still doesn't feel better.

I need something—anything—to make it go away. I search the stall looking for anything sharp, like the edge of the metal toilet paper dispenser. It's a desperate move, one that might lead to tetanus. I'm not sure if I can do it. As I move my wrist toward it, I catch sight of the buckle on one of the leather bands on my wrist. Viewing it as a better alternative, I place my other wrist above it and then drag it down, pushing hard. The skin splits open and the pain erupts up my arm. As the blood pools out, a calm blankets the inside of my heart.

I sit down on the toilet and let it bleed out onto the floor, splattering red on the tile near my feet. I let my hands fall into my head, feeling ashamed yet gratified and wondering how the fuck I got to this place and how I became this person.

I can track the compulsion back to when I was about twelve. It was right after my team had lost a baseball game, due to the fact that I'd struck out every time I was at bat. Part of me had done it on purpose out of spite because I knew it would make my dad angry. And even though it hurt, every time he got angry he was hurting too, on the inside.

I remember how calm my dad had been on the drive home, which made me nervous. His fingers clutched the steering wheel as he drove the car up the street to our home. The wind was blowing and kicking up a lot of dust. The sky was cloudy and I remember wishing that the drive would never end.

But all things do and too soon we were pulling up in front of the house. The grass had just been cut and the lawn-mowing guy was still cleaning up the piles of cut grass that the lawn-mower had spit out.

"Go inside," my dad had finally said and the low tone of his voice meant I was in deep shit.

I grabbed my bat and glove and climbed out of the car. With my head hanging low, I walked up the path, with my eyes fastened on my feet until I made it to the front door. I only looked up to open it and then I lowered my gaze back to the ground as I walked in.

I started to climb the stairs, hoping for once that he'd just let it go. But halfway up, I heard the front door slam and the wind from outside silenced. I kept walking though, hoping that somehow I'd learned how to make myself invisible.

"Do you want to tell me what the hell happened?" His voice slammed against my back.

I knew I should turn around and talk to him, but I panicked and only sped up. This was always a mistake. His footsteps rushed after me and by the time I reached the top of the stairway, he had taken ahold of my collar.

He jerked me back as he ran down the stairs and I struggled to keep my feet on the ground as the bat and glove slipped from my hand. "Do you realize how lucky you are?" He swung me around in front of him and I tripped over my shoes and slammed into the wall.

"Lucky?" I asked, getting my footing. "How?"

I usually didn't talk back to him, but my head was in a weird place. Someone at school had asked me what the bruise on my arm was from and I almost told them the truth. That my father had shoved me into the side of one of the shelves in the living room because I'd spilled soda on the floor. But I'd chickened out and through the silence a realization had occurred to me. My life was always going to be this way.

"What did you say?" My father stormed toward me, the vein in his neck bulging and his knuckles were white as he balled his fists.

"I said I'm sick of this," I muttered, with my chin tipped down. "I didn't do anything but lose a game."

The silence that followed my small voice's utterance was fucking terrifying and when I finally dared to raise my head I was shocked to find that his fingers had slackened and the vein had resided.

There was a brief instant where he almost looked human and I thought I'd finally gotten to him. But then his eyes reddened and he stepped forward. "Do you know what my father would have done if I'd lost the game and then talked back to him like you just did?" He stopped and waited for me to answer.

"No, sir," I said. "I don't."

He stepped forward and towered over me. "He'd have yelled at me right in front of all those people and told me the truth because the truth is what we need to become better."

Sometimes when he got angry, he'd mention his father and what he did to him, like he needed to explain his violence. I wondered if that's how I'd grow up, reliving his beliefs with my own kids. The idea terrified me, that I could become that. I didn't want to become that and make anyone suffer.

I held my breath, waiting for him to hit me, but his arm stayed at his side.

"I don't get you," he said. "You're such a fuckup. No matter how many times I try to teach you how to behave, you always mess up. And then you lose that game in front of everyone and make me look like a loser father who has a fucking pussy for a son. You don't deserve to be out there." The muscles in his arms protruded and the vein in his forehead pulsed. I wrapped my arms around myself, waiting for the impact. "You don't deserve anything. You're a piece of shit. And a fucking loser. You don't even deserve to be standing here."

He kept going on and on, ripping into me, but not touching me. Each word was a cut—a scar. On and on. Cut. Slash. Scar. Scar. Scar. I felt small and invisible just like I'd been wishing for earlier. When he was done, he turned away and left me alone in the foyer.

I remember thinking how much worse it felt that he hadn't hit me. In fact, I remember wishing he'd said nothing and had beaten the shit out of me. Then I could have curled up in a ball and slept the pain off. Instead, the pain was inside my head, my blood, my heart. I wanted it out so fucking bad and I did the only thing I could think of.

I ran up the stairs to the bathroom and found the first razor I came across. It was a replacement blade for one of my mother's razors. The edge was pretty dull and it had this strip of some kind of lotion shit at the top.

It didn't matter. It was enough. I put the blade up the back of my arm and made a slice. It took several times before it split the skin open, but each graze was gratifying. By the time blood seeped out, I felt better. I moved my arm over the sink and let the pain drip out.

I blink the memory away and rise to my feet. I need to get the hell out of here. Now. I need to bail on this fucking road trip and go home before I get too attached. I wipe the blood off my arm and rearrange the rubber bands and bracelets to cover the cut up. I hurry out of the bathroom and turn sideways to fit through the people, heading for the door.

I'll go back to the house, grab my stuff, and drive my bike home, back to that fucking house where I belong because I can't survive anywhere else.

As I push through the last of the people, I spot Callie and Seth on the dance floor. There's a slow song playing and she's holding onto him, saying something with her forehead creased. Her eyes look watery under the spotlight. I think about how breakable she is and I glance down at my wrist, thinking about how easy I break myself.

# Chapter Twelve

*#88 Don't hold back. Let it all out.*

## Callie

"Okay, I think I might have messed up" is the first thing Seth says to me as the bathroom door swings shut. There are a few women in there, but they're all holding beers and don't seem to mind that Seth's in there. Either that or they're so drunk they're mistaking him for a woman.

"What happened?" I lean against the bathroom sink. "Something with Greyson I'm guessing."

He nods his head up and down. "I panicked."

"I'm familiar with the term," I tell him. "But what did you panic about?"

"About—" He lowers his voice and moves aside as the door opens and a cluster of women enter. One shoots him a glare and he returns it with equal animosity. "About our relationship."

"Yours and Greyson's?"

"Yeah, I think I'm having flashbacks."

The women filling up the restroom are listening intently, so he grabs my arm and leads me into the handicapped stall. Locking the door, he lets go of me and runs his fingers through his hair. He looks uneasy, which is weird because he rarely does.

"Seth, whatever it is, please just tell me," I say, leaning against the wall. "You know you can tell me anything."

He pulls a wary face. "It's about intimacy."

I squirm uncomfortably at the word, like it's a reflex instilled inside my body. "I can handle it."

He shakes his head. "Are you sure?"

I step forward, straightening my shoulders. "Yes, I'm your best friend and you can tell me anything."

He sighs and starts to try to pace in the small amount of space. "I can't go through with it...and not because I'm worried about finally going that far. It's because I keep having flashbacks."

"About what?" I keep my voice calm.

He stops pacing and his arm falls to the side. "Of Braiden."

Braiden was Seth's very first boyfriend and the guy who was solely responsible for letting Seth's ass get kicked by the football team to avoid facing the rumors swarming about their relationship.

"Do you have feelings for him?" I ask, flicking the latch of the door with my pinkie nail.

"No, it's not that..." He wavers. "It's...it's about getting my heart broken."

All this time Seth has seemed so strong, but just like everyone else he has his own fears and I need to be there for him like he's always there for me. I step into his shoes for a minute and become the comforting best friend who tries to help ease the pain.

"It's going to be okay." I take a step forward and place my hand on his arm. "Greyson's not Braiden."

"I know that." He sighs and places his hand over mine. "But sometimes I find myself going back to that place where I'm lying in the dirt and they're kicking the shit out of me."

I wrap my arms around him and hug him, noting how safe I feel in the closeness. "I know, but sometimes moving forward is the only way we can escape our pasts, right? At least that's what you're always telling me."

"I know," he whispers and his arms circle around me. He pulls me closer. "And I know nothing will happen. Greyson's not Braiden and he loves me, but I just keep thinking about that God damn day. I was so fucking happy, thinking life was perfect, and then they showed up all piled into the back of that fucking truck like a bunch of robots all following what the other one does. And..." He drifts off and I can tell he's about to cry. "And I can't stop picturing his face—the hate in his eyes, like he was blaming me that he was part of it."

I hold very still and give him all the time he needs to collect himself. Seth being himself, it doesn't take him too long before he's pulling away. He wipes the corners of his eyes with his fingertips and he puffs out a breath. "Anyway, what I was going to say before I started bawling like a baby was that I was feeling a little scared about moving forward and I might have said some things to Greyson that weren't very nice."

I reach for a roll of toilet paper and hand him some tissue. "It could be...sometimes saying sorry is actually easy."

He dabs the rest of the tears away with the tissue and then tosses it into the garbage bin that's on the wall. "Yeah, but sometimes it's not."

"But sometimes it is."

That gets him to smile. "Look at you. Being all wise." He swings his arm around my shoulder. "I think it must be from all the time you spend around me."

I crack a smile as I unlatch the door. "It must be."

By the time we walk out of the bathroom, the room is even more crammed. I don't like it. It makes me feel anxious and ashamed about the dress I'm wearing. Each time someone brushes up against me, I cringe internally.

I grasp Seth's hand as he guides me to our table where Luke is talking to some girl in a tight black dress. Her blonde hair is done up, her cleavage is nearly popping out of her dress, and she's sitting in my seat. As we approach the table, her eyes scale me and then she looks away, disregarding me.

"Hey," Seth says before she can say anything. He reaches across the table and grabs two tall shot glasses from the eight that are circling the middle of the table. "I think Callie and I are going to take shots and dance."

Luke nods and then starts chatting with the girl. I step

behind Seth and he turns to me and offers me a shot. I'm distracted, and without even thinking, I put the rim up and tip my head back. The alcohol burns and tears at my esophagus.

"Blah." I gag, shoving the empty glass back at Seth. "I didn't mean to drink that."

Seth giggles at me and angles back his head, knocking the shot back. He takes my glass and his and puts them back on the table. One tips over, but he doesn't bother picking it up. He holds my hand and tugs me toward the dance floor.

"Do we really have to?" My head's a little blurry and my legs feel like rubber. "I don't feel very good."

Seth nods as he spins around, doing a little wiggly thing with his hips before striking a pose. "You and I need to relax."

I glance around at the people surrounding us who are grinding against each other to the low beat of the sultry song. "Dancing's never been relaxing for me."

He shuffles toward me, snapping his fingers and rocking back and forth. "Come on. I saw you dancing in the car ride when we were heading to Afton."

I shake my head, but my lips turn upward. I start to dance with him, not going too overboard, but enough that I feel my mood lifting. When the song switches to a slow one, Seth inches in and puts his hands on my hips. As we rock to the rhythm of the song and with each sway, a weight builds on my chest. My mind is going back to when Kayden and I danced and for a moment everything seemed like it was going to be okay. But it's not okay. Nothing is. Kayden won't talk to me and all I can ever picture is how he looked lying on the floor, pale as snow with a dying pulse. I can see the slits on his wrist and on his side. I can feel my terror and worry about him dying. How I don't want him to die. How I need him. How I need him forever. The weight on my chest bears down and I swear my ribs will splinter.

"Callie, what's wrong?" Seth brings his finger up to my cheek and grazes a tear that escaped my eye.

"I don't want him to die," I say through a choked sob. "I don't."

His eyes widen. "He's not going to die, Callie. He made it out alive."

"I know that," I say, knowing he won't understand. Kayden is like me in so many ways. He'll hide it inside himself until he breaks. And if he breaks, I might not make it to him in time.

Then what? I can't go on living my life without him, fighting through the pain every day. I felt what it was like to lose him back when I saw him on the floor. I thought he was dead and my chest nearly crushed into my heart as the pain slammed into my ribs.

I can't do it without him. I need to save him and myself and make us happy together.

## Kayden

When I realize she's crying, I move for her, shoving anyone who gets in my way. Seeing tears come out of those stunning blue eyes rips my heart in half and I no longer care about anything else but making her better.

When she sees me, her eyes enlarge and she reaches up to wipe the tears away from her cheeks. Seth turns and looks at me and then he lets go of her waist and backs away.

"You got it from here?" he asks me and I nod. He moves through the crowd and I take his place, positioning myself in front of Callie.

Her fingers start to slide down her pink cheeks to wipe the tears away, but I catch her hand and move it away. Bringing my free hand to her cheek, I trace my thumb down each tear and erase them.

"What's wrong?" I ask, pulling her closer. "Did something happen?"

She shakes her head, her eyes blinking fiercely as more tears threaten to spill out. "I'm okay, just a little tired."

"Callie, please tell me what's wrong so I can try to make it better."

She shakes her head and her throat is jerking as she works back a choke. "It's really...nothing." She starts to sob, her shoulders quivering with each tear.

My arms loop around her and I pull her against my chest. She buries her face into my shirt, clutching onto the bottom, and her tears are soaking through the fabric. I don't dare move, even though everyone around us is dancing. I run my hand along her back and down her hair.

"Shh..." I say, as I work not to cry myself. I don't know

221

why, but I can feel her pain, even though I have no idea what's causing it. I try to hold the tears back. I focus on the open wound on my wrist and concentrate on the lingering burn. But it's not working and soon I know I'm going to crumble—we both are.

I pick her up and she doesn't even look at me or seem stunned. Her legs hitch around my back and her arms slide up my chest and she secures her arms around my neck. People watch us in wonder as I shove my way through the crowd, making sure to hold the back of her dress down and keep her covered up. When I step outside, she moves to get down, but I tighten my arms and force her to stay against me. Now that I've got her, I can't let her go.

Holding onto her, I flag down a cab. The driver looks at me funny as I duck my head in, still carrying her, and sit down in the back seat. "552 Main Beach Drive," I tell him as I reach forward, rising up a little, and glide the door closed.

He's an older man, and I catch him eyeing us a few times through the rearview mirror. I bring one of my hands up and cup the back of her head, while the other I keep at her waist. She's still crying and her tears are making my shirt damp.

The cab moves forward and the meter up front begins to tick. I hold as still as I can and rub her back with my cheek pressed against the side of her head. About halfway home, when the streetlights from the main road change into porch lights, she raises her head and rests her chin on my shoulder, staring out the back window. I don't ask her what's wrong and she doesn't tell me. She just watches the twinkling lights blur by as we drive forward, into the night, knowing that eventually we'll reach the end and one of us will finally have to break the silence.

# Chapter Thirteen

*#89 Admit the truth and accept what it means*

## Callie

The song playing from the cab stereo is cheerful and the singer is professing his love to a girl he ran away from. I envy him because he can admit it to the world. I, on the other hand, just realized that I might be in love with Kayden and that there is no way I'll ever be able to tell him. Not just from fear of rejection, but from fear of the unknown. I've never been in love before. Never understood it. But I realize now that the worry and heartache I've been carrying inside me might just be love.

I clutch onto him, feeling his chest rise and fall underneath me as I watch the Christmas lights blur by in streaks of gold, silver, red, and green. It's such a pretty time of year, but I've never been a fan of it. It reminds me of a time when I used to get excited and run out to the tree to rip presents open. However, the Christmas I was twelve, presents only reminded me of my birthday and the terror that came with that memory would always surface.

I remember the first Christmas after it happened. I'd lain awake in my bed all night with my eyes open and my gaze fastened on the ceiling, wishing I'd hear reindeer on the roof, like I imagined I did when I was little. But there was no imagination or magic left inside me and all I heard was the dead silence of nighttime and the secrets lying in my heart.

When I heard my mother walk into my room that morning, I pretended to be asleep.

"Callie," she'd whispered. "Callie darling, wake up." She gave my shoulder a little shake. "Sweetie, I think Santa brought you some presents."

My eyelids lifted and I met her gaze. She was wearing a pink satin robe and her hair was braided at the nape of her neck. Her makeup wasn't on, but I thought she looked better without it.

"Good morning," she said with a cheerful smile. "Are you ready to go see what presents you got?"

I was exhausted from lying awake all night and I rolled onto my side, situating my hands beneath the pillow. "I'm not in the mood for presents."

She placed a hand on my back and I jumped, thinking about the last time someone had put a hand on me while I was lying in the bed. "Callie, are you all right? You've seemed so sad the last few months."

"I'm fine," I snapped. "I'm just sick of Christmas and

pretending that I believe in things when I really don't. There is no Santa, Mom. I haven't believed in him since I was eight."

"Well, of course I know that," she replied, lifting her hand from my back. "But it takes the magic and fun out of it if we don't all play along."

"Magic and fun doesn't exist," I said, wiggling away from her. "And I'm tired of playing along...I'm going to go back to sleep. I'm tired."

She sat there for an eternity, breathing in and out, and then finally she rose to her feet, the mattress rising as her weight left it. "All right."

That's all she said. Then she left and the room and the haunting memories took over again. Even now, I wonder why she never said anything. She had to be able to tell that something was wrong. One of these days, I'll find the courage to ask her. I have to. Otherwise I'll never know and the answer will always haunt me.

"Callie." Kayden's voice echoes through my thoughts. I lift my eyes, realizing I've dozed off. I elevate my head and glance around at the darkness outside and the ocean in the distance.

"Did I fall asleep?" I blink my eyes and then let go of his shoulders to rub the dreariness away.

He nods, sweeping a lock of my hair out of my face. "You did, but that's okay."

My cheeks and eyes feel swollen from the sting of tears. "I'm sorry."

His fingers linger on my cheekbone and he's looking into

my eyes, terrified. "I said it was okay, Callie. And I promise it is . . . I liked holding you . . . It made me feel calm."

I suck back the tears that still want to come out. "Okay."

He nods and there's a silent agreement that we're both okay for the moment and that being together is okay. I start to climb off his lap, but he grabs my waist and shifts me aside so I slide onto the seat. I put my feet on the floor, confused as he reaches for his pocket. He takes out his wallet and pulls out a twenty, and then he leans over the seat and hands it to the driver.

He starts to move back into the seat but then drifts to the side and grabs the door handle. Flicking it up, he pulls the door open and then hops out. He stretches his arms above his head and then offers his hand to me. I take it, feeling the warmth of his skin as he helps me out and doesn't let me go as he closes the door. We both stand in the driveway beside Luke's truck as the cab backs down the gravel path and out onto the street. Once he speeds off, Kayden looks at me.

"Do you want to go for a walk?" he asks, nodding his head at the shore.

I nod through a sniffle. "A walk sounds nice."

He gives me a tiny smile and laces our fingers together. We walk hand in hand past the house and step out onto the shore. Sand fills up my sandals and is cool against my skin. It's hard to walk, because they keep getting stuck, so I stop, giving a gentle tug on his arm.

"What's wrong?" he wonders, refusing to let go of my hand.

I wiggle my feet out of my sandals and bend over to scoop them up, hitching them on my finger before standing back up. He nods, understanding, and then we continue walking deeper into the darkness. I can hear the waves rolling like a lullaby and the sound of music drifts from one of the houses. The sand seeps through the cracks between my toes as I listen to every sound and feel the coolness of the air.

"Are you cold?" Kayden asks as we slow down just out of reach of the water.

I glance at my arms, feeling myself shiver, and in the moonlight, I see the goose bumps on my arms. "A little."

He sighs and then glances back at the house up at the top of the sandy slope. "Let me run back and get you a jacket."

I quickly shake my head and strengthen my hold on his hand. "No, please stay here. We need to . . . we need to talk."

He eyes me over skeptically and in the darkness his eyes look hollow. He rubs the back of his neck tensely and then he lowers himself onto the ground, guiding me down with him. He gives me a gentle tug to the side and maneuvers me onto his lap, settling me against him. I lean back, shutting my eyes, feeling safe, feeling like this is where I belong.

Kayden is the only guy who's ever made me feel this way, more than Seth, more than my own self. He is all I need and I hope he feels the same way too. But before I ask, there's something else I need to know—need to understand.

I summon a deep breath and then release it out into the open. "Kayden, what happened?"

Three tiny words, so heavy and meaningful that they crack the earth. He tenses and so do I, before I turn to look him in the eyes. He swallows hard and so do I. He takes a deep breath and it's nearly soundless as it eases back out of his lips.

His lips part and as his voice slides out, my heart nearly stops. "My father stabbed me."

## Kayden

I have no idea why I tell her. I wasn't planning on it. I was planning on keeping it a secret forever, just like everything else. But she's sitting there, waiting for me, trusting me enough to hold her and be close to her. She expects the truth and I want to give it to her. I want to give her everything.

"My father stabbed me." And just like that, I've shattered the box inside my heart and it fractures into a thousand jagged splinters.

Her eyes widen and her breath hitches in her throat. She's verging on crying again, so I wrap my arms around her and pull her against me. "Relax, I'm okay now."

Her skin is like ice. I rub my hands up and down her arms, trying to warm her up. She shivers, not from the cold but from my touch. Or maybe it's from the shock I've just given her. I suddenly wish I could take it back, because I never should have put it on her shoulders.

"I'm sorry," I apologize. "I shouldn't have put that on you."

Her hands wiggle between our bodies and she flattens

her hands on my chest. Pushing away from me, she looks me in the eye. "Yes, you should have... You should have told me sooner."

I shake my head, putting my hand onto the small of her back so she'll stay close. "Callie, you don't need to know this kind of stuff... You've got your own problems."

She looks angry suddenly, her eyes flaring and I lean back, concerned she's going to hit me or something. "Kayden... I don't..." She can't find the right words. She shifts her body, bending her knees so her weight is on my lap. She places her hands on my shoulders and with a steadfast look in her eye she says, "This is all my fault." I start to protest, but she puts her hand over my mouth. "You should have never hit Caleb... I should have never let you find out about him. If you hadn't, then none of this would have happened. We'd be back at the house lying in my bed."

"That's not true," I say, my lips moving against her hand. "It's good that you told me. He can't just go walking around living his life when he took yours."

She lowers her hand to her lap and sighs. "That's what your father's doing." She huffs a frustrated breath. "Does anyone even know?"

I shake my head and then shrug. "My mom, but she's known about everything... about the hitting, the beating, the kicking... She doesn't care."

Her eyes wander out to the ocean. "This isn't right," she mutters and turns her head toward me. "We have to tell someone." She starts to get up, but I dig my fingers into her side and hold her in place.

"Callie, there's no point telling anyone…and you…you need to stop worrying about me." My breath starts to tremble from my lips. God damn it. This is the hardest fucking thing I've ever had to say. But I need to say it. I need to make her understand who I am, deep on the inside. "I messed up. Big time. What I said at the diner about…about cutting myself…I'm broken. I don't know if I'll ever really be able to stop…to stop cutting. You need to stay away from me. *Please*, walk away."

Her eyes stay on me as she takes in my face and makes me feel unsettled on the inside. "No."

I shake my head. "Callie, you don't want this—"

"Yes, I do." She places her hand over my mouth, pressing her lips together as she slips a finger underneath one of the rubber bands on my wrist. "Kayden, you think I'm walking blindly into this, but I'm not. I think I might have known for a while that you…that you cut yourself, even before you told me."

My heart shrivels into nothing as she lowers her hand from my mouth. "How?"

Tears bubble in the corners of her eyes. "That night when we…when you and I…" Her breathing is unsteady. "When we had sex, I saw you had all those cuts on your arms, I thought…the thought crossed my mind that you might have put some of them there."

"Why didn't you say anything?"

"What was I supposed to say? 'Did you cut yourself?' Besides, I didn't want to believe it."

My shriveled heart has become a fucking pile of nothingness. "Because it's too much?"

She quickly shakes her head. "No, because I don't want to believe that you have all that pain trapped inside of you...I know how much pain it takes to go that far...to want to hurt yourself."

There's this mind-blowing moment when I realize something. Someone understands me. *Callie* understands me. She gets it and she's not afraid of me or what's inside me. And while I don't understand it, I want it—I want her. How is it even fucking possible that I've been walking around for years and years and years with her in the same town—the same school— and I never really saw her? What would have happened if I had?

"I'm too messed up," I press again, wanting her to fully understand. "I hurt myself and let others hurt me and I don't tell anyone."

"But you need to. You need to tell someone about your father. Even if they think you hurt yourself, people need to know."

"No one will ever believe me. I just got arrested for beating Caleb's ass and then I have my fucking scars that I put on my body myself. No one will get it."

"I don't care," she responds and her fingers dig into my shoulders as she clings onto me. "We'll make them understand."

I stop and look at her. How can someone like her exist? It's impossible, and yet she's here in front of me, looking as beautiful as ever beneath the pale glow of the moon. "Callie... but what about you and Caleb? You haven't told anyone about that." I feel like a jerk for saying it, but it seems like it needs to be said.

"I'm working on it," she utters and there's a quiver in her voice. "You and I, we're going to work on it... We're not going to let other people own us anymore." She seems to be making the speech to herself more than to me, but that's okay. I want her to tell someone so that piece of shit can stop walking around owning her.

She looks at me and I can tell she's about to cry. I don't want her to cry. I want her to be happy. "Callie, tell me what you need," I say and tuck a strand of her hair behind her ear.

"I need the world to stop being such an ugly place full of hurt." Tears slip out of her eyes. "I need to wake up and really believe everything will be okay instead of just hoping it will be. I want to be one of the lucky ones who has a good life."

I nod, because that's what I want for her, too. "You can still get that. Just tell me what you need to make you happy."

She looks me in the eye with tears streaming down her cheeks. *"You."*

I flinch because she just threw herself out there to a person who's hollow and cracked. I don't know what to do. I don't know if I can give her what she wants. I don't understand need or love. I don't understand what makes people's lives whole. My lips part and I honestly have no idea what's about to come out of them, but I never find out because she presses her lips against mine and silences me.

Maybe she knew it wouldn't be what she wanted to hear or maybe she just wanted to kiss me, either way I pull back. Cupping her cheek, I say, "Callie, you don't want me. Trust me. I'll get you nowhere."

All she does is shake her head and kiss me again, clutching onto my shoulders for dear life. This time I can't help myself. She's shaking in my arms and I want to make her better, so I kiss her back, slowly at first, but then this hunger takes over and I begin to kiss her fiercely and with all the passion I've kept trapped inside me.

We fall back into the sand. She's lying on top of me and our bodies are joined together as our tongues entangle. The heat of her is mind-numbing and I forget where I am. It's just me and her lying in the sand and I swear for one fucking moment that everything is going to be okay. That this will be my life. Just her and me.

Forever.

And for a second, the thought doesn't scare the shit out of me.

## Callie

I can tell I'm scaring him and I start to shy away, fearing rejection. But then I see something in his eyes put there by years of beatings and God knows what else. I suddenly get it. Kayden can't love me because he doesn't understand love. He understands pain and hurt and disappointment, but not love. I know right then that I can't tell him how I'm feeling, but I can show him.

Needing to be close to him, I gather every speck of courage I have inside me and kiss him. He kisses me back but then he's pulling away. My insides wind into knots, but I don't back down. I press my lips to his again and just like that, through a second chance, he's kissing me back.

At first he's gentle, his tongue soft against mine as he holds me on his lap. But suddenly the gentleness turns desperate and the next thing I know we're falling backward. I land on top of him, with our mouths sealed together and our bodies perfectly aligned. His hands are all over me, on my neck, my back. They glide down to my backside and then they're slipping underneath my dress, digging roughly into my skin.

I tense at the intimate touch, but then remember that he's seen and felt all of me. I relax, letting his hands explore my body. Without warning he turns us to the side and pulls my leg up over his hip. His hand slides higher, leaving a path of heat along my skin, and I almost burst into flames as he inches his fingers beneath my panties.

I start to shiver, from nerves, from the cold, from the anticipation, but each feeling leaves me when he slips his fingers inside me. I let out an embarrassing moan and my body arches into him. He starts to move his fingers and causes small whimpers to leave my lips. I feel myself verging toward the edge, about to break and be free. But he abruptly stops and then he's pulling away again. The moment starts to dissipate and fall into the sand as he sits up, moving me with him.

"What are you doing?" I stutter, feeling flushed. "Is something wrong?"

His fingertips burrow into my waist and he holds me firmly as he stands. Sand showers from our bodies as he wraps his arms underneath me and he holds me against his body. He hikes across the beach and toward the house, with me attached to his front.

"I'm taking you inside," he says softly, kissing me and then pulling back. "Before things get too out of hand." He presses his lips to mine and gives me a delicate kiss. "We don't want to be out in the beach...out in the open." He brings his lips to mine as his shoes scuff in the gravel of the driveway. He nips at my bottom and I shiver uncontrollably. When he pulls back, his lips quirk. "We don't want to be in the sand...it can get messy."

I try not to blush, but I've never been good at suppressing my embarrassment, and my cheeks are fiery hot.

He walks around Luke's truck and trots up the steps, bringing us into the porch light. He smiles as he takes me in and then moves one arm away from me to touch his finger to my cheek. "I've missed that, you know—the blushing. It's adorable."

I blush even more, but I let it be—there's nothing I can do about it. Smiling, he shifts my weight to the side, and I overlap my fingers behind his neck as he maneuvers the door open without setting me down. We stumble into the kitchen and his lips come down on mine as soon as his feet make it over the threshold.

His hand travels up into my hair as he kisses me and walks through the house, bumping into the corner of the countertop and knocking his elbow against the wall of the hallway. It's dark, but there's a lamp on in the living room and also in the bedroom and a soft trail of moonlight filters through the windows.

Kayden's hands run down my back and slip underneath my dress as he turns the corner and stumbles through the doorway into the room Seth and I are sleeping in.

"What if they come back?" I ask, breathless, and my lips feel bruised from all the kissing.

Kayden adjusts his arm so it's under my backside and I can feel his hardness pressing against me. All there is between us are his jeans and my panties. "We'll lock the door...unless... unless you don't want to do this." Without letting me go, he reaches back with one arm, shuts the door, and pushes the lock in.

I love that he asks. I love it even more that I want to do it. I want to be with him. I can be with him. Only months ago, the idea seemed out of reach, nonexistent, impossible. But now, with him, everything inside me has changed and my heart and soul aren't so shadowed anymore. He is my light and I hope one day that I can be his.

I move my lips toward him. "I want to be with you."

He doesn't say anything else. His lips collide with mine. He starts walking again as his hands stray to my waist, fingers dipped inward and leaving paths of sweltering heat on my skin. He lowers us onto the bed, sits up a little, and shoves Seth's bag off the edge. Then he maneuvers his body over mine and our lips reconnect with a shock of static. When his tongue enters my mouth, I knot my fingers in his hair and steer his face closer, wanting all of him.

"Callie," he groans as his hands round to my stomach. His fingers graze along my skin and send a coil of heat down between my legs.

My back bows up into him as I relish the feel of his tongue on mine. If I could wish for one thing, it would be that I could always feel this way, completely and blissfully consumed by someone else. No, not just by someone else. By Kayden. My legs move around his hips, so I'm opened up to him, and his weight bears down on me. He's holding himself up with his arm propped to the side of my head and his other hand moves up the front of my dress until it reaches the edge of my bra. For a split second I feel uneasiness choke inside me, but I remind myself that this is Kayden and he would never hurt me—he'll only ever protect me, no matter what it costs him.

His fingers sneak under and cup my breast and my nipple promptly hardens. My knees constrict around his waist as the pad of his thumb grazes across my nipple. My head falls back as I let out a moan and Kayden begins grinding his hips against me. He does it over and over again, our bodies connecting and colliding. There's undying passion in each movement and I forget where I am. I exist only in this moment and every other moment in my life is dead. My nails dig into his shoulder blades as I feel myself rising toward the stars outside the window and seconds later I fall back to earth. Panting loudly, I stretch my fingers out as he stills.

Then he's sitting up and grabbing my arm. Moving off the bed, he pulls me up so I'm sitting on the edge of the bed and he's standing in front of me. He reaches for the bottom of my dress, and with one swift movement, he pulls it over my head. My heart jumps inside my chest as my hair falls to my shoulders. He leans over me and his hand slides up my back to the clasp of my bra. My chest rises and falls as he flicks the clasp open and my bra falls off my shoulders. I'm choking up again, but whisper at my heart to calm down as I reach for his shirt. His breathing becomes unsteady as I slip my hand up his chest and bring my body up, so I'm standing in front of him and his shirt is pulled up. One of my hands rests above his heart, beating unsteadily against my palm.

I swallow hard as I take in the scar on his side, still heal-ing, and I trace a path around it. Tears sting my eyes as I think about how it got there, what he went through, what he must be going through.

"Callie…" Kayden says and he hooks a finger under my chin so I'll look up at him. He lowers his hand and his fingers circle my wrist. Bringing my hand up to his lips, he kisses the inside of my wrist and I shudder from the delicate touch of his breath. "I'm okay."

*No, you're not*, I want to say. *Your father stabbed you and you took the full weight of it. You can't be okay.*

He lets go of my hand and reaches behind his neck. With a soft tug, he slips his shirt off the rest of the way and drops it onto the floor beside my dress and bra. His hair is sticking up and his lips are red from kissing me so roughly. My gaze moves from his face to the scars. Most of them are small, but some aren't. The largest one tracks up his chest and looks coarse.

"I fell on a rake when my father hit me," he explains in a solemn voice, like it means nothing. Like it's something that just happens and he's moved on and forgotten it.

I want to cry for him. I trace my finger up the scar, feel-ing the bumps and imagining how painful it must have been. "Kayden, I—"

He silences me with his lips as he falls down on me and lays us back onto the bed. After his tongue searches every inch of my mouth, he pulls away again. "I know you want me to talk about it with you—and I will—but right now this is what

I want." He sketches his finger down my cheekbone and my eyelids flutter shut. "You're all I want for a minute."

His touch is driving my body crazy in ways I didn't even know were possible. I nod my head, wanting him to have me for a minute. There's a faint smile at his lips as he kisses my cheek and then he lifts his hips off me. He slips his jeans off and then his boxers before sliding my panties down my legs and pulling them off too. He grabs a condom from his wallet before tossing his jeans aside, and then he stills over me with his arms resting at the side of my head as he looks me in the eyes.

"You know, if you ever need anything from me—whether it's to stop or slow down or simply talk, I'm here," he says, trying to calm my nerves, which are a mess, even though I've done this with him before.

"I know." I inhale and exhale and I almost tell him I love him right there and then, because holding it in is nearly excruciating.

I don't though and then he's kissing me and sliding inside me. It doesn't hurt as bad as the first time we had sex and my legs more willingly open up to him as he rocks inside me. I fasten my hands around his back and hold onto him as my body drifts to that place again, the one where I'm free, the one where he and I only belong together.

I begin to sweat and the muscles of his arms and chest flex as he speeds up his movements. All thoughts leave my head. I wish I could grasp onto this moment, hold it in my hand and keep it with me forever, because then my life would be complete, breathless, real.

It would be perfect.

# Kayden

I don't have control when it comes to her. I'm quickly learning this. Whenever she looks at me, I swear she steals another piece of my soul. Unlike most people, she doesn't care if it's damaged. And once we kiss, I'm gone. The broken, soulless, empty Kayden who's existed since the first time his father beat him no longer lives. She owns me and I want nothing more than to be with her.

I pick her up and carry her into the bedroom, because what I want to do to her can't be done on the beach without things getting messy. I kiss her for as long as I can, rubbing up against her and then watch in fascination as she breaks apart. I need more, so I stand up and bring her up with me, undressing her. Then she reaches to undress me and I can tell she's looking at the scars and thinking about what put them there. When I take my shirt off, her gaze goes to the largest one right up the center of my chest.

"I fell on a rake when my father hit me," I tell her and I don't even know why. I hate talking about it, but suddenly I want her to know because it'll make me feel better and the weight on my shoulders will be a little less heavy.

She looks like she's about to say something that might ruin the moment, so I crash my lips against hers and steal both our breaths and voices. I fall onto her, holding my weight, noting how small and helpless she is underneath me.

I finish taking off the rest of our clothes and then she's lying underneath me, looking about as terrified as I feel, her eyes massive and I sense a small tremble of her body every time she breathes.

"You know, if you ever need anything from me—whether it's to stop or slow down or simply talk, I'm here," I say, trying to calm her nerves. And it's true. I'd stop if she asked me to. I'd do anything for her.

She doesn't say anything and I slide inside her, feeling her warmth and wishing I could just stay there and just feel her. It's calming, terrifying, perfect—it's so many God damn things I don't let myself feel except when I'm with her, and when I'm with her, feeling things isn't as hard.

I rest my arms by the side of her head and rock inside her. Her legs fall open and her hands tighten around me as I press deeper into her, knowing that nothing else will ever compare to this. I thrust inside her, watching in awe as her eyes glaze over and her head tips back. Her body starts to arch against mine and we collide into each other as I drive her further. She bites down on her bottom lip and her neck bows forward as her fingernails pierce my skin. I hate how fucking much I like it, but I can't help it. Even with her beneath me, it's still there, hiding inside me, the desire for pain instead of feelings.

"Kayden," she moans and loses herself in my movements.

She holds onto me, our skin damp, our breathing fitful as

I still myself inside her. My head is tipped down and her breath is hitting my cheek as her fingers draw up and down my back. When I get control of myself again, I kiss her cheek and then start to pull back, but she tightens her legs around my waist and holds me in place, refusing to let me slip out of her.

I lean back and look her in the eyes, searching for what's wrong. "Are you okay?"

She nods, with a funny look on her face. "I'm just not ready to let you go yet."

A smile reveals at my lips. And it's genuine and not for show like most of my smiles are. I kiss her deeply with every ounce of passion I have in me. "Give me a few minutes," I say and turn my hips to the side. "And I'll be back in the game."

This time she releases me and I lie on my back, with my arm behind my head as I stare up at the ceiling. I'm very aware of my scars at the moment and how each one feels smaller somehow. I'm starting to realize something...something I'm not sure I want to realize. She makes me feel better and I wonder if that means I'm supposed to be with her. I don't want it to mean that, though. I want her to be unrestricted.

Pulling the sheet over her, she rotates onto her hip and brushes my hair out of my face. "What are you thinking about?" she asks, grazing a finger between my brows and erasing the worry line.

I tip my head to the side and meet her gaze. "You really want to know?"

She nods her head, lowering her hand to her hip, and my eyes trace her thin figure. "I always do."

I pivot to the side so we're lying face to face. "I'm thinking that you should leave me."

Her breathing becomes ragged. "You want me to go?"

I quickly place a hand on her hip. "Don't think for a second that I want you to go. I never want you to go. I want you here. With me...but I don't want *you* to be with *me*. I want you to be happy, if that makes any sense."

She considers what I said, biting on her bottom lip, and all I want to do is lean forward and bite it too, but it would defeat my whole purpose of trying to let her go. "I get what you're saying," she says. "But I don't agree with it. You're the only person..." Her bottom lip shakes as she takes a deep breath. "You're the only person who I can ever feel whole with."

"You don't know that." I keep trying to push her away. "There could easily be other people out there."

She shakes her head. "There's not...a-and I don't want there to be."

"Callie," I say softly and place my hand under her cheek, rubbing a finger across her birthmark on her temple. "I'm not good for you. You deserve better." It gashes deep inside my chest to say the truth aloud. But it needs to be said.

"There's nothing better," she utters quietly, staring at the foot of the bed, blinking back the tears. "You just need to realize that."

"I just want you to be free…from all my shit and my fucking complicated life."

"I don't want to be free. I just want to be here. With you. I-I don't care about your fucking complicated life or your problems. I just want *you*…and I want you to be happy. You deserve to be."

Fuck. No one's ever said that to me. I don't even know if I'm certain what happiness is. I can't control myself anymore. Each one of my scars is throbbing and I need her to silence them. I lean in and grab the back of her head, bringing her lips to mine, and kiss her with so much intensity it rips my scars in half. I flip us over, pressing her down on her back as I run my hand down to her breast. She trembles as she moves her legs up so I fall down between her. I kiss her fervently, nipping at her lip as I touch her everywhere. When I finally pull away, I can barely breathe as I trail kisses down her jawline, her neck, her collarbone. I graze my teeth along her neck and suck on her soft skin as her legs latch around my waist. My head journeys down farther and her hips writhe up as I trace a circle around her nipple before sucking it into my mouth. She lets out a sexy whimper as her fingers tangle through my hair. I suck hard, needing more of her, before I travel to her other breast. I caress my tongue along that one too, until I can't stand it anymore.

I push back and grab another condom. Seconds later, I'm back inside her, wishing things would stay this way forever. Just she and I without the sounds and heaviness of the world. Without the fucking complications of life.

# Chapter Fourteen

*#10 Face the truth and let it go*

## Callie

We make love countless times throughout the night and then finally I slip Kayden's shirt on and he puts his boxers back on. Then we lie down in the bed and rest. Somewhere well into the early hours of morning Luke and Seth stumble into the house, drunk off their asses and making a lot of noise. Seconds later, Seth starts jiggling the doorknob and shaking the door.

"Oh Callie Lawrence, let me in," he says, banging on the door.

Then I hear Luke say, "Not by the hair on my chinny chin chin."

This is followed by a lot of laughter and then the sound of a glass breaking.

I glance up at Kayden, who has his arm around me and is playing with my hair. He smiles down at me as I rest my face on his chest.

"They're wasted," he says. "And I'm guessing that Luke probably dropped a bottle on the floor in classic Luke style."

"Does he do that a lot?"

"In the past, yeah. It's like he forgets how to use his hands or something."

I laugh against his chest and he kisses the top of my head. "Should I let him in?" I ask.

"Nah," Kayden replies. "Let them stay out there and annoy the shit out of each other."

I laugh as Seth continues to bang on the door. He does it for quite a while before he gives up and the house gets quiet. Even though the last few hours have been amazing, I still have a ton of questions on the tip of my tongue, but I'm worried about the consequences if I ask them.

"Tell me what you're thinking about?" He repeats my early words as he twists a lock of my hair around his finger.

I peer up at him, noting the small scars on his face, and I can't believe how many people don't notice. "I'm thinking that you should tell someone about your father."

He freezes and the strand of my hair falls from his finger. "Callie, I can't do that. No one will believe me."

With my hands flat on his chest, I push up and swing my leg over him. "Yes, they will. We just have to find the right person."

He shakes his head as he swallows hard and stares at the moon through the window. "I can't."

I put my hands on his shoulders and pin him down. "Yes,

you can...and do you know why..." I trail off because what I'm about to say is probably the second hardest thing I'll ever have to say. The first being what *I* actually have to say to someone else. "Because I'm going to tell someone too."

His eyes snap to mine and he assesses my face with great concern. "You're going to tell someone about Caleb?"

My heart is trying to kill me from the inside as it slams against my chest. "I am, if you will."

It's that simple, at least the theory in my head is. I'll promise to tell my family as long as he tells someone about his father—someone who will do something about it. Although, when it actually comes down to spilling those words out to the world, it'll be complex, complicated, rough, hurtful, aching, painful, shameful...I could write a list down in my notebook of everything that it will be and there wouldn't be enough pages.

"Callie, I think that's good," he encourages. "You should tell your parents."

"But I'm only going to if you tell someone about your dad." I know it's blackmail, but it's all I've got at the moment. "And you need to tell—*we* need to tell."

His eyebrows knit together. "You'd really blackmail me into it?"

My shoulders slump inward as I slouch down, feeling like the world's most terrible person. "I'm only doing it because I lo—care for you." My eyes widen at the word that almost slipped out.

I know he notices, but he pretends he doesn't. He stays calm underneath me. "And what do you think will come from us telling someone?"

Tears are forming in my eyes and one rolls down my cheek, dripping off my jawline and falling on him. "Freedom." I try to force the rest of the tears back, but the wall around me is crumbling rapidly and soon I lose all control over my emotions. I start to sob, again. He's probably going to start thinking that's all I do.

He pulls me down against him and I bury my face in his chest with my hands on his shoulders. Tears veil my vision as I stare at the wall to the side of me.

"Fine, I'll do it...I'll tell someone...I guess," he says so quietly the sounds of my tears falling almost drown it out. "But only for you. I'm only doing it for you."

I'm not sure I like his answer. I don't want him to do it for me. I want him to do it for himself because I want him to know that he's that great of a person. One who gets the weirdo-Goth-Satan-worshipping girl who everyone was always afraid of. One who can break down indestructible walls. The kind of person who can piece a person back together again.

The person I'm falling in love with.


## Kayden

I can't believe what I'm hearing. She wants us to tell someone. Confess together. Tell our dark secrets to the world and let everyone do what they will with them. It throws me off more than anything I've ever heard until she almost says she loves me. She stops herself quickly, like she's afraid to say it, but it's enough that I can tell she means it. And it'll mean something to me. I know that. It's not like back when Daisy and I used to say it to each other. It was just a word between her and me that meant nothing other than it was part of the script. If Callie says it, then I know it means she loves me and I don't know how to handle that. *Love... Love... Love.* What the fuck does the word mean?

I don't have a God damn clue and I don't like how enthused my heart got when the words just about left her lips, like it'd been waiting around silently for that one word to fall from her lips and jumpstart it to life again. It doesn't matter how I feel, though. She's told me she'll tell if I tell and no matter how much I don't want to fucking tell, it's done once she says it. Because I'd put my pain and shame out there to take hers away. I'd stab myself in the heart if it meant her life would be easier.

We lay in bed for a while, listening to the ocean crash against the shore. There are birds cawing just outside the window and someone is snoring out in the living room. I hold onto her while she falls asleep, wishing this is how things would always be. That I could just lie here with her and be at peace with myself and life.

But every nerve in my body is disturbed and adrenaline is coursing through me more powerfully than the waves outside.

I'm itching for a razor or something sharp because I took the damn rubber bands off my wrists. I try to pinch myself a thousand times, and then I finally stab my fingernails into my skin. The pain and feelings that come with it keep building like the waves outside. I keep thinking about how I used Luke's razor to finally shave off my stubble and even though I wanted to, I resisted the urge to cut my skin because I couldn't stop thinking about kissing Callie in the alley.

This time though, I can't shut it off. It's consuming me, the need, the compulsion, the overtaking desire to get it all out of my head and body. Finally, I can't take it anymore. I peek down at Callie, making sure that she's still asleep, and then I vigilantly lift my arm off her and place it beneath her head. Inching my body to the side, I scoot out from underneath her and then gently lower her head onto the pillow.

She incoherently mutters something as she twists to her side and tucks her hands below her cheek. I stand there for a moment, making sure she'll fall back asleep and then I walk quietly across the room to the bathroom in the corner. I flip on the light and shut the door. Callie's bag is sitting on the counter, and although I hate the idea of digging through it, I need a razor. The only other alternative is to slam my fist into something and that will make noise and I might break something.

I rummage through her bag until I come across a small pouch at the bottom. I take it out and let out a sigh of relief as I spot a razor in the midst of her makeup and travel-size bags of shampoo. I take it out and run my finger along the top blade, testing the sharpness. It looks a lot like the first one I used: pink, with a strip of something at the top. But it's sharper, and knowing that calms me.

I decide where the best place to make the cut is, the place where she won't notice. Finally, I slide the bandage down and put the razor to my wrist, not by a vein but to the side where there are already a collection of scars. My head is tipped down and I'm about ready to make the first incision when I hear the door open.

I freeze. No one has ever walked in on me while I was doing it. And what's worse is that it's Callie. I don't even have to look up to know it's her. I can smell her shampoo and I can hear the sound of her uneven breathing.

"Kayden." Her voice is alarmingly calm, not at all what I expected.

*Fuck. Shit. Fuck.* I don't want to look up because then it's real and she'll be able to see how weak I really am. Plus, she'll make me stop. And I've never had to stop when I'm almost there. I don't know how my body or mind's going to react.

Her feet shuffle across the floor as she inches toward me. I still have my head tipped down, my teeth biting hard on my tongue. Her bare feet appear in my line of vision and her legs are naked three-quarters of the way up and then my shirt covers her small-framed body.

"Kayden," she repeats, sounding so fucking calm it's unsettling.

I still have the edge of the razor aligned with my skin and

every muscle and vein below the skin has warped and convoluted into knots. "Callie, just walk out and shut the door. I'll be out in a minute."

There's a long pause and I think that maybe she's actually considering it.

"No," she says firmly. "I won't."

My hand trembles and my heart thuds brutally inside my chest. I don't want to snap at her, but I'm panicking and my feelings are controlling me. "Callie, I swear to God if you care about me at all, you'll turn around and walk back out into the room."

She takes another small step, reducing the already limited space between us. "I do care about you and that's why I'm not going to leave."

My head snaps up and rage bursts inside me, flames ripping through my body. I'm about to ruin everything but I can't stop it. "Just get the hell out!"

"No." Determination burns in her eyes. She doesn't even look like the Callie I know. She looks strong and confident. "I won't let you do it."

I lean in toward her with the razor still pressed against my skin and I notice her gaze flick to it. "If you know what's good for you, you'll leave. You don't get this...I don't need you. Now leave."

Her hand snaps out and she grabs ahold of my wrist, her tiny fingers encircling it firmly. "I do get it. You want to stop whatever the hell it is you're feeling and this is the only way you know how. And because I get that, I'm not going to leave. If you walked in on me when I was…when I was trying to…when I was trying to make myself throw up, I'd want you to stop me even though I know I'd try and argue and justify it with you." Her fingers pry into mine as she tries to steal the razor from my hand. "I get you!"

For a brief second her words stop the uncontrollable urge to stab the razor deep into my skin, but then I panic again. I jerk my arm back from her grip, ready to scream at her and probably say words that will scar her for life. But as I move my arm, she winces and she hastily withdraws her hand back to her. Her finger skimmed the razor and her blood is dripping onto the floor by her feet.

I no longer give a shit about the razor or getting rid of my emotions. I chuck the blade into the sink. "Callie, I'm so fucking sorry. I didn't mean to do that." I've fucked things up again.

She's clutching onto her finger and blood is spilling out and her face is contorted in pain. She looks at me through her bangs and I prepare myself for whatever she's going to say: rejection, hatred, anger. But then she doesn't say anything. Instead, she moves toward me and the next thing I know, she climbs onto me, hitching her legs around my waist and fastening herself to me. Then she wraps her arms around the back of my neck and presses her forehead to the side of my neck, right where my pulse is throbbing. I tense, but then a tranquil feeling rushes through my body. My heart starts to still as she hugs me resolutely, trusting me wholly. I've never experienced anything like it, especially in the middle of one of my meltdowns and I don't know what to do with myself except stand there with my hands lifelessly at my sides.

"Callie," I say, but she steals my voice as she clutches onto me and places kisses on my neck.

"It'll be okay," she whispers between each touch of her lips. "I promise."

I don't fully understand what it is she's promising, or maybe I do and I'm just not ready to admit it yet. Either way, I find that I'm calm enough to leave the bathroom. I walk back to the bed and lie us down. She refuses to let go of me even when I get us onto the mattress. She crosses her ankles behind my waist, latching onto me and making it impossible for me to escape.

But that's okay. For the first time in my life I'm content enough that I don't want to.

## Callie

I had one of those moments where I knew that every single thing I did mattered, from the way that I breathed, to the tone of my voice. Honestly, I am terrified out of my mind. I'd felt him wake up, but I didn't think too much of it, until suddenly I did. It snapped me out of my sleep and I went in there, knowing I was about to walk in on something that could potentially break me, just like I did when I was twelve. This time things would end differently though because I'd be strong and I'd save him, just like he's saved me.

He's pissed about it, which is understandable, but it doesn't mean I give up and eventually it ends okay. Well, other than the fact that I cut my finger open, something I'm painfully reminded of when I open my eyes.

The sun is sparkling through the window and paints the sky in contrasting shades of pink and orange. My finger is throbbing and I realize I never cleaned it up. There's blood on my hand, on my arm, on the bed, and on Kayden's chest where I am resting my hand.

I sit up, cradling it in my other hand, and blink my eyes until the room comes into focus. I'm still wearing Kayden's shirt and it smells like his cologne. Swinging my feet off the bed, I leave him to sleep as I head into the bathroom.

My hair is a tangled mess and there are dark circles under my eyes. I feel exhausted as I turn the faucet on and wince when the warm water runs over the wound, washing away the blood and part of last night. I rest my elbows on the counter-top and let my head fall forward as I keep my hand beneath the water.

"Are you okay?" Kayden asks and I whip my head up, startled.

He's standing in the doorway, with his boxers on, and in the bright morning light all of his scars are very distinctive against the outlines of his chest and ab muscles.

"I'm fine." I shut off the water and reach for a towel, then press my finger into it. "I just forgot to wash it off last night. That's all."

He steps into the bathroom and I tense as he extends his hand for the towel. He lifts it off and brings my finger closer to his face, examining it. "I'm sorry I hurt you," he says.

I shake my head. "You didn't hurt me. It was my own fault... and it was worth it."

When he glances up at me, he looks horrified, but then the look disappears and he lifts my hand to his lips. He places a tender kiss on my finger and then moves his mouth downward to kiss my hand. He continues to make a path of kisses across my forearm and all the way to the crook of my arm, and then turns upward, showering my skin in succulent kisses until he reaches the top of my shoulder. He gives it an affectionate suck and his tongue rolls out along my skin. The sensation of his zealous breath drives a shiver through my body and I place a hand on his shoulder to keep from falling down.

"You are the most amazing person," he whispers against my neck. "You really are."

I almost start to cry. "So are you."

His lips part again and he sucks on my neck, his tongue savoring the taste of skin and the edge of his teeth gently grazing it. My head distractedly falls to the side because it feels so good and my fingers dip downward, gripping onto him and trying to keep my legs from giving out. His mouth starts to progress upward to the arch of my neck, to the spot where my pulse throbs, then to the line of my jaw, the corner of my mouth. His moist lips dampen my skin and knock the breath out of my chest in ravenous gasps of air.

It's like we're locked in a box, protected from the world and our fears. We can keep our hands off each other. There are so many problems around us but all I can think about is him. When our lips join, he turns us to the side and backs us toward the bed. Maybe it's crazy, with everything going on, to be so absorbed in each other, instead of working on our problems. Maybe one day we'll look back and wonder what we were thinking. Or maybe we'll just remember the day we decided to escape the pain in the arms of each other.

We collapse onto the bed, our legs twined together like a snug vine. He's on top of me, his shirt is still off, and I trace my fingers along his firm chest, feeling the warmth of his skin and the dance of his heart beneath his chest. He scoots between my legs and the shirt I'm wearing rides up over my stomach. His fingers caress my skin right below my belly button and it tickles but it feels so overwhelmingly good at the same time. My knees lift upward as heat spirals downward between my thighs and I contemplate how far I've come in just a short while and how much I'm enjoying him touching me.

His fingers hook the top of my panties, and he starts to guide them down my knees. I'm still sore from the other times we've had sex in the last twenty-four hours, but there's no way I'm going to stop him. It's completely worth the pain. When my panties reach my feet, I kick them off and then his hands glide down my arms and he pulls me so I'm sitting up. With one rapid tug, he jerks the shirt over my head and throws it on the floor.

My lungs heave wildly as I take the moment in. I'm naked in front of him. Again. Me. Callie Lawrence. Every time I think about it, it gets to me. I start to lie back down while he takes his boxers off, but he quickly grabs my wrists and pulls me toward him. Then he sits down and picks me up by the waist. I gasp as he lies down and sets me on top of him, so one of my legs is on each side of his hips. Before I can respond to the abruptness, his fingers spread around to my back and he's drawing my breast to his mouth. He sucks on it repeatedly until I cry out and my legs press against him, and then his mouth leaves my breast and he lowers himself back onto the bed with this content, hungry look in his eyes that makes my skin swelter. He thrusts his hips upward and he enters me. I cry out again, biting my lip as my hands search for something to grab onto. Like he reads my mind, he takes hold of my hand and steers it to his shoulder where I grip forcefully and hold onto him as he rocks inside me again and again until I think I'm going to explode. Then he presses the palm of his hand to my back and pulls me down to his lips. With one last thrust, he slips his tongue inside my mouth and kisses me passionately as every thought in my head leaves me and my body spins out of control, soaring away before returning again.

When I come back down from the high, panting and sweaty, I think about how good it feels. And not just the sex. The connection. The contact. The fact that I'm here. With him. And I'm fine. More than fine. I think it might be time to tell. To get my freedom back. Because I deserve to have it. I deserve to be here in this moment.

## Kayden

"If you could have one wish, what would it be?" Callie asks, tracing a finger in circular motions along the palm of my hand.

It's late and the sun is up and beaming into the room. Seth and Luke haven't woken up yet; at least that's what I've determined by the silence in the house. Her head is relaxed on my arm, her leg is hitched over my stomach, and her hand is resting over my heart.

"That we could stay just like this forever," I answer truthfully.

Her head tips up and she meets my eyes. "That's really what you'd wish for?"

I nod, running my fingers through her soft hair that smells like strawberries. "Absolutely. It's peaceful."

Her cheeks start to flush and I wonder what she's thinking. "What would we do if we stayed here forever?"

It's fucking cute as hell that her dirty thoughts are making her blush. "Whatever you want," I say with a hint of laughter in my voice.

She angles her face down against my chest and gives my skin a kiss, sliding her tongue out. "I'd want to stay just like this."

261

I chuckle underneath my breath and it hurts my lungs because my muscles have been immovable for the past month. "Is that all you'd want to do? Because your pink cheeks are suggesting otherwise." I trail my finger across her cheek and she shudders. I love that she does, and yet I hate it at the same time because it shows how much I affect her. "Or did you have something else in mind?"

She's quiet for a while and then she finally looks up at me, her blue eyes large. Her cheeks are still pink and her hair frames her face and her shoulders. "I didn't have anything else in mind," she says. "I was just wondering."

She's lying, but I let her off the hook. Gathering some of her hair out of her face, I move it behind her ear. I'm about to tell her we should probably get up when there's a knock on the door.

"Um...I've been waiting as long as I can," Seth says through the door. "But at some point I have to come in there and get my stuff."

Callie pushes up from me and starts to kneel, with the sheet pressed against her chest. I grab ahold of the edge of the sheet and tug it down, then brush my finger over her nipple. She shivers and I feel gratified as she gives a shy smile, backing off the bed, naked.

She searches for her clothes, trying to cover her body with her hands. She is so small, thin, fragile. I can't help but think about how she said she made herself throw up and how I think maybe we need to talk about it, since we've been talking about my problems so much.

"Callie, please," Seth begs, sounding hoarse and hung over. "I really need to get my stuff."

"Just a second." Callie grabs a pair of shorts and a T-shirt from one of the bags Seth was carrying yesterday. She gives me another reserved smile before retreating toward the bathroom. "Will you let him in when you're dressed?" she asks, as I slip my boxers back on.

I eye her over. "What are you doing?"

She combs her fingers through her hair. "I'm going to take a shower. I have sand in my hair from last night."

A slow smile spreads across my lips. I know I've been kind of intense with her and she's probably sore as hell, but I can't help it. As images of her in the shower, the hot water dripping down her body, hair, nipples, appear in my head, I decide I need to take a shower with her. Besides, everything is perfect right now and I want to drag it along for as long as I can before we have to return to real life and our problems. "Yeah, me too." I stand up from the bed and she pulls a perplexed look from the doorway of the bathroom. She doesn't get what I'm saying and I don't expect her to. She's innocent and sweet and her mind doesn't instantly wander to the gutter like Daisy's would.

I walk toward her, loving that she's biting her lip. "You look lost," I say as I reach for her arm.

Her gaze skims to my chest and for a second I feel

263

self-conscious. "That's because I am. Do you want to take a shower first? I can wait if you need to?"

I smile and it's real, not plastered on. Touching my fingertip to her bottom lip, I bring my other hand up to her bare hip. "I'm saying I'll take a shower with you."

She lets out a startled gasp and I'm worried I've pushed her a little too far. Then her cheeks turn pink as her eyes quickly roam over my body and she chews on her bottom lip. She doesn't say anything when she meets my eyes and I can tell she's curious.

"Don't worry." I lower my finger from her lip. "It'll be fun. All soapy and wet and slippery." Her eyes enlarge as my fingers envelop around her hips and I scoop her up. She lets out a giggle and I smile as I back us into the bathroom.

"Wait a minute," she says right as I'm about to kiss her. "We need to let Seth in. He's going to get upset."

Begrudgingly, I walk back to the bedroom door and unlatch the lock. Then I hurry back to the bathroom, still carrying Callie, who keeps giggling every time my fingers touch her stomach. As I'm kicking the bathroom door closed, I call out, "Seth, you can come in." Then I seal my lips to hers and kiss her until we run out of air. Then we part, breathing ragged, and her fingers are brushing the nape of my neck.

I glance around, ready to turn the shower on. "Wait, where's the shower?"

She points over her shoulder at the corner of the wall that's framed with a narrow doorway. "I think it's back there."

"That's not a closet?"

She shrugs. "I don't think so. If it is…" Her eyes wander around to the sink, the toilet, and the towel rack. "Then I'm thinking there's not one."

Cupping her ass to hold her weight, I walk around to the doorway and round the corner. There's a small section that dips back with empty rods and shelves. I veer to the left because it's the only place to go and the room opens up. There are frosted glass windows on the wall and the ocean is right outside. There's also a massive oval tub in the corner that is raised up on a rectangular podium that is framed by tile steps.

Callie frowns. "There's no shower?" She tries not to smile. "That sucks. I was seriously warming up to the idea of it."

I give her a gentle pinch on the back of her leg and she squeals and clutches onto me. I make my way back to the tub without setting her down and turn the faucet on.

"What are you doing?" she asks, watching the water stream out as I stick my hand in and check the temperature.

"Taking a bath." I secretly love the fact that there's only a tub and no shower. The possibilities of what we could do in this big bathtub are endless.

She fidgets nervously, her body stiffening as she warily eyes the water filling up the tub. "We're going to take a bath *together*?" Her nose scrunches up and I'm about to tell her that we don't have to if she doesn't want to when she says, "Then we'd be, like, sitting in each other's filth."

I sputter a laugh and then step up onto the stair. "How dirty do you think I am?"

Every once in a while she'll get this conniving look in her eyes and it's appearing in full form. "I don't know." She scales up my body. "Guys are known for their filthiness, aren't they?"

I pinch the back of her leg again and she jumps, letting out a squealing laugh. The movement sends me forward and I stumble into the bathtub, slipping on the bottom. I try to land as gently as I can so she won't get hurt and I end up slamming my elbow into the corner of the tub and water splashes everywhere. She's laughing as I struggle to sit up in the water, with her straddling me.

"Oh, you think that's funny?" I sit up, still holding onto her waist, my fingertips delving into her wet skin. Beads of water are streaming down her body, her hair, her soft skin and it's even better than I ever could have imagined. We sit there for a while, listening to the water fill up the tub, looking at each other, waiting for the other one to speak.

"Callie, I have to ask..." I massage her hip bones with my thumbs. "About the throwing-up thing."

She stops breathing, but doesn't move away. "I'm working on it."

I let out a deep exhale through my nose. "You're too skinny...to be doing that."

"I told you it's not about that."

"I know it's not about that, but regardless, it's making you too skinny and I hate the fucking idea that you're hurting yourself." I'm being a hypocrite, but it's important that she knows how I feel because she always tells me how she feels.

"Maybe I should talk to someone," she says, conflicted. "Although I've been doing better."

"Talking to someone would be good." I shut my eyes and summon up some courage. "I've been...I've been talking to this therapist at the clinic. As much as I hate the fucking clinic and the reason why I was there, he seems like an okay guy." I shift my weight as the water gets higher. "I'm supposed to keep seeing him."

"That's good," she says, searching my eyes for something. "Maybe you should tell him about what your dad did."

My fingers pierce deeper into her skin. "I'm not sure if he's the right person."

"Then who is?"

She has a point. Who would I tell? My mom? My brother? After that, the only people I know wouldn't know what the fuck to do with the info. "Maybe I could."

"You're going to," she insists and runs her hand through my wet hair, smoothing it out of my face. "And I'll come with you."

I'm wary and hesitant, and honestly, as much as I care about her, I really don't want her there, listening to all the fucked-up things I've done. "Callie...I don't think that's such a good idea. I don't want you hearing the gory details."

"I saw the gory details," she says and tears form in the corners of her eyes. "I can handle hearing them...unless you don't want me to be there." Determination burns in her eyes.

"Callie, I really don't think you should be there," I protest, my insides clenching as I think about her hearing the inner workings of my screwed-up head.

She shakes her head and takes my hand. "Kayden, I can help you if you'll just let me... Please just let me help you."

It's hard to say no when she's looking at me this way, so even though I want to go alone, I hear myself saying, "Okay, you can come with me... but only if you promise me one thing."

She nods enthusiastically. "Anything."

"That I can be there to help you when you tell your family about Caleb."

She considers this, looking conflicted, but then she slowly leans in and lightly places her lips against mine. "Okay," she whispers against my mouth. "We can do this," she mutters and I'm not sure if she's talking to me or herself. "Because I think we're stronger when we're together."

I think about last night and how she managed to calm me down and stop me from cutting. She might be right. On so many levels. "I think we should head back today... I don't think I should have probably left in the first place... I kind of feel like I'm running away from everything."

She nods in agreement. "It might have been a bad idea."

"Not bad." I inch my fingers between her legs, causing her breath to falter. "What happened last night..." I lower my voice as I dip my lips toward her ear and run my fingers across the back of her hand. I want to get as much Callie-time as possible, just in case this doesn't end well, because in my world things generally don't. It's painful to think about, but realistic, and it could end up being reckless and damaging if I didn't see this way. "What happened over and over again..." I slip my finger inside her and her body curves into mine. "...was in no way bad at all." I kiss her cheek as her eyes gaze off. "It was amazing."

I start moving my finger until I drive her to the edge and she cries out my name. Then I slip my soaked boxers off and slide inside her, wanting every part of her, knowing that at any moment things can go wrong. But for once in my life, I hope they don't. I hope everything goes okay. What that means, I'm not sure, but I want to find out.

# Chapter Fifteen

*#26 Face the inevitable, whatever the hell it is*

## Callie

Bathtubs aren't as gross as I thought. I've never been much of a bather. The idea of sitting in water and soaking in your own filth grosses me out. But after the bath with Kayden, I think I've had a change of heart. After we get out, we get dressed and then prepare ourselves to head out into the kitchen. It's kind of scary, leaving the room. We've lived in this magical, safe bubble for the last fifteen hours and as soon as we step over the threshold it's going to pop, especially when we tell Seth and Luke we have to go home early.

I put on a pair of jeans and a T-shirt, pull my hair into a ponytail, and slip my shoes on. Kayden has on a plaid shirt, jeans, and boots. His hair's a little damp and he had to take the bandage off because it got wet in the bathtub. The wounds beneath it aren't healing and one of them looks fresh. He notices me staring at them as he rolls his sleeve down to cover them up.

"I'm going to work on it," he says with his head down as he buttons his sleeve. Pieces of his hair hang in his eyes and, unable to stop myself, I brush them away.

"I can't lose you." I'm not one hundred percent sure why I say it other than I can't stop thinking about him lying on the floor and how I felt when I thought he wasn't going to make it. "I need you."

He seems to grow uncomfortable with my declaration, fidgeting with the bottom button on his shirt. It doesn't matter, though. He needs to know. In fact, I think I'm going to tell him a lot just how much I need him and how great a person he is, because I don't think he's heard it that much.

"You ready?" he asks, finally looking up from his shirt. He reaches for a rubber band on top of the dresser and slips it onto his wrist.

I nod and open the door. "Seth's not going to be happy we're leaving."

"Yeah, Luke isn't going to be either." He winds around me. "But oh well."

I follow him out the door and down the hall into the kitchen. Seth and Luke are sitting at the table, looking exhausted: bags under their eyes, which are bloodshot, pale skin, and they look nauseous. Seth is dressed in cargo shorts and a gray polo, and his hair is stylishly tousled. Luke's got a pair of striped pajama bottoms on and no shirt. I immediately feel uncomfortable at the sight of his bare chest with tattoos all over it. Some of my old feelings of shame and guilt begin to surface, so I hitch my finger through one of Kayden's belt loops on the back of his jeans. I don't know why I do it, other than holding onto him seems to have a serene effect on me.

He glances over his shoulder at me, his emerald eyes glistening as he looks at me with concern. "Are you okay?"

I nod, avoiding looking in Luke's direction, biting at my nails. "Yeah, I'm fine."

He looks down at my finger in his belt loop, and then shrugs it off. I love him even more at that moment, especially when he swings his arm around my shoulder and pulls me up next to him as we stop near the counter, which is littered with beer bottles, ashes, and cigarette butts.

He slants in and brushes his lips across my forehead, before he announces, "So, we have to head back today."

Luke starts digging around in the fridge and then he moves back with a gallon of milk in his hand, kicking the door shut with his bare foot. "Are you fucking kidding me? We just got here yesterday morning."

"I know," Kayden says, glancing at me with a hint of fear in his eyes. "But... but there are a few things that Callie and I have to take care of back at home."

Seth puts a cigarette in his mouth, cups his hand around the end, and flicks the lighter. "Like what?" He drops the lighter onto the table and leans back, taking a long drag and then letting a thin trail of smoke escape his mouth.

"Like *really* important stuff," I say with pressing eyes, hoping he'll catch on.

And just like the good friend that he is, he catches on. "*Oh*, okay."

Luke shoots him a harsh look as he twists off the lid on the milk. "No way. I'm driver. Therefore I get final say."

Kayden exhales loudly and then moves his arm away from my shoulder. He walks up to Luke and places his hand on the counter, standing right in front of Luke. "Look, I know why you don't want to go back—and I really don't want to make you—but there's something I've been running away from that I need to return to."

I don't know if Luke understands Kayden's full meaning, but I think he might. He nods his head with a grunt, even though he looks annoyed. "Alright, if it's important, then it's important."

"Thanks." Kayden returns to my side. "You want to go pack your stuff?"

I nod and then motion at Seth to come with me. He puts his cigarette out in a leaf-shaped ashtray that's in the center of the table and then pushes the chair back. He gets to his feet, glancing at Kayden as he walks by, and then he links arms with me. We walk side by side back to the room. As soon as the door shuts, he turns around and puts his hands on his hips.

"All right, let's have it," he demands. "What's going on?"

I shake my head and bend down to pick up a pair of shorts and one of my shirts off the floor. "I can't tell you."

He gapes at me with his hands out to the side. "Why?"

"Because I can't yet." I ball up the clothes and stuff them into my bag, which is near the foot of the bed on the floor. "Part of it's that I'm not ready to and part of it's because it's not my thing to tell—it's Kayden's."

He doesn't press anymore. He starts packing his stuff as I gather up my clothes. I clean up a little, stalling, knowing that as soon as we walk out of the house, Kayden and I'll be stepping back into reality and all I can hope is that it'll be nice to us.

# Chapter Sixteen

*#15 Stop torturing yourself*

## Callie

I'm afraid to go home and face my mother, even with Kayden at my side. Halfway there I turn on my phone to find that I have thirty-seven new voicemails and fifty-eight text messages. All are from her and it's unbelievable and yet believable at the same time. She's never been good at handling things that don't fit into her world. And rebel-runaway Callie fits about as well as lone-Goth Callie did.

"We could get a hotel room," Seth suggests as we pull into town. "And keep the vacation going."

"Or at least avoid going home," Luke mutters, grumpily.

It's late, the trees in the park are flashing with lively red twinkly lights, and there's a huge inflatable Santa at the entrance welcoming us to town. Kayden has been really quiet the entire drive, staring out the window, lost in his thoughts and it makes me sad. Luke has been silent too, chain smoking the entire drive and Seth has been equally as bad.

I glance at Kayden, wondering what he thinks of the hotel idea, but all he does is stare out the window. "I feel like if I go to a hotel then I'm running away from my problems," I say. "I should probably go home and face the wrath of my mom."

"Why?" Seth asks, surprising me. I gape at him as smoke snakes from his lips and he takes out the cigarette and sticks his hand out the window, scattering ash into the street as he grazes his thumb across the end. "Callie, I hate to say this"— his brown eyes flick to Luke, then to Kayden, before he leans in and whispers—"but until you can tell your mom, and you-know-who will officially no longer be showing up at your house, it might be good for you to stay away from there. Stop torturing yourself."

I press my lips together as he leans back. "I don't torture myself," I mumble.

"You don't?" Seth flicks his cigarette out the window and then rolls it up. Luke's truck is really old and doesn't have automatic windows so Seth's arm fights against the tension in the handle.

Kayden glances at me with a frown on his face. "Seth's right," he agrees quietly.

I think about all the times I spent wishing I could just shrink into a ball, maybe become invisible, maybe disappear altogether. But if I could have just broken Caleb's hold over me, maybe I would have escaped from the tortuous years I spent locked away, living inside myself. Could I do it? Just free myself? Do I have that kind of power? I really don't have to go back unless I want to. I can go back when I'm ready to confess. "All right, let's get a hotel room." It's such a simple conclusion, yet it took me forever to get to it.

I don't have to go back home until I'm ready. I have choices, power, freedom. I can sever the ties with the things that hurt me. *You can do this.* I can do anything if I want to. I just have to *choose* to do it. Suddenly, I can breathe freely again. I'm smiling and Seth and Luke are looking at me like I've lost my mind.

Kayden glances at me, a forced grin at his lips. "Sounds good."

I offer him a smile, wondering why he's acting so upset. Everything had been okay when we left the beach house, at least I thought so. I lean into him and whisper, "Are you okay?"

He nods, giving me a puzzled look. "Yeah, why wouldn't I be?"

"I don't know," I say, eyeing the sadness in his eyes. "You look sad."

"Well, I'm not. I promise." He returns his attention to the window and my heart sinks in my chest, knowing there's something he's not telling me. But I don't want to press him in front of Luke and Seth, so I keep quiet.

Ten minutes later we're checked into a motel room with two queen-size beds, a retro décor, and air smelling of mildew. Seth and Luke start arguing about the sleeping arrangement and I take the opportunity to talk to Kayden about what's bothering him.

"Are you sure you're okay?" I ask, sinking down on the bed beside him.

He nods, fiddling with the remote, even though the television isn't on. "Yeah, I'm fine. I already told you that."

"But you've been so quiet," I say. "You've barely said a word since we left California."

"I'm just tired." He drops the remote down on the nightstand and stares out the window. He does look really exhausted, but I don't think that's the real reason. Like he senses my doubts, he places his hand on my knee and gives it a gentle squeeze. "Callie, stop worrying. I'm okay."

"Okay," I say quietly and then get up from the bed to use the restroom. I lock the door and sit down on the edge of the bathtub. I don't really have to use the bathroom; I just needed to gather myself. The urge to make myself throw up is rising inside me and I really want to give into it, because it's been a while and I'm really stressed out about Kayden and about telling my mom. I start bouncing my knees as I breathe through my nose and count to ten, reminding myself that I'm strong. That I can live life without making myself purge.

It takes me a while, but about ten minutes later, I calm down and walk out of the bathroom, surprised to find Luke on one bed and Seth on the other watching television and Kayden is nowhere to be seen.

"Where'd Kayden go?" I ask, walking between the two beds.

They both look up at me, blinking their eyes, and then they gaze around the room. Seth sits up with his brows furrowed. "Huh? I didn't hear him leave."

Luke yawns. "He went to get his bag out of the back of the truck," he tells me. "But he's been out there for a few minutes."

Panic surges through me as I round the foot of the bed and draw back the curtain. The neon VACANT sign lights up the parking lot where the truck is parked down below, snow falling on the hood and roof. I can't see Kayden anywhere, but I tell myself he has to be coming up the stairs, which are out of my view. Slipping on my shoes, I run out the door.

"Callie, what the hell?" I hear Seth call out as I leave the door wide open. I don't turn back, racing to the bottom of the stairway and out into the parking lot. When I reach Luke's truck, Kayden isn't there. I search the parking lot and even walk over to the lobby, wondering if maybe he went to raid the vending machines, but I can't find him anywhere. My mind is racing with a thousand thoughts of what's going on. Where would he go? Why would he leave? Why did he look so sad?

By the time I'm headed back to the stairway, Seth and Luke are walking down it. I'm about in tears, frozen without a jacket on. "He's gone," I sputter.

They meet me at the bottom of the steps and Luke's forehead creases as he stares at his truck. "What do you mean he's gone?"

"I searched everywhere." I wrap my arms around myself, shivering from the cold and my nerves. "I can't find him."

Seth's arms encircle me. "I'm sure he's fine. Maybe he just went for a walk."

"It's almost ten thirty at night and freezing," I say. "There's nowhere to walk to."

"Maybe he walked to a gas station to get something to eat." Even he sounds like he doesn't believe it. "I thought I saw one a few roads up."

"Hang on a second," Luke says as he removes his phone from his back pocket. "I'll call him and see if I can get him to answer and see what's up." He dials the number, puts the phone up to his ear, and wanders away toward his truck, leaving footprints in the snow.

Seth hugs me as I watch Luke kick at the snow with one arm resting across his stomach. He keeps walking and walking farther away from the motel. My legs grow weak and finally I have to sit down on the stairs.

Seth sits with me. "I'm sure everything's okay."

I shake my head. "He seemed so upset the whole drive. I think something was really bothering him." I pull my knees to my chest and rest my chin on top of them. What if he's going to do something...something hurtful to himself?

I slide my phone out of my pocket and try to call him myself. The phone rings four times and then goes to his voice-mail. I hang up and send him a text.

**Me:** Hey, where r u... I'm worried. You just took off.

I wait, but there's no response. I suck back the tears franti-cally wanting to escape, wishing I could curl into a ball and cry myself to sleep. I hurt everywhere. And I'm afraid. Not for myself but for Kayden and what he's doing. I can't get the picture of him trying to cut himself out of my head. What if he ends up hurting himself really badly?

Finally, Luke heads back toward us with a puzzled look on his face. Right before he reaches us, my phone beeps.

**Kayden:** I'm ok.

*He's okay?*

**Me:** Where R U?

"I got ahold of him," Luke says as my phone beeps again. "He said to tell you that he's okay, but that there's something he needs to take care of."

I glance down at the screen, trying to hold the phone steady in my shaking hand.

**Kayden:** There's someone I need to talk to and it can't wait...with my therapist...Look, I'll explain everything later. I'll come back and then we'll talk. And Callie, I promise I'm OK.

I don't understand. My hands tremble as I type.

**Callie:** I thought I was going to go with you...and it's late. The office isn't even open.

When he doesn't respond, I don't know what to think. Is he really seeing him? Or is he lying?

I stand up, brushing the snow off the back of my jeans. "We should go look for him."

Luke shakes his head, squeezing by us and heading up the stairs. "Callie, I'm sure he's okay...and he said he'll be back soon so I think we should just wait here for him."

I glance at Seth, wondering what I should do. Sighing, he swings his arm around me and leads me up the stairs. "I'm sure he's fine," he says quietly.

I clutch onto him, hoping with everything I have that he's right.

## Kayden

I am obsessed about telling the truth and finally having my secrets out in the open the entire drive home. The longer I thought about it, the more anxious I got until I felt like I was going to burst. I'd spent my whole life holding my emotions and secrets in and suddenly I needed to get them all out. Now.

Even though it was late, I knew if I lay down on that bed, closed my eyes, and went to sleep, my mind would probably change by morning. It was just one of those things where if I'd sat on it, I'd talk myself out of it. So as soon as Callie went into the bathroom, I slipped out of the room, muttering something about getting my suitcase out of the back of the truck.

I knew she'd be upset that I took off without saying anything, but I had to do it; otherwise she'd look at me with those sad puppy eyes, wanting to go with me, like we talked about, and I'd have a hard time saying no. Despite the fact that I told her we'd do this together, I realized on the way home that it's something I need to do on my own. Otherwise I'd hold back, and I want—no *need* to let it out. All of it.

I walk out of the room and run over to the park just a few blocks down, and then I stop and take out my phone and the card Doug gave me. When he gave me the card he said I could call him anytime and I hope he meant it.

It's late and colder than hell, the air stinging at my skin like needles. I let the phone ring, walking back and forth across the sidewalk, thinking about what this means. For as long as I can remember, it's always been about doing what my father wanted, with sports, with rules, with life. I'd always felt this obligation to go back to that house, no matter what. I don't know why and maybe I never will. But I'm hoping this is the first step to cutting the ties with that God damn house that's haunted by nothing but terrible memories and the soulless monster who put them there.

It's gratifying to think about.

I'm about to hang up after the phone rings for the fifth time, but then someone says, "Hello."

"Umm..." I can't tell if it's him or not. "This is Kayden... Is this Doug?"

"Oh, yes, Kayden." There's some ruffling in the background followed by some voices. Then it goes quiet. "Are you okay?"

"Yeah, well...no." I'm struggling and it feels like someone has their hands around my neck. But I mentally pry them off, shutting my eyes and picturing Callie. "I know it's late, but I need to talk about what happened that night."

There's a pause. "The office is closed but I can meet you at Larry's twenty-four-hour diner in about half an hour."

I take a deep breath and the cold air sends relief to my lungs. "All right."

We hang up and just like that I'm heading toward the starting line of my recovery.

The diner is not too far away and I choose to walk there even though I'm frozen and my fingers are turning blue. I get there earlier than Doug and order a cup of coffee. It's late enough that no one's there except a few guys with trucker hats and grease on their jeans and the cook and waitress. I select a corner booth away from them, the counter, the kitchen. I don't want anyone else hearing what I'm going to say—it'll be hard enough getting the words out of my mouth.

I start flicking the rubber band, wishing Callie were here holding my hand, just like we'd planned, but I know it's better being solo and leaving her out of this mess. The waitress is bringing me coffee when the bell on the front door rings. An icy breeze sweeps through as Doug walks inside, but it's okay. It kind of makes it all real and forces me to feel everything.

I rest my arms on the table as he heads over and I stab my fingernails into the tops of my forearms. He has on a jacket and a pair of jeans, along with a beanie. It's a little out of character for him, since I'm used to seeing him in suits, but then again it's eleven o'clock at night.

"Hello, Kayden," he says in an exhausted voice as he lowers himself into the booth across from me, taking his beanie off. His thinning hair stands up in every direction.

"I'm sorry for waking you up," I tell him and take a sip of coffee, feeling the burn all the way down to my stomach. "I was just worried that if I didn't call…that I'd back out or something."

"I'm glad you woke me up," he replies and slips his arms out of his jacket. "It's better not to wait on these things."

I wonder what he'll say when I tell him everything. I set the cup down and fold my arms on top of the table, returning my fingernails to my skin. "You were right," I hurry and say before I pussy out. My fingernails burrow farther into my skin and split sections open. Blood trickles out.

"About what?" he asks, but I think he really knows. He eyes the blood on my arm but doesn't say a word about it.

I flex my fingers and take in the bloody, crescent-shaped marks on my arms. "About what happened that night."

He crosses his arms on top of the table. "I don't recall ever saying what happened that night."

"Yeah, but you...you thought that my father..." God, this is so fucking hard. Why is it so hard? My dad's a fucking dick. He beat me all those years. *Just say it.* "He's the one who hurt me that night. Well, I mean I did stuff to myself too, but he..." I sound like a fucking kid. I tuck my fingernails into my palms, stabbing them into my skin. Every part of my body wants to escape, be alone, find something sharp and bleed the pain out of me. But I keep reminding myself *Callie, Callie, Callie.* "He stabbed me. That's where the cut on my side came from. He was pissed off because I'd got in a fight with Caleb and he had to pick me up from jail and everyone knew. So he took me home and started hitting me, which he's done a lot. But I hit him back, which I'd never done before. And then things got out of hand. We knocked some knives onto the floor and the next thing I knew he'd stabbed one into me. I'm not even sure if he meant to do it or if it happened by accident." The words pour out of me like blood, and with each breath I take, my lungs start expanding wider and more powerfully. I feel like I'm free for the first time in my life. Free from my childhood. Free from my scars. Free from the cuts, the bruises, the razors, the pain.

By the time I'm finished, I've stopped clenching my fists and my fingers are stretched out in front of me. I wait for Doug to say something, but instead he flags down a waitress with his hand.

She's a middle-aged woman with blonde hair braided at the back of her head. She's wearing a bright blue dress and a white apron. In her hand are a pen and an order book. "What can I get ya two lovely gentlemen tonight?" she asks, poising her pen over the notebook.

"I'll have some pancakes, toast with strawberry jam, and a tall cup of milk," Doug says and looks at me with a small smile. "Kayden, go ahead and order whatever you want. And make sure it's enough to get you through the next few hours."

"The next few hours?" I question. "Is that really necessary?"

He nods. "Yeah, I want you to tell me everything that happened."

*"Everything?"* It's an unfathomable, unreachable idea to me. "Like what? You want me to pour my fucking heart and soul out to you."

The waitress frowns at my language and also probably because the conversation has headed in a strange direction. I wonder who she thinks we are. And why we're here. I'm kind of wondering the same thing myself.

"Everything. I want you to start from the beginning," he

says and sets a menu down in front of me, giving it a tap with his finger.

I order a large stack of pancakes, bacon, and toast and the waitress smiles before walking away. I say nothing at first, fidgeting with the salt and pepper shakers to keep myself from scratching at my skin. I keep waiting and waiting for Doug to speak, but he just sits there silently, watching a television over my shoulder.

The silence eventually rips my sanity open and I trace the cracks in the table. "How far do you want me to go back?"

"Back to the very first time your father hurt you," he speaks calmly, looking away from the television to me.

My lungs expand as I inhale, preparing myself for what I'm about to do. "That was about fifteen years ago. You really want me to go all the way back?"

He has this comforting smile on his face. One I've never seen on any of the adults I've known. "I want you to tell me everything. Don't hold back. Let it all out."

I open my mouth, knowing that when I let it out everything will change. And I pray to God it's a good change.

## Callie

Seth and I are getting ready for bed, not saying much to each other, and Luke walked out to smoke and fill up the ice bucket. It's been about an hour since Kayden took off and I can't stop thinking about him and what he's doing; if he's really talking to his therapist like he said, and if so, if it's going well.

Seth walks out of the bathroom as I'm getting underneath the covers. He's wearing green and navy blue plaid pajama bottoms and a white T-shirt, and he's brushing his teeth.

For a second he just watches me. "I called Greyson," he announces, his voice a little jumbled because he has a mouthful of toothpaste.

I fluff the lumpy pillow and then turn on my side. "Did you work everything out?" From under the blanket, I cross all my fingers, hoping he did.

He nods, returning to the bathroom to spit out the toothpaste. He rinses his toothbrush off, sets it on the counter, and then climbs into bed with me. He rolls to the side, turns the television on, and clicks the lamp off.

"I told him I loved him," he says inaudibly and it takes a minute for his words to register inside my head.

"You *love* him? You never told me that?"

"I do. Like a lot."

I uncross my fingers. "And what did he say?"

"I love you too," he says and I hear the smile through his voice. He's happy, which makes me happy even under the circumstances.

I'm a little envious of him, for being able to say the truth and put himself unconditionally out there to someone. "Seth . . . I'm really happy for you."

Laughter flows from him. "I'm really happy for me too."

The room stills and a little while later Luke walks in and climbs into bed. It makes me a little uneasy with him sleeping in the same room as me, but it's not as bad as I thought when they first mentioned sharing a room—to split the costs—back when we were in the truck.

I toss and turn for another hour or so. The clock is glowing against the darkness and snowflakes start to strike the window. The heater is clanking and there's banging coming from the room next door. I can hear Seth's loud breathing—I can hear everything. It's almost one o'clock in the morning when I decide it's time to face one of my fears. I'm not even sure what brings me to the conclusion. Maybe it's Seth's bravery or maybe it's that I really need to get it off my chest. I've been placing too much on it already and perhaps it's time to clear the pressure completely.

I'm going to tell Kayden how I feel. Because he deserves to know that someone loves him, even if he doesn't love me back. I grab my phone and notebook from the nightstand and tiptoe over to the bathroom. Flipping the lights on and then shutting the door, I dial his number and open my notebook to his letter. It goes straight to his voicemail like it has the last few times I called him. I take a deep breath and begin reading out loud what I feel, admitting the truth and putting myself out there, even though it terrifies me.

Maybe, if I'm lucky, this step will help me get to the next admission in my future.

# Kayden

Doug and I are still at the diner when the sun starts to ascend from behind the snowy mountains. The waitress starts pulling the shades down on the windows as the sunlight shines into the restaurant. She flips off the neon signs both inside and out, preparing for another morning.

I sit across from Doug, finishing up a very long story, preparing myself to leave the comfort of the table. I haven't told him nearly everything, especially the darkest times that are locked deep away in the back of my head, the ones I won't let myself think about. Doug said that's okay and that I have time. It baffles me. I'd never really thought about my time. I took things day by day and was basically living the life my father wanted me to live. Halfway through, when I'm telling him about how my father choked me until I passed out, I started to cry.

He'd done it because I'd lost the remote. After hours of searching, I'd finally given up. And I was never supposed to give up. I didn't even fight him. He just started yelling and I stared at him, which seemed to piss him off only more. His face was bright red and he was screaming and then running at me. And I just stood there as he tackled me and wrapped his arms around my neck.

I remember looking up at him and thinking, *Please just kill me so it'll be over.* And when I woke up from my blackout, I found myself slightly disappointed.

"So what's next?" I ask, after Doug pays the bill, trying to wipe my eyes off on my sleeves as discreetly as possible.

He puts his wallet back into his jacket and slides the empty plates aside. "That's really up to you."

I pile my fork and spoon onto the stack of plates, and then I stare at the healing crescent-shaped wounds on my arms with blood dried over them. "This therapist in Laramie that you know, is he . . . is he as understanding as you?" I don't like the idea of opening up to anyone else.

"He might even be better." Doug smiles. "But Kayden, you can call me whenever you want. And be sure to come to your appointment next week."

I nod, scooting to the edge of the booth. "All right."

Doug tosses a few ones down on the table. "Kayden, I feel like I have to say one more thing . . . about your father."

I wince. Over the last several hours I'd said a lot of terrible thing about my father and even though I wish it weren't that way, feelings of guilt and betrayal lie within me. Maybe one day, though, they'll be gone. "What?"

He takes his time answering. "I think you should consider pressing charges against him. What he did to you that night . . . there's a lot you can do to him."

I shake my head. "I can't . . . especially since I might be getting charges pressed against me."

"You don't have to do it now," he assures me. "There's a somewhat lengthy time frame for these things . . . Maybe it's something we can talk about next week. If you feel up to it.

But that's the key here. I don't want to push you until you're ready."

*Press charges against my father?* I want to. The idea of throwing him out to the world is fucking appealing. But every grain of fear that's ever been inside me rises. "Okay, we can talk about it next week."

He nods and then gets up from the booth. I follow him outside, zipping up my jacket and tugging my hood over my head. I sling my bag over my shoulder as he gets into his car and drives away. I stand beneath the shelter of the carport watching the sunrise and the sky shift to a bright pinkish orange. It's blinding to look at but I can't seem to turn away. I keep staring at it until I see spots and then slide my hand into my pocket to call Luke, figuring I'll skip the cold, numbing walk in exchange for a car ride. I turn on my phone and instantly feel like an ass. Callie has called and texted multiple times, asking if I'm okay. I've been gone all night and she's probably worried sick.

My voicemail light is flashing so I dial into it and hold my breath, fearing what she has to say, fearing she'll say it's over and realizing that I don't want it to be over, a feeling that amplifies at the first sound of her voice.

*Kayden...*

*So Seth thought it would be a good idea for me to write everything that I'm feeling down and please, pretty please, keep in mind that I wrote this before the beach, but I'm sure I still feel the same way.*

293

She takes a deep breath and it sounds like she's about to cry.

*Before I met you, I was kind of a mess. Even though Seth had brought me out of my shell, I still felt so ugly on the inside and out-side…so broken…so ashamed I guess. Sometimes the pain was so bad that I couldn't take it, and it's part of the reason why I'd make myself throw up. It's part of the reason why I chopped my hair off in sixth grade. Why I wore baggy clothes for so long. Why walking through a crowd sends me into a panic attack. Why I hated being touched. It was basically the reason for everything that I did. And it was always there all the time…Sometimes I just wanted a break from it, but every time I looked forward to see if a break was possible, it never seemed like it could happen. I honestly thought I'd be that way forever, which sometimes made me wish that forever would be a really short time.*

She takes another deep breath and her voice falters.

*I actually thought about making it short a few times, but I never got further than the thoughts. I'm glad I did too, because despite all the ugly and heaviness and panic attacks, it was worth the suffering because I got you…You saved me from a lifetime of self-loathing and torture. You saved me from myself, from my past, from the painful, lonely future I'd set up for myself. And I thought everything would be okay. But then I found you on the floor… that night…and I realized how much you'd been hurting and how much you needed to be saved too. Not just from the injuries but from the pain I know you have trapped inside you.*

*I get it. I really do. And I'll do anything to help you. You just have to let me help. And I need you to let me help you because I need you. I can't... I can't....*

She starts to cry and it makes my own eyes water up. There are people walking in and out of the café and I'm standing underneath the carport in front of cars crying like a fucking baby. But it doesn't matter. The tears, the pain, the past, none of it matters. They're just things that exist inside me like the scars on my body. Sure, they'll always be there, reminding me of what I went through, but it doesn't mean I have to hold on to the pain. Scars fade and become marks on my skin. They weren't originally there and although they do alter how my skin looks, they don't change how *I* work and function.

Her tears quiet and she sniffles before speaking again.

*I can't do this without you. I... I-I love you, Kayden. And I don't expect you to say it back. I don't expect anything. I just wanted you to know because you deserve to know and you deserve to be loved.*

The line goes quiet. I hear her breathing for a moment before she hangs up. Her words echo in my head. It's like she knows. Knows that no one's ever said that to me before, except for Daisy and that wasn't the same. It was fake and easy to say back to her because it was just words to both of us. Callie means it. I can tell through the sound of her tears.

I don't know what to do. My heart is thumping in my chest as I glance around at the people getting in their cars and eating their breakfast inside the diner. I know what I *want* to do. I want to turn it off, make my heart relax, run away from the feelings nipping at my heels.

I get up, sliding my phone into my back pocket, and then I start to run down the road right as the wind kicks up. Snow flurries are falling on the sidewalk and road, but I run against them, pushing forward, unsure where I'm going. And that's okay. Sometimes the best things are the ones that aren't planned, the decisions made while living in the moment.

# Chapter Seventeen

*#1 Overcome your worst fear*

## Callie

"Have you heard anything from him?" Seth asks me. He's lounging on the bed, with the remote pointed at the television as he surfs through the channels. Kayden's been gone all night and I'm extremely worried about him. I text him a couple of times, but he doesn't respond. Everyone keeps reassuring me that everything's okay, but Luke left really early, saying he needed coffee, when really I think he went to look for Kayden. At least I hope he did.

I shake my head and set the brush down on the counter. "No, not yet."

I wonder if he's heard my voicemail, if he's heard me pour out my heart and soul. If he has, he's probably upset, or pissed, or maybe even scared. But I needed to say it. No more hiding. I love Kayden and he needed to know that.

I leave my hair down and walk back into the room. I drop

down on the bed, flat on my stomach, and stretch out. "I need caffeine," I say through a yawn. "I didn't sleep very well."

He tosses the remote onto the foot of the bed. "Maybe it's because you spent half the night talking to a voicemail."

I prop up on my elbows. "You heard that?"

He nods. "I heard the crying too." Leaning forward, he sweeps my hair out of my face. "Do you want to talk about it?"

I shake my head and pivot to my side. "Not really. I kind of talked about it last night."

He crooks his eyebrow. "On a voicemail."

I nod. "He'll hear it and that's all that matters."

"And then what?"

"And then he hears it."

Seth waits for an explanation. "And..."

I trace the floral pattern on the faded bedspread. "And then nothing...I didn't tell him because I expected anything. I just wanted him to know how I felt about him...He deserves that."

He presses his lips together, contemplating. "Did you tell him you love him?"

I look up from the bedspread. "Y-yes."

"Callie, I..." There are drops of pity in his eyes. He doesn't think this is going to end well.

I sit up and tuck my feet under me. "Seth, I promise everything will be all right. The very fact that I could tell him I loved him means something to me...It means I'm growing.

298

Do I wish he'll say it back? Yes. But either way, I'm glad I did it."

He gives me a lopsided grin and then brushes the tip of my nose with the tip of his finger. "That's good." He sits up and swings his feet over the edge of the bed. "But Callie, if he doesn't say it back, as your best friend and protector of evil guys who want to hurt you, I'm going to have to kick his ass."

I snort a laugh and cover my mouth. "Yeah, okay."

He stands to his feet and presses his fist into his hand, popping his knuckles. "I'm not joking. I'll hurt him for hurting you."

Laughter sputters from my lips at the sight of tall, thin Seth trying to kick Kayden's ass. "Well, thank you, protector. I appreciate *your* getting *your* ass kicked."

His nose crinkles as he scoops up a pillow and throws it at me. I duck and it zips above my head, landing on the floor. I start laughing at him, clutching onto my stomach as I roll onto my back.

"What the hell's so funny about that?" Seth sounds offended and he rolls up the sleeves of his gray shirt. He flexes his muscles and I just about die of laughter. "Well, I'm glad I can entertain you."

"I'm sorry," I say, wiping the tears away from my eyes. "It's just so funny to picture."

He glares at me, but it vanishes as someone knocks on the door. "Oh good, there's my breakfast." He heads over to it, collecting his wallet from the nightstand. "And if it's so funny to picture then stop picturing it." He grins at me as he grabs the door handle. "You know we're going to have to come up with a solution to the no-car dilemma..." He trails off as he opens the door and his jaw hangs to his knees.

Kayden is standing on the other side of it, with a thin jacket on, and the bottoms of his jeans are wet with muddy water and so are his boots. He has snowflakes in his damp hair and water beads off the end of each strand. His lips are purple, his eyes are red like he's been crying, and his hands are tucked up in the sleeves.

"Nope, not breakfast for me," he says, glancing at me. "I think this is what *you* ordered."

He's making jokes, but none of this is funny. Kayden's here after he took off and then I told him I loved him and sobbed on the phone as I told him my story. I don't know what it means or if I'm stable enough to find out. I want to believe I am though, that I'm not the weak girl I used to be. That I can handle anything.

Kayden runs his hand over his head, ruffling his hair and sending snowflakes to the floor. "Hey."

"Hey," Seth says, glancing at me from over his shoulder.

Kayden maintains his gaze on me, his emerald eyes sparkling in the sunlight flowing from outside. There is snow falling from the sun-kissed sky, something that occasionally happens when a small section of the sky is cloudy but the sun still can spill through.

Kayden lowers his hand to his side and I just stare at him as I remain on my back, letting the cool breeze sink into my body. I can't tell if he's listened to my message yet, but I hope he has.

"Um…" Seth coughs into his hand. "I think I'm going to go check out what's taking room service so long." He squeezes past Kayden, leaving the door wide open.

Kayden doesn't budge. He keeps looking at me with this perplexed, intense look on his face, like he's afraid to cross the threshold. The moment keeps building, bricks stacking on bricks, as we just look at each other, afraid to move, to breathe, to be the one to speak first.

I sit up, my hair blowing in the wind. "You can come in," I say and my voice nearly gets carried away in the wind and knocks the bricks to the ground in a pile of dust.

He doesn't disconnect our gaze as he bends his knee and steps one foot into the room. He repeats the movement with the other foot and then shuts the door. The wind ceases and the curtain is closed so the room is mostly dark.

"I got your message," he says, shocking me with his bluntness.

"Oh…" My throat feels like it's closing as I kneel up onto the bed, bringing a pillow to my lap to hug it. "Kayden, where have you been all night? Were you with your therapist?"

A breath eases from his lips as he rakes his hands through his hair, shifting his gaze to the wall just over my shoulder. "I'm sorry, but I couldn't do it with you there."

301

"Did you...did you tell him about your dad?" I ask and he just stares at me, with a strange look on his face, like he's really studying me. I don't know if it means he told him or not. I don't know what any of this means. I move my feet to the floor and stand, tipping my chin up to meet his eyes. "Kayden, you need to tell someone...I thought we...I thought we had a deal."

He gives me a small smile and then threads his fingers through mine. His hands are as icy as a breeze outside the room. "I did tell someone. I just didn't want you there when I was giving...all the gory details."

My shoulders jolt upward as I imagine him on the floor again. "But you did tell someone? *Really?*"

He nods and forces the lump down his throat with a hard swallow. "I wasn't lying in the text. I went to talk to my therapist and I told him."

"And?" I'm not sure what the right question is or if one exists. I feel like I should just let him tell me what he wants to.

He sighs and then lines form on his forehead as he presses a hand to his chest, massaging it over his heart. "And it feels kind of good."

I study his expression and realize that his eyes look a bit greener, his shoulders a little less stiff, like some of the darkness he keeps bottled inside has reduced and lightened. "What did your therapist say for you to do?"

He stares off into space, his hand coming up to my face.

He starts twirling a strand of my hair around his fingers and I don't think he's even aware he's doing it. "He said to think about pressing charges."

"And are you going to?"

"Think about it?"

"No, press them."

"I'm still thinking," he mutters. He unravels my hair from his finger and looks at me with depth in his eyes. "I want to, but it's hard. I just need some time," he murmurs, confused. "I really wish I had some help... What I really wish is that my brothers would be on my side, at least so I don't look like a complete liar."

"Maybe they will be," I say encouragingly. "You said it was the same for them, right? Maybe once they see you do it they'll want to stand up to him too."

He shakes his head, his gaze never wavering from mine. "Nah, Tyler's a crackhead alcoholic so I'd have to wait for him to sober up first, and Dylan's been missing for forever. Well, missing in the sense that he won't speak to anyone in the family."

"Do you know where he is?" I ask, sketching my finger below his eye and along the red streaks on his skin. He's been crying. I can feel the dried tears.

He shrugs, moving my hand to his mouth and closing his eyes. He places a tantalizing kiss on my palm. "I've never tried to find him." He opens his eyes and tilts his head. "Maybe though... I could try."

I nod, leap to my feet, and wrap my arms around his waist without any hesitation. "You should. At least I think you should."

He kisses the top of my head and inhales my scent. "I know you do. I wouldn't expect any less from you." He sweeps his lips across my head again, then slants his face to the side and relocates his lips to my temple. He kisses it delicately before traveling south to my cheek and then my jawline, sucking on my skin. My shoulder shudders upward as his breath feathers against my neck. He kisses me there too, sliding his tongue out and giving my skin a little nick.

"Thank you," he whispers against my neck as his arms encompass my waist. His fingers press into my back as he steers me closer, aligning our bodies.

I try to tip my head to the side to look at him, but one of his hands cups the side of my neck and he secures me in place. "For what?" I breathe as he strokes my collarbone with his lips, lightly grazing his teeth along the skin.

"For saying it." His voice is unguarded and he keeps peppering me with kisses all the way down my shoulder. I have on a tank top and some pajama bottoms and my skin is sensitive to his hungry touch.

"It was the truth." The last part comes out as more of a whimper as he slides the strap of my top down while his other hand glides up the front of my shirt, his cold skin mixing with the heat I'm radiating.

He starts backing me up to the bed with his hand resting on the outside of my bra. When the backs of my legs hit the edge of the bed, he lifts me up by the waist and lays me down on the bed. He draws back for a minute, staring down at me and I feel naked under his penetrating gaze. But I'm not nervous. I know he won't hurt me. And I think I know that deep down, even if he can't say it, he loves me.

He opens his mouth to speak and I hold my breath in anticipation. "You're beautiful. And amazing."

My cheeks grow warm at his compliment and I stuff down the harrowing connection my memories have to the word "beautiful," because the one and only guy who's ever said it to me is Caleb. "Kayden, no I'm not. I'm just an average girl and I'm happy with that."

Shaking his head, he traces his finger down the arch of my neck. "No, you're way beyond average, Callie."

I squirm under his gushing. "I'm not that great."

"No, you're amazing and perfect and caring and beautiful."

I offer him a small smile. "So are you."

He kneels down on the bed so he's straddling my hips. "Those things you said on the phone...it had to be hard to say them."

Pressing my lips together, I shake my head. "Not as hard as I thought." His face is masked and he looks perplexed as he struggles for words he's afraid to say, so I say them for him.

"You don't have to say it back. I just wanted you to know how I felt."

His lips start to separate and I push up on my elbows, grab hold of the top of his shirt, and crush his mouth against mine, so he doesn't have to deal with it just yet. Putting his hands out, his palms slam against the mattress and he braces his weight on his hands, stopping himself from smashing into me. His tongue pushes between my lips and slips powerfully into my mouth. He tastes like syrup and pancakes and smells like coffee and snowflakes. I breathe in through my nose, inhaling the scent as I kiss him. He sucks my bottom lip into his mouth and bites it roughly, sending a searing ripple to the center of my stomach. There's freedom in his movements, from the way he kisses me to the way he grabs at my breast. His happiness makes me happy and that's all I really need at the moment.

He draws his lips away, but before I can protest, he sits me up and grips the bottom of my shirt, yanking it over my head, and my hair falls to my shoulders. With a needy look in his eyes that sends a coil up my legs, he reaches behind me and flicks the clasp of my bra open. I notice there is a collection of rubber bands on his wrist and I wonder if his therapist gave them to him.

He notices that I'm staring at them and he stares down at them too. He slips his finger underneath one of them and flicking it looks up at me. "They're supposed to help me heal."

I nod, looking into his eyes. "I know."

A moment passes between us and then he's kissing me again, folding his strong body over mine as he pins me down below him on my back. He pushes his knee between my legs and skims his fingers up my inner thigh, propelling my body into an uncontrollable frenzy. I open my legs and let him rub his knee against me, probing my fingertips into his shoulder blades as he tastes my neck with his tongue. Little moans keep fleeing my lips as my body arches into his and unexpectedly he moves his legs away from me.

"Don't stop," I beg and he slants his head to look at me. I feel mortified for begging. And surprised at myself. "I'm sorry," I apologize, embarrassed.

"Don't be sorry," he says in a gravelly voice. He grabs my hip and turns us to the side. Reaching his hand down the waistband of my pajama bottoms, he slides his fingers deep inside me and a moan leaves my lips as my body clings to his. He cups the back of my neck and lures my lips to his, kissing me fiercely as he moves his fingers inside me, and I end up screaming out his name.

Once I come down from the high, I feel embarrassed by my outburst. My cheeks are warming and I know he can see it.

"You know you're adorable when you blush?" he says, outlining my damp cheeks with his finger.

I bite down on my lip. "I'm sorry I begged like that...and screamed."

He shakes his head and strands of brown hair hang across his forehead and shadow his eyes. "Don't be sorry for telling me what you want. I'll give you whatever you want, Callie."

Whatever I want? I want him to say that he loves me, but I won't ever make him *give* me that. So instead, I do something that is so out of character for me that it shocks us both. I lift my hips and start slipping off my pants, because what I want is for him to be inside me.

He watches my every move with this animalistic look in his eyes that I've never seen before and I'm pretty sure every speck of my skin is flushed with heat. I take off my panties too and then just lie there naked while he's still fully dressed. Despite the fact that I'm blushing, it's a huge step for me and the very fact that I did it says that I'm moving forward in my life. He starts tracing his fingers across my cheek, then draws a line to my neck, his skin searing hot when it reaches my chest. His eyes stay on me the entire time as he strokes his finger across my nipple and my breathing instantaneously picks up. He moves to the other one and then heads downward, skimming his fingers across my ribs, feeling each bump until he reaches my hip. It tickles, but in a good way and the insides of my thighs are scorching so severely I have to entangle them around each other to contain the heat.

He keeps his fingers on my hip as he swings his leg over me, his eyes never leaving mine. Once he has a leg on each side of me, he uses his free hand to reach around and tug his shirt off. I feel a little better now that he's not entirely dressed and I'm not the only one naked. As soon as my fingers come into contact with the lines of his lean chest muscles, his fingers drift downward across my body. Instead of putting them inside me again, he directs his hand to the upper part of my inner thigh.

He maintains my gaze, like he's afraid that if he looks away I might panic. "You can tell me if you want me to stop. You know that, right?"

I nod. "I know. I trust you."

Smiling, he moves his thumb back and forth and my body begins to tremble. He continues to do the same thing, moving his thumb up across my inner thigh, making a path across the center of my legs, and then moving it to the other thigh. Back and forth, his fingers never enter me, like he's teasing me. And it's driving me crazy, to the point that I've become mortified at the pleading noises that keep fleeing my lips and the way my toes curl every time he's about to slip his fingers inside me and then retracts them.

Finally, he moves his fingers away from my skin, and then he watches me, panting, and his eyes are blazing with something I've never seen before.

I don't know what he wants from me, but I can't take it anymore. "*Kayden, please*, please don't stop."

Apparently that's what he wanted, because a smile curves at his lips. He undoes the button of his jeans, grinning the whole time as he kicks them off. It's weird to see him this happy, but nice too. When he returns to the bed he lays his body down on top of me.

He studies my face for an eternity, like he's memorizing it.

"What?" I ask, self-consciously.

He shakes his head, still studying me. I'm worried he's going to start going off on how beautiful and amazing I am, but the corners of his mouth just quirk. "I was just thinking how I would have never gotten here if it hadn't been for you."

I wiggle my arm free from my side and run my finger along the outline of his jaw. "That's not true. I didn't even do anything really."

He turns his head and presses his lips against my palm. "Yes, you did," he whispers against my skin. "You saved me countless times. Not just from getting my ass kicked or calling the ambulance, but because you showed me that you cared." He shrugs and moves his mouth away from my hand, looking a little embarrassed. "You showed me that I'm worth caring for." His eyebrows instantly knit. "But I want you to know that you don't have to stick around. I've still got a ton of shit I have to work through, and you have your own. I don't want to put that on you."

I say the first thing that enters my mind. "Kayden, I love you." Then I press two fingers over his mouth, so he knows he doesn't have to say it back. The tremble in my heart matches the one in my hand as I move my fingers away from his mouth.

His breath hitches and falters and then his eyes start to water over. Mine pool with my own tears. It's amazing how one sentence—three single words, eight letters—can have so much power. In a moment like this, even our breathing stirs the sorrow, the agony, and the happiness that we'd both buried below our hearts, underneath the immense pain.

I'm looking into his eyes and he's looking into mine and I wonder if maybe it wasn't coincidence that brought me to him that night in front of the pool house. Maybe it was fate that guided me there so I could save him and he could save me and then it could lead us here to this moment where we are both completely content and free and glad we're alive.

He starts kissing me and I feel his tears drip against my cheeks and mix with my own tears. I open up my legs and he keeps kissing me as he thrusts inside me, slowly and perfectly in rhythm. I thread my fingers through his soft, damp hair, and then move my fingers down to his cheek, feeling his stubble and the slight unevenness of his jawline. His hands explore my body too, touching every inch of it, his palms callously against my skin, but I enjoy every minute of it.

Sliding his hand to my knee, he tips to the side and brings my knee up as he keeps rocking into me. I'm climbing higher, faster, and my hands cling to him, gripping onto his shoulders. He kisses me with more passion than he ever has before, delving his tongue into my mouth and then sucking my tongue into his. He bites at my lips, nibbles at my neck, and grabs at my breast until a passionate fire combusts inside me. I cry out as I arc into him and my head falls back against the mattress. I gasp, waiting for him to catch up with me, and then I shut my eyes and breathe in the moment, letting go of my second biggest fear and preparing myself to face my first.

## Kayden

I slide out of her and roll onto my back, feeling more of my shield crack apart. As insane as it sounds, I'm somehow becoming whole again—or becoming whole for the first time in my life. I want to keep moving forward, putting myself back together again and helping her heal too. I decide to take a baby step in that direction and get up off the bed. She watches me walk across the room naked and her cheeks are heating, which makes me smile.

"What are you doing?" she asks, pulling the sheets over her body as she sits up.

I unzip my bag that I dropped on the floor near the door and rummage through my clothes until I find it. The cold metal presses against my palm as I round the foot of the bed and lie down beside.

"What's in your hand?" she asks as she reaches for my fingers.

I let her pry them open and then watch her face twist as she stares at the necklace in my hand. "I found it when Luke and I were walking around in San Diego. It made me think of you," I explain.

She peers up at me through her lashes, chewing on her bottom lip. "How come?"

I turn my hand sideways and let the chain fall from my hand and dangle from my fingers. At the end is a four-leaf clover, stained a shiny metallic. "Because you've brought me nothing but luck, Callie Lawrence."

She immediately frowns. Sitting up, she brings her knees to her chest and wraps her arms around her legs. "I've brought you nothing but bad luck. You almost wound up dead because of me."

I shake my head, then move behind her, putting a leg on each side of her and sweeping her hair to one shoulder. "Every single second I've spent with you has been worth it. Besides, I probably would have wound up dead anyway." She starts to turn her head in shock, but I put my hands on her shoulders so she can't see past my arms. She can't be looking at me when I say this. "Before you, there was just pain and emptiness and I really didn't care if I lived or died. I was just there, existing at the surface of the water, not quite drowning but not quite able to breathe. And then you came along and I could finally breathe. Without you, I probably would have just kept cutting until I finished my body off."

"But so many bad things have happened to you since I came into your life," she says, sounding choked up.

"Those bad things were because of my own choices and from problems that existed well before you came along." I put my lips beside her ear. "But you showed me something I'd never seen before." I kiss the tip of her earlobe and she shivers, her shoulder moving upward against my cheek. "You gave me good...I've never had good before." I place a soft kiss on her neck and whisper, "You showed me that it was okay to feel both the good and the bad. It just took me a while to get it balanced." I suck her earlobe into my mouth, thinking about how she poured her heart and soul out to me on the phone. I want to say it to her, to let her know that I feel the same way, but the words won't roll off my tongue, so instead I say, "I want to be with you, Callie, more than anything."

Her head falls against her knees and she starts to sob, her body heaving. I slide my arms underneath hers and then steer her back with me as I lean against the headboard. I listen to her cry and it matches with the rhythm of my heart. I feel how much I want her—need her. I feel how much she means to me. I feel the pain that coexists with my feelings for her. I feel how much I want to run a razor down my arm, feel the skin split open, and watch the blood pour out, and then I feel how much I don't want to do that because of her. I feel how much I want to live and be with her.

My heart opens up and I feel it all. Every single emotion that's ever been inside me starts pumping through my veins: the good, the bad, the painfulness, the heartache, the loneliness, the happiness, the need, the knowing that there's more out there to life than what I grew up with.

And for the first time in my life, I feel it all and tell myself that, in the end, I'll still be okay.

## Callie

I cry myself to sleep and when I wake up, I feel different. Kayden's pressed up against me, with his arm around me, clinging onto me like I'm the most important thing to him in the world as he sleeps off his overwhelming day. I have a necklace around my neck that he gave me because he thinks I'm good luck. Seth is still gone and again I wonder if he has spy cameras all over the place because it's like he knows what he'd be walking into if he came back to the room.

I also feel lighter—braver. I want to be free from the one thing that still pushes me down. I want to tell my family about Caleb, not just because I want them to know, but because I want to free Kayden from the burden of letting his father buy Caleb off.

If I tell my family, then they'll be on my side—and Kayden's—once they understand why he beat Caleb up. At least that's what I hope. Honestly, I have no idea how it'll all turn out. Maybe they'll crush me and decide not to believe me. But whatever the outcome, it's time to face my worst fear and not allow it to own me anymore. Then maybe Kayden and I can move forward, together, with a little less weight on our shoulders.

I decide to check my voicemail but give up after the fifth repetitive message and switch to texts. Skimming through them, I come across one that catches my attention. After numerous threats from my mother, she finally finds my weak spot, although I'm not sure how she knows it exists.

> **Mom:** Callie, I don't even know who you are anymore. You run off with those boys who are nothing but trouble. I'm not going to let them ruin you and neither will your brother or Caleb. We've all decided that Caleb should press charges. You need to come home and side with this family. We're going to be there for him.

I drop the phone and get out of bed. I get dressed in jeans, a long-sleeved thermal shirt, and my coat. I write Kayden a note and leave it by the pillow.

> Please don't freak out when you wake up, but I had to tell them by myself and I know you'll understand. I'll be back soon. I promise.
> Love,
> Callie

I slip my shoes on and then sneak out the door, letting him sleep. As much as I would love for him to come hold my hand

and be my security blanket, he's already dealt with enough today and I'm going to force myself to be brave all on my own. Besides, after that message, I know my mom will attack him the moment he steps foot in the house.

I walk the quiet streets underneath the clouds and the sun, hoping that ultimately they'll part and let the sun shine freely. *This is all your fault, Callie. If you ever tell anyone, that's what they'll think.* I keep walking, quickly and determinedly, one foot in front of the other until I reach my house. *You better keep quiet. I swear to fucking God, you'll regret it if you don't.* The snow has been shoveled from the driveway and my dad's truck is parked in front of the shut garage. The curtains are open and the steps have been sprinkled with blue salt. *One foot in front of the other. Just keep going.* I open the side door and stand in the doorway, taking in the overwhelming memories rising in my head. *Come with me for a second, he says. I have a present for you, and I skip after him, excited.*

My mom turns from the sink. There's a dishrag over her shoulder and her hair is done up in a bun. Her skin is bare of makeup and she has a pair of slacks and a pink sweater on.

"Callie Lawrence," she says, tossing the towel onto the counter and placing her hands on her hips. "Where the hell have you been?"

I turn to my father sitting at the table, wearing a hooded sweatshirt with the high school's logo on it. He's eating eggs and toast and drinking juice and my brother is next to him, texting on his phone.

"I need to talk to you," I tell my dad in an uneven voice. I'm not quite sure why I choose him, other than that we used to get along really well when I was younger and I know he'll be more stable than my mother. "Alone."

Glancing up at me with confusion in his eyes, he sets his fork down and without arguing he rises from his chair. "All right, honey."

My brother scowls at me as he sets his phone down on the table. "Aren't you even going to tell Mom where you've been? She's been worried."

"It's not important where I've been," I say. "It's only important why I'm here."

He frowns at me and then shakes his head before returning his attention to his phone. My mom starts shouting that I need to explain where I've been and I'm surprised when she doesn't follow my dad and me to the living room. Once I've settled down on the couch, and he's sitting in his tattered leather recliner across from me, I give myself a final quick mental pep talk. I look at the photos around the room, the ones with our family and some even with Caleb.

"That was fun, right?" I point at one photo of the two of us wearing jerseys and standing in front of a stadium with smiles on our faces. I was eight and I was happy.

He tracks to where I point and then a smile turns up at his

lips. "That was a good day." His forehead creases as he looks back at me. "Honey, your mother and I have been really worried...about what happened that night and then you just ran away with those boys you barely know."

"Those boys are like my family, Dad," I say truthfully. "They've really been there for me."

He fiddles with the string on his hoodie, tightening it and then loosening it. "Yeah, they always seemed like they were good kids." He smiles. "They kicked ass on the field too."

I know right then and there that I've made the right choice by telling him first. He's looking past the fact that Kayden beat up Caleb and maybe that's because he's looked a little deeper into the situation.

"I have to tell you something." I clear my throat. "And it's going to be kind of hard, not just for me to tell you, but it's going to be hard to hear."

"Okay..." He's puzzled and uncertain, which is understandable.

I take a few deep breaths and then I take some more, until I feel like I'm going to pass out. And then I stop breathing all together. *You better not fucking tell, or I swear I'll hurt you.* I clutch the clover hanging on my neck in my hand, needing to hold on to a part of Kayden so I can have strength and courage. "You remember my twelfth birthday?"

This seems to confuse him even more, his head slanting slightly to the side, his blue eyes getting a little squinty and his forehead scrunching up as he assesses me. "Yeah...didn't you have a party?"

Pressing my lips together, I nod. "And there were a lot of people there."

"You know how your mother likes a show," he says with a heavy sigh. "She's always loved her parties and get-togethers."

I nod again and then push forward before my pulse and my thoughts can catch up with my voice. "Something bad happened to me...that day." My thoughts drift back to when he pinned me down and I start to shake. *Please get off me. It hurts. I'm breaking. Please. Help me. Help me. Help...*

He sits up straighter and scoots forward in his chair, like he's about to go kick someone's butt or something. I don't want him to, though. I just want him to know.

"Dad, please stay calm when I tell you this." I fidget with the bottom of my coat, unzipping the pockets and then zipping them back up, and then I return my hand to the clover. "I need you to just stay calm."

His fists clench on his lap. "I'll try my best, but no promises. Callie honey, you're really scaring me."

"I'm sorry." I run my hand down my face and then up it, drawing my hood off my head as I remember how I felt that day. *I wish I were invisible. I wish I didn't exist. I want to die.* The room lightens up a little as the clouds part from the sun just outside the window. I grip onto the clover and grasp onto the feeling Kayden has given me. "I was raped." Just like that it's out there, in the air, for him to hear, like tearing off a Band-Aid, lifting skin, wounds, everything with it because there's no way to prepare anyone for this.

My father stares at me for an eternity and a thousand emotions rush across his expression: wrath, rage, frustration, pain. Then he does something I've never seen him do. He starts to cry. He's sobbing hysterically, with his head hung in his hands, and I don't know what to do, so I stand up, cross the room, and throw my arms around him.

He keeps crying, but my eyes stay dry. I've cried enough over the last few years and I really don't feel like shedding anymore.

❧

The conversation with my mother doesn't go as well as it did with my dad, especially when I have to tell her who did it.

"No, no, no," she keeps saying, like if she repeats it enough the denial will be real. She keeps tapping her feet against the ground as she sits in the chair in front of the window. "It didn't happen...There's no way..." But every time she looks at me, I know she knows it's true. She's probably going through every detail of my past, when I chopped off my hair, started hiding out in my room all the time, when I changed my wardrobe to "hoodlum clothes," as she put. She's probably thinking about when I stopped talking to almost everyone. When I stopped crying. When I stopped living.

We're in the living room, sitting on the couches. My father is next to me, close, like he thinks he can still protect me from everything bad in the world. Jackson left the house right after I took my dad out of the room so he doesn't know yet, but I wonder what he'll do when he finds out—if he'll believe me or take his best friend's side.

"Yes, it did," I say, surprised by the strength in my voice. "You were outside and everyone was playing hide-and-seek. And he...Caleb told me he had a present. He took me into my room and then...and then it happened."

She's shaking her head over and over again and my dad starts crying again. "There must be a mistake. I wish it were a mistake."

"It's not," I say simply. "It happened and here I am telling you...I really wish...I really wish I could say it was a mistake, though. But wishes are just wishes, Mom. I know that."

She keeps tucking her hair into place and smoothing the wrinkles from her sweating, like she needs to fix something. "Why didn't you tell us when it happened, Callie? I don't understand."

I'm not sure she ever will. My mother loathes dark, ugly things that exist in the world and her defense has always been to ignore them. And now her daughter is telling her that these dark, ugly things have been living in her house, eating her food, smiling at her, charming her, and slowly killing her daughter.

"Shame...guilt...fear," I say, trying to explain the best

322

I can, focusing on my pulse and the feel of the metal of the clover as it rests against the hollow of my neck. "The sheer fact that saying it aloud makes it real."

"Damn it!" My dad pounds his fist on the armrest and then pounds it into the wall, making my mom and me jump. His eyes are red and his skin is pale. "I'm going to fucking kill him!"

"No, you're not, Dad," I say, shaking my head as I touch his arm, trying to calm him down. "Killing him will get you nowhere but in jail. I don't want you to go to jail."

Tears stream from his eyes and it's so strange to see. I watch them fall onto his lap as he says, "Is that why he did it? Kayden?"

I nod my head once. "He wanted to make him pay...for what he did. And it was...it was the only way he could think of to do it."

My dad rises to his feet and shadows over me. He's not that large of a man—medium build and height—but right now he seems enormous. "Oh, he's going to pay. I'm going to call the police."

I jump up and grab his arm, wrapping my fingers firmly around his elbows. "You can't...It won't do any good...It's been too long, Dad."

My mother starts to bawl, taking hysterical breaths as she buries her face into her hands. "This is so wrong...This can't be happening...Oh my God..."

"But it is," I say, and she stares at me through her tears. "Sorry, but it's the truth."

"How can you be so calm?" Her voice is wobbly. "I don't understand."

"I'm not that calm," I correct her as my hand leaves my dad's arm. "I'm just…I'm just trying to move on. Besides…" My eyebrows knit as I realize how strong I'm being at the moment. "I've been weak for long enough and I don't want to crumble anymore."

She takes her phone out of her pocket and starts punching away at buttons. "This is so ridiculous. This is not happening. No, it can't…It can't…"

"Mom, what are you doing?" I ask, and when she doesn't answer, I trade a questioning glance with my father.

He wipes the tears away from his eyes with the back of his hand. "Honey, I think the texting can be put on hold for a moment."

She shakes her head and she hits the last button. "I'm telling Jackson to come home."

"Why?" I ask warily.

"Because he's part of this…this…this…I don't even know what this is." Tears flow from her eyes and drip to her lap, staining her slacks. Her eyes are swollen, and if she keeps crying, she won't be able to see.

I glance up at my dad. "She doesn't need to cry, Dad… Help her stop."

He pats my arm in a comforting gesture. "She's upset." His jaw tightens and he looks at me. I wonder what he sees.

"And so am I. No, I'm fucking pissed. This is such bullshit. All this time…under our roof…" He starts muttering incoherently under his breath, the veins in his neck bulging. He paces the floor and I stand there in front of the couch and watch the madness unfold like a building getting knocked down.

Finally, my mom gets up and crosses the room, heading for the doorway with a determined look on her face. "That's it…"

"Where are you going?" I chase after her. "Mom?"

She dabs her eyes with the bottom of her sweater. "I need to do something…I need to fix this somehow…I just need a minute."

Shaking my head, I position myself in front of her with my hands out to the side. "You can't fix it, Mom. It happened. There's nothing you can do about it, except for be my mom right now."

She analyzes my face for a moment and then returns to crying again, throwing her arms around me. It's been forever since I let her hug me and I stand awkwardly, telling her it will be okay. When her eyes dry, she backs up into the chair, with her face in her hands and her shoulders hunched. The denial and the crying goes on well into the late hours of the night. My dad starts yelling again, going on and on about how Caleb's not going to get away with this. There's no conclusion at the end of the crying and ranting. Caleb still raped me and six years have gone by while he walked around getting away with it. There's nothing that will change that, not even from saying it out loud. But it changes me, alters my life in an irreversible way. It shatters the chains around my wrists and finally I'm free.

Jackson never does come home and I'm not sure what that means. I eventually get up from the couch to leave the house, despite my mother's protests. She wants me to stay there and let her cry over me while she figures everything out. She's so determined that she can erase it somehow, but I'm not naïve enough to believe that's possible. Besides, I've got somewhere else I need to be—want to be. Someplace where I can be happy.

"Wait, Callie, please don't go," she begs, getting up from the couch to follow me to the kitchen. "We can stay here and talk about it some more."

I shake my head as I walk for the door. "Mom, as much as I know how you need to try and work through this, I've already found a way to cope and I kind of need it right now." I more than need it actually. I have to be with him.

She keeps shaking her head and my dad gives me the keys to the truck so I don't have to walk and then tells me he's still going to call the police, just so they know. His eyes are red and puffy and his lips are chapped. I tell him okay, because that's what he needs to hear at the moment. As I step out the door, I wonder what will happen, if Caleb ever shows up again, if he was with Jackson when my mother told him.

Once the door is shut behind me and I'm by myself, I spread my hands to my side as I stand on the top of the porch, underneath the light. The sky is clear, the stars twinkling against the black backdrop. What will happen with my life? I don't know. But I'm eager to find out because for once I'm looking into my future, not my past, and I smile at the endless possibilities.

# *Chapter Eighteen*

*#65 Watch fireworks with someone you love*

## Kayden

"I still really wish I could have been there with you," I say. It's been a couple of days since she told her parents and she seems okay, stronger, more confident. But even though I'm glad she did it, I wish I could have been with her, to support her, comfort her, do whatever she needed.

We're sitting outside on the hood of her father's truck that's parked near the lake. There's a New Year's Eve party going on a ways down and I can see the bonfire through the trees. The stars are out and the sky is a little hazy but the moon shines full. It's way below zero, and the truck's hood is glazed with snow, but we have a blanket draped over us and the warmth of our bodies to keep us warm. "I wanted to be there for you."

"But I had to do it alone," she says, staring at the sky. "Besides, it's over now and I'm ready to move on."

When I'd woken up in the hotel room by myself, I'd nearly panicked and the feeling multiplied when I read her note. She'd gone to tell her parents what happened *by herself.* The idea of Callie standing there telling them alone crushed me. I wanted to be there with her, help her, comfort her, but in a way, I guess I understood why she did it alone. I think Seth's always been right. She's a lot stronger than she looks.

"How do you feel?" I ask her, wrapping my arms firmly around her waist while she presses her cheek against my chest. I get a whiff of her hair, strawberries and something else that's only Callie.

She considers my question in silence. "Weightless."

I smile. "Me too." I had my Monday appointment with Doug yesterday and I feel even lighter than after our meeting at the café. I wonder how much lighter I'll feel down the road after more therapy.

"There's still so much stuff to deal with, though," she adds, turning her head so she can look up at me. "And I worry what Caleb will do when he finds out I told."

My muscles vine into blistering knots. "He'll never hurt you. I won't let him."

"I know you won't," she says, surprising me by how much she trusts me. She nuzzles her face against my shoulder and her warm breath seeps through my coat. "I think...I think we should try and find your brother."

"Dylan?" I tilt my chin down to look at her. "Why?"

She angles her face up and her lips are close enough for me to kiss and the feel of her breath is comforting. "Because, I think it'll help you with your father...when you decide to press charges."

I try to contain my breathing as I think about actually going through with it. What if he gets mad? What if nothing happens and he hunts me down and hurts me? What if he kills me? The idea of death isn't very settling anymore, which confounds me. "I'm not sure if I can."

She inhales and a sigh escapes her lips as she releases a breath. "Yes, you can...I know you can."

I'm uncertain if she should be so confident about *my* confidence. "And what if I don't? Will you..." I trail off, clenching my hands and then flexing my fingers, and then I shake out my hand. "Will you still love me?"

She lowers her head back onto my chest and rotates onto her back. "I'll always love you."

I breathe in the sound of the words and her voice and I have to stop the tears that appear from the overpowering feeling it sends through my body. I wish I could say it back to her. I even get my lips to part, but no sound will come out. "I want to say it," I say quietly.

She shakes her head. "Don't. Only say it when you really mean it." She slides her hand down my chest and interlaces our fingers on top of my stomach.

We breathe through the chilled air, underneath the stars, listening to the sounds of laughter and music from the party.

Minutes later, the sky lights up with an explosion of colors. Every year, this town puts on a huge fireworks show over the lake. When I was a kid, I used to watch it, wondering what the hell the big deal was. Fire in the sky. *Okay.* I didn't get it. But now, lying here with her in my arms, it's starting to make sense. *Freedom.* Things are starting to make sense.

"Happy New Year," I whisper to the air as sparks rain down on the lake.

## Callie

I'm having a moment. I've been having a lot of them lately. The kind where everything connects: pieces puzzling together, stars shining in sync, hearts beating rhythmically. Everything is perfect and although I in no way believe that it will last, I'm going to cherish the moment forever.

"Happy New Year," Kayden whispers underneath his breath as fireworks boom and drift to the water in front of us.

"Happy New Year," I reply, even though I am pretty sure he's just thinking aloud. I prop my chin up on his chest as fireworks boom. "What's your New Year's resolution?"

He makes an outline around my lips as he contemplates my question. One of his lean arms is tucked behind his head and his hand is in mine. "To not think about the past."

"That's a great one," I say with a smile. "Can I make it mine too?"

A grin forms on his lips and he shifts his arm, moving his

hand out from behind his head. He holds out a fist in front of him. "Pound on it."

I contain a giggle as I remove my hand from his and move to bump fists, but he pulls his hand back at the very last second and I frown. "What's wrong?"

He bites on his lip as he sits up and my head slides to his lap. His eyes mirror the colorful fireworks as he lifts me up off his chest and then pushes on my shoulder until I'm lying on my back, against the windshield. The frost nips against a spot of my skin on my lower back where my shirt has ridden up but I don't move as he leans over me, propping an arm on each side of me. Lowering his mouth toward mine, I wait in anticipation for him to kiss me, but right as he's there, right as our lips are about to make contact, he pauses.

"This is nice, right?" he asks and I nod, resisting the urge to grab the collar of his shirt and jerk him down to me. "We should make it a tradition for next year."

My stomach flutters with a thousand enthusiastic butter-flies as I think about being with him for an entire year. "Okay." I cross my ankles over each other, trying to contain the ner-vous energy created by the flush of our bodies.

"So we're on for next year?" he checks, and I nod without any contemplation. I know what I want and I'm not afraid to say it. No more living in fear.

"Good," he says and then leans in to kiss me, whispering, "Thank you for saving me."

"Thank you for saving me too," I say, and seconds later his lips engulf mine.

The fireworks explode and boom above our heads, vivid and colorful against the dark sky, but I think about nothing but him.

# Chapter Nineteen

*#11 Say good-bye and move on*

## Callie

The next two weeks are pretty uneventful. Between the road trip, the recovery, and the confessions, Kayden and I are drained and we spend the rest of our winter break avoiding our houses, and hanging out in the hotel room, diner, or café as much as possible. Seth and Luke hang out with us a lot too. It's been snowing quite a bit, but the air feels warm. My mom calls me every morning and every night. At first I wouldn't tell her where I was staying, because I didn't want her tracking me down, but then I finally fessed up that I was staying with Kayden and Seth in a hotel room.

She isn't very happy about this, but I'm almost nineteen years old, which is what I tell her.

"Callie Lawrence," she says after I finally tell her. I'm sitting on the hotel room's bed in shorts and a T-shirt and Kayden is lying behind me, making shapes on my lower back with his fingers. Every once in a while, he hits a ticklish spot and I giggle.

"This isn't funny," my mom says, sounding irate.

I cover my mouth with my hand to stifle the uncontrollable laughter. Once I settle down, I lower my hand to my lap. "I know, Mom."

"You need to come home... We need to talk about what happened." She sighs. "Callie, the police said they can't do anything about it and even if they could Caleb...he...No one knows where he is still. Jackson thinks he might have taken off."

"I already knew the police couldn't do anything," I tell her, lying down on the bed beside Kayden. He has his boxers on with no shirt and when he snuggles against me the warmth and sturdiness of his chest soothes me. "And I'm not surprised about Caleb."

"But..." She's frustrated and I hear something crash to the ground. "Shit," she curses—she's been cursing a lot lately. "I broke a damn cup."

"I'm sorry," I say, arching my back as Kayden draws hearts on my spine, his hand drifting up my shirt to the area between my shoulder blades.

"You don't need to be sorry, sweetie," she says and then sighs. "It's just a cup."

As much as my mother and I have never gotten along, I have to give her credit for how nice she's being through all this. After her meltdown, she's been less teary eyed and she's never once tried to put the blame on me. Sometimes my thoughts wander back to my twelfth birthday and my head fills with what-ifs. What if I had told her then? What if I'd never had to suffer in silence for the last six years? What if my life had been different? But I always shove the thoughts right out of my head. What-ifs aren't important. I can't go back through time and change things, but I can move forward and create the life I want.

"Callie, did you hear me?" she asks, sounding a little annoyed.

I blink away my thoughts. "Yeah...no...huh?"

Kayden snorts a laugh from behind me as he traces the length of my spine. "You're so going to get into trouble." He makes a silly airhead voice when he says it.

I reach back and pinch his arm and he laughs even harder. "What, Mom?"

She sighs exhaustedly. "I said, have you thought about going to that therapist friend of mine in Laramie when you get back to school? I think it'll be good for you."

"I'm not sure...I'm worried what it might bring up if I do."

"Callie, I think it's important...after all the things you told me...I think you need to get some help. I really wish you'd just consider staying here with us and take a semester off."

"I need to go back to school," I say. "I need to move forward."

She gives an elongated pause. "Then please just go see the therapist..." She's on the verge of crying. "I need to know you're okay."

I glance over my shoulder at Kayden. "I'm okay, Mom. But if you really want me to go, then I will."

"Good." She sounds relieved. "And you call me every day. And stop by here today before you leave."

"Yes, Mom."

"And you'll call me whenever you need anything?"

"Yes."

Kayden starts laughing hysterically, rolling away from me so she won't hear. I've told him how controlling she is and apparently seeing it in action is humorous to him.

"Who is that?" my mom wonders. "The person in the background who keeps laughing?"

Craning my neck, I peek over my shoulder at him and he smiles. "Kayden."

"Oh." She pauses and I hear clicking in the background, like she's tapping her fingernails on top of the counter. "Callie...are you...are you sleeping with this boy?"

Heat rushes through my body. *"What?"*

Kayden must have heard her, because his laughter kicks up a notch and fills the room. "I have to give her credit," he says between laughs. "She's very entertaining."

"Callie," she says. "I'm not going to judge you...I just want to make sure you're being careful."

Oh my God. This is so mortifying. My cheeks are as hot

as the heater below the frosted window and I tuck my head down with the phone still pressed up to my ear to hide my blushing face. "Yes, Mom."

"Yes, Mom, you're sleeping with him?" she asks. "Or you're being careful?"

"Tell her you're being careful right now." Kayden laughs in my ear and it tickles my neck, causing my shoulders to shudder. His arms snake around my waist and then he's pulling me back, lifting himself up from the bed with one arm. He tucks me underneath his solid body and then lowers himself down on me.

I laugh into the phone as he starts to tickle my sides and I squirm, trying to keep the phone beside my ear. "Mom," I say through laughs as his fingers trail high up on my ribs and then halt next to the sides of my breasts.

"Tell her you'll make sure to be careful every day," Kayden teases, his green eyes flashing with untamed desire. He pinches my sides and then moves his hands up my arms and then down them, stopping when he reaches my wrists. He cups each one with one of his hands and then tugs on them.

"Mom, I got to go," I say quickly. "And yes, I'll stop by on my way out." Before she can respond, the phone falls from my hands and Kayden gathers my wrists together and brings them above my head.

For a brief second, panic claws up my throat as I'm hurled into the past when I was pinned down on the bed and my heart beat unstably. He must see it on my face too.

His grip starts to loosen. "Do you want me to let you go?"

I shake my head. "Just kiss me, please."

His mouth turns upward and his lips connect with mine as he bends his back and leans in. And just like that the panic and the memories slip from my thoughts and it's just he and I. No one else in the world exists.

❧

"So what have you been up to?" Seth asks as he hops cheerily into Luke's truck beside me.

It's a bench seat and a compacted fit, but it's not that bad. In fact, it's kind of comforting to be squished into a car with three strong guys who have been there for me in their own wonderful ways.

"Well, you'd know if you hadn't disappeared." I flash him a playful grin as he fastens his seat belt.

He smirks with doubt in his eyes. "I highly doubt I was missed." The seat belt clicks and he sits back, tugging the sleeves of his black-button coat down to cover his arms. "Besides, I wanted to give Kayden and you some space."

"You didn't have to. We didn't really do anything."

He arches his eyebrows, accusingly. "Yeah, right. You two have been locked in that room since the new year started. You're like newlyweds or something, going at it like rabbits."

I turn my face away from him as I feel the blush creeping up and try to restrain my smile. "Seth, stop," I say and he giggles.

Kayden opens the door and the hinges squeak as he scoots into the seat beside me, but he pauses halfway in, with one of his feet still on the ground as he examines my reddened face. "Okay, Seth, what did you say to her this time?" he jokes, and brushes the pad of his thumb across my cheek. He grins at me as I stand up a little so he can climb onto the seat.

"Nothing I haven't said before," Seth responds with a wicked glint in his brown eyes. "She just reacts the same way each time, which makes it so much fun."

I swat his arm and then sit down onto Kayden's lap, immediately overwhelmed by the scent of his cologne. He slings an arm around my shoulders and pulls me into him as he guides the seat belt down from behind himself and fastens it over both of us. It's snowing outside and fluffy flakes are stuck in the brown locks of his hair. I run my hand gently along the top of his head and dust them out. Some of them melt from my body heat and his hair ends up with this wet, sexy look.

"So where do we still have to go?" Luke asks as he tosses his bag into the back of the truck that still has Kayden's motorcycle in it, and then he hops in and slams the door. The truck is already running and he turns up the heater and hot air blasts out from the vents.

"To my house," I say. "And..." I look at Kayden. He hasn't been home since we took off to San Diego and I can tell he doesn't want to go back. But he has to go back and get his clothes and stuff and I think deep down he might want to talk to his brother Tyler. "And to Kayden's, I think."

The cab becomes silent and then Luke sighs and drives out onto the main road, flipping on the wipers. The roads are a little slushy and slick so he reaches to the small shifter in the center and shoves it into four-wheel drive. The truck makes a loud thud and jerks as it slides into gear.

"Jesus." Seth makes a face as he turns his legs to the side and adjusts his seat belt, which has tightened. "It feels like it's going to fall apart."

Luke pats the dash. "It's fine. It's just old."

Seth rolls his eyes and then crosses his arms. We all remain quiet as he veers off roads and makes turns down the narrow streets. The radio plays "Wonderwall," by Oasis, and then "Hands Down," by Dashboard Confessionals. When he pulls into the driveway beside my house, Luke puts it into park and mutters, "Hurry up."

"Relax," Kayden tells him, flipping the handle and pushing open the door. He brings his foot to the ground and climbs out, moving me out with him. Once my feet are planted firmly to the ground, he releases his grip on me and slams the door.

I don't ask questions when he takes my hand and walks up the driveway with me. He never said anything about coming inside, but I think in his own head he's protecting me. We walk up the steps and I try not to think about the haunting memories inside and out. Instead, I think about the good ones that I spent with Kayden and Seth.

By the time we reach the top of the stairs, my mother is swinging the door open. She has on an apron over a floral cream skirt and a white shirt trimmed with lace. Her hair is curled up at the ends and she has a string of pearls around her neck. She also has a plate of chocolate chip cookies in her hand and she's smiling brightly. I can tell Kayden's trying really hard not to laugh at the *Leave It to Beaver* theme she's got going on.

"I'm so glad you decided to stop by," she says and then pulls me in for a hug while balancing the cookies in her hand. She moves back and then hugs Kayden too. He pats her back, awkwardly exchanging a confounded look with me.

But all I can do is smile. At that moment, I love my mother, the cookies, and the 1960s dresses and all because I'm pretty sure no one has hugged Kayden like that besides me. She urges the plate of cookies at us, and shaking my head with a tiny smile, I take one to make her happy. I had accidentally let it slip during a phone conversation about my throwing-up problem and I'm pretty sure for the rest of my life she will probably try to overfeed me.

The good-byes are quick and my dad and Kayden even chat a little bit about football. They don't ask him questions about what happened with Caleb or his dad, even though the gossip around town is spinning into stories full of suicide, attempted murder, and every felony charge imaginable.

We're heading out to the truck when Jackson's car pulls into the driveway. My initial reaction is to run away from him, because he's usually got Caleb attached to his hip. But there's no one sitting in the passenger seat so I relax and let out a loud breath.

"You coming?" Kayden asks, and I realize I'm standing in the middle of the driveway, staring at my brother.

I hold up a finger, indicating I need a minute. "Just a sec."

He eyes me with worry in his green eyes. "Are you sure?"

I nod as my brother climbs out of the car. He's looking at me and I can't read his stoic expression at all. "Yeah, I just need to talk to him."

Kayden nods and then he heads for the truck, passing Jackson along the way. They mutter a hello and then Kayden climbs inside. He never takes his eyes off me as I wander over to the steps and take a seat on the bottom stair, the light layer of frost on the cement seeping through the backside of my jeans.

Jackson walks up to me with his hands stuffed into his plaid hooded jacket. His brown hair hangs over his ears and his sideburns look like they could use a trim. He rocks back on his heels, appearing apprehensive as he looks at me.

"Look, Callie, I don't even know what to say," he starts. "I guess . . . I guess I'm sorry."

I'm a little shocked by his declaration and my gaze darts to the ground, my forehead creasing. "You don't need to be sorry. It's not your fault."

He drops down on the steps and stretches out his legs in front of him and then crosses his ankles. He smells like cigarette smoke and booze. I didn't even know he smoked, but then again, I don't really know him, not really. Even when we were kids, we were kind of competitive, and then when the thing with Caleb happened any hope of a brotherly-sisterly bond shattered.

"I turned him in," he finally proclaims. His cheeks suck in as he inhales and then they puff back out as he releases a breath.

"Thank you," I say. "But the police won't do anything. They really can't. It's been too long and it's basically just his word against mine."

He shakes his head and rubs his hand across his stubbly jaw. "Not for that...I already knew that wouldn't do any good." His hand drops to his lap. "I turned him in for growing pot in his parents' basement. I even told the police where he keeps his own stash."

I'm stunned. Speechless. Unsure. Happy. Amazed. Thankful. "So he's...so he's in jail?"

"No, not yet." He sighs heavily. "When Mom told me about..." He clears his throat at the uneasiness of the topic. "About what happened to you, I was at a party with him. As soon as I confronted him, he totally fucking bailed on me before I could even get in a good swing. He didn't even try to deny it." His eyes glaze over as he recollects. "Anyway, he's been dealing for a while, here and back home, so I thought I'd try to get him in trouble for something. If he ever shows up, he'll be in deep shit. On top of growing, he had, like, five pounds stashed in his floorboards, which is considered drug trafficking." A ghost smile rises on his face at the thought.

"How did you know it was there? The weed?"

"Let's just say I took a lucky guess."

"Didn't the police question you?"

"I called in an anonymous tip."

I'm grateful, but also really sad. Warm tears force their way out from my eyes and I turn my head so he won't see me cry. Kayden starts to open the door, but I shake my head and then shut my eyes as the tears stream out. *If* Caleb ever comes back, he'll be in trouble. *If* not, he'll roam around free. Regardless, my brother did this for me and I'll be eternally grateful.

"Thank you," I whisper, wiping my tears away with the sleeve of my coat.

"Don't thank me," he mutters and I detect a hint of guilt in his tone. "It doesn't fix anything."

"It's not your fault," I say, drying off the last of the tears and then I look at him. "It's not."

He doesn't respond, instead rising to his feet. "But it kind of is, you know. I feel like we all kind of saw what we wanted to see and I blamed you all that time for making everyone in the family stressed."

I stand up too and brush the snow off the back of my jeans. "People generally do see what they want to see, but it doesn't make them bad."

He presses his lips together and then runs his fingers through his overly long hair. "Yeah, I guess so." He huffs out a breath and then blinks as he looks at me, changing the subject. "So are you headed back to school?"

I nod and walk backward toward the truck, staying in my

footprints to keep from sinking in the snow. "Yeah, school starts on Monday."

He gazes at the people in the truck. "Are you driving back with them?"

Smiling, I nod. "Yes."

"With a bunch of dudes?"

"Yes."

"Is that safe?"

My smile expands into a face-consuming grin. "I'm safer in that truck than I am anywhere else."

He crooks his eyebrows at me with cynicism. "Well, okay then." I wave at him as I start to turn, when he calls out, "I'll let you know what happens."

Glancing over my shoulder, I nod again, knowing all I can do is hope everything will work out, that I'll get a little bit of justice and Caleb will have to pay. But no matter what happens, I spoke up, made a voice for myself, freed the haunting memories that have owned me every day for the last six years. I found my courage.

## Kayden

"I don't fucking understand" are the first words that leave my lips when I enter my house. It's empty. Cleared of all the furniture, pictures, books, plates, and food, and the cars aren't even in the driveway. The floor is bare of rugs and the few dressers that are left have been emptied out as well, including my clothes. My parents took them too, probably to punish me for existing.

"They even took the blinds down," I say, astounded, turning in a circle in the living room. "Why would they do that? I mean, there's no for-sale sign, no nothing."

Callie steps up beside me beneath the chandelier and right in front of the bulky marble fireplace and she threads her fingers through mine, giving my hand a squeeze. "They never mentioned they were moving?"

I shake my head slowly, her hand feeling so diminutive in mine, yet enormously comforting. "I haven't even seen my dad since he beat the shit out of me." I think about the itinerary papers in the trash bin. "Did they just bail?"

"What about your brother?" she asks. "Could he still be here? Maybe he knows where they went."

Shaking my head, I tug her with me as I rush toward the open front door. I trot down the stairs and round the corner of the house to the basement. Kicking the snow out of the way from the front door, I grab the doorknob.

It's not like I'm upset I'll never see them again. I'm pissed off because I was starting to warm up to the idea of pressing charges and now… "I have no idea what's going on," I mutter as I open the basement door and find that that room is empty too. The leather sofa Callie, Luke, and I played truth on is the only thing that remains. The mini fridge, the television, and the futon are missing. I walk in, still clinging onto Callie's hand and it soothes the loneliness and feelings of abandonment rising up in my body.

I stand in the entryway with my jaw hanging open, just staring at the room I spent countless days hiding out in. "What the fuck?" I don't move or breathe. I can't even think straight as my thoughts become jumbled. There's a crack in the wall just outside the farthest corner where my dad rammed my head through the Sheetrock and then didn't patch it up correctly. I had a concussion from a "collision with another player on my baseball team" my mom had told the doctors. There's a hole in the carpet that was once hidden by a recliner. Tyler had dropped his lighter when he was smoking weed and it had burned a hole. To cover it up from my dad, we'd moved the recliner over it.

"Can you try and call them?" Callie asks. "Maybe not your parents, but you could try your brother."

I shake my head in disbelief. How can this be happening? How can he walk away to Puerto Rico or Paris or wherever he ended up? And why? It's not like he'd definitely be in trouble if I spoke up. He could easily deny it.

"I don't get it," I mutter, turning back to Callie. Her hair is twisted in a clip at the back of her head and pieces of her bangs frame her face. Her lips are turning purple because the low temperature in the room almost matches the winter air outside. "We should go," I say, shaking my head as I attempt to sort through my rapid, disorganized thoughts.

She tightens her grip on my hand and holds me in place.

"Are you sure? We could look around and see if we could find some clues or something."

I sigh. "Callie, this is real life. There won't be any clues, and even if there are, none of it matters. To anyone. It's better if I just walk away from it . . . move on." I feel the hole inside my chest developing again and the need for infliction is surfacing. "I really just need to go."

She quickly nods, understanding what's going on inside me, and she leads me outside. I stop to shut the door, watching the room slowly disappear, inch by inch by inch until the lock latches into place and the room vanishes.

We walk back to the truck and climb in. Callie sits on my lap, and even though everything seems about as shitty as it can get, I know it's not. Because I'm not lying on the floor bleeding to death, giving up my will to live. I'm here, sitting with her, and she's amazing and keeps my heart beating. She gives me a reason to live without pain, without sadness. And she gives me hope that maybe this will work out somehow.

# Chapter Twenty

*One month later...*

**#6 Take a leap of faith**

**#38 ~~Finish~~ Get somewhere with a major project**

**#44 Eat chocolates, have a lot of sex, and enjoy Valentine's Day, the day of LOVE!**

## Kayden

"Oh my God! Oh my God! Oh my God!" Seth comes running up to me shrieking like a psychopath. The library is pretty empty, but the librarian, a younger woman with square-framed glasses and fluffy brown hair, scowls at us from behind the counter. There are paper hearts all over the shelves and walls and even hanging from the ceiling. Valentine's Day is in a few days and I'm still trying to figure out what to get Callie, because I want it to be something special, something perfect, something that will represent her.

"Seth." Angling my chin up, I nod my head at the counter. "Watch the shrieking."

He's holding a crinkled paper in his hand. I've been searching the library for about an hour for a book on Darwinism. Usually, I'd use a computer, but Professor Milany is totally old-school and always requires one book reference.

"Who gives a shit?" he says and then scrunches his face at the librarian, who *tsks, tsks* him in return. He unfolds the paper and shakes it out, trying to get rid of the creases. "I got fantastic fucking news."

I put the book I'd been holding back onto the shelf. "No, there's no way you've found him yet...Fuck. You have... no..." I'm kind of stuck on words because it's unbelievable. It can't be possible. But the look on his face says otherwise. "Shit."

Grinning, he hands me the paper. It's been printed up from the computer and has an article beneath it. Above the article is a face that resembles an older version of the brother who left my house years ago: dark hair that's thinned a little, the same green eyes as me, and a nose still crooked from when he broke it from getting slammed into a wall. I'm stunned beyond words as I stare down at the picture of him.

I hadn't expected this to happen so soon. I'd returned from the therapist only yesterday evening and told Callie that I think I was ready to start searching. My therapist, Jerry, an older guy who wears a lot of Hawaiian-print shirts and loafers, suggested it might be time for me to start searching for Dylan. I put up a pretty good argument about why I shouldn't, including the fact that I'd slipped up the other night and kind of rammed my fist against the door in a fit of rage when I got a call from my father's old boss who was looking for him. No one knows where they are, why they left, and it's surprising how little people care. My dad's boss was only looking for him because he said my father had something of his. I don't even know how he got my number and the call reminded me of everything wrong outside my Callie-Seth-Luke-school world. I messed up, but I told the therapist. And Callie. And somehow Jerry thought it'd be a good idea to start searching for Dylan, even though I was worried of what he might be, or what he might not be.

"You'll be fine," he said, chewing on an Altoid, which he always has on him. "It'll be good to have someone to talk to about what you're going through and maybe he can help the abandonment issues you're dealing with."

"What abandonment issues?" I'd played dumb. "I'm glad they left."

"Yeah, I know you are," he replied and scratched down some notes on a piece of yellow business paper. "But I think you also feel abandoned. Even if they've done terrible stuff to you, they're still your family and I think you feel connected to them."

"Or stuck to them," I muttered in response, slumping back in the lumpy leather chair I always had to sit in.

He wrote down something else and then shut the manila

folder and shoved it aside with a stack on the corner of his desk. "How about this?" He overlapped his hands on top of his desk. "How about we just try to look for your brother? It doesn't hurt to try, right?"

I rolled my wrist until it popped and gave a burning aftershock, something that's been happening ever since I cut them open. "And what if we find him?"

He opened the tin of Altoids on his desk and popped one into his mouth, leaning back in the chair. "Well, that's really up to you."

After sitting in silence for about fifteen minutes, listening to the wall clock tick and the traffic rush outside, I'd agreed. When I went out to dinner that night with Callie, Seth, and Luke, they decided to take it upon themselves to look for him.

I just didn't expect Seth to find him so quickly.

"He kind of looks the same," I note, taking in his green eyes, which resemble mine in an eerie, uncomfortable kind of way.

"He's married," Seth says, tapping his finger on the top of the paper. "And he's a teacher."

I gape at him. "A teacher? Fuck, really?"

Seth's eyebrows knit. "Why are you so surprised?"

I shrug and then head for the exit, winding around the book cart blocking the path. "I don't know... It just seems so fucking normal." I slam my palm against the door and push it open. The area around and underneath my scars aches a little and I massage my thumb across it as I walk out into the sunlight with the paper in my hand. The sun is gleaming and melting the snow off the grass and the sidewalks. It's nice to see, but it makes everything a watery, muddy mess. The gutters near the streets are flooding the sidewalks and the grass looks like a pond.

"So what are you going to do?" he asks, hopping over a puddle and then he kicks a rock off the sidewalk.

I shake my head and sidestep a large hole in the sidewalk filled with murky water. "I don't know."

"You don't know?"

"I don't."

He doesn't get it and I don't expect him to. But there is one person who will. "Is Callie at her dorm?" I ask.

Seth nods as we veer around the side of the humanities building and hike diagonally across the lawn toward the sidewalk that borders the street. The trees are raining down droplets of water and they land on my shirt and the paper. There's a light spring breeze blowing against my back. "She's working on some paper that needs to be turned in by the end of the year, but she's hit a"—he makes air quotes as he walks backward—"writer's zone."

I smile at the thought of her locked in her bedroom, scribbling away in her journal, naked. Although I'm pretty sure the last part isn't true. But if I really wanted it to be, I could probably strip her down and have her write naked for me. She's trusted me a lot lately and our relationship has been heating up immensely. But I never push her—I don't ever want to.

"I'm going to head over and talk to her." I swing around a jogger stretching near a tree. "Are you coming?"

He shakes his head, stuffing his hands into the pockets of his tan pants. "Nah, I got a date." He hurries off, with a spring in his step, toward the parking lot on the opposite side of the main office, the puddles splashing up beneath him. When he reaches his car, there's a guy waiting for him with a big teddy bear in his hand. It makes me smile, thinking of Callie and the teddy bear at the carnival.

I pick up the pace, taking as long a stride as possible, allowing the wind to take me where I need to go.

᪣

I knock on the door several times before her roommate, Violet, answers. She's kind of a scary chick, with studs on her clothes and one in her nose. Her black hair is streaked red and she has a dragon tattoo on her neck. She wears a lot of black and she always has this look on her face like she's about to start a fight.

Violet walked in on us one time when we were having sex. Callie was absolutely mortified, although I thought it was kind of funny. Violet didn't think so, though, and she chewed us out, saying we needed to hang a scarf on the doorknob next time. I was a little surprised by her reaction. Violet has a reputation around the campus and it seemed a little unfitting for her to get so worked up over sex.

"You're not Jesse," she says, with her hand on the doorknob, frowning. She takes me in with her eyes and then she

355

fiddles with the diamond stud above her upper lip. "Do you two ever take a break?"

I roll the paper in my hand, making a cylinder as I shake my head and shrug. "Nope, not really."

She rolls her eyes and then steps back to let me in. I wipe my wet boots on the rug in front of the door and then stand in the center of the narrow room between their beds. Instead of closing the door behind us, Violets leans over and grabs her jacket and bag off the chair next to her bed and then heads out the door.

"You don't have to leave." I turn to her. "I just need to talk to her."

She raises an eyebrow, looking at me and then at Callie, who's sleeping on her bed. "Yes, I do . . . You two are a little too much for me." She walks out and slams the door. The white-board on it falls to the carpet and I pick it up. It's Callie and Seth's list of things they have to do before they die.

I'm surprised at how many have been crossed off, especially number eleven: do a dance in your underwear. Laughing underneath my breath, I hook the board back onto the door and then stand next to Callie's bed. She's lying on her back, with her arm draped over her stomach and her shirt folding up at the hem so I can see a sliver of her soft pale skin. She's wearing the necklace I gave her—she always wears it—and it makes me smile every time I see it because it makes me feel like she's mine. Her journal lays open beside her head and there's a box of chocolates next to her. Somehow she's managed to fall asleep with a chocolate in her hand. She's put on a little weight since Christmas break and seems to me to be doing better. I think it might be her therapist. She's always a little happier when she comes back from her sessions. It hurts, though, sometimes, thinking about what was done to her and all those years she spent in solitude. It's probably the biggest regret of my life. That I didn't *see* who she really was back when we were kids. Maybe if I had, then her life wouldn't have been so hard.

I drum my fingers on the side of my leg, deciding the best way to wake her up. There are tons of ways, from using my fingers to my tongue, but I know I have to be careful. She sometimes still has nightmares and if I surprise her in her sleep, it could upset her.

Kneeling down on the bed, the mattress caves beneath me. I set the paper down on the nightstand beside the bed and then lean over her, resting one of my arms next to her head. With my other hand, I trace her temple, the one with her birthmark, a small brown spot beside her eye that makes her even more perfect.

Her eyelids flutter and she lets out this cute little moan that gets me a little too excited. Grinning, I slant closer to her and brush my lips across her forehead.

"Kayden," she murmurs, not fully awake, and yet somehow she knows it's me.

I'm enjoying this way, way too fucking much, my cock instantly getting hard. But oh well. Moving my lips down to her temple, I lightly kiss the birthmark I'd just been tracing with my finger, and then I move to the side and place a gentle kiss on her fluttering eyelids. Her body shivers beneath me and she lifts her chest and presses it against mine. My mouth travels down her nose to her mouth, where I part her lips with my tongue, delving it into her mouth and licking a path to the inside. Her eyelids lift up and her massive blue eyes catch in the light flowing into the room and they sparkle. She sucks in a sharp breath through her nose and I straighten my arm, putting a little distance between our bodies so she can regain her breath.

She glances around the room and then directs her attention back at me and the sleepiness in her eyes starts to dissipate as she blinks up at me. "How did you get in here?"

"Violet let me in," I say and lean down to kiss her. She responds instantly, opening her jaw and letting my tongue deep into her mouth. She tastes like chocolate and smells like strawberries as my tongue explores every inch of her mouth.

By the time I pull away, we're both panting, with fire scorching in our eyes, and I've got my hand up her shirt. Keeping my fingers near the bottom of her bra, I roll off her and lie beside her on my hip. She glances down in her hand at the piece of chocolate melting in her palm and then her face contorts with disgust. She puts it on the nightstand and then wipes her palm on the side of her jeans.

"Okay, that's embarrassing," she says with a timid smile. She reaches for the box of half-eaten chocolates and starts to set them aside.

I grab her arm and stop her, glancing at each piece that has a bite taken out of it. "Okay, I have to ask. Did you eat an entire piece or just taste them all?"

She sighs and throws the box next to her lamp and then presses her body down on my chest, with her chin above my heart. "I don't like any of the flavors except for the strawberry."

"I guess that works then." I grin at her. "Who gave them to you, though, by the way? It's making me look bad."

Her eyes glimmer with a slight bit of haughtiness that comes out only on extremely rare occasions. "What if I said it was some guy? Would you be jealous?"

"Yes," I say truthfully. "In fact, I think I'd have to kick some ass."

"No kicking ass."

"All right, but only because you said so."

She smiles and then her tongue slips out of her mouth to wet her lips. "Greyson gave them to me last night."

I stare at her luscious lips, shimmering from the afterglow of her tongue and they're so fucking enticing it's driving my body crazy. "Seth's Greyson?"

She nods. "The three of us went out last night. He's really nice."

I frown, remembering why I came here in the first place. "I actually just ran into Seth."

"Where?" she asks. "I thought he had a date."

Sighing, I reach for the paper on the nightstand. Unrolling

it, I hand it to her. There must be a very close resemblance because she knows right away who he is.

"Where did you get this?" she asks, sitting up and reading the paper.

I push up and sit in front of her, crossing my legs. "Seth came running into the library today like a lunatic with it. I guess he was pretty easy to find, which makes me wonder if my mom or dad ever really went looking for him."

She bites her lip as she meticulously studies the paper. "It says he lives in Virginia."

I nod, tracing the whitish scars on my wrist. They're fading rapidly, but they are still there as little reminders of everything that happened. "I know."

"That's far."

"I know."

She lowers the paper onto her lap and studies me for a moment. "Are you going to try to get ahold of him?"

I shake my head and shrug my shoulders, thinking about the past. I'd never had a stellar relationship with Dylan, and besides, he ran away and never tried to get ahold of me. "What if he doesn't want me to get ahold of him? I mean, there's a reason I haven't talked to or seen him in years. And it looks like he has a family and everything. At least that's what the article says."

Callie's silent for a while and then she reaches her hand over and fixes her finger underneath my chin, tilting my chin up so I'm looking at her. "But what if...what if he does want to see you? What if he was just staying away from your parents and the house? Or what if he tried to get ahold of you and your parents wouldn't let him?"

I remember when Dylan left the house. He'd just graduated and gave up a football scholarship, partially to spite my dad and partially because he didn't want to play football. My dad was fucking pissed and had told him to never come back. *Ever*.

"Yeah, maybe." I'm still not fully convinced, but if I were to talk to my therapist right now, he'd say that I was doubting myself more than Dylan. He says that a lot. He says I have low self-esteem. It makes me feel weak and like a fucking pussy and kind of proves his point.

"I'll call him for you," Callie says, scooting closer on her knees toward me. "If you want me to."

I spread my fingers on top of her legs and frown at her. "You'd do that for me? Call a complete stranger?"

"I'd do anything for you." She positions her hands on top of mine. "Because I love you."

"I know you would," I reply, both hating and loving that she said she loves me. I still haven't said it to her yet. I don't know why. I've tried a thousand fucking times, but I can't get the words to come out of my mouth. She never says anything about it either, which makes me feel like an even shittier person. She's so happy having it one-sided. "I should be the one to call him."

Her shoulders elevate with her eagerness. "So you're going to call then?"

I nod, deciding to take a leap of faith and see what happens. "Yeah, I'll call him tonight after I'm done with you."

She brings her bottom lip in between her teeth, biting it nervously. "When you're done with me?"

Nodding, I lean in for her mouth, but then veer left and breathe hotly on her neck. "Yeah, I really want to work on number forty-six on your list."

"Forty…six…" She's breathing profusely as my mouth makes a wet trail down the side of her neck. With each sweep of my tongue, I gently nibble on her skin, bringing it into my teeth and then licking it.

"Eat chocolates…have a lot of sex," I say, reminding her what it says as I arrive at her collarbone and glide my hand up beneath her bra.

She lets out a breathy moan. "That one's for Valentine's Day…"

I run my thumb across her nipple and it instantly perks. Giving it a gentle pinch, I start massaging her breast. "So what? We'll celebrate it early…" I trail off as her head falls back and she becomes consumed by my touch. I slip my arm around her waist and guide us down to the bed, laying her beneath me. "And then we'll celebrate it again on Valentine's Day."

"Okay," she says with a look of ecstasy on her face, and then her eyes shut. "Whatever you want."

And she means it. She would do anything for me—she already has. She gave up her secret, she gave me herself, she gave me her love. And even though I can't tell her yet, I feel the same way about her. She owns me completely, uncontrollably, irreversibly.

## Callie

I'm so happy for him, and yet scared for him at the same time. He's found his brother and I just pray to God it goes well for him—that his brother is a better person than the rest of the family.

Things have been going pretty well for the both of us. We've both been seeing a therapist and I haven't thrown up since before the incident at the hospital over three months ago. I'm happy. And the feeling is wonderful and amazing and scary.

It's not always easy. Sometimes I have nightmares, especially when the therapist makes me dig really deep into my hidden thoughts. There was also one instant when I flipped out when Kayden decided to try something new on me while we were having sex and it momentarily threw my thoughts back to that horrible day. He was great about it though and he held me while I cried it off.

I've also been talking to my mom more, which hasn't been too bad. My dad and Jackson even call me. Caleb's still missing and I have a feeling he may be missing forever. I'm still not sure how I feel about that. There's a lot of confliction. Part of me wants him to suffer in prison, but part of me is glad he's not in my life anymore.

After Kayden tells me about his brother, we talk a little bit about what he's going to do, and then he starts to undress me. After he runs his tongue over almost every spot of my body while I cling onto him, he slips inside me and rocks his hips against mine.

"I love you," I keep whispering through my moans as I knot my fingers in his soft hair.

He nibbles at my neck and massages my breast with his hand as he thrusts inside of me. "I know."

It's all he ever says. Or sometimes he doesn't say anything. It's a one-sided conversation for now, but I keep saying it because he needs to hear it—needs to know that he is loved. I hear it from my parents, my grandparents, Seth, and sometimes even Jackson. I'm lucky and I want him to feel lucky too.

Our hips writhe harmoniously together until we're falling over the edge. We both moan and I let out a whimper, which always gets him excited. After we're done, he lays inside of me, with his arms resting to the side of my head. Our sweaty bodies are pressed together and our hearts race with lingering adrenaline.

Eventually he lowers his head to my chest and rests his cheek against my breast while I trace the back of his neck with my finger. "What were you writing about?" he asks, staring at my journal shoved to the side of the bed.

"Nothing," I say. "Well, nothing fantastic. I was actually writing a paper for the creative writing club. It's supposed to be nonfiction and I'm not very good at it."

He pushes up off me and pulls himself out of me. Flopping to his side, he extends his fingers for the notebook. I quickly sit up and snatch it from his hand, hugging it against my bare chest. "No way. It's private."

He sits up, his skin glistening with sweat. His bare chest is covered with jagged scars, small and big, dark and light. Sometimes I stare at them while he's sleeping, wondering where each one came from. It's kind of like a horrible painting of his memories that will always exist, no matter what happens.

He crosses his arms over his chest, his muscles flexing, and he frowns. "Oh come on, Callie. Just let me read one page. I'm curious to see what you write about all the time."

"It's private. Some of the stuff . . . you might think I'm crazy."

"I already think you're crazy," he jokes, lowering his arms onto his lap. He slides across the bed toward me until he's right in front of me, and his face softens. "Please, just one page." He's using his sexy voice on me, the one I have a hard time saying no to.

Sighing, I fan through the pages until I come across the nonfiction story I've been fighting to get out of my head and into coherent sentences. "This is the story I've been working on. I'm not very far into it and I'm not even sure if it makes sense yet."

He takes the journal from my unsteady hands. It's the first time I've let anyone read anything I've written and it feels like I'm letting him have full insight into my head. Holding it in his hands, he clears his throat and begins to read aloud.

"*Where the Leaves Go.*" He glances up at me and smiles. "Nice title."

I shake my head and lie down on my back, staring at the cracks in the ceiling and trying to still the tempestuous beat of my heart. "Please just hurry. You're making me nervous."

He chuckles underneath his breath and then starts to read. "*I remember when I was a child being fascinated by the leaves. They were always changing: green pink, orange, yellow, brown. And then eventually, when the air changed and chilled, they turned into nothing. They'd fall from the branches of the trees and either crumble and become a part of the ground or blow away in the wind. They never really had any power over their movements. They'd just go with the weather and wherever the wind would take them, helpless, weak, incapable of control.*

*I remember when I was young, about thirteen. It was a rainy spring day and the raindrops were splattering fiercely against the earth and the wind was howling. I was sitting at my window, watching the street flood and the leaves get carried away with the rage of the water. They were all a flourishing green, in the prime of their life, just blooming, yet the rain and wind was destroying them.*

*But there were these two leaves stuck to my bedroom window that wouldn't budge. They remained in place through the windstorm and the temper of the rain, even when the water was falling so heavily I couldn't see through the glass.*

*I kept staring at the leaves, unable to take my eyes off them, fascinated by their determination, even when the sky darkened* and the wind howled so violently it shook the glass of the window. I kept thinking about how strong they were and how they were only leaves. Pieces of a tree, a plant, these little things that couldn't think, make choices, do anything of their free will, yet they wouldn't give in to the wind and rain and leave that damn window. In a strange way, I envied them, the determination, passion, sheer will not to give in and let something else take them to the end of their life.

At the end of the storm, I fell asleep in my bed. When I woke up, the sun was out and the land was drying. The leaves that stayed attached to the tree branches were green and dewy. To my surprise the leaves were gone from the window and it made me kind of sad and I felt hopeless. The idea that they could survive against the storm was bringing me a sense of comfort.

However, when I look back at it now, I wonder where they went. Maybe they didn't give up and let the wind and rain take them away. Maybe they somehow found their way back to the trees. Maybe they reconnected themselves to the branches and continued to grow and flourish even after their temporary break. Maybe they were strong enough to take control of their lives again, revive themselves from their approaching death, force themselves to start breathing again..." Kayden stops reading and looks up at me with an indecipherable look.

I take my journal from his hands and cuddle it against my chest. "I know it's not really a story, just my thoughts. But it's all I can come up with at the moment."

He nods and doesn't say a word. He drapes an arm around

my shoulder and steers me with him as he lies down on my bed and rests his head on my pillow. I nuzzle my face against his chest, breathing in the scent of him as I hug my notebook. I listen to his heart in his chest and shut my eyes and inhale and exhale with the sound of it.

"Callie," he says after a long stretch of silence has gone by.

I inch my face closer to him and place a kiss on his chest. "Yeah."

"I think the leaves made it back to the trees."

# *Epilogue*

*Three Weeks Later...*

## Kayden

Virginia is a pretty nice place, green, with lots of trees and wildlife roaming around. It's a little warmer than in Wyoming. At least from what I can tell. I've only been here for about an hour and most of the time I was stuck in the airport. I flew out alone, even though Callie wanted to come with me. As much as I wanted her to, I didn't need to disrupt her life and her progress. "I'm only going out for a week," I told her. "And I think it might be something I need to do alone." She seemed a little hurt, but she understood and let me go without any more discussion of it.

After a very strange, somewhat awkward reunion with my brother at baggage claim, we got in his midsize SUV and headed out to the freeway. He looks a lot like me, only older with thinning hair and fewer scars on his face. He's dressed in slacks and a polo shirt and the inside of his car smells like fast-food.

We keep the conversation light for about the first ten minutes, talking about school and his family, and then suddenly I have to know.

"Why didn't you ever call?" I ask, holding onto the handle of the door for support.

He looks at me with the same green eyes as mine. "I tried to, but Mom and Dad changed the number when I left. And then when I did get it, they would never answer and if they did they would hang up. I wanted to get ahold of you after you moved out...but I don't know...life just kind of got in the way." He pauses and his hands grip the steering wheel and he forces a lump down in his throat. "How bad was it?"

I shrug, staring out at the warehouse lining the side of the freeway. "I don't know."

He doesn't press me for the details, but he can tell by my tone that it was bad. And he knows about what happened in the kitchen, when my father stabbed me, and that story tells a lot. "Have you heard from them at all since they took off?"

I shake my head and place my hand over my side on the last scar my father ever gave me. "No, but I wonder why... and where they went. It's like they were running away from something."

He nods, with a pensive look on his face. "Yeah, I know... I think it might be that they were worried you'd speak up."

"What would it matter if I did?" I question. "Even if I did, there isn't a whole lot I could do. Even if the police believed me, and I could press assault charges, he could get off by only paying a fine. And he probably would, knowing him."

Dylan shakes his head as he turns the car for an off-ramp. "Try attempted murder or even manslaughter. He stabbed you, Kayden—beat the shit out of you. He beat the shit out of all of us." He touches his cheekbone and runs his finger over a small straight scar on his cheek. "Someone should have spoken up a long time ago and not let him get away with it."

Silence takes over as we both drift back to our childhood. It's weird being around someone who understands what it's like.

"We were all scared," I say quietly and he nods in agreement, his eyes focused on the road. "How do you get over it? How did you move on with your life?"

He shakes his head and slows the SUV at a stop sign. "I haven't yet, but it gets easier with more time away from him. That stupid fucking power he has over you will go away."

I suck in a deep breath and then let it blow out. I tap my fingers on the door, watching the houses move by in a blur and wonder what his place will look like. I know he's married and doesn't have any kids. His wife is a teacher too. It seems so normal and strange to me, considering how Tyler turned out. But I guess that's life. Not everyone ends up the same way, even if their circumstances are the same, because not everyone thinks and reacts the same.

Finally, he pulls the vehicle to the side of the road in front of a field and shoves the shifter into park. I'm surprised though by where we are, not by houses but by a prison that's hidden behind a tall chain-link fence with coils of barbed wire.

"Ummm…" I glance at Dylan, perplexed. "What are we doing here?"

He turns down the stereo and takes his seat belt off. He stares at the building for a really long time before he speaks. "You remember Dad talking about his dad sometimes and it always kind of sounded like he pretty much treated Dad the same as he did us?"

I nod, staring at the guards outside. "Yeah, I guess."

"Well, you want to know the truth?" he asks and looks at me. His eyes are a little glossy and I wonder if he's about to cry or something.

"I guess so."

"He was actually worse, if you can believe it. Dad had a brother and his dad—our grandfather—killed him…beat him to death."

My heart stops beating inside my chest and for a moment I'm thrown back through time into the kitchen. The knife enters my side. It hurts. Not just the pain. It hurts because he's my father. He's not supposed to do this to me. He's supposed to protect me, not destroy me.

"And now he's here," my bother says, nodding his head at the jail.

I pause as I take in the building and the fence around it. "How did you find this out?"

"I wanted to know…where we came from. Why we had such a shitty life. Was it just a freakish fucking coincidence that we were born into a crappy home with crappy parents? Or was it inevitable?" He pauses, staring at the fence and the sharp barbed wire. Then finally he cranks the wheel to the side and flips a U-turn, the tires spinning as he floors the pedal and drives down the road.

I'm not sure what to do with what he said or if there's anything to do, but I have to wonder if I'll end up just like my dad, just like he ended up like his. I wonder if Dylan thinks the same thing. I wonder if he prefers physical pain over feeling emotions. I wonder if my dad does. I wonder a lot of things at the moment and it starts to pile up on my chest. Everything I've worked so hard to get rid of over the last few months is returning, the silent storm stirring.

But then I wonder if my dad could have changed his life, knowing the outcome. He could have made himself feel things and be a better person, just like I can. I don't know why I choose that moment to do it. It's probably a little fucked up and twisted, but the need to get it out of me is more overpowering than anything else. Instead of reaching for a sharp object, I reach for my phone. I dial Callie's number and when I hear her voice the storm in my chest calms.

"Are you having fun?" she asks with hope in her tone, wanting me to be happy.

I take a deep breath and say it with all the emotion I have in me. "I love you."

She's quiet for a moment and I can hear her breathing, in and out. "I love you too."

For a moment, everything makes sense in the world. For a moment, the darkness in my life lights up. For a moment, everything is perfect and still.

## Callie

I have a silly grin on my face when I return back to the benches. I just got off the phone with Kayden and he told me he loved me. I wasn't too sure about him going out alone to Virginia. I was worried about him meeting another family member who would let him down and hurt him. But it has to be going well. Because he said he loves me. Loves me. I'm practically skipping.

Greyson, Seth, Luke, and I are at a basketball game. The crowd is really loud, and whistling and shouting fill up the stadium, along with the sounds of sneakers scuffing along the court. The air smells like peanuts, popcorn, and sweat.

"Where are Greyson and Luke?" I ask when I sit down in my seat next to Seth.

Seth points down at the bottom of our section where Luke and Greyson are standing near the railing, chatting about something. Greyson keeps waving his arms animatedly and Luke keeps shaking his head in disagreement.

Seth's brown eyes scan my face as he reaches into his popcorn bucket. "What's with the silly grin, my darling Callie?"

My smile grows as I grab a handful of popcorn. "Kayden just told me he loves me."

He almost throws the popcorn bucket onto the floor as he reaches to wrap his arms around me. "I'm so happy for you," he says, hugging me.

I embrace him back, laughing as we squish the popcorn bucket between our bodies. "I'm really happy for me too."

He pulls away with a grin on his face as he sweeps the spilled popcorn off his lap. "I know you are, which is good. I really didn't want to kick Kayden's ass."

I laugh softly at the idea of it. "I'm sure Kayden's grateful too."

A large man behind us starts yelling at Luke and Greyson to "sit the fuck down!"

"Shut the hell up," Seth chimes in, giving him a dirty look over his shoulder as Luke flips him the middle finger.

I hold my breath until the tension clears and then Luke and Greyson start talking again. Luke's been hanging out with the three of us for the last few days and always seems comfortable, never out of place.

"Sometimes...I wonder if Luke..." I lean in to Seth and lower my voice. "If Luke...likes...guys."

Seth sits there for a moment, crunching on popcorn as he chews noisily. Then he starts laughing so loudly it nearly drowns out the crowd. Then he stops and says in a low voice, "Luke's not gay, Callie."

"Are you sure? Maybe he's just afraid to come out, like Braiden was."

"Yeah, I'm sure." Seth's shoulders slump with his sigh and he shakes his head. "You want to know what I think?"

I nod and grab a handful of popcorn. "Yes, please share your all-knowing thoughts."

He offers me a smile as he leans into me and whispers, "I think that Luke's been through something that makes him more understanding and accepting than the average person. And I think that sometimes people misinterpret understanding and acceptance and make it into something that it isn't."

He's completely right and I feel terrible. "You're right and I'm sorry. I should never try to guess things about people."

"You don't need to apologize," he says, jabbing me playfully in the side with his elbow. "Besides, you're one of those people."

"What? Understanding and accepting?" I shove a handful of popcorn into my mouth.

His smile lights up his whole face. "The kind of person who can see things in a different light, who's been to hell and back. The kind who has had and gave redemption."

I return his smile with equal happiness as the crowd goes wild around us, shouting and clapping and jumping up from their seats over a three-pointer. Seth starts clapping and I move my hands together, but then my phone rings from inside my pocket. "Cumbersome," by Seven Mary Three.

"It's my brother!" I shout over the noise of the crowd as I

get to my feet. "I'll be right back. He's been trying to call me all night."

I hurry down the stairs, making sure to move to the other side when a group of guys comes walking up. Even through all of the recovery, crowds and unfamiliar guys make me nervous. But the important part is I'm here and not hiding.

I quickly answer it as I enter the food area and the screaming of the crowd fades out. "Hey," I say.

"Hey." He doesn't sound happy, but he usually doesn't. I've actually noticed that my brother has a very grumpy tone, but that it's just him and shouldn't be taken personally.

"Sorry I didn't pick up earlier." I head to one of the empty metal tables in the middle of the room, sink down on a bench, and rest my arm on top of the table. "I'm at a game and it's loud."

"It's all right." He gets quiet and then he sighs. "Callie, I don't know how to tell you this—and Mom thinks I shouldn't—but you're friends with Luke and you're going to find out."

A lump starts to form in my throat and I swallow hard to force it down. "What's wrong?"

He takes a loud breath and blows it out. "Well, after the police searched Caleb's house they found a few things...notes and journals and stuff...and, well...do you remember Amy Price? Luke's sister? She was only a couple of years older than you and she committed suicide when she was sixteen."

"I didn't know she...I didn't know that." My chest starts

to compress as I remember the one time Luke mentioned his sister.

"Well, she did and no one really knew why," he says. "I remember some of the kids in my grade saying she was a slut and super weird and a pothead, but no one really knew her outside of that."

Change a few words and Amy's story matches mine. "Jackson, what was in those journals they found?"

He keeps puffing out breaths and I wonder if he's smoking or something. "Notes about people, you, her...and the stuff he did to you...her...other girls."

I sit there, frozen in time, like a statue made of cracked and chipped stone. "How do you know this?"

"Dad's friend, Denny, the cop, came over for dinner the other night and told Dad, even though he's not supposed to talk about it yet until further investigation. He thought Dad should know since there was stuff in the journals about...you."

He keeps talking, but I barely hear him. I barely hear anything over the sound of my heart. I'm not even sure what's striking the nerve. Whether it's the feelings manifesting inside me, that Caleb actually wrote about me, that he did stuff to others, or that Luke's sister killed herself...and that maybe... and that maybe she did it because of her internal suffering. Maybe she just couldn't hold on any longer.

I cut the conversation short and head back to the stadium. I walk back to the bench and my eyes instantly go to Luke. He looks at me and cocks an eyebrow with interest and I feel my heart transfer to him. I don't know how I think or how I feel. Because even though I got my redemption, Luke's sister wasn't so lucky.

I grab at the clover hanging around my neck and hold onto it with every single speck of hope I have in me and I tell myself just how lucky I am. Yes, I went through a lot of pain, heartache, breaking. But I'm here breathing and my heart is beating. I'm thriving. I'm not alone. And I'm loved.

## THE END

Are you ready for the next bit of the story?

Turn the page for a preview of

*The Destiny of*

*Violet & Luke.*

# Chapter One

## Violet

*(Freshman year of college)*

I've got my fake smile plastered on my face and no one in the crowd of people surrounding me can tell if it's real or not. None of them really give a shit either, just like I don't. I'm only here, pretending to be a ray of sunshine, for three reasons: (a) I owe Preston, my last foster parent I had before I turned eighteen, big time, because he gave me a home when no one else would; and (b) because I need the money; and (c) I love the rush of knowing that at any moment I could get busted, so much that it's become addicting, like an alcoholic craves booze.

"You want a shot?" the guy—I think his name is Jason or Jessie or some other J name—calls out over the bubbly song beating through the speakers. He raises an empty glass in front of my face, his gray eyes glazed over with intoxication and stupidity, which are pretty much one and the same.

I shake my head, my faux smile dazzling on my face. I wear it almost like a necklace, shiny and making me look pretty when I'm out in public, then when I go home I can take it off and toss it aside. "No thanks."

"You sure?" he questions, then slants his head back and guzzles the rest of his beer. A trail drizzles from his mouth down to his navy blue polo shirt.

I'm about to say yes I'm sure, but then stop and nod, knowing it's always good to blend in. It makes me look less sketchy and people less edgy and more trusting. "Yeah, why the hell not." I aim to say it lightly even though I loathe the fiery taste of hard alcohol. I rarely drink it, but not just because of the taste. It's what I do when it's in my system, how my angry, erratic, self-destructing alter ego comes out, that makes it necessary that I stay sober. At least when I'm sober, I have control over the reckless things that I do, but when I'm drunk it's a whole other ballgame, one I don't feel like playing tonight. I already have a barely touched beer in my hand and have no plans on finishing it.

Jessie or Jason smiles this big, goofy, very unflattering smile. "Fuck yeah!" he practically shouts, like we're celebrating and I want to roll my eyes. He lifts his hand for me to high five and I slam my palm against it with a frustrated inner sigh, even though it's a good sign because it means he's veering toward becoming an incoherent, drunk idiot.

It's always the same routine. Get them drunk and then I can get more money. It's what Preston taught me to do and what I do pretty much every weekend now, hitting up the parties around the nearby towns. Never in the town I go to college in, though. That would be too risky and way too easy to get noticed according to Preston.

I'm wearing a tight black dress that shows off what little curves I have, along with my leather jacket, and thigh-high lace-up boots. My curly black hair that's streaked red hangs down my back, hiding the dragon tattoo and two small stars on the back of my neck, each star drawn to represent the people who have loved me in life. I usually wear my hair down because guys always seem to like to run their fingers through it, like they get their kicks and giggles from the softness. Personally, I have no opinion about it, although a lot of girls seem to gush over guys playing with their hair. Let them touch it if they want, just as long as I get paid at the end of this charade.

J, as I'm going to call him because I honestly can't remember his name, pours two shots of tequila, spilling some on the countertop. When he hands it to me I slam it back without so much as flinching, filling up my mouth with the disgusting drink, then I quickly move my beer up to my lips, pretending to chase the shot with it, when really I spit the tequila into the bottle. I smile as I move the bottle away from my mouth and set the empty shot glass down on the counter. Preston would be so proud of me right now, since he taught me that little trick as a way to stay sober when everyone else is getting drunk to avoid mistakes with the deal. And I'm glad because mistakes with Preston never go over well.

"Another?" J asks, pointing a finger at the glass.

I decide it's time to move on from shots and onto taking care of business. I dazzle him with my best plastic smile as I set my beer down on the counter. I stained my lips a bright red before I left and my dress is low-cut enough to show a sliver of my cleavage, created by a push-up bra. It's all a distraction, a costume to keep them focused on something else besides the deal. Distractions equal mistakes.

I grab the bottom of his shirt and bat my eyelashes at him as I lean in, trying not to scrunch my nose at the foul scent of alcohol on his breath. "How about you take me to your room?" I breathe against his cheek. "So we can take care of some business."

He blinks his blue eyes through his drunkenness, alarmed by my bluntness. Most people are. And that's what I love about it. Throw them off. Never let them know what's really hidden in me. Never let anyone in because no one really wants to get in, not for good reasons anyway.

"Okay," he slurs, dropping the bottle of tequila down onto the countertop, and then he drags his fingers though his clean-cut blond hair.

I keep smiling as I grab a lime slice from off the counter and shove it into my mouth. I suck the juice off so that I can get the damn tequila taste out of my mouth. It tastes bitterly sweet, but better than the burn of the alcohol. After I'm done with it, I discard it onto the counter and scoop up the bottle of tequila.

"Lead the way," I say to J and he gives me another one of

those goofy drunk smiles of his, probably thinking he's going to get lucky after we make the deal. Most guys do which is why Preston loves having me do this for him. *You're a distraction*, he always tells me. *A very beautiful, enticing distraction.*

Deep down, I know I could do it. Fool around with J and probably feel fine afterward. I can turn off everything I'm feeling in the snap of a finger and put it away, only bringing it out when needed. I wouldn't feel a single part of it, which makes doing things I don't necessarily want to do easier. Plus J's not that bad looking, although he's a little too athletic and preppy for me. He's tall, with broad shoulders, and lean muscles, his entire body screaming that he spends way too much time at the gym. I wonder if he's a jock, but I'm not going to ask him. Just like I'm not going to fool around with him.

He takes my hand, his palms clammy, and he leads me through the crowd of college-age people packed in the townhouse living room, where a game of beer pong is going on. A few of the girls shoot me dirty looks, like I don't belong with a clean cut guy like J who's wearing a collared shirt and a watch that probably cost more than all the money I've spent in my entire life. And I'm fine with it, too high on the thrill of what I'm doing—what I'm about to do. The danger. The instability. The adrenaline.

When we reach the hall, we disappear out of the sight of all the judgmental eyes and lucky for me, J's not doing that great. His feet can barely carry him as he stumbles his way to the last door in the hall, hauling me with him.

"Whoops." He giggles like a girl as he turns the doorknob. "I'm sorry."

I have no idea what he's sorry for, but I just smile. "It's fine."

He grins again, stealing the bottle of tequila from out of my hand. He tips his head back and knocks back a mouth full, gagging as he moves the bottle away from his lips. Then he aims it at me.

Not having my beer to spit it back in, I grab the bottle and set it down on a small bookshelf nestled in the corner. "Let's take a little break from drinking, okay?"

"Sure," he says, trying to stun me with an award-winning smile. "How 'bout we just get ya in here and get ya out of those clothes of yours." His gaze scales my body and I briefly contemplate clocking him in the face. I know that look way too well, just like I know what he wants way too well.

I give him a little shove so he stumbles across the dark, empty bedroom. I follow him as he continues to stagger back and then lands on the bed. I shut the door and lock it without taking my eyes off him as he lies there on the mattress. Soft moonlight filters in through the window and lights up the dazedness on his face.

"Come…here…" He props up on his elbows, working to keep his head up.

I saunter toward him, glancing around at the clothes scattered around the large room decorated with a dresser set that matches his kind size bed.

"How about we talk some business," I tell him, positioning myself in front of where his legs hang over the edge of the mattress.

He shakes his head determinedly, and then flops his hand toward the leather belt looped through his slacks. I watch him fight with the buckle for a while and then growing impatient, I finally unhook the buckle myself, and jerk it from his belt loop.

"I knew you'd like to play rough." He laughs and starts to sit up, his fingers seeking my waist. But I gently shove him back by the chest so he's lying flat on the bed.

I toss the belt onto the dresser. "I didn't come here to play."

"Preston promised you'd take…you take…" he blinks around the room, looking lost. "That you'd take care of me first."

I roll my eyes. Damn it Preston. I hate when he promises stuff. If he'd just be vague about what was going to go down, then I wouldn't get in so much trouble when I don't follow through. Then again, most of them can't remember that much about what happens anyway.

"I will baby," I lie, cringing at my endearing term, but doing what I have to do to smooth things over. I reach for my jacket pocket and take out the small bag of pills. If I'm lucky he'll try one and then quickly pass out. "But first I need you to pay up."

Shifting his weight to the side, he snatches the bag out of my hand and then scoots back so he can sit up. He totters as he sits up straight, then when he gets settled he opens the bag. He glances inside it, pretending like he's checking to see he's not getting ripped off, even though it's too dark to count the pills.

"You got the cash?" I scan his room, his stereo on the nightstand, the open closet overflowing with clothes, and the closed armoire in the corner. I can't see a wallet anywhere, so I'm guessing he's got it tucked in his pocket. Things just got a little complicated if he decides to be a pain in the ass about paying.

"Cash comes after we play," he says, but I shake my head, ready to be done with this deal. I'm about to tell him to pay up, when he has an abrupt burst of energy. He throws the bag of pills aside and his fingers quickly jab into my waist. He jerks me toward him and I lose my balance and fall down on him as he collapses back onto the mattress.

He starts sucking my neck, his wet tongue placing sloppy kisses all over my skin as his hands start to wander up my leg toward the bottom of my dress. His breath reeks of tequila and cigarettes. "God, you smell so good." His fingers pinch down into my skin and it kind of stings. "I bet you like it wild...you sure as hell look like you do."

I roll my eyes. If I had a penny for every time I heard that, I wouldn't have to be here dealing.

Turning my head, I lean to the side and try to slip out of his grip. His hold on me starts to loosen, but he continues to kiss my neck, his hands moving all over my ass and slipping between my legs. I'm starting to get bored, my mind wandering to homework, finals, moving back in with Preston in a few weeks.

J moans against my mouth. "I'm so hard for you right now, baby." He rubs the evidence that he is against my leg and runs his fingers through my hair.

I get a little annoyed by his pet name and that I've become a humping post. I'm about to gently knee him in the balls and get rid of his hardness for him, ending this tiring situation, when he stops kissing me and slumps backward. He mutters something about me being a cock tease and then his head flops against the mattress. His eyes drift shut and seconds later he's passed out, his chest rising and falling as he breathes loudly.

"Thank God." I slip out from his arms and climb off him.

Although the situation has gotten more complicated, I'm glad he passed out. After a lot of deliberating on what I should do, I decide it's best to leave it up to Preston so I take out my phone and dial his number.

"What's up, beautiful?" he asks after three rings.

I climb off the bed and pace in front of it. "I got a dilemma."

"What'd you do now?" he asks in that flirty tone he uses on everyone. Even guys. It's just how he is and I know he really doesn't mean anything by it. Besides, he's eight years older than me.

"I didn't do anything." I glance over at J. "Well, not really . . . J . . . that guy you were having me deliver to, passed out."

"And?" I can hear the laughter in his voice.

"And I want to know what you want me to do." I stop

pacing and look down at J with his legs and arms sprawled out to the side. "Do you want me to just grab his cash or really screw him over and take the pills too?"

It takes Preston a while to answer. I can hear voices in the background, which probably means he's at a party. "What do you think you should do?" he finally asks me.

"I know what I want to do," I answer, biting on my fingernails, a bad habit of mine I can't seem to break. "But I mean, it's really your thing. I'm just doing it as a favor to you and I'm done once I finish paying for my tuition. You know that."

"A favor to me, huh?" he deliberates. "How disappointing. All this time and I thought you were doing it because you secretly were in love with me."

I roll my eyes at his twisted sense of humor. "You did not."

"I did too."

"Did not."

"Did—"

"Stop." I cut him off because this could go on forever and J is starting to stir. "Look, I really want to get out of here. I've got a final to study for. And a life to get back to." The last part is kind of a lie, but it sounds like a good point to make in theory. "So should I take the pills and the cash or just the cash?"

He pauses. "How much does he have on him?"

I sigh and pat the front pockets in J's slacks, but they're empty. Pressing the phone between my cheek and my shoulder I use both my hands to rotate him on his side and then I check his back pockets and find his wallet in one of them. I take it out and step away from the bed, opening it and counting the money inside.

"There's a hundred bucks in his wallet." I frown, knowing what it means.

"Well, isn't that interesting, since I told him it was going to be two hundred bucks for a bag," Preston replies in a calm voice.

"So you want me to take the pills too," I say flatly. Sometimes when I'm doing something I'm not totally comfortable with, like stealing from an unconscious guy, my conscience tries to wake up on me.

"I think it's only fair," he replies simply. "Especially since he was obviously going to screw you over."

"Maybe he has the money somewhere else," I suggest, but even I can hear the doubt in my voice.

"Or maybe he was just going to try and fuck you over," he says. "Literally."

I blow out a breath and take the cash out of the wallet, feeling the slightest bit guilty. Then I drop the wallet onto the bed, reach over J, and snatch up the bag of pills. I put the cash and pills into my pocket, then head for the door.

"Give me like a half an hour and I'll be at your house," I tell Preston, opening the door.

"Sounds good," he replies as the music in the hall drowns over me. "And Violet, remember, I'm a nice guy and everything but don't try to screw me over." He always says this as a warning, reminding me that business comes before our friendship...our foster-parent bond...whatever the hell we have. He used to not be this intense when I was younger, but now he'll say just about anything. It makes me nervous and uncomfortable, but I never say anything about it, worried I'll lose the only family that I have.

"I remember." I step out into the hall, but halt when I spot a group of guys I'm pretty sure I've scammed before, standing at the end of the hall. "Look, I got to go." I hang up and stuff the phone into my jacket pocket.

One of the guys with a really thick neck points at me, saying something, and the rest of their gazes wander in my direction.

"Hey, I know you, don't I?" the tallest one says as he strolls down the hall in my direction. "You're that girl, right? The one who sold me the stuff at that party a month ago. The one that fucking screwed me over." I spot anger in his eyes at the same time I note the thickness of his arms that can easily hurt me. For a moment, I just stand there, letting the group of them get close to me, feeling the beat of my heart accelerate inside my chest, alive and thriving—finally awake.

But when they're almost within arm's reach, I whirl around and run back into the bedroom where J's sleeping. I lock the door and then search through the dark for a solution.

"Open the door you fucking cunt!" One of them bangs on the door as they shout loudly over the music and J lets out a loud snore.

It's not the first time I've been in this kind of situation, and I doubt it will be my last. I wonder what my mom and dad would think of me if they were here now? Would they be ashamed? But they're not here and there's no one else in the world that really gives a shit what I do with my life. I can't just wait around here and wait for something—or someone to show up and miraculously help me. I'm in this on my own, which is for the story of my life.

Striding over to the window, I pry it open and pop the screen off. Tossing it onto the floor, I lean over the edge and look down the two-story drop to the wooden fence right below the window. It's not that far of a fall, but if I land on the fence things could go badly, like one of the pieces of wood could get lodged in my body or I could land the wrong way and hit my neck or head on it. They're such morbid thoughts, but my mind always goes to that dark place. The what-ifs of death. Those random occurrences that no one can control. Most of my life has been based on one random occurrence of death.

I know if I jump, either I'll safely land on the grass just over the fence or I'll mess up and get hurt, maybe even killed if random occurrences really hate me. Either way, I don't care what the hell happens to me, so I climb up onto the window-sill, letting destiny take over as I slide my legs over the edge. I hear the lock on the door click and open. My time here at this place is up.

My heart speeds up and I breathe in the rush of knowing that something tragic could happen to me. It makes me feel alive and without any hesitation, I jump.

# Luke

*(Freshman year of college)*

My night has been filled with shot after shot. Empty glass after empty glass. I knock back one after another as the sound of the music vibrates inside my chest. With each scorching swallow of Bacardi, tequila, Jäger, I feel more at ease, letting all my worries and the fact that I haven't checked my insulin slowly erase from my mind. My tongue becomes numb. My lips. My body. My heart. My mind. It's a fucking beautiful state of mind to be in and I wish I could never leave it—most days I don't.

After I lose count of how many shots I've downed and how many asses I've had grind up against me, I ditch the club with the woman I've been dancing with for the last two songs, debating what to do—fuck, wander around, go find a place to gamble. There's a familiar burn inside my chest as I drown into a sea of alcohol, where nothing bothers me. I relax and breathe the cool night air and just exist without all the weight of my past inside me. I've been drinking more frequently, especially since my past has been forcing its way into my life again. Stuff's been happening with my sister, Amy, specifically questions about her suicide that happened eight years ago. I thought it'd been put to rest, but it was brought up a month or so ago, questions mainly about what really drove her to throw herself off the roof that night. Plus, on top of it, my dad's decided he wants to become a huge part of my life again, after being pretty much absent since I was five. It's bullshit and I don't want to think about it or deal with it. I just want to get trashed, fuck as many women as I can, and live my life the way that I want to.

I lose track of how much time has gone but somewhere along the lines I stop walking and end up with my back against the tree. I'm not aware of too much going on but there are three things I'm sure of: (a) It's nighttime, since I can see the stars, (b) I feel very relaxed and in control at the moment, and (c) there's a blonde kneeling down in front of me with her mouth on my cock.

I have a fist full of her hair as she sucks me off, muttering something incoherent every once and a while. As she moves her mouth back and forth I feel myself verging closer to exploding and I let myself go as I approach it. It's the only few moments of peace that I have, where I don't have to think about the past, the future, just the goddamn moment. Once I'm done though, the silence of the night tears at my chest as there's nothing left to do but think. I'm back to that place where my past and who I am haunts me. The only thing that gets me through is the fact that my body is numbed by the potent amount of alcohol in my bloodstream.

I zip up my pants as the blonde gets back up to her feet. She mutters something about that being amazing, biting her lip as she tracks her fingers up my chest, looking like she's waiting for me to return the favor. I'm not going to, though. I only do things for myself and no one else. I spent too much time when I was younger living under restrictions, never living for myself, never enjoying things, and I refuse to go back to that place again.

I shove her hand off and head down the sidewalk, hoping she'll just stay behind. But she follows, her high heels clicking against the concrete as she rushes to keep up.

"God, it's such a beautiful night," she says with a contented sigh.

"If you say so," I say. "Don't you need to go back to the club and catch a ride home?"

"You said you were going to take me home," she reminds me, rushing to keep up with me.

"I did?' I sway as a maneuver around what looks like a bush in the middle of the sidewalk…no, that can't be right. I bump my hip on a fence and stumble off the grass and back onto the sidewalk

"Yeah, you said you'd love to give me a ride." She braces herself by grabbing my shoulder, then giggles. God, I hate gigglers. I really need to start paying more attention when I pick them up to avoid getting stuck with a Miss Fucking Giggles.

"I'm pretty sure you misunderstood me." I move my shoulder out from under her hand, stepping back onto the grass, and causing her to miss a step. She looks stunned, but still grins at me as she adjusts her boobs in her dress, pushing them up so they bulge out. I'm sure she does it on purpose, trying to remind me what she's giving me if I take her back to my place, but what she doesn't realize is that I've already had it. A lot.

And I don't care about what she gives to me as much as I care about what I took from her back behind the tree.

There's a party going on in one of the townhomes nearby and music booms and vibrates the ground. We're walking in the ritzier side of town, made up of two-story townhomes, the yards matching, and the sidewalk is lined with trees and a fence. I'm not even sure how I got here, nor do I know the way back to my dorm. Sometimes I wonder how the hell I get into these messes.

*I really need to stop drinking.*

I laugh at my own absurd thought as I stop to retrieve my cigarettes from my shirt pocket. The only time I can actually deal with the chaotic aspects of life is when I'm drunk, otherwise I panic for some structure. I never had structure when I was a kid. I had a crazy mom who did crazy shit and dragged me into her crazy world, making me feel crazy with her. I still have nightmares about some of the stuff I saw or heard her do and I need order, otherwise the vile, sick feeling I experienced when I was a kid owns me.

I pop a cigarette into my mouth and light the end with a lighter I dig out of the back pocket of my jeans. I light the end, deeply inhale, and blow out a cloud of smoke. I start walking again, zigzagging back and forth between the sidewalk and the grass just to the side of it, running into the fence a few times

"Where are we going?" The blond asks as she tugs on the bottom of her dress as she hurries to keep up with me.

I graze my thumb on the end of the cigarette and ash it onto the ground. "*I'm* going to my place."

"That's cool," she says with a slight slur to her speech, not taking my not so subtle hint. "We can just walk wherever."

She doesn't look that drunk and she only drank girly fruity drinks at the club, but her voice is portraying otherwise. She's putting a lot of trust in me at the moment, to get her wherever it is she's going and whatever it is she's looking for. Maybe sex. The best orgasm of her life. A fleeting escape from reality. Maybe she's looking for love or someone she can connect with. From the needy, I'll-do-anything-you-want look in her eyes, I'm guessing it's the latter. And if it is, she's not going to get it from me.

I consider my two options. I can take her back behind a tree again and just bang the shit out of her until she's crying out my name and I get a few more moments away from the helpless, drowning feeling inside me—get the control I need. Or I can call my friend and roommate, Kayden, to come pick my drunken ass up, because I'm getting exhausted.

I'm battling my indecisiveness when I hear this strange swooshing sound coming from above me. I look up just in time to see something tumble out the window of the townhome we're passing.

I stagger back onto the grass as it falls toward me and stick out my arm out to push Blondie back. The tips of a pair of clunky boots clip my forehead, and I stumble over my feet as something lands on the grass in front of me and rolls down the shallow incline toward the sidewalk.

"What the hell," Blondie says as she rolls her ankle and

her foot slips out of her shoe. She quickly works to fix her hair, smoothing her hands over it.

Catching my breath, I shake my head, which is going to hurt like hell in the morning when I sober up. Usually when I'm this wasted my heart goes still, but my pulse has forced its way through the multiple shots I hammered back and suddenly I feel sober.

Blowing out a tense breath, I focus on whatever the hell just fell from the window as I mentally tell my heart rate to shut the fuck up. At first I think I'm seeing things, so I blink my eyes a few times at the . . . person . . . a girl lying on her back, groaning as she clutches her ankle.

"God damn it . . . that hurt," she moans, rolling to her side.

My heart is still racing and I move my hand toward my mouth to take a drag, hoping nicotine will settle it down but realize I've lost my cigarette somewhere. "Shit, are you okay?" I drag my fingers through my cropped brown hair as I glance up at the window she fell from, then back at her, wondering if I should help her up or something.

She releases a grunting breath as she gets up on her hands and knees and pushes to her feet. Her legs wobble as she gets to her feet, then she limps forward, trying not to put weight on her right ankle. "Yeah, I'm fine." Her voice is tight, and normally I'd back off from her leave-me-the-fuck-alone attitude, but she just fell out of a fucking window and a painful sense of déjà vu hits me square in the chest as I wonder if Amy fell the same way.

"Did you hurt your foot or something?" I follow after her as she limps down the sidewalk. Blondie calls out that she can't find her shoe, but I ignore her, walking after the girl. I'm not even one-hundred percent sure why other than I'm worried she might be hurt or that she might have been trying to hurt herself on purpose, like my sister Amy did, only she never walked away from it.

"I'm fine," she says and then picks up her pace when a guy shouts something from the window she fell from. "Now go away."

I look down at her ankle, hidden under her boots. It's obvious it's causing her pain, by the way she won't put pressure on it. "You shouldn't be putting weight on it if it hurts. You could fuck it up more."

At the corner of the sidewalk, she veers to the left, and steps into the light of the lampposts surrounding the parking lot. I finally get a good look at her and recognition clicks. She's got long black hair with streaks of red in it that match the shade of her plump lips. She's wearing a leather jacket over a tight black dress and her boots—the ones that put a lump on my head—go all the way up her long legs, stopping at her thighs.

"Hey, I know you," I state as we step off the curb. "Don't I?"

"How should I know?" She peers over her shoulder at me, giving me a once-over. I can tell she does know me, by the recognition in her expression, just like I'm almost certain I know her.

She continues to hobble toward a row of parked cars and I walk with her.

"Wait...I've seen you around at UW...We have Chemistry together." I make the connection as she stuffs her hand into the pocket of her jacket. "And I think you're Callie Lawrence's roommate?" I point a finger at her. "Violet...something or another?"

She shakes her head as she removes her keys from her pocket. "And you're Luke Price. The stoically aloof and somewhat intense manwhore/football player who dorms it up with Kayden Owens." She stops in front of a battered up Cadillac. "Yeah, we know each other. So what?" She extends her hand toward the lock on the door, holding the key, but I grab her arm and stop her.

"Wait, stoically aloof?" I ask, slightly offended. "What the hell does that mean?" I've crossed paths with her quite a few times, but never actually talked to her. I've heard Callie say she's intense, which I'm getting right now. But people say that about me too and it's for a reason. A dark reason I don't like to talk about. I wonder if she has a reason too or if she's just a bitch. Plain and simple.

"It means whatever the hell you want it to mean." She jams the key into the lock and unlocks the door, glancing over the roof of the car. "Now will you please let go of my arm?"

I'd completely forgotten that I was touching her and I instantly let go, tracking the line of her gaze to the sidewalk at a guy heading toward us. When I look back at her, there's panic in her eyes, but when she notices me staring at her, the look quickly disappears and is replaced by indifference.

"Is that guy messing with you?" I ask. "Because if he is I can kick his ass if you need me to." I cringe as I say it because most of the time when I start swinging punches I have a hard time stopping.

She seems shocked for a very intense, split second but then again the look vanishes. "I can take care of myself." She leans into the car and falls into the driver's seat. She puts her hand on the steering wheel and takes a breath before looking up at me. "Look, I'm sorry I kicked you in the face during my fall." She carefully pulls her leg in, wincing from the pain. "I didn't mean to."

I touch my finger to my forehead, feeling the forming lump. "It's not a big deal," I tell her. "But I'd really like to know why you…fell out the window." I'm not sure if fell is the right word. She could have jumped. On purpose. For so many reasons.

"I didn't fall…I jumped." She stares up at me and I see something in her eyes. I have to search my hazy brain for what it is, but finally I get there. Detachment. Like she feels and cares about nothing. For a brief second I envy her.

Before I can say anything else, she glances through the windshield at the guy who's reached the border of the parking lot and then she slams the car door. She revs up the engine and I have to jump back as she peels out of the parking lot, driving away like her life depends on it and all I can wonder is what the hell she's running from.